Allegory of Malad City
A Novel based on
Actual Events in 1986

Praise for *Allegory of Malad City*

One caution. You may be tempted to read too fast, to find out what happens next. There is a great deal of suspense woven into this story. Don't rush to find out how problems are solved, traumas are dealt with. Savor the journey. It is well worth paying attention to the way things unfold.

Characters come alive and act out their roles only through the spirit and vision of the author. This author tells a story that in turn delights and tears at the heart, sometimes simultaneously. It is a story and a lesson in how one can completely disagree with what another believes while still honoring and recognizing the other's right to the choices they make.

-Charlotte C. Anderson, Ph.D., a farm girl from Aberdeen, Idaho

***

Ruby Campbell Stroschein keeps the reader captivated with the Rebekah's story and the unique way it's told using different narratives. The mid-eighties were trying times for farmers and ranchers struggling with debt, low prices, foreclosures and life-style changes. This story captures the turmoil of hard times interwoven with religious beliefs. Rebekah's life becomes complicated as she faces challenges of a bad marriage and a run-in with her church elders while trying to save her family's bank from a FDIC takeover. I feel like I've meet all the characters in Ruby's novel, which makes this story a captivating read for folks, especially folks born and raised in south Idaho. -Randy Neiwirth, native of Malta, Idaho.

ALLEGORY

OF

MALAD CITY

A Novel based on Actual Events in 1986

by

Ruby Campbell Stroschein

Other Books and Renderings

by Ruby Campbell Stroschein

Out of the Box Anthology *2006*

Stroschein Sheep Stories *2012*

Juniper Boys *2015*

Down the Rabbit Hole *2013*

Chalk Elk Speaks Anthology 2013

7 Forks in a Cheesecake *2015*

Chalk Elk Speaks Anthology 2015

The Multiple Murders
of Mary Kelley Campbell *2017*

For Tom,

who found me, kept me,

and inspired me;

and

for my children

Matt, Katie and Sarah

who survived despite me;

and

for my siblings who love me in spite of me.

in memory of

another life.

My sincere thanks goes to Sue Benier, who held my hand through ten years of writing this book, and never let go; and to Becker Gutsch who tirelessly edited my book, twice; and to Chalk Elk Speaks Writers' Group who listened to chapter, after chapter. A special thanks to Terry Hager who created the graphics for the cover and the genealogy page. A sincere thanks to Ron Slavick who gave me permission to use his aerial photo of Malad City.

Finally, thanks to the writers who toil to tell their stories.

Ruby Campbell Stroschein

TABLE OF CONTENTS

Ruby Campbell Stroschein

Genealogy of Allegory of Malad City Characters

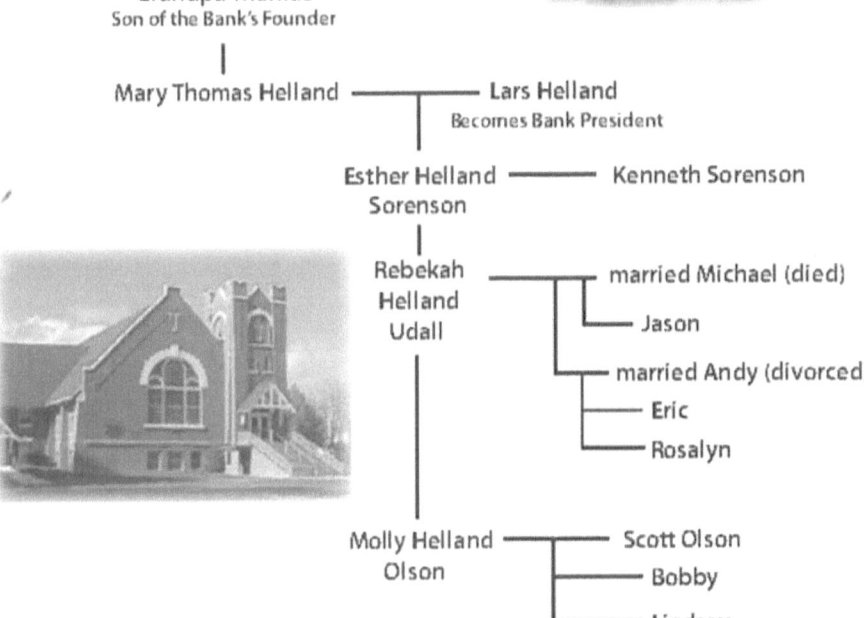

Grandpa Thomas
Son of the Bank's Founder

Mary Thomas Helland ———— Lars Helland
Becomes Bank President

Esther Helland ———— Kenneth Sorenson
Sorenson

Rebekah Helland Udall ———— married Michael (died)
— Jason
— married Andy (divorced)
— Eric
— Rosalyn

Molly Helland Olson ———— Scott Olson
— Bobby
— Lindsay

Melanie and Lance McDonald
[Molly and Scott's best friends]
McDonald Children
Dylan
Erica
Grace Marie
Lillian Grace

Ruby Campbell Stroschein

Forward

I didn't move back to Malad City after I left to get my degree, and eventually my license to practice law in Idaho; nor did I request to have my membership in the Mormon Church reinstated. Through all that happened in Malad during 1986, I gained a new testimony from which I worship:

I know my Redeemer lives. She lives in me, Rebekah, and not out there somewhere in the clouds. She releases her energy in ways I cannot explain when I tune into my core beliefs and live in harmony with who I am. When the static persists, and the energy is compromised, I know She patiently waits for the channels to be tuned, and signals restored.

I believe between birth and death, love and trust are all we possess of any significant value. Like the heartwood of an oak tree, my core is fortified by first, love of self, and then, love of family. When I truly love, respect, and defend me, and my family, I show love and honor to the God who made us.

I believe after reaching the age of accountability, there is no one person—man or woman—who has dominion over my mind and soul. I submit to no one. Even God, who has dominion over the world, is one with me, because She is me, and I am Her. My only submission is to be still and listen.

I believe I create my own realities.

I believe the value of womanhood is akin to life itself, yet, mine belongs to me, and no one else.

I believe harboring resentment and hate weakens who I am. I know if I build my core with a belief in myself, no one person or thing can break me, or amputate my spirit. Moving to a place of complacency or indifference creates far greater power than constantly flailing in the fury of a bitter heart.

I believe the only true armor I can gird myself with in life is education.

By learning the science of the earth, we sustain life.

By learning the science of man, we sustain health.

By learning the science of business, we sustain wealth.

By learning the science of society and law, we sustain order.

By learning the science of mind and soul, we sustain happiness.

By learning the science of music, we play the melodies and sing the songs in order to make our heart beat; and

By learning the science of communication, we preserve and pass on our stories.

Only when we know all this, can we know God.

Through my journey, I retained one article of faith from my days as a member of the Mormon Church serving as my beacon of light, dictating the choices I make:

We believe in being honest, true, chaste, benevolent, virtuous, and in doing good to all men; indeed, we may say that we follow the admonition of Paul—We believe all things, we hope all things, we have endured many things, and hope to be able to endure all things. If there is anything virtuous, lovely, or of good report or praiseworthy, we seek after these things.

We study the trails we forge. We study the journals our ancestors penned. We listen to the stories, and we sing the songs.

This journal is the Allegory of Malad City in the year 1986. While it may seem contrary to this one article of faith, remember, it was my journey of suffering, pain, trial, and tears that brought me to this place of peace. *-Rebekah*

Chapter One: Rebekah

I start the fire with a spark of my uncontrollable urge to run. Like a fleeing prisoner, the fear of getting caught, or running free, extolls the same charred nightmare: my life will never change. So, on a frosty October morning, in the mountains of Idaho, when my soul normally fades into winter dormancy, once again, I flee. Somewhere between retreat and resolve, the sheer ecstasy coursing through my veins keeps me moving; moving swiftly away from the same life I am running to, carrying an ever-heavier satchel. Woven with a different design on each panel, my travel bag seams are frayed. Now, on this cold, fall day, I lug two marriages and three children stuffed inside.

At the outskirts of Pocatello, I stop to fill-up with gas, then drive the loaded mini-van west on I-84 toward Twin Falls. As I pass the Pocatello airport, I look long in the review mirror—a mistake. I learn the hard way, "where you look is where you go" and will think of this exact place in reverse, weeks later.

After two more hours on the road, I exit the interstate, pulling into a rest stop the other side of Twin Falls. Eric is awake, moaning, "I have to pee." He grabs himself, pushing down to stem off the urge.

Rosalyn's flush face rests against the wing of her car seat. She forces herself to breathe through a stuffy nose, unconsciously opening her mouth from time-to-time to catch a deep breath. Her eyes flutter when I bring the car to a stop. I keep the engine running hoping she stays asleep, attempting to make it to Boise before the rental office closes for lunch.

My bladder is full, yet I don't dare leave the kids alone in the car, not knowing if I am being followed. I look at Eric. "Can you go in yourself?"

"Sure, mom. Dad lets me do it all the time."

I point to the east side of the building. "Go in the women's room and I'll keep watch."

"Ah, do I have to? I'm old enough to go in the men's' room by myself. Dad said so."

"Okay. But don't talk to anyone, and come right back out." I watch the five-year old run up the walk just as a trucker enters from the other side. Eric turns and gives me a thumbs-up before entering through the door the man is holding open for him. The trucker then looks at me, and he too gives me the thumbs-up. I return a weak smile and nod my head as if to say, 'thanks, and I'm watching you' at the same time.

Jason is laying in the back seat next to Rosalyn. Somewhere between Pocatello and Burley, Jason released his seatbelt and shed his ski parka, using it as a pillow. I don't make a fuss. Most of the time I don't make him wear his seatbelt anyway. "Only sissies wear seatbelts," he argues. "Andy says so."

I can understand Eric saying something like that, but it confuses me why Jason does. I reach over the seat and lay my hand on his bicep near a purple-black bruise. "Hey honey, need to pee?" I keep my voice soft, like the dog-petting voice I use when I stroke Parker, the blue heeler we reluctantly left behind because he belonged to Andy, before he belonged to all of us. Jason jerks his arm away and winces. I leave him alone.

Eric skips back to the car, jumps in and buckles his seatbelt. "Let's hit the road, Mom," he says with a grin. I smile back. With our lives in free-fall, it seems strange Eric is the same loving, adorable little boy, bearing none of the scars, external or internal, Jason and I do. Eric exudes everything attractive about Andy; his soft dimples, dark hazel-blue eyes, square, chiseled jaw, and a kindness we mined out of Andy from time to time—something foreign to a Marine Corps drill sergeant.

With the sun heating the asphalt, the world feels warmer in the parking lot of the Boise K-Mart on Americana. I change Rosalyn's diaper and bolt her back into her car seat, giving her an animal cracker for each fist. This innocent child renews my resolve this is the right thing to do when she grabs the very place on my shoulder her father gripped two days earlier. The pain shoots past the cavern in my heart where the good memories lay, reminding me, I don't have to live with his war demons any longer.

"Jason, you watch the kids. You all be good and we'll go buy some pretty stuff for our new house when I get back. It'll be fun. I'll be just be a few minutes." Jason frowns. Eric is still asleep. Rosalyn is chewing on what is left in her right hand, looking hard at the cracker clenched in her left.

I dash across the street to the property management office with fifteen minutes to spare. It is an early-era bungalow converted to commercial space. The whole place needs paint and upkeep, which should have been my first clue about the kind of property they manage. The heavy wood door sticks on a hump in the warped linoleum. I give it a push with my hip and the bell above the door jingles. Squinting to adjust my eyes in the darkened room, I spot a tall figure in her early twenties with curly auburn hair circling perfect features set in flawless fair skin. Her body is hidden beneath baggy blue jeans and a Boise State sweatshirt. Her purse slung across one shoulder, a large cloth book bag across the other, gives her the look of a pack mule. She jangles her keys against a notebook in her hand with disgust when I walk in.

"I just drove three-hundred miles without stopping to get here before noon," I say, trying, in a nice way, to express to her the need to set her things down and take care of me. "I'm here to pick up the keys for the trailer in Green Acres. Whoever I talked to said they'd leave them in an envelope with my name on it. Rebekah Udall. I mean, Rebekah Helland."

We stare at each other for a moment. She says she has class in twenty minutes. I tell her my three kids are in the car alone, and I need to use a bathroom while she finds the key. She points down the hall.

Letting the tepid water run over my hands, I look in the cracked mirror over the bathroom sink, hoping for hot water to make up for the lack of hand soap. My black lashes and dark brows contrast my olive skin. "You're the lucky one," my sisters complain because I don't need makeup. I splash water on my face and wipe with the much-used cloth towel next to the sink. I pull the band from my ponytail, combing my hair with my fingers. In that reflective moment I study the Welsh features of my mother's ancestors, straight, coarse black hair, hazel eyes, and a square jaw. My height and long neck come from my Norwegian father. I quickly re-band my hair when I hear the nervous tapping of car keys on the counter.

The impatient student is holding an envelope in her hand and says she needs a check for a hundred and twenty-five dollars, a signature, and a telephone number.

"I don't have a phone yet."

"Then give me somebody's number who knows you."

I write down my sister, Esther's, number in Malad City.

"Anything else?" she asks.

"Yes. How do I get there?"   .

"Out Franklin five miles, turn left on Five Mile, then right on Overland, and left on Cloverdale. It's space number 175. You can figure it out from there."

"OK," I say, running the directions over in my mind. "Can I get a copy of whatever I just signed, and will you write your phone number and name on the back, please?"

She checks her watch, rolls her eyes and turns on the copy machine. We both know she is already late for class. Pulling back the faux silk curtains I see Jason standing outside the car stretching and Eric climbing out of the front seat to join him.

I open the front door, yanking it past the hump and yell, *"Hey. You two. Back in the car. Now!"*

I discard the notion of asking where the employment office is. I take the copy of the rental contract out of her hand, pick up the keys, and rush out the door. I don't think to look at the contract before I leave, nor do I think to look before crossing the street.

Screeching tires, and a blaring horn causes me to freeze in place. I drop my hand on the hood next to a Cadillac emblem. I look up and smile weakly at the man behind the wheel whose face is as pale as his frazzled white hair hanging out the window.

"You're lucky I didn't kill you, young lady. You need to pay attention. Hear me?"

"I know. Sorry. I'm in a hurry to get back to my kids." I point to where Jason is standing, holding Eric from running out into the street to rescue me.

"You didn't even look! I could have hit you! Then what would your kids have done? Huh? You need to pay attention!"

In a trembling voice, I utter I'm sorry. He looks in his rearview mirror, making sure no one else is behind him and waves me on. I wave back and run to my kids. Jason turns loose of Eric who instantly grabs me around the waist.

"Mom, what on earth?" Jason cries.

"It's okay, honey. That's the reason I tell you kids to look before crossing the street."

"Well," Jason says to me, "you're sure not setting a very good example ya know."

"Jason, honey, just watch what I do. Okay?" I shake my finger in his face. "Because whatever it is, it's not the right thing to do. Got that? I am the antithesis of the right way to live."

"What's an-tie-theesiss mean?" He struggles at the word, mispronouncing it.

"It means opposite," I say, thinking to myself. *It means don't get a girl pregnant in high school. It means don't marry her if you don't love her. It means don't think money means security; or someone with position will give you happiness. It means don't depend on someone else to give you what you need in order to find yourself.*

"Mom," he says, "its ok, you're a great mom. You got me out of there. You got us all out of there."

I grab hold of him, bursting into tears. He holds me, not saying a word while Eric stares at both of us in silence, trying to understand.

"Just please don't go back." He rubs my arm, then gasps. "Oops, forgot. Sorry," knowing he aggravated my bruised shoulder, and decides to pat me on the head instead.

I pull away, lift the corner of my jacket and wipe my cheeks, trying to smile through a deep, dry, sobbing breath.

5

"Thanks, Jason. Now let's get some bed sheets and blankets and a few groceries. We really should have a look before buying stuff we don't need."

I look at the back of our minivan packed with plastic garbage bags of clothes and toys scraped together and thrown into the rear cargo bay early that morning. It looks like we are either vagabonds, or fleeing for our lives. From behind, it looks despicable. I can see my parents looking at the disheveled heap of what I collected as my life's staples and keepsakes, shaking their heads.

Chapter Two: Rebekah

My parents live in a sprawling ranch house outside Malad City where my dad pays the Mormon Bishop's boy to clean the horse barn once a week and mow the massive lawn in the summer. Mom spends hours trimming landscape, replanting tulips the deer root out for fall food. The white plush carpet in the living room is still as pristine as the day the man from Ogden laid it in 1970, when the house was built.

A few months after I turned sixteen, we moved five miles west of Malad City, to St. John, from my maternal great-grandfather's old Tudor-style brick home on North Bannock Street. It was my younger sister, Molly, who inspired my parents to find a place she could have a horse, a barn, and an outdoor arena to practice barrel racing. There was no place suitable enough for the family who owned the regional bank, so they built one. Dad felt guilty for spoiling Molly with a purebred Paint quarter-horse, a pickup and horse trailer, so he bought me a shiny red Mustang, ripe for stashing beer and breeding unwanted babies.

My mother was an only child of an only child: An outlier in a Mormon community and an anomaly for descendants of polygamists; but then, so was owning a bank.

My Grandpa Thomas doted on Mom after my grandmother died at the age of forty-two. I never knew her. In my Mom's quest to heal her mother's breast cancer, she held my grandmother's hand every day until she died. Soon after the funeral, she left home to earn a degree in nursing at University of Utah in Salt Lake, wanting to heal everyone's mother.

My father used to be a Lutheran until he met my mother at college. His dad's family moved from Minnesota to Montana; broke out prairie grass to grow wheat; got a mortgage to buy farm equipment and then in 1930, my dad was born.

My dad's father lost their farm to the bank during the great depression. The bank evicted my father's family from their Montana property, and my dad watched his parents pack up their belongings, fleeing the wildfire of doom and devastation of the depression. There was hardly a day he didn't hear his father curse the Bank of Montana, and the guy in his fedora hat and fancy suit yelling at my grandfather to pack up and get off the land as he waved foreclosure papers in his face.

It was likely much the same way my children witness me as I flee my own nightmare earlier that morning. The difference is, back then, they didn't have garbage bags to pack their belongings in.

I don't think of all this while standing out in the parking lot at K-Mart in Boise. But I did think about it all the way there; about my father being the same age as Eric when they drove away from the flatlands around Havre, Montana; watching his mother cry, his dad grip the steering wheel, then pounding on it like he wanted to pound on that banker. I don't know what it was like to be a child not knowing where you will live, or sleep, or go to school. I thought about this while glancing at my five-year-old son leaning against the door, sleeping, as we ferried across a wasteland of rock, sagebrush and parched earth of the Snake River plain earlier that day.

After leaving Montana, my father, Lars Helland, spent the rest of his years growing up in Ogden, Utah, attending the St. Paul Lutheran Church, a scarce congregation of steadfast Norwegians who migrated there during the thirties. His father planted trees for Franklin Roosevelt's Civilian Conservation Corp, and then hand shoveled the foundation for the new federal forestry building in Ogden.

In the early forties, when the war started, his father found work at Union Pacific Railroad and grew numb to the loss of his land. Dad later told me he was grateful for subsistence from the FDR New Deal. It would forever shape his life.

When my father met my mother, he discovered her father owned the bank in Malad City, Idaho. With a smile he reflected, "it may take some time for my father to get used to the idea of his son marrying a banker's daughter." Worse yet, it would sever his relationship with his family for many years when he announced he was joining the

Mormon Church.

My father toiled at being a faithful Latter Day Saint. When I was caught with beer in my car after a high school football game, he admitted taking a nip or two of stiff whiskey to pass exams while finishing his MBA. His confession seemed to relieve his conscience more than mine.

The hardest part of being a Mormon for him was coughing up the ten percent of his earnings required to get the Temple admittance paper from the Salt Lake City Bishop. He married my mother in the Salt Lake Temple in 1951, much to the consternation of his family who weren't allowed to witness the ceremony. My sister, Esther, was born a year later. I came along three years after Esther, and Molly a year after me.

After graduating from University of Utah with his MBA, Grandpa Thomas asked my father to work for him at the Idaho First Bank of Malad City. It was 1954, the year my father turned twenty-four; the year I was born.

Chapter Three: Rebekah

I waste too much time looking for cheap goods in the bottom-feeder store in Boise; things I don't want or need, things feeding my hunger for change. I fill one cart to overflowing, then another. I instruct Jason to follow me with the second cart, telling him he will ruin everyone's day if he bumps the cart into my heels, and to "by god pay attention." He laughs, hunches his shoulders and makes a threatening motion. When I put a six-pack of beer in my cart he scowls. Then I grab one more while his head is turned, reprimanding Eric for not keeping up with us.

I load a large bag of Halloween candy and ask the boys if we should look at costumes. They frown in a disappointing way making me ask, "What?"

"You're not making 'em?" Eric complains. I pull out a lollypop from the cache of candy and hand it to Rosalyn to chew on.

"With what?" I say. "A needle and thread? I don't have a sewing machine anymore."

Then I wonder why I didn't think to bring it. It could keep me busy while I wait for calls on a phone I don't yet own; calls requesting job interviews on jobs I haven't yet researched, let alone applied for.

In Lava Hot Springs, where we lived the past two years, my children always wore award-winning costumes created and sewn by me. The rural elementary school held an annual Halloween Carnival with prizes for best costume, and we took home the first place prize two years in a row.

We moved to Lava the spring of 1983 from Camp Pendleton, California after Andy retired from the Marine Corp. He agreed to move me to Idaho on the condition it would be at least fifty miles from my family who were steeped in a religion he wanted nothing to do with.

We bought an old farmhouse on fifty acres, fifty purebred Suffolk ewes and two bucks. I was finally doing all the things I loved, what my instincts thrived on—gardening, canning, sewing and weaving. It is in my veins, as profound as the genetics of my Welsh heritage

Andy loved spending his days wandering the foothills of the Rocky Mountains or fishing off the banks of the Portneuf River and evenings sipping sixteen-ounce aluminum cans of Coors, finishing a six-pack-a-day. At this point the past would rise like cream in a bucket of fresh Guernsey cow's milk—Vietnam. We all paid the price of that senseless war. Over—and over—and over.

"Six hundred forty-five dollars and sixty-two cents," the cashier says to me, twice. I look at the bags full of crap; everything defining me at that moment. I write out the check and the wire-thin woman in her blue K-Mart smock looks at me, and then at my children.

"It's good," I insist.

Peering over the glasses she moves a pencil from the nest on top of her head and pauses before initialing it. "Didn't say it wasn't," she barks.

"OK kids, let's go see where we're living."

The drive west on Franklin Road takes us to the fringe of Boise, past a new housing development, then a pasture, another development, then a cornfield rife with the browns and grays of October. At Five Mile Road I turn right, another half mile, then left on Cloverdale. There is a Circle-K store at the corner and I make a mental note to come back later and use the pay phone to call my sister, and Pacific Northwest Bell to order phone installation.

By now, Andy is likely home from early morning bird-hunting, reading my note, calling my family, asking if they'd seen me and the kids today. I decided weeks ago if I got up the nerve to leave Andy, I'd go to Boise instead of Malad. I knew I needed to take care of my problems on my own. I didn't want my family cleaning up the mess I got myself into. I no longer view these escapes as a road to freedom, but only a passage back to the beginning to start over again.

My older sister, Esther, moved back to Malad in the fall of 1984. Her husband, Kenny Sorenson, was a full partner in a well-known law firm in Pocatello. When our mother's breast cancer returned,

Esther, the sister who takes care of everyone, insisted they move close to Mom to care for her.

Like our mother, Esther believes mothering and nurturing is her calling in life. She finished her education degree at Brigham Young University in Provo, Utah and taught second grade for five years, getting pregnant nearly each of those years—losing each of the babies in the first trimester. She constantly pined for a baby, loved children, finally resolving her students would be her children; until the year our mother became her child.

Esther is a midget next to me. Her mousy brown hair is layered in a bouffant, entirely too large for her slight frame. Her emerald eyes, and dainty nose duplicate our mother's. She truly believes everyone, including me, is a special child of God. "Even Andy," she said after he cursed in front of her when the neighbor's German Shepard chased our sheep. "God damn son-of-a-bitch," Andy yelled, grabbing his rifle, leaving Kenny and Esther staring at the door he slammed behind him.

"He means well, and he certainly makes beautiful babies," Esther said as she held her tiny niece close to her. She said my new baby girl looked like a rose. It was Esther who picked the name, Rosalyn. When Andy brought me home from the hospital after she was born, Esther stayed at our farmhouse in Lava Hot Springs two days, cooking and cleaning, but mostly just holding Rosalyn. When she went home she sewed Rosalyn six new dresses, all of them with different patterns of roses on the bodice. She worked every night for a week designing a wardrobe not really suited for a baby living in the dry scrubby hills of Idaho. I dressed Rosalyn in those outfits every day until she outgrew them.

Every time Esther and Kenny came to visit, they'd bring the boys gifts; baseball gloves, bats, and pocket knives. Esther always wrapped Rosalyn's gift so she could rip off the paper, discovering a stuffed lamb or baby quilt Esther handcrafted.

Esther quit teaching when she and Kenny moved to Malad to help Mom. She started doting on our baby sister, Molly, and her two little kids. One day she called to ask if I knew Molly's diabetes was getting worse. She worried when Molly started working for Dad at the bank, wondering if she was taking her insulin shots on time and eating right. "Molly is so thin," she said to me several weeks earlier. "And Molly doesn't need to solve all Scott's family problems." .

I reminded Esther, besides her and Kenny, Molly and Scott have the strongest marriage in the Malad Valley. She says she knows, "but Scott needs to take better care of Molly, not the other way around." We all think if Molly has one more baby, it will kill her. Esther retreats, saying the Lord will take care of us, chastising herself for not having more faith.

Esther was Malad City High School Valedictorian of the class of 1972, and was awarded a full-ride scholarship to BYU. It pleased my parents; not because of the savings, but more, the bragging rights. Finding Kenny Sorenson at BYU is a prize we all cherish.

Kenny is the brother I didn't have, and, if truth be told, he is my best friend. He is tall, gangly, and I imagine what Abraham Lincoln looked and talked like—without the beard and the top hat—though I have no idea what Lincoln sounded like at all. I assume he talked slow, in a quiet tenor voice, making dry jokes, just like Kenny. Kenny's hair is always mussed and his shirttail hangs out, driving Esther batty. His bulky nose and elongated chin punctuate his smile, exposing oversized and tilted teeth. I can't say a thing to rattle him. He listens, doesn't judge, laughs, and gives thoughtful responses. His only hell is their empty house echoing the sounds of their dead babies he yearns to hold.

I need to call Kenny, I think, as I drive past the Circle-K. He can file a restraining order and divorce papers for me. Once the car is unloaded and Rosalyn settled for a nap, Jason can be in charge long enough for me to come back to the pay phone.

On Peppermint Lane, the mobile home park begins revealing my inability to make good choices. I take a deep breath and shake my head. This is like driving out of purgatory into the eternal depths of hell. There are rusted out cars sitting in front of drab trailer houses with broken toys strewn around postage stamp-size lawns. Garbage cans overflow with beer cans and McDonalds wrappers.

"Mom, are you serious?"

"Oh, be quiet, Jason."

"It looks okay to me," says Eric, eyeing the plastic big-wheel trikes, obviously thinking about potential playmates.

"Don't even think of making friends here," I tell him, then make a correction. "I mean, we're not going to be here long, so don't get attached."

"Don't worry, Mom," I feel Jason giving me an eye-roll through the tone of his voice.

"Look for space number 175, guys."

My heart is sinking fast. *What was I thinking?* Trouble is, I wasn't thinking. I was reacting. I didn't think about any of it: not who my neighbors might be, what the house might look like; not one thing except leaving. Ignoring consequences has always been my problem; like when I drank too much beer in high school, giving Michael cause to think he could rip off my clothes in the back seat of my Mustang. Answering a letter to an unknown soldier, which, by the way, has a whole new meaning. Maybe I am more like Esther than I give myself credit; always thinking everything is going to be fine, and believing people are kind, and loving (in a good way).

The number "175" is attached to a single-wide mobile home with red paint hemorrhaging to a pale pink, and duct tape holding a cracked window together. The front stoop is rotted, rough-cut lumber shoved against the front door. This is the moment I make a vow I will, from this day forward, think about consequences. *If-then… if-then…if-then.* I say it over and over in my head, like I can change it. I look at my kids, and say, "Well, here we are." And like my loving sister Esther would say, "…so let's make the best of it."

The key pushes in hard. I wiggle the knob. It doesn't turn. I look at Jason who is standing anxiously next to me, holding Rosalyn.

"Let me try," he says as he hands Rosalyn over to me.

He wiggles it again, and it unlocks. Opening the door slowly, he sticks his head in and yells out, like a Marine on reconnaissance, "it's all clear."

Eric bolts past him into the elongated edifice while I reluctantly step into the dark, dampness. There, in this den of gloom, are walls of bowed dark wood paneling, press-wood cabinets chipped at the corners, wood kitchen table with four vinyl-covered chairs, and a worn velvet orange couch with a matching flowered chair. Worst of all, olive green shag carpet stiff with the residue of dried carpet shampoo.

"OK, guys. Here's the plan," I say. "Eric, you and Jason unload the car and I'll start making beds and putting groceries away. When things are in order, we'll all go out to eat, maybe pizza? How 'bout that?"

I recall from a trip I'd made to Boise as a chaperone with Jason's fourth grade class to study Idaho history, we stopped at the original site of the Overland Stage, where only a plaque and a pizza parlor acknowledged its existence. I remember passing Overland Stage Pizza at the intersection when I turned off Five Mile. It is not too far, and I can remember the way.

Wiping Rosalyn's nose with wadded tissue from my jacket pocket, I pull her face close to mine. She is hot. "Oh, honey. I don't have any Tylenol." I hold my hand on her forehead like I am holding it on my own head trying to think rationally about what I need to do for her.

The boys pile K-Mart bags and garbage bags in the center of the living room. I feel devastated and alone, but relieved and free, all in a single deep breath. I have a sick baby on my hip, a sick life in my heart, and three children all looking at me like baby birds with their necks stretched and their mouths open, waiting for me to feed them with health, and life, and happiness, and love, and security, and food and a good time at Overland Pizza. I'm not sure which they need first, or if I even have any of it to give to them. I'll call Esther, I think. I'll go and call Esther and Kenny. A lump rises in my throat. I swallow hard and wipe the tear rolling down my cheek.

"Leave it all here," I say. "We need to get Rosalyn some meds."

In an empty minivan, Jason holds Rosalyn's hand, covering his eyes playing 'peek-a-boo.' She laughs and coughs at the same time, a deep croupy croak.

"Mom, maybe we should take her to the hospital," Jason says. "I think she's really sick."

I look at them in the rear-view mirror.

"Let's get some Tylenol and a thermometer first, and I'll call Grandma."

Truth is, I know I'm not going to call my mother. She has stage three breast cancer. It's the reason I didn't take the kids to Malad. God, I wish I were there. I'd be taking off my cowboy boots, walking stocking-footed on her white carpet. Esther would take the kids while I fall across the flowery comforter on my bed; the same one I left nearly thirteen years earlier.

I want to pull back the blanket and slide into clean, crisp ironed sheets, smelling like summer. The bed where I dreamed every dream a young girl does, then douses them with buckets of guilt and angst; always wishing I could be Esther, good and smart; or Molly, gifted and focused. I wish I could hug my mother, leaning against where her breasts used to be, missing them. Missing them because it's where she would lay my head, her hand cradling my cheek, pressing me against her, feeling her heart beat, telling me things would be fine. I'd be fine. I want her to live long enough to tell me what to do.

"Can I help you?" I hold Rosalyn in my arms while Jason sits with Eric in the waiting room of the St. Al's Hospital emergency room.

"My baby's sick."

"What's wrong," the woman at the desk poses the question like a statement, not a question implying concern.

I am running out of patience. Hadn't I come to a hospital? "Well, look at her. She's hot. She's got a croupy cough. She's flushed. She can't breathe."

"Do you have insurance?"

"No."

"Without insurance, St. Al's requires partial payment at time of service. If you pay in full, there will be a 10% discount."

"I can do that," I shift Rosalyn to my other hip.

"OK. Fill out these papers," she hands me a clipboard with a pen dangling off the metal clip. I hand Rosalyn to Jason, and sit down next to him.

Address. Dear God, I have no idea what my new address is. Space number 175, somewhere on the outskirts of Boise.

While Jason is looking over my arm, I write down my mom and dad's address.

"That's not our address."

"Hush." I put my finger to my lips, and whisper, "I can't remember our address."

"Shithole trailer court, Boise Idaho."

"Hey, watch your mouth, young man." I can see Eric smiling. The worst part is, I know where he learned it.

"I mean it, Jason. We might live in a shithole, but you don't need a mouth like one."

"Sorry, Mom." He is still grinning, one side of his mouth turned up like he's gotten away with something.

"It's OK. Let's get this done and get out of here."

"It's a good thing you brought her in, this could develop into pneumonia overnight." The doctor looks at me hard and asks, "You OK?"

"I'm fine," I lied. "Just need some sleep." Then I think of the stack of bed sheets still in packages in shopping bags in the middle of the floor of a run-down trailer house.

Fifty-dollars seems like a lot of money for ten minutes with a doctor who takes an hour to see us. I fold the receipt and prescription and shove them into my purse. Rosalyn is rubbing her shoulder where the nurse gave her a shot of penicillin.

Outside the night air is October crisp. It is dark. "Mom, you promised pizza," Jason whines.

"I know," I say, belting Rosalyn into her seat. "OK, let's go, but no complaining when I tell you it's time to go home."

In the arcade connected to Overland Stagecoach Pizza, Rosalyn and I watch the boys go crazy knocking down miniature bowling pins, crawling through tunnels, playing pinball machines, and jumping in cages filled with air bags. When she laughs at them, she coughs, and people stare. Knowing they place vigilant guard at the front door to keep children in, I slip to the corner of the restaurant near the bathrooms and look for a pay phone.

As I move Rosalyn to my left hip, I wonder what women do when they have no support system. I pick up the phone, hold it to my ear, and listen for a dial tone. "No Rosalyn, don't touch." I pull the receiver out of her hand. I push operator, wait, and then slowly set the phone back in the cradle. I go find the boys to tell them it is time to go home.

Chapter Four: Rebekah

"Mom? Mom! Are you OK?" Jason nudges me lightly with his foot. Lifting my head off the green vinyl floor, I try to bring him into focus. He's holding Rosalyn. I have a towel with the price tag still attached laying over me like a blanket, but I'm freezing. I sit up, shivering, and pull the towel tight around my shoulders. Running my fingers through my hair, small pieces of bile collected from the floor fall into my lap. Jason flushes the toilet to get rid of the putrid stench, then puts his hand out to help me up. My hand slips, and I fall back against the bathtub. This time I push myself to my knees, and holding onto the tub, I force myself to my feet. I lean against the wall with my eyes closed, trying to figure out where I am, why my head is pounding, and why is it so damn cold.

By 10 o'clock the night before, the beds were made with new linens and Scooby-Doo comforters in the boy's room. I settled for a cheap lime-green comforter on my bed I'd bought on a blue-light special with the rest of the K-Mart gear.

Eric was delighted to sleep on the top bunk. I put Rosalyn in with Jason on the bottom bunk, tucking her "Auntie Ether blankie" around her. I promised Jason I'd come get her when I finished putting things away in the kitchen.

At midnight, I finally sat down at the table with a can of cold beer, taking a sip. I reached up to the top shelf of the cupboard grabbing the bag of Halloween candy. I remember thinking I'll have one more handful of candy and one beer, then I'll get Rosalyn and go to bed. As I sat at the table, one by one, the ghosts started arriving, and insisted on staying until I finished most of the candy and two six-packs of Budweiser. The last ghost wanted to talk about my excommunication from the Mormon Church after Michael, my first husband, got me pregnant in high school. It took several more beers to quell the pain.

My brother-in-law, Kenny, found out about my excommunication after he and Esther moved to Malad. He was called to the position of Ward Clerk, the keeper of the records, so to speak. He asked me about it after Thanksgiving dinner at my parent's house the year Rosalyn was born. Andy was watching football with the boys and Dad in the family room. Mom and Esther went out to the barnyard to feed chickens, gather eggs, and feed Mom's horse. Kenny and I were alone in the kitchen with a stack of dirty dishes. At first, I was defensive. I told him I didn't want to talk about it. I told him nobody in my family knew, and I wanted to keep it that way. Kenny brooded.

"Really, Kenny? You really want to know?" He nodded his head. I warned him he wasn't going to like what I had to say. I was sorry I told Andy, and vowed it would be the last time I would recite the story. It left a dark shadow of resentment over the way Andy viewed my family's religion; but I told him it was Bishop Fuller abusing his position, not the church.

It's difficult to explain to people, specifically people like Andy, how the Mormon Church operates. The Mormon religion is different than main stream protestant or Catholic churches. Lay people run the church. In a place like Malad, the community is the church and the church is the community, with basically two kinds of people: Mormons and Jack-Mormons, who are non-practicing Mormons.

I was born and raised in a community of Mormon-Welsh descent with a self-empowered hierarchy. A system, I believe, that leaves people vulnerable to having their lives destroyed out of vengeance or fixation of power, particularly if the wrong man is in charge.

It doesn't mean this doesn't happen in other religions, but in the case of the Mormon Church, depending on status in the secular world, wielding spiritual and secular power in a small town can quickly become a double-edged sword. At least it is how it was in my case, and later, my sister's.

Qualified men are called to serve as Stake leaders with a Stake President and twelve counselors, like the twelve apostles, called The High Council. In every Stake are Wards run by Bishops. Bishops have two counselors. Besides hearing confession, the Bishop hands out admittance documents to those who meet the requirements for entrance into the temple after, among other things, making sure everyone pays ten percent of their income to the church. If a person commits a sin the Bishop or Stake President disapproves of, they get excommunicated. Well, basically. I'm not sure it's like that everywhere, but it is like that in Malad, especially since my family owns one bank, and the Bishop's family owns the 'other' bank, making my family their nemesis.

When Michael got me pregnant with Jason, my senior year of high school, Leon Fuller was the Bishop of the Malad Ward. He wasn't just the Ward Bishop, he is the brother of Clarence Fuller who owns Malad Community Bank. God only knows why Malad needs two banks, but both banks started competing in every small town in Southeast Idaho: Preston, Downey, Lava Hot Springs, Grace, and Soda Springs.

My great-grandfather started the first bank in 1907, which is why it is called Idaho First Bank of Malad City. I asked my Grandpa Thomas why Fullers started a second bank. He couldn't recall exactly, but he said it's the reason he asked my dad to move to Malad and work for him.

Leon Fuller's brother, Clarence, ran the bank with their father, while Leon started buying up more and more land. Every time a farm came up for sale, or a farmer was getting foreclosed on, Leon Fuller would buy the land. I saw him come in the bank after hours and talk to my father while I was in the bank doing janitorial work.

Cleaning the bank was my after-school job while I was in high school. I was emptying trash cans and sweeping floors when I saw Bishop Fuller leave Dad's office flushed, and breathing hard. Dad muttered "crazy son-of-a-bitch" under his breath. From what I could tell then, and learned later, he wanted to borrow money from Dad's bank to buy up the Showell place in Juniper; but he wanted a hundred percent of the purchase price and my Dad told him he would not make the loan. I wondered why he didn't just borrow it from his brother's bank.

When Bishop Leon Fuller called me in to his office the Sunday before my wedding, I assumed it was to visit about the wedding ceremony. My mother, sisters, and I cobbled together a small

23

celebration to take place the next Saturday, a week and a day after my high school graduation. Mom wanted to have it in her garden full of spring tulips, daffodils and petunias she planted. She said it was important to celebrate my union with Michael, the father of my "conceived out-of-wedlock child" with a traditional ceremony. She insisted on inviting their close friends and my father's family who are all Lutherans and delighted I wasn't getting married in the temple so they could attend the ceremony

My sisters and I worked in tandem sewing my dress. We made little candies using mom's old recipe, and ordered colored napkins with *Michael and Rebekah June 6, 1973*, printed in italics on the corner. Mom was supposed to ask Bishop Fuller to perform the ceremony because my dad refused to talk to him. She mailed him an invitation with a note attached instead.

There are things I insisted on having, and things Mom insisted on having. My mother says I have a proclivity to jump into things, and this is another one of those things. To her consternation, I insisted on wearing a white wedding dress. Thank goodness, the most popular design was a princess-style bodice flaring ever so slightly below my full, aching breasts.

The choke collar was covered with the same summer lace layering the bodice. Esther spent hours sewing miniature faux pearls into the lace and painstakingly covered domed buttons running the length of the sleeves and up the back of the dress.

Molly helped me try it on, carefully placing the loop over each button. When she finally stood back to admire me, I got sick. She grabbed a towel and draped it over the front of me while Esther held my hair back. Leaning over the kitchen sink I wretched until only clear fluid came out.

So, when I went to church on the Sunday before I marred Michael, like I always did, Bishop Fuller was standing at the door. He asked me to meet him after church in his office. I figured he wanted to talk about what scriptures to read at my wedding, what songs are being sung, maybe have Esther or Molly read a poem. You know, that sort of thing. I sat next to Molly and my friend, Angie, in Sacrament meeting. When they passed the sacrament, I didn't participate. I knew sinners were supposed to refrain, you know, pass it on and not take any. I saw Bishop Fuller eyeing me, and when I caught his eye he turned his head away with a jerk. I suppose that's how the Bishop knows who to call into his office for confession.

I sat on the turquoise padded folding chair in Bishop Fullers office and locked the heels of my pumps on the bottom brace, leaning forward onto the baby roll in my stomach. I wrapped my bulky cable-knit sweater around me tight, hiding my shame.

He said to me, "Please, Rebekah, sit down," waving at the chair. I was already sitting down, making me wonder if he knew I was even there.

People joke about short men and their personality glitches, and in the case of Leon Fuller, abbreviated at five-foot, seven inches, it's true.

I do not believe any woman, let alone an eighteen-year-old girl, should feel the wrath of the Almighty being unleashed on her when she she's about to bring forth a baby; a new life moving inside her—building its body and soul from her blood, her breath, and her soul. If she dies, the baby dies, and not just in body, but in spirit. A sincere spiritual leader caring for the very soul bringing forth a new life should have put me on a pedestal, told me I might need to make some corrections in my life, but the most important thing is the new life I am bringing into the world. He should assure me I am going to be a wonderful mother and wife, which is exactly what Kenny said to me. Instead, the damage Bishop Fuller unfurled less than one week before my new life as a wife was to begin, prematurely poisoned any hope of my marriage to Michael ever working. I walked out of the Bishop's office that day feeling like a discarded, worthless soul.

Whatever shield I built as a child, armoring myself with hope, the love of Christ, and the nurturing of my church community, was stripped away from me by this one little man. Six days before my conjugal day, which accidently got mixed up with my conception day, I was told by Leon Fuller I'd be excommunicated for fornication, "a sin next to murder."

As his lips moved, his eyes grew narrow and fierce. I listened to him for several minutes, then I sat up straight, leaned over and slammed my hand on the large custom-made mahogany desk. I looked Leon Fuller straight in his squinty eyes, forcing him to turn toward the window to avoid my fiery glare.

"You can do whatever you god-damned well please, Bishop Fuller, but you are never to speak of this to anyone. And, if you *ever* violate your oath of confidentiality, I'll hire an attorney and sue you for every dime you have!"

I didn't flinch when I said this to him. In an effort to react, he suddenly flung himself back in his chair like I'd shot him in the chest. But I wasn't finished. "You do what you have to do, but under no circumstances is my family ever to know about this."

Bishop Fuller finally spoke. "This isn't the contrite spirit I expected, Rebekah." Then he added, "don't your parents know about the baby?"

"Yes," I shot back. "Of course they do. And they are excited beyond belief they are going to be grandparents."

I may have overemphasized their feelings about the baby, but I was done talking. I stood erect, letting my stomach protrude, and without looking back, I yanked open the door and slammed it shut behind me.

I hated rehashing the story and told Kenny I didn't want him to bring it up again. I thought I had buried it deep enough inside me it wouldn't continue to haunt me, but here it is, reminding me this is likely the outcome Bishop Fuller hoped for. I told Kenny every time I thought about it, it felt like having a part of me amputated, and even though the limb is gone, the pain persists.

***

I growl at Jason for not turning up the heat. He doesn't answer. Then I tell him I'm sorry. He still doesn't say a word. Keeping the towel wrapped around me, I find the thermostat and move the lever to 75 degrees. Nothing. I walk back into the bathroom, turn on the hot water tap, and hold my hand under the stream of unending cold. I need to make a phone call, but first I need a shower, and we have no hot water. I tell Jason to take Rosalyn back to bed with him and stay under the covers until I figure out what to do; then I snap, "You too, Eric."

I force my head under the cold water, washing candy-laced vomit out the best I can, then pull my hair back, binding it in a scruffy-looking ponytail. I grab my rental agreement and drive to Circle-K to use the pay phone. I look for my wallet to get some change and remember I pulled it out the night before and set it on the counter. I scrounge through my purse for the two dimes I need to make the call. I find one dime, one nickel, and two pennies. I run my hands between the seats in the back, then in front. I find two more pennies. "Shit," I mutter and bend over to look under the seat. I am cussing and blindly running my hand in circles when a voice says, "Excuse me, can I help?" An aged man leaning on a cane peers at me.

"Oh you startled me! I need to make a phone call and I left my wallet at my house." I open my hand showing him my scrounged change. He reaches in his pocket, pulls out a handful of coins holding them out to me. I take a nickel and say thanks.

"Happy to help." He puts the change back in his pocket and walks away.

"This is Rebekah Helland at the trailer house 175 in Green Acres."

I still don't know the address. I look on the contract again, searching for the girl's name who helped me the day before.

"I have a problem. I don't have any heat or hot water.".

"Do you have your contract?"

"Yes. I have it here."

"Look at the third paragraph. Electricity is included, but heat and hot water must be turned on at Intermountain Gas. The phone number is there for you to call."

I put the receiver back in the cradle without saying goodbye. My head hurts and I feel nauseous. I lift up the receiver and listen for the dial tone to call the gas company. "Shit, shit, shit!" I look around for the man with a pocket full of change. He's gone.

I go inside looking for something to buy with a check so I can get change. I'll start looking for a job, I think, so I pick up a Boise Statesman newspaper and a pack of Wrigley's spearmint gum and lay it on the counter. I pull out my checkbook I keep in the side pocket.

"Nothing for less than two dollars," the clerk says.

I walk to the cooler and take out a six-pack of beer. "Will this work?"

"That'll be twenty-five cents for the paper, twenty-five cents for the gum, three eighty three for the beer, and four percent tax, comes to exactly four dollars and fifty cents," he says as he puts each item in the brown paper bag.

I write out a check for five dollars, hand it to him, and ask for five dimes in change. He asks me for my ID.

"It's in my wallet at home," I say. "If I had my wallet, I wouldn't need to write out a check."

"No, that's not it," he pauses. "I need your I.D. for the beer."

"Please," I plead with him. "I gotta get back home to my kids. They're home alone."

This clean-cut twenty-something is asking *me* for ID to prove I am old enough to buy beer? If I weren't so desperate, I would laugh.

"I need dimes for the payphone. I need to call the gas company to get heat in the house I rented yesterday. Right now, my kids are home in bed trying to stay warm. Please, just give me my change and let me get outta here! I have a 12-year-old son. Obviously, I am older than 21."

He opens his cash drawer and hands me the five dimes. I call Intermountain Gas, still looking for the physical address on my rental contract to tell them where to come.

"Ms. Helland," the lady said. "If you haven't been a customer before, you need to come down to our office and fill out an application," she pauses, "and, we'll need a fifty-dollar deposit." I scrounge for a pen and scribble the address on the rental contract. I sit in the car letting the morning sun warm me. I pull out the newspaper from the bag. I reach in again, take hold of a can of beer, pulling it from the carton, then let go of it. What am I doing? I put the newspaper back in the bag and drive home.

I change Rosalyn's diaper, dress her, and tell the boys to get dressed. Jason asks me if he shouldn't be in school. Eric asks when will his dad be coming to live with us. I realize I didn't buy milk or breakfast cereal. I think to buy more beer, and forget my kids have nothing to eat—not even the Halloween candy I consumed the night before.

At the Intermountain Gas office on Cole Road, I tell Jason to keep the kids in the car. I fill out the application. It asks for employer and monthly income. I am caught in a web I can't crawl out of, so I lie. I write down Bon Marche, hoping I spelled it right. $750 a month.

"Oh," she says, "my cousin works there. Emma Jean Smith. Do you know her?"

"Sorry," I say. "I'm new."

I'm glad Jason isn't looking over my shoulder to make auditable corrections. I write out the check for the deposit and ask the woman—who looks like my sister Molly—when they'll be out to turn on the gas. She tells me they need to wait for my check to clear.

"Oh, my god," I say, "I have three little kids." I look out the office window toward my car, hoping she'll see them waiting for me in the car and take pity.

"If you can bring me a cashier's check, I'll try to have someone out this afternoon." She is kind and I am desperate. I tell her I'll be right back.

Rosalyn is screaming when I get in the car. Jason has her out of her car seat trying to get her to stop. She has green snot all over her face. She keeps trying to push him away, and wants me to hold her. I know my kids are hungry, but If I don't get the cashier's check right away, they may call my fabricated employer. Rosalyn is screaming so hard her face is beet-red. I pull her across the seat and hold her. She quits screaming, but continues to sob. I get a tissue and wipe her nose and face. Her face is hot, but I can't tell if she's running a temperature again or if it's from the crying. She needs her diaper changed, and I forgot to bring her diaper bag.

I carry Rosalyn back inside the Intermountain Gas office and ask where the closest First Security Bank is located. I am doing math in my head. After writing out checks for rent, K-Mark, the hospital, and the six dollar check I wrote earlier that morning, I should still have over twelve hundred dollars.

I stop at McDonalds, buy hamburgers, french fries and three small cartons of milk. I let Rosalyn eat hers any way she wants. I don't care. I'll clean it up later. Jason puts a handful of fries in her lap.

I go in the bank to get a cashier's check made out to Intermountain Gas. The cashier takes my check to a bank officer who picks up the phone and makes a call. I wait. When she returns, she looks down, hands me the check, and says, "I'm sorry Ms. Udall, but your account has been closed."

Chapter Five: Rebekah

The place we call our home has no heat or hot water. I feel stupid for not opening my own checking account before leaving. It is an account we use for our sheep operation to buy feed, or vet supplies at the Cal Ranch store in Pocatello—that sort of thing. I am the only one who uses it, so I figure Andy won't think about it. I planned on setting up a new account once I got to Boise. I look in my wallet—$43.65. It occurs to me if Andy gets copies of the cancelled checks, he'll know where to find me. Worse yet, I worry he'll close the account before the checks I've written clear. If he finds me, will he come to the door with a dozen roses, or a gun?

The sun warms the trailer. We leave the blinds open to garner as much passive heat as possible. I tell the boys to wrap up in their blankets while I figure out what to do next. I ask Jason if he'll read a book to Eric. Rosalyn fell asleep in the car, so I lay her on my bed. I forget I haven't eaten. I take a beer from the fridge, pop the top, guzzle the whole can, crush it in my hand and throw it at the wall and drink two more. I walk to my bedroom and crawl under the god-awful lime-green comforter next to Rosalyn.

I stir when I feel a soft hand on my forehead, then on my cheek. I think it's my mother. Opening my eyes, I think she's smiling at me. Confused, I try to sit up. "What are you doing here?" I ask the stranger sitting on my bed.

"Your boy came over and asked to borrow a heater. He said you're sick."

"No, I'm okay." I sit up and look at the empty place in the bed next to me. "Where's Rosalyn?"

"She is in the living room with your boys. I'd like to take them over to my place and give them some dinner and let you get some rest. Would that be okay?"

"What? Who are you?" You don't have to…," I start to say.

"I'd like to. If you'll let me. I'm just right there." She points.

By the way she consoles me, I know she knows. She can't help but smell it. Sour beer breath is something I smelled every morning when I woke up next to Andy. Now here I am, passed out and don't even know my baby is gone. Dear god.

"You go back to sleep and get feeling better and I'll take the kids with me. I've got diapers for your little girl," she smiles. Then before she leaves my room she turns around, "I've been where you are. I mean to hell and back. It's a lonely place to be."

I stare at the ceiling as tears fall, some collecting in my ear; the rest snaking around the back of my neck and falling onto my pillow. I feel the damp as she turns out the light. "By the way, my name is Ruth Callahan. Get some rest and I'll bring the kids over later."

When I wake, I hear Ruth Callahan's voice, guttural and hoarse and smell the faint odor of cigarette smoke. She tells Eric and Jason to get ready for bed. I stand and fall against the wall. "Are you alright?" Mrs. Callahan asks, opening my door.

"I'm a bit weak," I say. I realize I haven't eaten for two days, vomited most of the night before, and now I'm famished.

"I brought you some stew. Come have a bowl."

"I will," I say. "I need to use the bathroom first." She's sitting on the couch, holding Rosalyn when I come out of the bathroom. When Rosalyn sees me, she whimpers and holds out her arms to me. Mrs. Callahan starts singing. "Itsy bitsy spider went up the water spout," and she walks her fingers up Rosalyn's arm, making her giggle.

There's a pot on the stove. I can smell oregano, green peppers, and tomato. The oven door is open and the coils are red hot, the heat penetrating the room. I am angry with myself for not thinking of the oven as a source of heat. There's a bowl and spoon on the table. I dish up the stew and sit down, looking at her. I take a bite and it tastes like kindness and compassion.

I study Mrs. Callahan and smile as I take another bite. Her black polyester pants are snagged and her faded cotton smock has multiple stains above her sagging breasts. Her dyed red hair is no secret with two inches of gray roots sprouting from her scalp. Rosalyn grabs at her thick, red-framed glasses. She grasps her tiny hand and says something to distract her. I finish my stew, run cold water in the bowl and leave it in sink.

"Mrs. Callahan, will you stay for a bit?" I ask as I take Rosalyn from her. "I'll put her to bed, and come right back."

"Sure, dear. Take your time. I have nowhere to go but back to a lonely trailer house."

I look in on the boys. Eric is asleep. In a low whisper, Jason asks if I'm feeling better. I choke and finally say, "thanks for doing what you did." Until now, I had no idea how much he is capable of solving.

"She went right to sleep," I say to Mrs. Callahan when I return.

I offer her the only thing I have— a can of beer.

"No thanks. I quit," she says." I just wish I could quit my other nasty habit." I tell her it's fine with me if she wants to have a cigarette, that I have one myself from time to time. "My husband smokes," I say

"Oh? Where is he?"

I frown. I don't want to tell her. I don't know her. I don't know if I can trust her not to call him and tell him the grave danger I've put my children in.

"You don't need to tell me," she says to me. She reaches into the pocket of her smock and pulls out a pack of Salem menthols, lights one, and looks around for an ashtray. I pull an empty beer can from the trash and set it on the table. She holds out her pack to offer me one, and I shake my head. I want to drink a beer, but don't.

Finally, I say "Thank you Mrs. Callahan. You saved me today."

"Ruth," she says, exhaling her name into the air with the smoke.

I don't know what to say. I don't want to start gushing, so I stay quiet.

"You know," she finally says, "I told you I've been in this place. No heat, no money, no job. Children taken from me. Nothing but a bottle of Vodka."

I want to tell her that is not where I'm at. I'm not that person. I just haven't had time to apply for a job. My husband closed my bank account. It's not my fault.

"Rebekah," she says, "let me help you." She finishes her cigarette and lets it fall into the beer can. It sizzles when it hits the bottom, surprising me I'd left that much beer in the can.

Chapter Six: Rebekah

I wake early. It's still dark outside. The house is cold, but tolerable. I left the bedroom doors open the night before to let the oven heat circulate. Ruth left her small electric heater. I boil water on the stove in the large pot I bought. I can't recall what I thought I'd use it for when I put it in the shopping cart. This morning I'm glad to have it. I fill the bathtub a quarter full with cold water and add enough hot to give us each a lukewarm bath. The boys take a turn, I bathe Rosalyn, then I refresh the water and go last.

We are ready by eight when Ruth knocks on the door. She is going with us to show me where to enroll the boys in school, then to Ada County Welfare office on Jefferson across from the county courthouse to get emergency aid. I think how different it is to climb my mountain with these heavy burdens on my back if just one solitary person stands next to me. What seemed insurmountable yesterday, is today possible.

One moment I'm in a deep, dark place with no doors or windows, no way out; and today the path is clear, thanks to Ruth Callahan. I still need to look for a job, but I'll get things worked out. It's one small step at a time. I know I need to call Kenny and Esther, but I want to be able to tell them, without lying, not to worry about us; we are doing fine.

The welfare officer with a gimpy leg limps to the counter and hands me an application. It appears I qualify because of my kids and my situation is considered an emergency. He hands me vouchers and explains what they are for. One for food at Fifth and Main Market, one for Intermountain Gas, and one for five gallons of gas for my car. He lays them down like a royal flush. I look at them, turn them over, read the back, then read the face of the voucher again. I do not have any idea what I am supposed to do with them. I decide to put them in my purse and ask Ruth, who is waiting in the car with Rosalyn.

Ruth shows me how to use the voucher at Intermountain Gas, then at the grocery store. The voucher won't allow me to buy beer, and I'm not going to spend my last few dollars so selfishly. Ruth offers to buy me lunch. "Not anything fancy," she says. "Maybe a bowl of soup." I tell her I will if she'll come to supper tonight. We need to be home by two o'clock to meet the service man to turn on the gas for our furnace and hot water.

"How do I thank you?" I ask putting my hand on Ruth's hand. A network of dark veins web across and around brown age spots. She makes a twisted grin. "Don't need to," she says, getting out of the car. She un-belts Rosalyn from her car seat and walks her up the make-shift stairs hanging on to both hands while I unload bags of groceries. As she leaves to go, I ask her for one more favor.

"Sure," she says.

"I'll get a phone as soon as I can, but if you see a blue GMC short-bed pickup truck parked here, will you please call the police for me?" I pull back the neck on my sweater and she sees the bruises. She shuts her eyes tight, grimaces, and shakes her head. The creases in her face show the harsh erosion of her past. It's painful to think about. "Just call them, please, and don't come over. You don't need to get involved."

Again, the autumn sun is shining at a slant through the dirty trailer windows, warming the kitchen and living room. I lie on the couch and put Rosalyn on my chest, holding her until she falls asleep. I listen to her breathe a soft wheeze, in and out. I feel her forehead and it's better than the day before, almost normal. I roll her gently off me and onto the cushions, trying to remember what day it is. I think of the newspaper, trying to remember where I put it. I need to start looking for a job. I need to file a restraining order and divorce. I need to call Kenny.

Someone knocks at the door and I jump. I breathe a sigh of relief when I peer out the front window and see it's the gas man.

"Afternoon, Ma'am, I need to see your furnace and hot water heater to light the pilot lights. I also need to make sure they're working properly."

I have no idea where to find either and tell the man in the blue uniform he is on his own. "No problem," he says, "I know where they are, or at least where they should be." He walks in the house, sees Rosalyn sleeping on the couch, and looks at me apologetically for talking so loud.

"It's okay," I whisper. "She has two older brothers and she's learned how to sleep through anything."

The man is rattling what I assume to be the furnace cover down the hall. I fold the first three sections of the paper without looking at them and lay them face down, opening the classified section. When I feel the sensation of warm air coming through the register next to the table, I smile to myself. The man comes back into the living room, gives me two thumbs up, smiles, and closes the door very gently behind him as he leaves. Yes, I think, two thumbs up for today.

When Jason and Eric get off the bus at 3:45 that afternoon, the house is clean, three job possibilities in the paper are circled, and fresh baked chocolate chip cookies are stacked on a plate on the kitchen table. It doesn't make up for the agony these self-induced disasters caused, but I hope it will help them forget, at least for a while.

I fix spaghetti for dinner and I tell Jason to run over and tell Ruth dinner is ready. After dinner, Ruth reads to Eric and Rosalyn while I wash dishes. Jason works on homework at the kitchen table. I ask Ruth if I can drop by her house in the morning to make some calls. After the kids are in bed, I show her the newspaper job offerings I'd circled and watch the wrinkles around her mouth deepen as she purses her lips.

"Rebekah, you're more talented than this. A clerk at Smith Food King?"

"I don't have any training or higher education."

She scans the listings. "Why not try this one? Legal assistant. Or bank teller at Idaho First National Bank."

I don't want to tell her my family owns a bank, not as large as Idaho First National, but my father helped expand Idaho First Bank of Malad to six regional branches; and my brother-in-law is an attorney. Worse yet, I don't want to admit the only experience I have working in a bank is janitorial work. Instead I say to her, "You're not going to believe this, but I don't even own a dress and now have no money to buy one."

"You know what job I'd love to do?" I say, as Ruth continues to scour the listings. "Work at a farm and ranch supply store. You know of any close by?"

Ruth writes down the names of two stores in the margins of the newspaper; one on Fairview and one in Eagle, and draws a miniature map giving me absolutely no idea where I am supposed to go, but I don't tell her. She takes out a cigarette and lights it. This time I salvage the lid from the jar of spaghetti sauce to use for an ash tray, and I smoke a cigarette with her. She offers to watch Rosalyn the next day while I drive to the feed stores and see if they have any openings.

Before I go to bed, I lay in a tub of hot water filled to the brim. I stare through the steam at the pattern in the buckled Formica wainscot around the tub, making out profiles of witches with twisted noses, and deformed ogres. The next morning I wake at 5 o'clock and slip out of bed without disturbing Rosalyn. Making a cup of instant coffee, I come back into the bathroom, close the door, and sit on the toilet lid, staring at the thin-lined squiggly patterns around the tub again, trying to figure out how to live on less than $45 until I get a pay check. Moreover, I promise myself I'll call Esther and let her know we are okay and ask how Mom is doing. The only thing I don't think about, and should have, is what I will do if Andy finds us.

I finish my coffee and go to the kitchen to scan the job opportunities once more. I pick up the stack of newspapers off the top of fridge. One of the sections of the Boise Statesman falls to the floor and I stoop to pick it up. I see the headlines, and drop the rest of the paper. Opening the business section, I lay it on the table, smoothing it with my hand.

Idaho Department of Finance Downgrades Malad City Bank.

I read the headlines and have to sit when my legs start shaking.

Idaho First Bank of Malad City, a state chartered bank, supervised by the FDIC was audited by the Idaho Department of Finance in September. As of last Friday, Idaho Department of Finance has downgraded the bank, originally chartered in October 1907, requiring FDIC to start monitoring the bank beginning January 1, 1986 unless the bank stock holders or directors can liquidate non-cash assets to satisfy the auditor's requirements. According to IDF Director, Tom Rowberry, the bank is not in eminent danger of being insolvent or the assets being seized by the Federal Deposit Insurance Corporation, known as FDIC, however it will be monitored quarterly by the state auditors.

My heart is racing as I read to the end, then read it again. My stomach begins to hurt. My life, once again, is in freefall.

Toddling down the hall, Rosalyn is calling for me and I switch my focus to the clock. It is late. Really late.

"Jason, Eric. Get up," I yell. "It's quarter after eight. Hurry."

We hear the diesel engine of the school bus while putting cereal bowls, Shredded Wheat, and milk on the table. It stops, loads, and leaves.

"Moooommmm!" Jason yells. "We missed the damn bus."

"Damn it, Jason, I told you not to swear, and I mean it. I'll take you to school. Just get out here and get something to eat."

I'm still in my night gown when I hear a knock on the door. I slide up against the wall and peer out. It's Ruth.

"Hey, Ruth," I say as I open the door, nearly knocking her off the front stoop.

"Need me to take the boys to school?" She asks. "I didn't see them get on the bus."

"It's been a bad morning," I say. "I don't want to talk about it."

Ruth raises her eyebrows, saying she'll be waiting in her car. I rummage through my purse and hold out a gas voucher for her to take. She waves it away. "Against the law to do that," she says. "Those are for you, and only you." I reach for my wallet to get out some money and she tells me to put that away too.

"Come on, boys," she says, "Let's get you to school. We've got twenty minutes until the bell rings. Rebecca, did you sign up for free or reduced lunches at school?"

"No, didn't know I was supposed to."

"It's okay. I'll go talk to the gals in the kitchen and make sure they feed the boys. I ran that place for thirty years, I guess they'll still do what I tell 'em. We can sort it out later."

The boys scramble to find coats, shoes, and Jason's homework while Ruth starts her car and pulls in front of the house. I hold the door open for them, giving each of them a tap on the back as they go, and shut both the doors, forgetting to lock them again. I can only think of my family's failing bank and an even stronger urgency to take a shower, get dressed and go find a job.

I take Rosalyn with me into the shower and ignore the haunting, squiggly lines of the tub surround closing in on me. I put shampoo on my hair and rub a little on Rosalyn's head when the shower curtain flies open.

"What the hell makes you think you can hide from a Marine?" a tired and hoarse voice whispers. Andy's bloodshot eyes are staring into mine.

Somehow it doesn't surprise me like I thought it would. I don't scream. I look at him in disgust, pick up Rosalyn and hold her under the shower head to rinse out the shampoo while she screams bloody murder, as I'd intended. Then I hand her to Andy while I try to stay calm and think.

"Well, since you're here, find a towel and dry her off and get one for me. They're in the hall closet."

I hide the quiver in my voice. I try to sound authoritative, but I know it won't last long. I only need it to last long enough for Ruth to come home, see his truck and call the police. But did he park it where she would see it? My heart is thumping in my chest.

Andy comes back into the bathroom, hands me a towel and has the other one wrapped around Rosalyn. "Hey, baby," he says to her. "How's my little girl?"

"Daaddee," she squeals.

I don't remember much after that, only praying Ruth won't stay long in the school kitchen, talking to her old friends. I remember asking Andy to dress Rosalyn, and thank god, he did. I tell him there is a comb in the bathroom, to please get it and comb her hair. As I put on my underwear, I holler out to him to get her a bowl of cereal.

Pulling on my jeans, I feel his hot breath on my neck and the smell of stale beer.

"Just who the fuck do you think you are, sneaking out on me like that? Taking my kids from me! Did you think I wouldn't fucking find you?"

I try moving away from him but my legs are tangled in my pants. I can't maintain my balance. I have no idea if he tries to catch me, or if he pushes me. I remember the piercing pain when my head hits the sharp edge cantilevering over the built-in drawers. I recall seeing blood on my hands when I grab ahold of my head. Then I remember nothing.

When I wake, the smells are antiseptic. The room is dark. I hear a beeping sound, then feel the pressure of a cuff on my arm tightening, then releasing. I groan at the throbbing pain in my head.

"Rebekah?" It's Kenny's voice.

"Kenny? Is that you? Where am I?"

"Don't talk. You've got a bad head injury and concussion. You need to stay quiet, and keep your eyes closed."

"Okay, I won't talk, and my eyes are closed, but you need to talk to me. Where am I, and what are you doing here?"

I hear someone open the door. Their shoes squeak on the floor when they walk. Mr. Sorenson," she says. "You need to call your wife."

"Rebekah, I'll be right back. I need to call Esther. The kids are fine. They're with Mrs. Callahan. And, Andy's in jail."

That's all I need to know for now. I hear Kenny open the door and softly close it behind him. I don't wake again for another eighteen hours. When I do, I see Kenny's silhouette in the dark room

41

vigilantly waiting for me to heal.

"Kenny," I whisper.

He stands and walks to my bedside, taking my hand.

"I'm here."

"Is Dad losing the bank?"

"Don't know. Too soon to tell, but we're working on fixing the problem. This is not your worry, Rebekah."

"What happened to me? I mean how did you get here? How did you know I was here? I was going to call you. I was taking a shower and was going to go out and find a job, and then I was going to call you and Esther."

"Rebekah. Shhh. With your head injury, you're going to be here at least another week. We'll have a lot of time to talk."

"No, Kenny. You don't have to stay. You need to go home and help Dad with the problems at the bank." I don't want to ask, but I have to. "How's Mom?"

Kenny is silent. I look up and in the dim light from the bathroom, I see a tear fall.

"Is she dead?" I whisper.

"Soon."

"Ah, Mom." I cry.

"Rebekah," he says, "your dad and Esther commissioned me to stay at your side until I can bring you and the kids home. Your mother promised Esther she will stay alive long enough to see you before she goes. And, knowing your mother, she's not leaving without telling you goodbye."

Chapter Seven: Rebekah

My mother dies on a Wednesday morning in 1985. The November sky is blue and the sun shines through the south facing French doors from her bedroom to her garden, also now dead. She dies looking at her three daughters who promise their father they won't cry in front of her. She dies in the arms of her husband of thirty-four years lying on the bed beside her, his arm around her, running one finger down the hollow of her cheekbone. She tries to whisper something before taking her last breath. My father shakes with silent sobs as our mother's flat, scarred chest pushes out one more breath of life, then stills.

Like everything she did in life, she planned her death to perfection. Esther scribed it on three by five cards precisely the way our mother dictated it.

Number One:. Call Bishop Williams. 336-2412
Number Two: Call Sister Hughes-Relief Society Pres. 336-6402.
Number Three: Call Evans Mortuary, ask for Danny. 336-4550.

Mom talked to Danny on several occasions. Once he came to the house so she could show him how to usher her body out the French doors through her garden for her to have one last look, and bypass the living room where she knew her grandchildren would be sitting. "Don't let them see the body bag," she told him. "It will scare them to death."

The next card describes her wishes for her casket: 'A velvet rose-colored lining inside a pine box. Wild flowers and sagebrush on the lid, which surprises me, because she so loved the domestic flowers in her garden.

For the front cover of the funeral program, she picked a picture of her and Dad taken at my second wedding. On the back cover, she requested the poem I wrote to her on her birthday the year before. Inside, on the left insert, she wants the 23rd Psalm inscribed from the Old Testament of the King James Version of the Bible.

The next card lists the outline of the program: music, with oversight by Molly; and speakers, with oversight by Kenny. It isn't a ceremony to memorialize my mother in some grandiose way, as some might guess by the way she planned it, but a ritual to keep her part of us in an everlasting, heartfelt way. Knowing what I now know about our family's failing bank, I assume she wanted to take the burden of organizing her funeral off my father.

She told Esther to spare me the embarrassment of not being allowed to touch her sacred temple clothes when Esther and Molly dress her for the casket. I don't have a temple recommend and only my sisters qualify for the job. I don't know if she knew about my ex-communication. I asked Dad later, and he said he knew but they'd never talked about it and he never told her. I didn't ask Dad how he found out. I assume Kenny told him. The only reason I didn't want him to know was I didn't want to give Fuller the satisfaction of thinking he hurt my dad.

Esther tells me Mom wants me to do her hair and makeup and put on her temple garments, bra, and slip. Temple garments are special underwear Mormons wear who have taken temple vows. I can touch those without the Bishop's permission. Mom told Esther she thought I'd know how to stuff her bra so it looks like her breasts. Esther says she laughed when she said it. I don't laugh when Esther tells me. I'm not sure why she thought that was my forte. I have nice, plump breasts and don't need an added buttress; but I fix my mom with nice looking breasts, the way she asked of me.

When the mortician, Danny Evans, arrives to get my mother's body, Dad retrieves his consecrated oil. He calls for Kenny and Scott to come into the bedroom and together they give her body a blessing, the way they did over and over while she was alive, asking God if he wasn't ready to will her home yet, please make her well. It is a ritual Priesthood men perform in the Mormon Church, and I'm okay with that ceremony, even if I don't agree with everything Mormons do.

The lonely sound of Danny zipping the bag is final. The men of my family emerge teary-eyed as he wheels my mother through the

French doors on the mortuary gurney, as she directed. Dad hugs each of his grandchildren. He holds Jason the longest, pulling up his chin to meet his eye. Dad smiles at him, tussles his hair, and without saying a word, he leaves in his over-sized Mark III black Lincoln, looking much like the hearse itself, following Danny Evans into town.

Molly breaks the silence, "I wonder if I should go into work,"

She works for Dad because she needs the money to support her family and their failing ranch. Dad gave her the job instead of handing her money, which he knew would insult Scott and his parents. Molly married one of the local rancher's sons she fell in love with in high school. Scott served a church mission, mostly because Molly asked him to. She majored in music at Utah State University while he was gone, and when he came home, they got married.

Scott tried college for a semester while Molly continued her music degree. By the next summer, they were back in Malad asking Scott's dad to find a way to make room for them on his small cattle ranch. I know my father's bank fronted the money for Olson's to buy the neighboring farm.

I know Molly thinks since Dad won't be at the bank the rest of the day, she should be. Scott agrees and takes their kids home. Scott takes eight-year-old, Bobby, with him most days to help feed cattle, bale hay, and irrigate, when he's not in school. Scott's mother, Sarah Olson, watches five-year-old Lindsay while Molly works. Molly pays her mother-in-law a portion of her paycheck because Scott's parents need the money as much as Scott and Molly do.

Esther, Molly, and I stand in Mom's kitchen, holding each other, crying until we know Mom wants us to stop and go about the business of living. Rosalyn is asleep on her 'blankee' on the white living room carpet. The sun moves across the southern winter sky, shining through the large picture window on the sleeping child while Jason and Eric play in the basement. Esther studies the three by five cards to be sure she has everything right.

I take the opportunity to call Ruth Callahan in Boise, talking laughing and crying for an hour, telling her the wound on my head still hurts, but is healing. I tell her the wound in my heart today hurts worse. I thank her again for calling the police when she did. She tells me she misses us and wants to drive over to Mom's funeral and see the children if the weather permits. I tell her I'll be over to Boise in a week for Andy's preliminary trial and we can spend time together then.

I wasn't lying to Ruth when I told her I didn't own a dress. It is a blessing to me to have Mom's large walk-in closet full of the finest clothes sold in Salt Lake City and most not worn for a very long time. Over the past year, she withered to a frail 90 pounds of bones and sagging skin. I ask Esther for my mother's black wool Pendleton suit to wear to the funeral. "Of course, honey. Take whatever clothes you need. Well, ask Daddy first, but I'm sure he's okay with it."

These beautiful, well-tailored clothes prove to be a god-send to me, and I am sure she is proud I find them attractive. When I put them on, I feel as though they are my mother herself shrouding me from the world, like the way her temple garments were to her. I learn to temper my foul mouth when I wear the Armani grey suit, knowing she wouldn't chastise me, but she would feel bad if I dressed in her lovely skirt and jacket she purchased for two-hundred dollars and let my filthy language soil them like dripping hot butter down the front.

I soon learn Mother's don't just die—they leave one small piece at a time. It is years before I stop driving to her grave every morning to have coffee with her, though I know she doesn't condone the coffee. I do know she enjoys the company as much as I do.

We decide the funeral should be on Saturday, which, essentially, was out of my mother's hands since she didn't know what day of the week she would leave us. Regardless, she directed Danny Evans to conduct the viewing at his mortuary the night before the funeral, from 6 o'clock to 8 o'clock. The viewing on the morning of her funeral should start at 10 o'clock AM in the Relief Society room at the ward church house until 11:45, at which time the family is to hold the family prayer, to be given by Scott.

Our ward church house is also known as the Malad Stake House, which is a complicated pyramid of hierarchy. Organizational structure aside, the Malad Stake House building is the most interesting building in all of Malad, and to me, a second childhood home. I attended two sessions of church on Sundays, primary once a week on Mondays after school until I was in Jr. High School. Then it was M.I.A. which stood for Mutual Improvement Association, but we called it just Mutual. It is a religious study for girls, and Boy Scouts for the boys, and church parties and events for both boys and girls from time to time. We met on Tuesday nights. Esther drove us until she graduated and left for college. By then I was old enough to drive.

We filled the car with the neighbor kids from St. John, mostly the Jenkins and Driscoll kids. The Jenkins's were like wild hyenas, making it easy for me to understand why their dad lost his lower arm and hand in the hydraulic hitch on the tractor. They screamed and kicked the back of the car seat, and I often threatened to make them walk. The Driscoll kids were quiet, and said "thank you Rebekah," when I picked them up and "thank you, Rebekah," again when I dropped them off.

Once I turned to the Jenkins's and said, "see, you little shits, the Driscoll's behave the way you're supposed to." They told their mother what I said, who told my mother, who told me she didn't blame me, but she reprimanded me, telling me I should watch my mouth.

With this kind of history it seems easy to understand why it is sad for me to be expelled from a place I cherish so. The memories I associate with this building, where I tell my mother goodbye for the last time, has very little to do with the way I choose to worship God; but everything to do with the way I worship life itself. This shrine, this beautiful old building with dark mahogany wooden benches and the old pipe organ delivered from Boston in the early 1900s and installed pipe-by-pipe, makes the chapel feel like a sanctuary when Molly begins to play the organ.

I try lumping everything together to describe it. Then I realize it's not the whole, but the parts I love: The steep sloped A-line roof over the entry way, the long stairway to the front doors where I sat many summer nights talking to friends after Mutual with the sound of frogs croaking along the ditch banks, and the smells of fresh-mown alfalfa hay lingering in the air. I even love the propane tank hidden by the back door where gas distributor, Grant McDonald, painted "No Smoking" in black block letters. Then someone spray-painted below it, "and no drinking." After which some high schooler spray-painted "and no fornicating." But Brother Jenkins painted over everything except the "no smoking" part with white water-based paint that wore off every year.

By Wednesday afternoon, Mom and Dad's closest friends, Betsy and Niles Ogden, come to the house. They live in Samaria, about 15 miles south of where we live. Betsy hands me a meat loaf and mashed potato casserole. She tells me stories about her shopping excursions to Salt Lake and Ogden with Mom. Each tale is treasure. I ask her how her son Paul is doing. She tells me he joined a big architecture firm in Chicago.

Paul and I spent many nights together on the back roads of Oneida County emptying cans of beer, or bottles of cheap wine. He was not a lover, just a friend, and a good one, though we lost touch. The last we talked, I ask him to be my maid of honor at my first wedding. He laughed. I knew he was gay, and he talked to me a lot about it. Though the rumors exist in the undercurrent of our community, I never discussed it with anyone, including my family. I suspect Betsy talked to Mom; and Niles discussed it with Dad, but I am glad she seems proud of him. He deserves that kind of support.

On Thursday night, I talk to Dad about wearing Mom's clothes and he tells me she'd love it. Yet, he doesn't say how he feels about it; and that is what's important to me. Late Friday afternoon we are getting dressed to go to the mortuary for the viewing, which seems like an odd thing to do—file past the dead body just to have a look at them—but everyone does it, so in accordance with Mom's instructions, we will be doing it as well.

I come out of my bedroom in the black two-piece gabardine wool suit from Mom's closet. When Dad looks up at me, his face drains and he begins shaking his head, ever so slightly. Then I see him smile.

"Oh, Rebekah, you look lovely." He says it as if it's the first time he's ever seen me in a dress.

"Come here," he says, walking into the master bedroom. He opens my mother's top dresser drawer and pulls out a green velvet box.

"Turn around."

He drapes the two-stand pearl necklace around my neck. The white pearls fall against the black wool jacket. "Here are the earrings that go with the necklace." He hands me two large pearls with a diamond at the bottom.

This is out of character for him to display so much tender emotion, but this is an emotional day for him.

"Thanks, Dad," is all I can say. I tuck away his approval with a deep sigh, hoping he understands how much it means to me.

"I gave these to your mother as a wedding gift," his voice cracks. "I want you to have them. Well, I suppose I mean, your mother and I want you to have them."

I don't need to ask him how he feels about me wearing my mother's clothes. I don't have to ask him how we will go on without her. I give him a kiss on the cheek and say, "we're going to be fine, Daddy. We're going to miss her, but we'll be fine." And I mean it. I am done feeling sorry for myself; done beating myself up for the mistakes I've made; and I am ready to be Lars Helland's daughter. One he can be proud of, though he already is.

"I'll get the kids and let's go," I say. Rosalyn is in her high chair where I left her. She picks up cheerios with both hands and stuffs them into her mouth. The boys are sitting in front of the television, their new white shirts tucked into black cotton pants we found at the Evans Merc on Main Street.

"Are you just in town for the funeral?" Allison Hess asked me when I laid the clothes on the high wood counter near the cash register, the day before.

"No," I said. "I've moved back to Malad."

"For good?" she asked.

"For now," I said.

Chapter Eight: Rebekah

For all the people coming in droves on a cold Saturday morning in November to tell my mother goodbye, the one person who attempted—not on one occasion, but later two—to destroy what she created from her body and spirit, all she nurtured from her body and spirit, and all she instilled in dignity and self-respect—that one man—sends his condolences to my father.

Leon Fuller said he would be out of town on Saturday and regrets not being able to attend. Dad doesn't mention it, but among the hundreds who fill the chapel, Leon Fuller's absence was vastly apparent to others, and a relief to me.

My mother's death and her service deserve detail because it's a good way to introduce the people who this story is about—the people of Malad Valley who feed from the veins of Malad City like the veins of a mountain spring, running from the drainages to the flats, where one-hundred and fifty years before the year 1985, lay barren and benign.

Malad Valley is geographically defined by elevation, mountain ranges, and the skiff of water draining from the winter snow pack. It is about 200 square miles, delineated by the Utah border to the south, the Malad mountain pass to the north, the Blue Springs Hills on the West and Malad Range, the northern extension of the Wasatch Range, to the east. Malad City is geographically 100 miles north of Salt Lake City, Utah; 60 miles south of Pocatello, Idaho; 50 miles northwest of Logan, Utah; and 50 miles to and from Morton Thiokol, the government-funded source of employment on the salt flats of northwest Utah. Thiokol is the subsidy for local farmers who cannot make a living on land 4,700 feet above sea level with 15.6 inches of precipitation and 125 frost-free days in a good year.

While the greater part of Idaho slopes toward the Columbia River and it's affluent, only Malad, Preston and Bear Lake tributaries, such as the Bear River, flow to the Great Salt Lake where the fresh mountain waters of Idaho become brine. Malad River, a tributary of Bear River, is where the beaver would subsist on wild parsnip or meadow fennel, a poisonous plant when eaten by the early French trappers who killed the beaver for their pelts, became deathly ill. And, while it could have many meanings, which it did through the years, Malad is French for sick, or ill.

After the death of over four-hundred, mostly women and children, at the battle of Bear River to the east of Malad, in 1863, the Indians, The Shoshone Weavers of Grass Lodges, with the aid of the Mormon Church in the newly established Salt Lake City, settled the Malad Valley. It would prove to be an important north-south passageway, especially in moving goods into Montana for gold miners to subsist and, would soon require a bank to feed the temporal needs of the people and a church to feed the spiritual needs.

The people attending my mother's funeral are the children of the children of the children who settled this valley. Most of them Mormon, most of them Caucasian, and most of them of Welsh decent with a proclivity for believing in magic.

These are the people who assemble on this cold November day to mourn our loss, and the loss of our Grandfather Thomas' only child. These are also the very people, for the most part, who darken the door of my father's bank, that was my grandfather's bank, and my great-grandfather's bank. I have since come to believe their ability to survive in Malad at all is because of the Bank they can borrow money from, and the Church they can borrow hope from. It is where they go to renew their faith, believing next year will be a better crop, or higher wheat or cattle price next year; and Morton Thiokol as their back up to help pay the bills.

The congregation gathers in the chapel while we kiss our mother gently, all those who wish to do so. My father's brother, Uncle David, and his wife Nancy, who live in Ogden, are the only ones from my father's family who attend the funeral. The rest either passed on or moved farther away.

We follow the Pine casket down the hall and into the chapel where Molly sits the organ with pipes blaring, the vibrations pounding at my heart while she plays *God of our Father*. As it rings out, I see people's lips moving to the words. Dad carries Rosalyn up the aisle, Esther holds Eric's hand and Kenny has his hand on Jason's shoulder as they walk side by side to the front bench—we call them benches, not pews, and I'll never know why. Scott holds his children's hands, Bobby on one side and Lindsay on the other.

I walk with Grandpa Thomas, taking his right arm as he maneuvers his cane with his left hand. We walk between Kenny and Scott, me in my mother's black gabardine wool suit with her double strand pearl necklace around my neck and her pearl earrings hanging from my earlobes. My black, straight hair is pulled up and twisted in a bun covering my head wound. My mother's black high-heels make me as tall as Scott, standing out like I am announcing to the world I'm back in town. My closer friends will wonder why Andy isn't with me. My mother's friends will wonder why I am wearing her suit. I walk next to my grandfather, who has shrunk to somewhere around five and a half feet, making me an odd companion for him.

We sit in the order we walked down the aisle and wait for our small family procession to finish filing in. Danny Evans, and his young intern, usher the family to their seats. Dad asks the bank employees if they will join the family, because, as he tells them, they are family to us.

We ask Niles and Betsy Ogden to sit with our family; and Scott's family, Lester and Sarah Olson, along with Lance and Melanie McDonald and their three children, whose names I didn't know on the day we bury my mother, but would, by summer's end burn forever in my heart.

 Lance and Melanie are Scott and Molly's best friends. Lance played football with Scott at Malad High School. On more than one occasion after a victorious football game, I drove him home, along with Scott, when they were too drunk to drive. We all ended up at Deep Creek reservoir to hide out and celebrate. In southeast Idaho, we didn't have lakes. We dammed up what little water flow we had for controlled water usage. Recreation was the by-product, particularly for high schoolers looking for discrete places to engage in a variety of furtive activities.

Because my mother is an only child, with only one aunt, the first ten rows of the chapel are not going to be filled by our immediate family the way they are by most funerals in Malad, so Danny Evans ushers the final grievers in as Molly completes round three of *God of our Fathers* and decides to play a song she thinks our mother will like, *Come, Come Ye Saints*. It is not on my mother's song list, or seemingly appropriate for a funeral, but appropriate for that moment. Molly knows it by heart and plays it with purpose. It is Molly's favorite song. I watch her lips move to the words as she plays—words soon to become the mantra of our family as we face our challenges in the months ahead: "All is well. All is well."

Sitting on the front row, I think about the people sitting behind me and wonder who they are; what their faces look like now. It has been twelve years since I stepped inside this church house and I don't realize, until now, how much I miss it. Like Molly, I love the organ pipes and the rich, full sound they make. I love the amber glass light fixtures hanging on long chains from the ceiling, the masterful woodwork, the high ceilings. I wonder if my old high school friends are here. My ten-year high school reunion was two summers ago, but I didn't go because Andy refused to spend time with what he called *a bunch of lunatics belonging to a cult religion.* I quit arguing with him about the definition of a cult religion and though I thought of going alone, I stayed home to avoid yet another argument.

I wonder how many of the class of 1973 are still in Malad. I know of a few. Some came back to teach school, or farm when college didn't work out, or just stayed and made the 100-mile round trip to Morton Thiokol, getting paid decent wages and retirement benefits.

I wonder how many of the former Malad football team came home from their missions, married, and were later called to be Ward Clerk. Like Kenny, I wonder if they rifle through permanent records and smile to themselves when they read my file. Was it Devon Naylor, who bragged on getting a taste of Jackie Olson, Scott's older sister; or Terry Owen who claimed he nailed Janice Jenkins, one of the four daughters of Brother Jenkins, the one-handed janitor of the church.

I know I seem bitter, and clearly, I am. I can't let it go; yet I know my excommunication was Fuller's way of trying to gouge my dad. I wonder if Devon and Terry confessed to Bishop Fuller about their one-night stands before leaving on their missions. Did Fuller forgive them and say, as he should have said to me, God and the Church forgive your youthful indiscretion. Or did he believe since no babies were made, no harm, no foul. And after they made their confession to him, did he call in those girls and ask them to describe graphic positions, the same as he asked me? Or did he just smile and shake their hand for not getting pregnant, which would have caused the boys to relinquish their mission calls to stay home and get married instead.

Or perhaps their guilt was remediated or encapsulated by some other type of penance or denial. After all, their deeds were only recklessly bragged about in high school locker rooms, not buried in church archives for all who have a key to the records to see.

While I sit in my mother's funeral, mulling this over in my mind, I think what I resent most is, no matter how many times I slip out the back door of my life to run away from myself again, I am reminded of where it all started. At the tender age of eighteen, my running shoes were forced onto my feet and, even now, I can't figure out how to get them off.

Chapter Nine: Rebekah

November, I think, is not a good month to die; though January to March is worse. The thought of someone you love—someone who shivers at the slightest wind, or wears bulky socks around the house all winter—going down into the cold November earth makes me want to place one of the many quilts Mom made in her lifetime into the casket to tuck around her. I want to keep her warm until the quilt, her temple clothes, the stuffing I placed into her bra, and the flesh and muscles all become one unified dust of the Malad Valley, leaving only the structure of her frame to defy decay. It is this frame that shaped us; this pelvis that carried us, this rib cage that held her heart, this skull that caged her brain. I believe this frame will remain in place forever, the way it protected the tender parts of her she gave to us; Esther, and me, and Molly.

We bury my mother on a Saturday in November near the row of Poplar trees struggling to survive in the harsh high mountain plain. The trees manage to thrive sufficiently to break the severe late-autumn winds, the blowing winter snow in January, and give shade in the heat of July.

At her request, Mary Thomas Helland isn't buried in the Malad City Cemetery, even though her mother is. The city cemetery is located so close to I-15, the interstate cuts off one corner. She told Esther between the noise of the semi-trucks and the proximity of the Malad High School football field raising the dead at Friday night home games, she couldn't stand the thought of being buried near that much chaos. At her request, Dad bought two plots at the St. John cemetery in the exact place she picked out.

With headlights on, the procession moves slowly from the Malad Church to St. John. They turn right and then left in vertical and horizontal patterns following the Government Survey section lines across the Malad Valley to the St. John Cemetery. It is a grand sight. The moment we immerge from our vehicles, the stinging wind ceases to blow and the warm waning sun in the southern sky lingers just a while longer. This would please her, which I believe it did.

The Relief Society President, Bishop Williams, and three other women carry flower baskets, placing them around the mound of displaced earth covered with the green turf blankets. Grandpa Thomas and the children sit in the padded chairs the mortuary provides. Dad, Molly, Esther and I stand next to the casket holding on to each other while Kenny gives the dedicatory prayer.

Kenny's prayer is brief, but simply beautiful. "Father, we dedicate this grave as the final resting place of Mary Thomas Helland, until that glorious day her body becomes whole once more. Amen."

We linger hugging friends and neighbors, which in and of its self, keeps us warm. Jason tells me to take my time, and he escorts Rosalyn and Eric to the car. "I got this Mom," he says.

I now regret wearing four-inch heels penetrating the half-frozen earth, accentuating my presence. Attracting members of our ward I have not seen for years incites questions. I develop a simple answer, "the kids and I are staying with Dad for a while." No one asks where Andy is, but then no one really knows him or remembers his name, except Sister Jenkins, the church janitor's wife, who asks if my husband, Andrew, will be joining us. "No. We have a large flock of sheep on our farm in Lava that need tending."

It isn't a lie. The Powell's are taking care of my sheep until I get livestock trucks to move them to Dad's place where the kids and I will be living. Kenny and I will be back in court in Boise the following week for Andy's preliminary trial, postponed due to my mother's death. We will also vacate the trailer and move my scant belongings to Malad.

I catch Kenny's eye across the top of the crowd and he clears his throat. "Folks, can I have your attention," he says loudly. "It's cooling down and we need to let the mortuary finish their job, so let's all meet at the cultural hall at the church for the wonderful meal the Relief Society Sisters have prepared for us." I wink at him and excuse myself from Sister Jenkins to fetch Grandpa Thomas.

On Sunday, none of us go to church, except Molly and Scott only because Molly plays the organ for the choir and congregational hymns. Kenny and Esther come over early and fix breakfast. The smell of bacon lures me to the kitchen, asking in a teasing voice, "got any coffee?"

Kenny produces a small bottle of Folder's Instant Coffee with a wink. I give him a kiss on the cheek and put a small sauce pan of water on the stove. In a practicing Mormon household, coffee isn't a staple, nor will the kitchen be furnished with a coffee pot or a tea pot. Regardless of the arcane way I prepare it, it tastes delicious.

"You know, you don't have to feed my bad habits." I smirk as I take a sip.

"Ordinarily we wouldn't," Esther says, "but Kenny doesn't want you grumbling about not getting your caffeine fix for the day.

"You know," I say, "if all the folks in Malad Valley were like you guys, this would be a great place to settle down for a long, long time."

"Oh, but Rebekah, they are," Esther says with a sweet nasally whine while Kenny stands behind her, smiling, shaking his head.

"What can I do here?" I ask.

"Sit down and drink your coffee. Breakfast will be ready in about five minutes. Or, go wake up Dad." As I turn to leave Esther looks at me. "I see you're wearing Mom's earrings."

I whirl around and look at her with a frown. I start to say, "Dad said Mom wanted me…," but she interrupts.

"I know, Rebekah. I just wanted to say how beautiful you look with them on, even in your t-shirt and sweats."

"I hope she gave you something special," I say.

"Oh, honey. For the past year, she gave me those parts of her heart, soul and mind the cancer couldn't take. I have her stories and her secret recipes, which she said I could share with you and Molly, by the way. And I thank my Heavenly Father every day I have a husband who was willing to give up his law practice to come here with me to be with Mom this past year."

In that instant I feel guilty as hell. I look at the floor because I can't look at my sister. I hadn't spent the time with Mom I should have—couldn't leave Andy with my children, or trust him not to abuse them in his fits of drunken anger. My angst and regret are revealed. She takes my coffee cup from my hand and hugs me. Esther gives Kenny the signal with a jerk of her head to take the kids out of earshot.

"Mother loved you more than you'll ever know. Her prayer every day was for you to find the courage to leave Andy. When I told her you were in Boise with the kids, she said to me, "I can go now. As soon as Rebekah comes home so I can tell her goodbye, I can go.""

I bury my head in the curve of her neck and sob like a wounded animal. She rubs my back then wipes my face with the dishtowel. "Go tell Dad it's time for breakfast."

"Hungry?" I ask Dad, distracting him from the morning paper.

"Not really, but I'll join you for breakfast." He folds the newspaper but doesn't move. He is staring out the large picture window framing the brown fallow fields as he chews on the place where the tender flesh protrudes under the lower lip. It's the piece of excess flab God installs in us to bite on, keeping us from saying things we shouldn't say, or to making us look like we're thinking because we don't know what to say, or sometimes to keep us from crying. "It was a nice service, wasn't it?"

"Because it was exactly what mom wanted," I reply, perhaps a bit too abrupt. I don't know what else to say. I can't think of anything nice about having her gone, or anything nice about a funeral. I want to ask him about the problems at the bank, and I'm sure he wants to ask to me about the ordeal with Andy.

Kenny walks into the living room. "Come on, Dad and Rebekah. Let's have breakfast." It is as though he is reading our minds. "Rebekah, please go get Jason. Eric said he's still asleep."

We rise from our seats to carry on with life that Sunday morning, the day after we bury my mother in the cold November ground on a hillside overlooking the Malad Valley. It begins a very sad and trying year for everyone, starting with my impulsive departure to Boise, followed by the tragic end of my second marriage, and my mother's life. Like my family, I am glad Mom wasn't here to see the devastation yet to be unleashed in Malad City in 1986.

Chapter Ten: Rebekah

I wake on Monday morning still facing the mess I created in my life. I resent having to spend the rest of the week mopping up instead of grieving. We need to be at Andy's preliminary hearing on Wednesday, clean out the trailer house, visit the doctor to examine my head wound, and I want to spend some time with my friend, Ruth Callahan. I still need to call Easterday's to have them truck the sheep to from Lava to Malad. I write down on my list to call my neighbors in Lava, who are tending my sheep, to coordinate the shipping. More than anything, I'm proud of myself for making a list. Thinking, instead of reacting.

Eric and Jason are enrolled in their third school this fall. The school bus picks them up at the end of the gravel driveway. Dad leaves early for the bank, otherwise he said they could ride into town with him. Dad tells me he can take care of the boys while we are in Boise, but Molly insists they come stay with her. The boys like it here, in Malad. I don't dare tell Jason the sheep are being delivered the end of the week.

I meet with Kenny late Monday morning and review the details of Andy's attorney's offer to settle. They want me to drop charges if Andy agrees to move out of state, never to enter Idaho again without my permission, or knowledge. I keep the livestock, my car, the farm truck, and livestock trailer; and he keeps his GMC truck. We will sell the house in Lava, and split the equity.

I worry about how this is going to affect Eric. I want him to have a relationship with his father. Rosalyn is too young to remember him, but Eric loves him, and I know he loves Eric. I want Rosalyn to know her father, but not like this. I'm surprised Andy does not negotiate a child custody or visitation agreement.

I tell Kenny I really don't think Andy pushed me that morning in the bedroom. I was trying to get away from him and I fell. But it doesn't excuse his intrusion, or the previous abuse. I don't know what Andy would have done about calling for an ambulance. He didn't have time to do anything. When Ruth saw his truck, she called the police immediately. Despite telling her not to come over, she did. The details aren't clear, I only know she got Dad's contact information from Andy, who cooperated with the police. She told me tears were rolling down Andy's cheeks when they loaded me in the ambulance. In the eight years I was married to Andy, I have never seen him cry. A twinge of caring tugs at me when she tells me, but I quickly force it to move on.

We end up not going to court on Wednesday. We agree to the settlement with one additional stipulation; Andy will get some help. I said if a veteran's facility could give him counseling, I'll consider letting Eric visit him, but I'll need some evidence he has worked on his anger issues. I don't say alcohol issues because he knows I have the same problem, and I don't want to openly address it right now. I hope with him out of my life, it is something that will take care of itself.

His attorney explains Andy plans to settle in the Ogden area, near Hill Air Force Base, where they have veteran's facilities to help him, and to stay close to Eric and Rosalyn. It gives me hope. He agrees to a reasonable monthly child support, including money for Jason, who he legally adopted after we were married. I said he could have the furniture, except my sewing machine, the loom my parents bought me, and my dinnerware.

Kenny, Esther and I travel to Boise and clean out the trailer house my children and I occupied for less than a week. We give most of it to Deseret Industries, the local LDS thrift store. I am embarrassed about the trash still in the kitchen; over a dozen empty beer cans, one empty jar of spaghetti sauce, and several cigarette butts. "Not mine," I say when Esther sees the makeshift ashtray.

Ruth comes over when she sees my car. I hug her for a long, long time, feeling her large breasts against me, longing for my mother, happy she had been a mother to me when I needed one.

"Promise you'll stay in touch."

"I will," she says. "But you'll go to Malad and forget all about me,

"I will never, ever forget you, Ruth Callahan. Ever. You are my angel. You saved my life." I hug her again until I know she needs to let go of me.

Chapter Eleven: Rebekah

I can understand why Molly loves what she's doing at the bank, building computerized farm cash flows. She runs her fingers across the computer keyboard the same way she does her piano at home, and the organ at church. Having learned DOS and Microsoft software programs in less than a month, she builds spreadsheets computing profit and loss, automatically adjusting the numbers without an erasure or having to manually re-add the entire column. It completely baffles the auditors who still use a ten-key adding machine.

While Molly works at the bank, I spend my days in sweat pants and a t-shirt, cooking for Dad, feeding sheep, and nursing my self-inflicted wounds. "It's not enough Rebekah, it is time to challenge yourself." Kenny scolds me for my laziness. He points out the doctor gave me a clean bill of health, so, "Get to work!"

"I need help at the law office and Esther has no interest in learning to run a computer. Besides, she's chomping at the bit to take care of Rosalyn." Quietly, I think Kenny is hoping this might rejuvenate Esther's reproductive organs, though I believe Esther has privately given up all hope of ever having children and is happy to help me raise mine.

I wonder exactly when it was that I became interested in the legal world and the agriculture business world all at the same time. I know some things about agriculture, and always found myself talking about crops and sheep and cows with local farmers in Lava when I would stop by the feed store.

Before I loved all the things about farming and ranching, I loved the cowboys; which is what got me in trouble with Michael and Andy. I never paid much attention to what Dad does at the bank, and I never took a second look at a guy in a business suit, unlike my older sister and mother.

It may be ancestral, a bequest running deep in my veins mixing agriculture, banking, and politics in this valley. The political boundaries of Malad City enclose an area of one square mile. Hollow drainages define the mountain range flanking the east side of the interstate highway hovering over the town. Inside Malad City my family's two-story bank building was built on a triangular corner where Bannock and Main Streets converge near the waters of Deep Creek.

Outside Malad City live the bank's borrowers and their wives who sign their names on promissory notes living in communities without the zip codes named Holbrook, Juniper, St. John, Daniels, and Samaria. The names aren't so much towns as they are people defining the place they take root. These are not necessarily the names of towns the FDIC will eventually use to mail the delinquent notifications on the promissory notes the people signed.

It is much the same way the borrowers think about the amount of money they owe the bank when they put their name on the paper with an address tracing them to the name of a town where they don't really live. And yet, they sign the promissory note and write down an address indicating they live someplace different than the place they water their crops and feed their cows and care for the children they take to church on Sundays where they pray to the Lord for money to repay the bank.

What is perplexing about this is very few of the bank's borrowers live inside the city limits of Malad City and yet, this story I am telling is, by all accounts, the allegory of Malad City without connection to its political boundaries, or zip code.

Malad (pronounced "Ma" like the slang word for mother, and "lad" -a young boy) named by French fur trappers who ate the poisonous roots along Deep Creek causing them to fall ill. Deep Creek—the perennial flow of drainage water from the mountains to the east, flows along the edge of my grandfather's back yard, and the parking lot behind my family's two-story bank building.

At the west side of the Malad exit, on Interstate 15, is a refurbished motor hotel newly named The Village Inn. It is a single row of white-washed clapboard bunkers with green shutters tucked under massive elm trees disguising the place as quaint.

Across the street is Ballard Oil, the town's only service station, opening at 6 o'clock in the morning, and closing at 5 o'clock every afternoon, except Sundays. The Village Inn patrons, though generally scant, often complain about the service bell the early-bird customers set off, or the air gun Bob Ballard uses to loosen and tighten lug bolts from tires, or bolts underneath cars on the hydraulic lift in the service shop. It is especially noisy in summer when the overhead door of the service bay is open.

Farmers, up early to tend to irrigation water or bale hay while the patina of dew is still on the windrow, stop at Ballard's if they need a tire changed, or a tank filled with gas, triggering the bell Bob Ballard sets unusually loud because he is hard of hearing. Bob jumps out of his skin when someone taps him on the shoulder from behind to fetch him to fill their tank with gas. He hates it; always imagining it's someone with a gun pointed at his head, wanting to clean out the cash register he keeps locked while he's working in the garage.

To the west of the gas station and motor lodge are several older homes, including my grandfather's house. My grandfather, who is somewhat hard of hearing anyway, finds Ballard's bell pleasant to listen to at the break of dawn through his bedroom window, left open to bring in the cool nighttime air.

However, older women, find the constant buzz of the air gun grinds on their nerves, and tell Bob as much. He can't hear what they are saying, so, lifts his dirty orange cap with our Malad Dragon mascot on the crown, nods, smiles, and then goes back to work

The central business district of Malad City is located on Main Street, all within a two-block stretch. These two blocks encompass early era one and two-story brick and stucco commercial buildings, mostly vacant. To the northeast of Main and Bannock Streets, where our bank is located, is the hill where the century-old Oneida County courthouse is perched overlooking the modern brick bank building with its state-of-the art three-lane drive-through canopy.

Many in Malad City feel the structure is a sign of self-indulgence in a town badly needing facades exfoliated and roof-tops re-mopped with tar. Across the parking lot from the back door of the bank is where my Grandfather Thomas still lives. It is a modest thirties-era brick home framed around the periphery with a black wrought iron fence. My 88-year-old grandfather walks all way around the bank, back to the gate every day, and then sits at the tall wood-framed window, looking down on the cars driving through the canopy. Like the watchman in a watch tower, he keeps an eye out for pending danger, though he mostly watches for Dad or Molly to stop by for a visit after work.

He is not sorry he agreed to build the new bank, but he is sorry it wasn't built soon enough for him to enjoy the massive feel of it, or sit in the large second floor office my father now occupies. Instead, he sits by his window, his starched white shirt buttoned to the top of his poorly shaven neck, his V-necked red cardigan smoothed over this thin torso. Using his mahogany cane as a fulcrum, he rocks back and forth in his high-back Victorian velvet chair that looks like a throne, peering at patrons and employees who come and go all day. If a small child looks up while riding with their mother through the last drive-up lane, they will likely scream at the frightful face of an old man looking down at them.

He covets the ten or so minutes Molly spends stopping in to say hello after work. She usually brings fresh-baked oatmeal and raisin cookies like Mom used to. When I start working for Kenny's law office in mid-January, I make a habit of stopping by to visit Grandpa at lunchtime. His caretaker, Mrs. McMillian, fixes an incredible lentil chili on Wednesdays and chicken soup with homemade noodles on Fridays. Grandpa Thomas calls her McMilly. "Good soup today, McMilly," he says. He loves having his granddaughters stop in, though he has less patience for his great-grandchildren.

"Those Fullers got us yet?" he asks me, at least once a week.

"Well, Grandpa, we're just not going to let that happen." I rub his hand and kiss him on his chafing baldhead as I go back to work at Kenny's law office.

When Kenny and Esther moved back to Malad to take care of Mom, Kenny remodeled the old building the bank vacated on Main Street. Grandpa wanted to give it to him, but Kenny insisted on putting twenty-thousand dollars into Grandpa's private care fund, though the building, as it was, was hardly worth half that. It had been vacant for years.

After remodeling the building, Kenny, rented half the space to Farm Bureau Insurance, and used the other half for his law office. He kept the stately old oak counter with intricate carvings for the credenza in his private office and salvaged the sturdy desks, retrofitting them for personal computers. The crumbling moldy carpet is gone, exposing the original hardwood floors. He pulled out the false acoustic-tile ceilings and accented the brick walls and high ceilings. Esther discovered a rich Brissac Jewell fabric she fashioned into period-appropriate drapes.

In addition to the lobby-waiting room and two private offices, there is a bathroom and a small break room plus the old walk-in safe we now use to store files.

Kenny considered bringing a partner in with him, but few attorneys are interested in joining a law practice in Malad, Idaho. In the meantime, he is happy to train me as a legal assistant. In March and April he suggests I should think about going to college and getting my law degree. By early summer he says I am not allowed to go anywhere.

I suspect Kenny is financially well off. He won a significant lawsuit against one of the big mining companies in Soda Springs in 1983 when his client received a three million-dollar settlement of which Kenny's law firm retained close to a million. From my limited anecdotal evidence, Kenny is in a good position financially and does not press destitute people, now coming to him, to pay hefty legal fees for helping save their farms and ranches.

I hear him say to his clients, "if the steer in your pasture is unencumbered, I suppose Esther and I can use half a beef in our freezer." He says his clients need to believe they have an obligation to pay for his services to maintain their own dignity.

Here is what I think. I think as much as we in the West believe we are independent, we are not. When the people of Malad Valley—and everywhere else for that matter—suffered from twenty percent interest rates in the late 1970s, and wheat prices dropped to a third of what they were in 1977, a perfect storm was created. A drought a year earlier caused the price of wheat to rise over seven dollars a bushel and everyone assumed it would remain at that price.

The farmers, in their zeal for more seven-dollar wheat, and with the encouragement of USDA wanting to fill commodity storage facilities, planted fence-row to fence-row. Prices plummeted to near two-fifty a bushel while farmland values were still escalating. The phenomenon resulted in a collision of disastrous commodity prices with the real estate market exuberance of the 1980s. Farmers leveraged their high-value farmland to absorb over-due short-term debt with no ability to repay the new debt they created. I believe it took the revenues of Kenny's settlement from a large corporation to subsidize the legal fees of these destitute farm families caught in this economic scourge to keep them from losing everything they owned.

It was the collective tax payers of the United States who electrified Malad, and the rural areas around it, because truth be told, there was no money emanating from these humble agrarians to pay for that kind of infrastructure. I tell Kenny and Dad, loud enough so the Farm Bureau people next door to our office can hear, they can be as politically conservative as they please, but we, in Malad City, Idaho, already live in a socialized society. It started with Brigham Young, and continued by Franklin Delano Roosevelt. "I'll never know," I say, "why it takes five years of a farmer's backbone touching his belly button to vote for a Democrat, but mark my words, in 1986, the democrat, Cecil Andrus is going to be our next governor."

Kenny agrees. His best friend, and old law partner is a Democrat, and Kenny is sure someday, if he is not a general authority of the Mormon Church, his friend will likely make a run for congress or governor. I frown at him saying, "I thought I was you best friend." He laughs and teases, "wrong."

The first time I sit down with one of Kenny's clients developing a bankruptcy expense plan, or, as we call them, "work-out budgets" I go down the list of questions he provided. He told me I could take over that sector of his practice if I did a good job. After our first case settled, our service assisting farmers under water spread like wildfire. Kenny's name came up in small circles of conversation; primarily on Sunday mornings when men gathered after Priesthood

Meeting to buoy each other up, or just listen quietly garnering a glint of hope of finding a rescuer, or a miracle worker, the way Ruth Callahan had been to me.

Some days, Esther, who insists on watching Rosalyn while I help Kenny, asks Molly's friend, Melanie McDonald, if she will watch Rosalyn while she helps answer phones at the office.

Lance and Melanie McDonald are still Scott and Molly's best friends, a relationship lasting since high school. They have a sixty-cow dairy in Daniels, ten miles northwest of Malad. They have three children near the same age as mine. Her youngest, Grace, is the sweetheart of the valley. Everyone calls her "Gracie", or "Amazing Grace" when Melanie brings her to church, or to town to go shopping. When Melanie picks up supplies at Malad Feed and Grain, where she used to work after she and Lance were married, all the men who work there dote on Gracie. Gracie is a perfect companion for Rosalyn. She is happy to play the afternoons away with her new friend. At 5 o'clock I drive out to Melanie and Lance's dairy farm to pick up Rosalyn. Gracie, who is almost a year older than Rosalyn, always gives Rosalyn a hug and kiss on the cheek before we leave.

The days in the office are long with paperwork and by late February, I start taking files home to work on after the kids go to sleep. First, we eat the pizza I pick up in the frozen food department at Dan's Grocery. Dad rarely arrives home before midnight, so he eats whatever is left. Esther fixes a casserole and leaves it in the fridge if she has time; or Dad slips over to Grandpa's house around 6 o'clock to eat dinner with him.

After dinner, we dress in our insulated chore coveralls I bought at Cal Ranch Farm Supply Store in Pocatello the week after Christmas when the coveralls, buckets and feed tubs were all on sale for half-off. We look like a family of brown ducks, all bundled up from large to small, following the worn pathway from the house to the farmyard to feed the sheep. We often push through snowdrifts wafting up to Eric's waist, frozen in place like giant waves on the ocean. Every night I thank my family for rescuing me from that trailer park in Boise. Any amount of snow, wind, and bitter cold is heaven compared to where we nearly ended up. I just wish Ruth Callahan lived in Malad. We all miss her, and I tell her so when I call her for a weekly update.

The barnyard floodlight shines on the livestock pens with enough filaments to easily see while we break bales of frozen alfalfa hay, pulling apart the sheaves and fighting hungry ewes as we fill the manger rows. We leave Rosalyn sitting on top of the stacked hay to keep her safe. Jason feeds the small pen of rams separated from the flock and then grains the dry and yearling ewes.

The herd of pregnant ewes stays in the large common area, securely fenced with the barn along one side, and a door opening into the yard. In the barn are six small empty pens we call jugs, awaiting mothers with new babies.

In the next few weeks, the thirty or so ewes will start lambing. I make two or three visits to the corral each night, caring for the mothers in labor, pulling a lamb when necessary. It requires getting the moms and their new babies into the jugs in the barn. The kids and I clean and scatter fresh straw in the pens during the first few weeks in January. Eric carefully places the new galvanized metal water buckets and black rubber feed tubs in each pen.

It seems to me the ewes prefer to lamb in the wee hours of the morning after they eat, take a long drink of water, and relax. I don't mind being there alone in the middle of the night, watching the snowflakes fight with the streams of light. I bend over a laboring ewe, grabbing her legs and pulling her toward me, gently laying her onto her side. Breaking the wax from her teats, I give her new baby easy access to its first meal. More often than not, there are two babies, and sometimes three. In that case, I graft the third onto a single or a mother whose lamb did not survive.

I am witnessing new life at its finest. There is no judgment here, no remorse, no regrets, only love. These expectant mothers only answer to their babies. That is it. A nice system, I think, as I watch in the cold night air. The steam pours off the hot, wet mucus of a newborn lamb lying on the frozen ground. A mother nuzzles the new life worrying only about survival, mothering, and love. Bringing her offspring safely into this world seems to be the only focus of this ewe breeding and baring her young without contrition or guilt.

Jason doesn't mind the sheep so much anymore. It is Andy he dislikes. I tell Jason he shouldn't be tough on Andy. He did the best he knew how. It was the demons of Vietnam we need to hold accountable, reminding him Andy is getting help.

It is heartwarming being together at night, talking, laughing and watching our animals munch and thrive. After chores, the kids take their baths, then take turns reading a story to Rosalyn. Long before lights out, she is asleep. Jason and Eric work on their homework while I pour through files full of sorrow and distress. I cannot imagine the fear and anguish these families are enduring every day, especially the children.

By early spring, the US Congress creates a special type of bankruptcy for small family farmers, reorganizing their debt, allowing them a chance to stay their debtors. Kenny becomes the expert, and he teaches me how to prepare the paperwork required for credit counseling, meeting the preconditions of filing a Chapter 12 Bankruptcy.

All very boring to most people, but I happen to find it fascinating, the same as Molly. I do the cash flows and balance sheets on my new computer Kenny purchased. Molly teaches me the short cuts, and how to code the spread sheet to make the job easier. As the weeks go by, I am doing more and more. Our clientele grows by the hour. Kenny is like Jesus feeding the five thousand. He refuses to turn anyone away while making promises requiring miracles.

"Rebekah can handle that," I hear him say. "I'll just set up a time Rebekah can meet with you and she'll put together all the required paperwork." By the first of May, I have forty-five new lambs. In addition, we have one-hundred thirty-seven clients, all of them destitute farm families crying out for someone to help them. Hard as we try, Kenny and I do not know how to stop the bleeding.

Chapter Twelve: Rebekah

Every year the Samaria Mountains announce spring has arrived sending out a powerful rumble heard throughout the valley. Geologists from Idaho State University in Pocatello believe the groaning is air trapped in small fissures or caverns throughout the mountains. The Washakie Indians believe the rumblings are awakening spirits of the mountains. Niles Ogden, my father's best friend, and chairman of his Bank Board of Trustees, has lived in Samaria his entire life. He says the rumblings this spring are louder than he's ever heard. Perhaps the spirits are trying to warn us.

This is also the time of year on the high mountain desert the aroma of lilacs begins to mix with hints of budding honeysuckle while tender diamond-shaped leaves from Lombardy Poplars shoot forth. These deciduous cottonwoods line farmsteads like fortresses around the periphery of our sedate farming community of less than two thousand people. But, like the unsuspecting Sho Ban Indians, slaughtered in 1863 as they camped along the Bear River, what appears sedate and inconsequential, is sitting directly in the crosshairs of the FDIC

The U.S. Congress created the Federal Deposit Insurance Corporation (FDIC) as an independent agency to maintain stability and confidence in the financial system of the United States, much the same way Coach Evans maintains stability and confidence in assuring our community he upholds a solid football program at Malad High School. The FDIC insures deposits, they examine and supervise banks, and they manage receiverships. That is technically who they are and what they do. It hardly describes what they did to us.

At an elevation of 4,700 feet, the water on the surface of St. John Reservoir freezes, thaws, and freezes again in any twenty-four-hour period in March, and often as late as mid-April. It frequently leaves pockets of low-lying farm fields full of frozen winter wheat. But, the six-hundred plus files describing assets frozen by the FDIC on a

Friday in May leaves farmland fallow and families bankrupt throughout our small community. As reality thaws, the raw carnage begins to leach from the ruins of the bank, perched at the edge of Deep Creek, trickling financial and emotional ruin throughout all southeast Idaho.

On the second Friday in May, I ask Scott to feed the sheep while the kids and I take Dad to Salt Lake for the weekend. We are ready for a day out of town, and Dad is confident he is gaining ground at the bank.

Knowing Grandpa Thomas keeps vigilance over the bank from his living room window, Dad warns him weekly if they come, it will be on a Friday afternoon at closing time. He should not be alarmed or fear for Molly, him, or the others if, or when, it happens. But as Dad gains confidence the pending crises is waning, he reminds Grandpa less and less.

Through the long winter and spring, surviving day to day without my mother, my father is confident he proved to the state auditors on their last go-around they are moving the right direction. He gets the impression after a private conversation with an old friend who works in the Department of Finance, the Fullers are pushing for a shutdown and takeover. One night in March, we are all sitting in the law office after hours trying to measure probability of a takeover by the Fullers.

"Doesn't it ever bother you, Dad to have the Fullers chipping away at our family like this?"

Dad said he admits it seems undemocratic to have Fullers own the conglomeration of both banks and run the church as well. With a wink, Kenny reminds us God runs the church.

Our conversations go like that, off and on, through the harsh, winter days of January, February and into March. All the while, Kenny is taking on more and more clients, working through mediated financial restructure with Farmers' Home Administration or Federal Land Bank, who is also in a crisis, now asking congress for a bail-out.

We work on cases involving two delinquent loans at the Fuller's bank. They refuse to budge an inch, forcing Kenny to file bankruptcy on their behalf, calmly responding, "we'll just have work this out in Bankruptcy Court then, Clarence."

Dad wonders if that incident pushed the Fullers to meet with the Department of Finance to assure them there is a standing offer to buy out the solvent assets of the Thomas family bank as soon as they pull the plug. Kenny reminds Dad it is against the law for Fullers to coerce the Department of Finance to force a shutdown. I say, under my breath, "when did that ever stop them?"

Every Friday evening, week after week, we have an auspicious celebration when the FDIC does not show up. A calm that makes us believe we cleared the most recent audit. Molly seems the most pleased saying, with her best humility, her spreadsheets are making a difference. Even the auditors tell her they help clear issues they are having. But there always looms that one mega loan, the one my father can't shake, or get another investor to buy out to get it off the bank's books. It is the highly speculative loan his board approved for land development at Bear Lake, going against the advice of my father and Niles Ogden.

It is a warm Friday evening in May. I am cleaning off my desk and getting ready to pick up Dad and the kids to go south. No one sees them coming: The five black Chevrolet Suburban's with charcoal tinted windows speeding past budding alfalfa and stooling grain, moving in unison along Interstate 15 into southeast Idaho as I finish up the last spreadsheet for the week.

From both parking lot approaches off Bannock and East 50 South Street, the small Suburban militia surrounds my family's wheat-colored bank-building at exactly 5:07 PM on Friday, May 9, 1986 taking Dad, Molly, Ruthie, Dixie and three girls just out of high school working the teller cages, hostage.

Kenny and I are leaving the law office when Sheriff Benson informs us there is a blockade of federal vehicles surrounding the bank. Federal Marshals, the FDIC Asset Manager and Assistant Manager, federal attorneys, and accountants have stormed the building. Dad, from his office on the second floor, pulled the alarm, not knowing who they were. The Sheriff told us when he responded from the courthouse on the bluff above the bank, he was informed the bank was under siege by the FDIC and to move away from the area.

Kenny rushes out the front door past the Sherriff with me trailing behind. He tells me to stay back as he tries to approach the front door of the bank telling the armed Federal Marshal he is legal counsel to the bank president. Immediately he is escorted away and told not to come back. "I don't think they can do that," he says to me walking back to the office. "In fact, I'm sure they can't." He looks through his telephone card file on his desk, saying he is going to call Congressman Stallings' office in Pocatello, or Governor Evans, who is, incidentally, from Malad. I tell him I'll call Esther and Scott. It isn't until the next day I learn the whole story from Molly.

At five o'clock, that Friday afternoon, Molly inserts the keys in the front door-lock to close the bank when, like a scene from Desperado, the parking lot fills with black vehicles. Doors fling open and people jump out. The front men are crouched with guns poised to shoot, running toward her. Molly quickly locks the door when she sees the hoard of black suits converging on her. Her hands are shaking. She doesn't know if she should keep the door locked or let them in.

She stares at a middle-aged tall, dark-blond man on the other side of the window now holding his badge against the glass. He mouths the words "open the door." She looks back at Ruthie and Dixie for confirmation. The man pounds his fist against the door shouting, *"Open the god damned door. Now!"* Fumbling with the keys she hears Ruthie in a low-pitched battle cry, "sons-a-bitches. You sons-a-bitches!" Tears well in Molly's eyes as she tries to steady her hand to turn the key. As the lock releases the masses catch Molly in the rush, pushing her back into the lobby. All she can think is to go find our dad.

The tall, husky man with prominent nose and piercing hollow blue eyes begins shouting orders as soon as he is inside. *"Everyone freeze, stay where you are. No one move!"* He holds out his hand toward Molly and motions with his fingers for the keys. She timidly sets them in the palm of his open hand.

He yells at the five women staring at him, *We are the Federal Deposit Insurance Corporation and your bank is under seizure. You need to know all exits are covered by armed US Federal Marshals who have been ordered to shoot anyone attempting to leave. No one will go out and no one will come in until you are personally released by either Jack Whittaker or myself.*

He reads the insolvency notice from the Idaho Department of Finance pronouncing it Malad—like salad, but with an M. He says Idaho First Bank of Malad City (like salad) over and over. That is when Ruthie Swenson, the interim bank manager, corrects his mispronunciation despite the nine millimeter handgun slung across his chest.

The other guy, described by Molly as a slightly shorter, soft-spoken sturdy man in his mid-thirties with dark hair and a receding hairline, leans into the taller one and audibly whispers, "Benny, I know you love doing this, but I'll take it from here."

Dixie is scared, and Ruthie is mad. The nice guy speaks in a more professional tone.

"Hi everyone. My name is Jack Whittaker and this is Benny Schnabel, Assistant Manager. I am the Asset Manager for the Federal Deposit Insurance Corporation. We were notified by the Idaho Department of Finance this lending institution is insolvent. We need to go through a procedure to put this bank into receivership so we will be taking over. We have agents at each branch collecting all files and assets that will be consolidated here at the main branch over the next couple of days."

Molly said Dad warned all of the employees it might happen. Ruthie is Dad's strongest supporter, becoming more protective of him after Mom's death. She is brazen toward the intruders, not seeming to back down. She looks toward the second story doorway, and pointing with her head, she says, "the bank president's office is on the second floor. I'm guessing he's gone. I think I saw him leave." She chops her sentences like she is dicing onions with a meat cleaver, knowing he is still upstairs in his office.

The Asset Manager looks at Ruthie. "What's your name?" he asks. She stands like a stubborn stone and doesn't answer. He says he knows this is difficult but he needs to brief her on the process.

Checking the name-plate on her desk, "Ms. Swenson?" Ruthie just looks at him. She is not familiar to the term "Ms." "Is the manager here Ms. Swenson?"

"Well," she drawls, then briskly wipes her nose with her embroidered handkerchief, setting off the trinkets for each of grandkids on her charm bracelet, "I s'pose that's me."

The Asset Manager who introduced himself as Jack Whittaker asks Ruthie if there is a private office where they can talk. She motions reluctantly for him to follow her. Before closing the door, he instructs several people to secure the vault and impound the records. He looks around the room, then at Molly. Feeling faint, she sits at her desk, her face drawn and pale. He gives her a smile, kind of an assurance there wouldn't really be a shootout, and asks her to take Dixie to the break room with the other three tellers. Dixie wants to know if she can call her mother to let her know she won't be coming home right away.

"Sorry, this is a secure federal shut-down. No calls in and no calls out. It can take several hours. I will try to get everyone cleared as quickly as possible."

An hour later, an FDIC intern standing guard at the break room door keeping the women sequestered, notices Molly beginning to tremble as beads of sweat form on her forehead. The girls catch her as her eyes roll back and she falls to the floor. It was long past time she should have had something to eat to stabilize her sugar levels.

A knock on Dad's office door interrupts the dressing down by the assistant manager, Benny Schnabel. The intern tells him Molly passed out on the floor in the break room. Dad jumps out of his chair and tells them she is his daughter, and she is likely in insulin shock. Benny yells at my father, "Sit down!" The nervous young man says he can't find Jack.

These are all important details because they will come up over a year later, in the trial. We should have written it down when Dad and Molly tell us the story. We could not guess in our wildest dreams how ugly things will get.

The intern, a sturdy boy as tall as Benny with tangled dark-red hair and a boyish freckled face, wrings his hands, asking Benny what he should do. Benny huffs, "Boy, that is not my problem here. Just use your prestigious Stanford education and come up with the answer. That's why we brought you along."

Dad stands again, insisting he needs to go to Molly. "She is my daughter for Lord's sake!" This time Benny physically pushes him back in his chair and tells him he isn't going anywhere.

Running down the stairs, the intern yells across the room, "Hey. Everybody. I've got an emergency here. Where the hell is Jack?" Attorneys and accountants behind the teller's cages, their heads together, quietly buzzing, all look up at once with blank stares and open mouths. Someone must have directed him to the manager's office.

When Jack gets to the break room, Molly is lying on the floor with her head cradled in Dixie's lap. Dixie is rocking back and forth sobbing. "We're gonna die. We're gonna die." The three young girls in flat shoes and cotton dresses have bunched in the corner of the room. Ruthie tells Jack in no uncertain terms, he is going to have to either call Scott Olson, Molly's husband, to bring food and insulin or call an ambulance. Jack yells at the intern to clear Ruthie to make the call. "Have her husband bring something to eat and his wife's medication to the front door and I'll go out and get them from him."

When Dad tries a third time to get up, Benny pulls a gun from his shoulder holster and tells him to sit back down. "Mr. Helland, listen. I'm not trying to be tough on you, but people pull all kinds of pranks to get information in and out of failed banks." Dad asked him what information? "There isn't some kind of a coo going on, except from your side. My daughter has severe type-one diabetes and if she isn't taken care of she'll die."

Benny tells him, as my father will later testify in his deposition, "I'm very sorry, Mr. Helland. That's not my problem."

Jack yells after Ruthie to make sure Scott brings a syringe. He asks Dixie and the girls when Molly ate last and they don't know. He asks if anyone has an orange, or orange juice.

One of the tellers opens the small fridge retrieving a carton of half-empty orange juice. Jack asks her to put some in a glass and hand it to him. He pulls off his suit coat, loosens his tie and kneels next to Dixie. Jack holds Molly's head up and cradles it in his arm, prying her jaw open with his thumb, then pours a couple of drops on the side of her mouth. "We need to be careful to not choke her. I had to do this for my mother more than once."

When Molly's body starts jerking and her eyelids start fluttering, Jack asks if there is a hospital in town. "Yes," Dixie answers, but you'll have to wait for EMTs. It'll be easier to lift her into one of your vehicles in the parking lot and drive her." Molly stirs and her body calms.

Jack asks for a towel to wipe her forehead. As she opens her eyes and sees Jack's face, she begins apologizing to him as though she had done something wrong. He says he's sorry for letting Benny do the takedown, whatever that means. "Sorry about all the commotion," he adds. His voice stays steady, and professional.

Molly finishes the juice on her own. Jack helps her and Dixie up off the floor. "I'll go out front and wait for your husband to get some food and the insulin for you," he says to Molly. "Is everyone else okay?" he asks, looking around the room. The girls nod in unison.

He tells the intern, "good job." The intern asks Jack if he should tell Mr. Helland his daughter is okay, then leans close to Jack's ear and whispers, "that guy, Benny, the one who's upstairs giving the bank president hell? He is an asshole."

"I know, Will," he says, "but the first lesson you need to learn is to try to get along with everybody. Even assholes. Now go up and tell the lady's father she is okay, then come back and keep an eye on her." Jack gives the intern a light slap on the back as he walks away.

It is dusk when Scott shows up and the bank parking lot entry is still blocked. Bobby and Lindsay are in the truck with him. Scott parks on the street, leaving the door open as he runs across the parking lot. Bobby said it was like the time the wheat field caught fire and his dad jumped off the combine running for the fire extinguisher in the pickup. Bobby and Lindsay both follow him. The Federal Marshal standing guard starts to pull the gun from his holster when Jack stops him.

"Don't," he said. "He's bringing his wife's food and insulin." The Marshal starts to protest. "You don't know what he has in that paper bag." Jack turns and stares the Marshal down until he puts the gun back in his holster.

Scott is wearing his blue jeans, worn lace-up leather work boots, a faded greasy T-shirt with "USU Aggies" on the front and his baseball cap with "Malad Dragons" on the crown. He thinks Jack looks like a California city boy and is as out of place as Kenny used to be when he first moved here.

"Is Mom is okay?" Bobby is anxious to know. He knows what diabetic shock does to her. " Dad taught me how to care for my mom when this happens." Jack assures him he gave his mom some orange juice and she is doing fine. Jack formally introduces himself to Bobby, Lindsay, and Scott.

"What's your mom's name?" Jack asks Bobby.

"Molly," Bobby says. "My mom's name is Molly Olson. Bobby returns the question, "What's your mom's name?" Jack chuckles. "Beverly," he says.

Jack hands the paper bag to the Federal Marshal, telling him to take it to the break room. "Give it to the lady named Molly" The Marshal opens the bag and frowns. "There's a syringe in here."

Jack's patience grows thin. "Yes, I know. I gave instructions for Mr. Olson to bring it."

The Marshal objects. "I don't think I can allow this in."

Jack pushes his suit coat back and put both hands on his hips. "Marshal, how the hell do you think she's going to get that insulin in her?"

The U.S. Marshal with a gun strapped across his chest is four inches taller, with a chest four inches wider, whimpers, "I am just following the rules.

Jack reminds the Marshal he has the authority to override the rules. Then he says in a low monotone, "Marshal, go take that food, medication, and the syringe, into the break room to this man's wife, right now. Please."

Jack watches the Marshal walk across the lobby and disappear out of sight. Turning to Scott and the kids he apologizes, "Sorry about all that." Holding out his hand he says, "I'm Jack Whittaker, FDIC Asset Manager." Scott shakes his hand, "Scott Olson. Malad Valley Rancher. Jack studies Scott's cap. "Dragons, huh? I don't believe I have ever seen that used for a high school mascot."

Removing his hat, Scott examines it like he can't remember what it says. "Yea, they picked it because Malad was settled by a bunch of Mormon Welsh immigrants with a thing for dragons. It's supposed to make us fearless and strong. And, once in a while, we are."

"Well, my ancestors were neighbors to the Welsh in the old days. My dad's side is English and my mom's English-Dutch. Catholic." Jack asks Scott if he is a Mormon. Scott nods. Jack confesses he imagined Mormon's looked more like the Amish people.

"Yup. We're just ordinary folks," Scott says, and pauses like he's afraid to ask. "How long you keepin' em locked up for?

"It will be likely be close to mid-night if things go smoothly, but so far, it has been a bit rough."

Jack explains the procedures. "Our first priority is to protect the deposits, safe deposit boxes, and the records. When all that is secure, accounted for, it is turned over to the acquiring bank and that bank takes charge of the employees. The acquiring bank decides which employees show up for work on Monday. After that they will be released to go home."

"Who's the acquiring bank?"

"I am not at liberty to say."

There is a long silence. "Oh, say, Scott" Jack asks, "do you know all the women who work here at the bank?" Scott nods. "Will you call their families and tell them they will be home late. Federal regulations will not allow calls in and out. You are the exception because of your wife's acute health condition."

Scott does not have to speculate about who is taking over the bank. Just as he is leaving, Clarence Fuller's Cadillac pulls up and parks behind his truck.

When the Federal Marshal returns to guard the front door, Scott takes Lindsay by the hand, and gives Jack a slight wave as he leaves with Bobby following behind. They walk past Clarence Fuller, who is staring at the ground, not saying a word. Before getting into his truck, Scott looks back, hoping to catch a glimpse of Molly through the front window, but doesn't see her.

"Come on Dad, let's go home and pray for Mom and Grandpa Lars," Bobby says to his dad. Scott tells him he's his mother's boy, always finding a way to fix things, or make them better.

Scott calls when he gets home to update me after Bobby leads them in prayer. "Ahh," I say. "He's such a good kid. I was doing the same," which wasn't completely the truth, and it wasn't really a lie either.

After I hang up the phone, I check on the kids. I sit for a while, then work on some files from the office. Sometime after midnight, I go through the house turning on all the lights making it look like a beacon on the hill, of sorts, so when my father drives up the gravel driveway, he can see the lights on the horizon burning and not feel like he is lost in an abyss of darkness.

I wait up for him. It is after 2 o'clock in the morning when I see headlights in the driveway. I don't ask him any questions except one. "How's Molly?" He says she is fine. He tells me they would have let her leave at midnight, but she insisted on staying with him. "I followed her home to make sure she got there safely," he says.

"I kept supper warm for you in the oven." He sits at the place I set for him at the kitchen table. I dish up a plate of food and set it in front of him. Then I sit down with him to keep him company. He stares out the window into the black of night. I finally ask if he wants to pray. It is out of character for both of us, but it is the only thing I can think of to say.

A weak, harrowed smile crosses his face, "sure, if you'll say the prayer."

I study this wonderful, kind and gentle man from a farm long ago in northeast Montana; this man who refused to wear a fedora hat, a double-breasted silk suit, and pound foreclosure papers against the chest of his neighbors telling them to pay up or get off the land.

"Sure, Dad," I say, "I will say the prayer."

Chapter Thirteen: Rebekah

Like a typhoon, it takes weeks to sort out the damage the bank closure caused. Unlike a typhoon, or an earthquake, or a tornado, the damage isn't as physically evident, at least not right away. It manifests itself in sudden and unexpected ways no one can predict. Dad and Kenny spend all day Saturday with FDIC. The bank board of trustees, including, and especially, the board chair, Niles Ogden, Dad's confidant and closest friend, are called in.

While Dad and Kenny are in meetings with the FDIC, Molly, Scott, Esther and I spend the morning going over the details of the night before. We learn that on Monday morning, Molly will be going back to work at our bank the Fullers now own, and Dad will not. Dad will be spending several days with Jack Whittaker and his team going through a rigorous process of sorting out details, and, as we soon find out, assigning blame.

We are all surprised Clarence Fuller let Molly stay. She said he didn't ask, he simply said if Molly wanted to stay on to operate the computer until she trained someone to take her place, he would let her. He let all the others go: Ruthie, Dixie and the tellers, because, as he explained, he is combining the two banks in Malad, and all his personnel are moving into our bank building starting Monday.

"That old bastard," Scott says. Molly frowns and tells him to kindly watch his mouth.

"I don't want the whole town hating each other," she says. "This is the way the devil takes over our lives. I thought about saying 'no' to him," she pauses. "I thought about telling him how much I hated him for taking over my grandfather's bank. But I don't hate him. I don't hate anybody. I think he kept me on as a good-will gesture to show the community our families can get along. I'm going to respect that."

I am thinking to myself, she is so damn naïve. I shake my head, more out of pity for her innocence than stupidity.

"Ah, Molly. That's so Christian of you. You are such a wonderful example for all of us It's hard not to feel bitter, but we all need to be more like you." Esther reaches across the table and takes hold of her hand, smiling at her. I can't sit and listen to my sisters any longer. Their talk of love, and forgiveness, and Christianity makes me want to throw up. I leave the room without saying anything, mostly to keep me from saying something I'll regret. I don't understand how they can believe this shit, let alone swallow it. Scott finds me sitting at Dad's desk in his den and shuts the door.

"Scott, I know god damned well Clarence Fuller kept her on for one reason, and one reason only; to use her for his own gain. He did his homework. He knows exactly what he's doing. He's using her." I'm am so furious I'm trembling.

"I know, Rebekah. I feel the same way. I hate it as much as you do. She may look sweet and innocent, but trust me, her head is as hard as yours. When she makes up her mind to do something, she's gonna do it come hell or high water."

I look up at him, surprised, and start laughing. I'd never thought of my sister that way, but looking back, he is so right. It's a subtle trait, and yes, innocent to the point of being naïve at times, but so, so, true. Yet, her hard-headedness often involves her acquiescing to others, instead of standing up for herself.

Molly relinquished her passions years ago when she gave up her music and her barrel racing for Scott. She came back to this god-forsaken place trying to make a living on land that can't produce a respectable crop two years in a row. Molly can call it "the devil" if she wants, but it is just plain fate and geography—and in the end, Molly, and women like her, blame themselves for not being able to fix it, or change it. I feel my own scars, and resent that my mother, good as she was to forgive me for my transgressions, did not teach us to lord over our own bodies, our brains, and our independence enough to take a stand for ourselves. She did teach us to not blame ourselves for not being able to fix the things we're not responsible for.

My sisters are forever making themselves the victims by being the rescuer; rendering themselves as servants to these kinds of men for the good of the church, or the good of the community. Yet, in so many ways, how is it any different than my life?

"C'mon, Bek. Don't make her feel bad." Scott says, opening the door, waiting for me. " Come back to the kitchen." I reluctantly go back, pour myself a cup of coffee, and sit down at the table.

"You don't have to work for him, Molly," I finally say. "Kenny and I have stacks and stacks of files that need to be entered into the computers. We could use you in the law office."

"No," she says. "I need to go back. I need to show our community the Helland's can get along with the Fuller's. I need to do it for Scott's family. I need to do it for our children. I need to do it for unity in the church, especially since President Fuller is our stake president."

I was okay up to the point she said she needed people to stand behind President Fuller. I shut my mouth and keep it shut. I figure Molly has no idea what Loren Fuller did to me. She doesn't know this is a deliberate take-over orchestrated by both Clarence and Loren: Clarence taking control of the bank, and Loren buying up the farms and ranches from FDIC when borrowers can't produce the money to pay them off. Molly can say she doesn't hate anyone, but I hate the Fullers. The whole lot of them—and sadly, for a long time, this is the cancer that seeps into my soul, a cancer far worse than the cancer that killed our mother.

I make myself believe I have a solid case for hating them. I know for a fact Molly had no idea Fuller's refused to take over any of the loans that she worked feverously to restructure—what FDIC referred to as the underperforming assets—frequently having nothing to do with reality. It means the Fullers can decide which loans they take and which ones they pass on to FDIC. I am certain she does not understand the FDIC will then take ownership of those loans, making them due and payable immediately. It means if the borrowers can't come up with the money, in full, the assets will be liquidated to the highest bidder.

Farmland, livestock, and farm equipment will all be sold for pennies on the dollar to anyone with the cash, except the person who owns them. As we soon find out, borrowers in this dilemma are Scott and his father, Lester Olson, Lance and Melanie McDonald, and about five hundred and ninety-eight other families. I have a perfect understanding of how it is going to work because it is what Kenny and I have been trying to prevent for the last five months. Oh dear god, how the flood waters of hell have been unleashed, and my poor baby sister has no idea how to hate anyone. I don't know how to tell her in a way she can understand. It may have saved so much heartache for her in the months to come.

I can't help but think of how history seems to repeat itself, much the way I managed to do in my own life. I indulge in reading a lot of books, some fiction and some historic with different authors; some white-washing events, or some with selective, or prosthetic memory, infusing myth, and some with outright bias. My favorite book, because, in my opinion, it was written without bias, is *The Gathering of Zion* by Wallace Stegner.

I read a lot of different accounts on what some called the 'Battle of Bear River' and others called the 'Massacre of Bear River,' which was, as later determined by academic historians, both. What started out as a battle on the Bear River on January 29, 1863 turned into a massacre of unprecedented human slaughter. Over four-hundred sixty-two Native Americans who came together to celebrate the winter dance, perish at the hands of mere Indian-haters. To me, more later than in that moment, it felt similar to what happened to us, in Malad, though obviously not as literal. In fact, I believe that not since Colonel Patrick Edward Connor and his California volunteers massacred the entire Shoshoni-Bannock Indian Village, the region had not been more invaded.

Without giving consideration to the entire truth of their mission, it seems to many in the Valley that the FDIC is here to do to the farm families of south Idaho what Connor did to the Indians four generations earlier. Both California-based armies (Volunteer Army of 1863 and the FDIC) are likely well paid by government vouchers and some, crassly, assumed they are immune to indictment for engaging in undisciplined behaviors, though each one carries a different type of ax.

What happened just twenty miles to the east of Malad City was this, in a nutshell: At twenty below zero, mounted horses led by Colonial Connor forged through snow in the early morning shadows, before sunrise on January 29, 1863. Howitzers were slowly being moved toward the precipice overlooking the sedate winter camp site. Soon, the howitzers became hopelessly stuck in the overburden of windblown snow and were abandoned. The cries from Chief Bear Hunter as he yells a final warning to stay away from his people echoes across the confluence of Beaver Creek and Bear River sparking the largest slaughter of a peaceful Indian village in the history of the West. "Sons-a-bitches," he yells. "Sons-a-bitches."

Five hours later the frozen white tundra oozes searing blood-red rivers. Warriors are shot point blank after raising their arms in surrender. Women are raped, their plump breasts heavy with milk laid open by the sheeting of steel blades, steam curling into the freezing air while the men of the California Volunteer Amy curse and spit. The horror worsens as children's skulls are crushed against rock outcroppings.

The seizure of one-thousand bushels of wheat and flour and one-hundred seventy-five Shoshoni horses from dead Indians resonates over and over in my mind in the weeks and months ahead as the FDIC begins processing asset confiscation and liquidation. What resulted from a few settlers asking an over-zealous Indian-hating US Army Colonel for intervention on their behalf was later recounted by most, including Brigham Young, himself, as senseless and tragic human slaughter.

After this horrific event, there is a deliberate effort on the part of Mormon settlers migrating north to make reparations with the Indians, to bring Indian children into their homes to clothe, feed, and school them or to offer friendship and supplies during the harsh winter months. As the settlers continued to arrive and create communities like Malad City, they receive little resistance from the Sho-Bans. More and more these new agrarians began to suckle on—and eventually galvanize—veins of water from the Portend, Bannock, Bear River and Malad Mountain Ranges to grow their grain, pasture their cows, and fence off their fields. When the agents of the government heed the call again, in 1986, some would believe the consequence levied against them was the manifestation of God's word in Exodus:

And the LORD passed by before him, and proclaimed, The LORD, The LORD God, merciful and gracious, longsuffering, and abundant in goodness and truth,

Keeping mercy for thousands, forgiving iniquity and transgression and sin, and that will by no means clear the guilty; visiting the iniquity of the fathers upon the children, and upon the children's children, unto the third and to the fourth generation.

Chapter Fourteen: Rebekah

"I'll make sure the sheep are watered and fed, Mom," Jason says as he walks by.

I give him a spat on his behind. "You are absolutely the best kid ever." He turns, in a shy way, and smiles at me, "don't worry, Ma, I'll get even."

"Oh, I'm sure you will."

His job is not as strenuous with the sheep on spring pasture close to the house. All he needs to do this time of year is hay and water the pen of rams and give the lactating ewes a little grain. We set out salt, and the automatic watering troughs are great, but need to be checked.

Jason and I decide we'll pick out his 4-H lamb for the county fair, along with one for Melanie and Lance's oldest son, Dylan. I promise to help Melanie run the 4-H club; demonstrating how to shear and clip the lambs to get them ready for the showing and fitting competition. Melanie's husband, Lance, offers to get a good feed mix figured out for them. "Not too hot," I say to Lance, referring to the feed mix. "We can't put too much weight on them." I remind both Jason and Dylan they need to walk the lambs every day to have them fair ready by August.

Jason raised 4-H lambs in Lava, but this is Dylan's first year. I receive several calls in April from families who want to buy 4-H lambs for their kids, and I wonder how they will pay for them. I figure I'll be like Kenny getting legal fees from his clients. I'll wait to get paid when the kids sell them at the Oneida County Fair livestock auction. Honestly, I'm fine with that arrangement. I don't need the money; but, like Kenny, I feel strong about the kids understanding their responsibility to pay.

Eventually, this is a lesson in human nature I must reconcile in my own mind. Three weeks after going to work for Kenny, he set up an appointment with Ferron Hansen to meet with me. He told Ferron to bring in tax returns and a list of his assets and liabilities. Kenny explains in detail we need to know how many mother cows he owns; how many yearlings; how much hay is on hand; how much grain is in the bin; and so forth. When I meet with Ferron, I am sitting in front of my computer, filling out the spread sheet Molly helps me create just for this task. I tell him I'll ask him the questions and I'll fill in the numbers on my computer. He seems puzzled by this new kind of process. I tell him, "look, I enter the numbers and hit F9 key on my keyboard and it will automatically calculate." I warn him if I don't have a twenty percent margin in the cash flow, I'll have to go back and start figuring out how to either cut more expenses, or create more income.

At first, Ferron doesn't take his hat off, a light-gray felt cowboy style with sweat-stains above the band. I knew Ferron when I used to live in Malad, but not well enough to make light conversation with him. Kenny warned me it would take these guys a while to warm up to me "on account of me being a woman and all," is how he said it. He cautioned me to stay on point and professional, or these guys might take something I say the wrong way. I think he's worried I'll start speaking my mind about President Regan and how he didn't give a rip about family farmers going down right and left. Turns out, Ferron likely agrees with me.

Ferron finally sheds his brown canvas coat, laying it across the empty chair next to him. I notice the elbows in his cotton western shirt are patched with a red-colored material matching the floral design of his shirt. His blue jeans are worn, but clean and lightly starched, pressed with a crease. I wonder how his wife lets him out of the house with that horrid sweat-stained hat he refuses to remove from his head. His bulbous cracked hands shake as he rifles through papers he spreads out on the desk in some semblance of order. He places bifocals on his nose, tilting his head back as he searches for magnified answers to the questions I ask. As the afternoon wears on, he becomes frustrated, and by 4 o'clock he has shifted blame for his financial woes from the feed lots, to the banker, and finally to the government who put all those dairy cows on the market, pushing down beef prices, crippling ranchers. By the end of our session, I am a bit disheartened he takes no personal responsibility.

Part of the problem, I tell Kenny later, is people like Ferron believe if he gets up earlier and works harder, his financial problems will be taken care of. But he hates paperwork, and I doubt he'll ever put a pencil to his cash flow except to figure prices will surely go up next year. I care deeply about the plight of these family farmers, but like the kids trying to buy my lambs for a 4-H project, they need to learn the business side of their project just as much as the effort it takes to feed, water and care for their lambs. They need to know the government isn't always going to be the reason they fail to make a profit. It isn't just hard work, losing a finger in a baler, or having the government dump cows on the market, though, granted it doesn't help. Eventually, you have to take responsibility for your own fate. "We all create our own realities," I said to Kenny. "I've certainly created mine."

This is a particularly hard truth for the Helland-Thomas family to accept, the second week in May of 1986, when the FDIC absolved them of their ownership of the oldest bank in Idaho and transferred the performing assets, what few there were left, to the Fullers.

Chapter Fifteen: Rebekah

On Sunday morning I slip out to check the ewes. The bucks managed to overturn their manger during the night. I wrangle it around, standing it upright, putting some grain in the corner for them to fight over while I straighten out the mess they made. The sun is peering over the eastern mountain range, casting red reflections across the aluminum irrigation wheel lines, catching a glint from the old wind mill Mom left on our small farm after they bought it.

The plentiful spring rains produce a lush pasture, so we leave the irrigation water off for now. I wonder where the neighbors will find the money to turn on their pumps to water hay and the grain crops now beginning to stool. With no operating capital from the bank, the prospects of finding short-term cash requirements look bleak. I worry about Dad. He was so melancholy when he came home from his meetings with FDIC on Saturday. He seems to be in his own Gethsemane, taking the blame for trying to keep the valley afloat.

I crawl behind the wheel of my truck parked next to the barn and, knowing Rosalyn won't be up for another hour, drive down the road to the cemetery. The large granite stone with my parent's names engraved at the top sparkles in the morning sun. Mary Thomas Helland, b. November 15, 1932 d. November 6, 1985. Lars Helland b. May 20, 1930 d. blank. Lowering myself down onto the wet grass, my ankles cross, my arms wrap around my knees and I rock back and forth for a while.

"Happy Mother's Day, Mom," I finally say.

I wait to feel her to say "thanks," and, "same to you, dear." I forget it is my day to celebrate too, though I don't feel I deserve it, or have earned it the way she did.

I talk out loud and don't feel shy about it. I tell her about the bank being taken over by FDIC and the Fullers, and about Dad. As I talk, I see dust roiling behind a truck on the gravel road and watch as it approaches. I wave at Ralph Withers as he drives by, saying to the headstone, "there goes Brother Withers, Mom. I think he wants me to tell you 'hi'."

I ask her what I can do for her on Mother's Day to make her happy. I wait for her to answer me. I stand up, brush the new mown grass off my soaked pants and say, "OK, Mom, I'll do it, but I don't really want to, and I know you know that. I wouldn't do it for anyone else, but, I'll do it for you."

I am okay with going to church once in a while. I like listening to Molly play the organ; and singing songs about forgetting all our earthly cares. Walking to the truck, I take in a deep breath of the still Sunday morning air, climb in, start the engine, and drive back to the house.

Dad started drinking coffee with me in the mornings and he didn't mind when I bought an honest to goodness coffee pot to perk a decent cup. He is up, sitting in the kitchen. The newspaper is spread across the table, but he's staring out the window when I walk in from the utility room.

"Where you been, sis?" he says, stirring out of his deep thought

"Checking the sheep, and went down to tell Mom 'Happy Mother's Day'."

"Oh."

I pour a cup of coffee and sit at the table with him. "How'd it go yesterday?"

He takes a deep sigh, then a long sip of coffee.

"I can, and will, take their abuse," he finally says. "A lot because I believe Kenny knows what he's doing and he is confident my board of directors will not be personally liable for losses the FDIC will end up taking. But the Assistant Manager is way out of line. He threatened the board yesterday the same way he threatened me on Friday. When he was in my office, he held me at gunpoint to keep me from helping Molly. He's ruthless."

"I am so sorry, Dad." I don't know what else to say. "Is there anything I can do for you?"

He looks out the kitchen window again, and I follow his gaze. The sun is full up across the eastern sky, filling the landscape with colors of spring. The green filaments of the pastures and budding grain fields blossom in the full morning light.

Dad is quiet for a minute, but I can tell he wants to talk, so I wait in silence until he's ready. "This has been hell, Rebekah. And I don't mean for me; it's been hell for Grandpa Thomas, for Molly, for my board of trustees, especially Niles. Kenny talked to him last night before he went home, assuring him these are, for the most part, empty threats. It's a game they play, and Benny Schnabel loves playing it. He spews out threats of leaving all of the directors penniless. He got right in Niles face and told him he hoped he had a 'god-damned good attorney'."

Before they left Saturday night, Jack Whittaker explained to Dad they are required to investigate the failure and its causes, but it generally takes up to two years to conclude any personal liability for an institution's losses. Jack told Kenny they won't file suit against directors, officers, and third parties unless the claim is both meritorious and cost effective. He said that overall, investigations have resulted in filing against directors in about a fourth of bank closures they conduct. It would be difficult to make a case for our bank given the culture of failing banks across the U.S., particularly in agricultural regions.

Before Niles left for home, Dad and Kenny both talked to him. They repeated everything Jack Whittaker iterated to them, but the veins in his neck stood out, purple and pulsating. He left in stone-cold silence, without uttering a word.

Dad says, as if talking to no one, "I wonder if Kenny and I should go out and have a talk with Niles again this morning."

Niles Ogden is my father's closest friend, his confidant, his fishing and hunting buddy. They spend every fall in the Wind River Mountains in Wyoming with a hunting guide, searching for trophy elk, which Niles finally bags and Dad is the happier for it. They especially love to hunt birds up along the west banks of the American Falls Reservoir where they lie in duck blinds for hours, waiting for a flight of geese. Dad knows Niles' heart, and Niles knows Dad's.

If we were Catholic or Protestant, instead of Mormon, I'm certain Niles and Betsy Ogden would be my god parents. Niles is larger than my father, with a ruddy face, a completely bald head he has the barber shave once a week, an overly-large stomach, and a larger than life kind of laugh. I would say 'like Santa Claus' but Niles is far too tall and hairless to be compared to Santa.

Through my difficult years as a teenager, Niles was my friend and protector on more than one occasion. One night, while I was out with his youngest son, Paul, drinking a six-pack of beer, we got picked up out by Deep Creek Reservoir. Niles drove to the Sheriff's office to get us after the Deputy Sheriff called him. Sheriff Benson locked me and Paul up in his office and told us he wasn't letting us out until Paul's dad got there. We were completely inebriated. Niles thanked the Sheriff, and then took me and Paul to their house where he and Betsy put Paul to bed with a pan on the floor near his head to throw up in, then sobered me up and took me home.

When I saw Niles at church the next morning, he just put his arm around my shoulder and asked, "How's my little pumpkin doing this morning? You're a little green around the jowls, dear." Then he tapped me on the head, grinning, knowing I was in pain.

I love Niles as much as my father does, but for different reasons. In both cases, he has always been there for us, through our happy times, our problems, and our sorrows.

"Want to go to church this morning with me?"

Dad looks at me with wide eyes, wrinkling his forehead. It is a mocking sort of look, like he thinks I'm joking.

"I'm not joking," I tell him. "I think we need to listen to Molly play the organ. We need to hear her music. It always makes me feel like there's hope. Besides," I say, "I promised Mom this morning that I'd take you. We'll see Niles there, and maybe Niles and Betsy will come out for dinner. I'll get a roast out of the freezer and put it in the oven."

"Sure," Dad finally says. "I'll go. Want some help getting the kids up and ready?"

I was at the sink, rinsing out our coffee cups. "No," I say, "they

102

bathed last night. We can get ourselves ready in no time. Call Esther and tell her they don't have to stop by to pick up the boys, we'll see them at church." Esther and Kenny stop by on Sunday mornings to pick up Jason and Eric for church since we moved in with Dad. I think the boys like being with their new friends at church, and it makes them fit in better at school. I understand how that works, but I also understand it only works for them if they go with Esther and Kenny. It is how the Mormon religion works.

I don't mean to sound cynical or demeaning but it's the one thing about the Mormon faith that is true. They are a church for families, not half-families or broken families, but whole families. That's why it works so well for Esther and Kenny to have surrogate children; my children. That works. I don't.

I took the boys and Rosalyn to church once, in early April, on Easter Sunday, when Esther and Kenny went to California to his niece's wedding. I didn't realize how awkward it would be, seeing all our clients with their families. Men (and some of their wives) who sat across my desk exposing the rawest of their financial failures to me as I transcribe their misery into digits in rows and columns. And here they are, in church, trying to gather courage and faith, perhaps looking for the miracle they expect to arrive any moment—or praying Kenny and I will be their miracle.

But when I walked in with my boys, carrying Rosalyn on my hip, even Scott barely spoke to me. Lance and Melanie were the most hospitable, asking us to sit with them. Molly was in her assigned seat at the organ bench, and eventually Scott brought his kids over, sitting next to Lance, filling in the bench.

I see how Scott might feel strange, sitting with me and my children while Molly plays the music, afraid of what people might think, or even say out loud. After that experience, I stayed away from church and don't say anything about how I feel, not even to Kenny, who doesn't usually care what people say. I know it's best for me to just stay away. Besides, I have no interest in clawing my way back only to find out acceptance requires having a husband in tow. Even the Bishop who took Leon Fuller's place, Eldon Williams, a sweet, kind, adoring man with a large frame, stubby fingers, and a round face capped by unruly strands of hair—even he treats me different at church than he does when I compile the statistics on his embarrassing alfalfa hay yields and under-producing calf crop.

But now, as I tell this, perhaps I see it a little differently. What I may mistake as being shunned by our clients, and my neighbors, at church, is the humiliation I remind them of by just being there. Perhaps I am being too hard on them. Regardless, it's better for me not to be there, knowing all I do about them. I am the person they can bare their secular soul to without judgment or recrimination, so by showing up in the one place they feel dominance and self-importance, or perhaps reprieve from their earthly cares, leaves their pride vulnerable.

It seems I spend too much of my life whining about not getting the respect I deserve, yet I fail to understand how a man's pride and self-dignity is his strength. In a place like Malad Valley, where land owners feel obligated to make their grandfather's or great-grandfather's farm viable, when it never was, Church (or the local tavern) may be the only place a man can refortify himself to go back out and give it another go.

***

I look through Mom's closet and choose the double-breasted strawberry pink Chanel suit with navy-blue collar and gold buttons, similar to the iconic article of clothing Jackie Kennedy wore that fateful day in Dallas. It was an honest coincidence, however, looking back, very fitting for Mother's Day.

Even though it was Mom's favorite outfit, she quit wearing it when a few Kennedy admirers—and in Malad, Idaho, I mean very few—commented on the unfortunate resemblance. She said she hadn't made that connection when she bought it, though admitted there was a strong resemblance once she thought about it; so, she decided to stop wearing it. Mom confessed she spent far too much money on the suit. I assume it's why it has remained in her closet for years; but it is still in near-new condition. Pink, I think, will be a wonderful way to brighten the world, though pink is definitely not the color of my character. While I would never buy the suit for myself, I admit it looks striking against my dark hair cascading straight, half-way down my back. And once again, I wear her three-inch matching navy-blue heels, bringing me to my father's height.

We all look stunning; Dad in his gray suit, a pink shirt and matching silk paisley tie, the boys in white shirts, ties and dress cotton pants, and Rosalyn in a white dress with a pink ruffle around the skirt and pink eyelet-lace bodice with matching pink ribbons in her hair. Esther made the dress for Easter and I am pleased Rosalyn can wear it again before growing out of it. Beyond a doubt, I look the finest in my mother's beautiful strawberry pink suit and coordinated heels.

It is a fact women in Malad, on Sundays, always look their finest. Many have standing weekly appointments at Shawna's Beauty Salon on Friday or Saturday. While most sew their own clothes, others forage through discount basements at Z.C.M.I department store in Pocatello or Ogden to find the hidden treasure making them look more sophisticated than the lifestyle they live.

Most of the women come to church looking extraordinarily well-dressed for a farming community, with their stiff coiffed hairdos, and deep tanned skin. It seems out of place for this isolated, wind-blown high-mountain prairie in the middle of nowhere to have a chapel full of women with impeccable taste in clothes, shoes, and hair styles, all looking as though they just came from the beaches of Mexico. The truth is, many just crawled off a tractor or a horse on Saturday, driving to their hair appointment to be spiffed up for Sunday. Myths of plain-clothed, simple looking Mormon women hiding in houses, out of site, are just that, myths. I believe they have a lot of work to do on the inside to recognize they are human beings, like everyone else; but on the outside, they exude pure class and elegance. At least in Malad City they do.

When we arrive the church parking lot is full. So full, we have to park down the street. People are lined down the front stairway waiting to get inside. I see my father hold back, staring at the crowd. I suddenly feel his pain. This is incredibly humiliating to him to come here and meet his borrowers and depositors face to face in disgrace. I don't think anyone with money in his bank lost any, but there are now hundreds left without a bank.

I will never forget that morning when Brother Withers, our neighbor who passed the cemetery earlier, came ambling across the street out of the line of folks waiting to get into the chapel. As he approaches us, the entire crowd on the stairs turn to watch him. He doesn't just shake my father's hand, but with a flushed face and tight lips, he embraces my dad, holding him for a long time the way he did when my mother died. My father's eyes grow misty as he let him go. Ralph says in a hushed voice, looking Dad in the eye, "Lars, we're gonna get through it. One way or the other, we're gonna get through it."

Dad doesn't say anything at first. I doubt he knows what to say. He gives Ralph a weak smile, touches him on the back. "Thanks, Ralph. You will never know how much this means to me."

Then Ralph Withers shakes my hand, "Happy Mother's Day, Rebekah," he says. "What beautiful children." He gives the boys a hand shake and Rosalyn a little pinch on her cheek as she shies behind my skirt. Ralph isn't a client of Kenny's, and if he had financial difficulties, he never came to the Sorenson Law office for help. I have no idea if he even had an account at my father's bank.

Esther pokes her head out the side door of the church and waves at us. When we are within ear-shot, she tells us to come with her. She saved a bench for us. I am grateful she spared Dad from walking through the crowd on the front stairs on such a challenging day. I am so proud of him that morning, not cowering from the humiliation.

We walk past the Sunday School classrooms and through the side door, following Esther, who always wears flat shoes, and walks fast. Walking past Betsy Ogden who was squeezing into the last single seat on the bench, Dad stops.

"Where's Niles?"

She looks up at him, her eyes empty, her face drawn and shakes her head, trying to compose herself. "He wouldn't come this morning," she finally says in a whisper. "I left him sitting in his chair in the living room. He was dressed for church, but said he just couldn't come face everyone." She got quiet. "Not today, he said to me."

Just as Niles is my father's best friend, Betsy was my mother's. She was the same height, but contrasted my mother's dark blond hair and blue eyes with a rich chestnut red she kept artificially colored for several years to accent the reds over the browns, hiding the gray. Her hair is short and professionally styled, like most of the women here. She has deep-bedded freckles she softens with a layer of translucent face powder. Her lips are highlighted by her pink lipstick, but unlike my mother, it is the only makeup besides face powder she wears. Betsy's dark-brown eyes set off her fair complexion. I have always thought she was beautiful, not so much in a Sophia Loren way, but the way a feisty determined red-head is beautiful, and yet, it is more her complexion, her beautiful dark eyes, and her character than the actual color of her hair.

She is wearing a well-tailored two-piece suit, similar to the one I am wearing, except it is a light blue V-neck with a scarf tucked in around her neck. She and Mom always shopped together, and while they tried to buy different styles, they often liked the same outfits, so settled on different colors.

It is the look in Betsy's face, I believe, that startles my father, causing him to ask Esther where Kenny is. "In the clerk's office," she says, pointing toward the front doors of the chapel. Dad pushes the boys toward Esther, picks up Rosalyn who is beside me, hanging onto my skirt. He gives her a kiss on her cheek, then hands her to Esther and says, "Rebekah and I need to get Kenny and go out to see Niles. You take the kids and we'll see you after church."

I don't know why my father asks me to go with him. Well, he didn't ask, he just handed me the keys from his pocket and told me to get the car and meet him and Kenny by the back door next to the propane tank.

They are both on the far side of the driveway waiting when I drive around back of the church. Dad sits in the front passenger seat, and Kenny in the back. I exit out of the parking lot, picking up speed as I turn right, then right again onto the road to Niles Ogden's house, four miles west of town. Dad is shedding his coat and tie. Kenny is doing the same. I don't ask. I know.

When we pull into the driveway of the Ogden's ranch-style home, one similar to my parents, built the same decade, but smaller, Niles GMC pickup truck is in the driveway. The garage door is open. Dad commented that Betsy must have left it open when she left for church. The Ogden's garage, their yard, their garden is the way I picture the Garden of Eden. Betsy, like my mother, loves to garden, keeping her home and yard the way Niles keeps his shop. The shop, driveway, front yard and house are at road grade. Behind the buildings, the land slopes downhill toward the livestock sheds and hay cover, and corrals. The corrals continue to slope toward the Deep Creek drainage, designed so the corrals will drain, and the cows can water from the creek.

The garage floor is painted a ship-deck navy-gray. There are three stairs leading to a landing, then the door into their utility room. Next to the door is a multi-colored braided rug where boots are lined against the garage wall. Dad tells me to stay in the car. He says he wants to go in with Kenny and talk to Niles alone.

"Rebekah," he says, looking at me, "if Betsy comes home, and she might if she figures out why we left, stay outside with her, will you?" I nod my head.

Dad stands on the landing inside the garage, taps on the door, then opens it and sticks his head inside. I hear him call out Niles name. He calls out again, louder. Then he goes inside, Kenny following him. In less than thirty seconds both are bolting back out the door they just went in, Dad carrying a small piece of paper in his hand. They turn and both exit out the back door of the garage leading to the livestock sheds below the house. I hear Dad hollering, *Niles. No. No. Niles!*

I see Betsy's rubber chore boots sitting on the rug in the garage. I kick off my mother's navy blue heels in the car, run in my nylon feet to the garage and slide my feet into Betsy's boots. As my left foot sinks into place, I hear Dad cry out. I run down the path, screaming for my father, and then Kenny. When I round the corner of the shed, my father is on the ground, bending over Niles. Kenny is picking up the shotgun, and they both look up at me in shock and horror. In Lava, before Rosalyn was born, I was an EMT. I saw horrible things. But this is one of my dearest friends lying on the ground, bleeding to death, his head covered in blood, skin, and shattered bone.

Kenny, give me your shirt and you go call the Sheriff. Get an ambulance out here, I yell. *And grab me some towels from the house. Hurry, Kenny!*

I look at Dad on the ground. "Dad, move over!"

Kenny hands me his shirt as I kneel, pushing the shirt against Niles head to stop the bleeding.

Dad sits back against the support post, laying his head against it sobbing. I feel for a pulse in Niles neck, and then hold my hand on his chest. I gather Niles into my arms, and pull him against my body, and I cry. Our dear, kind, loving Niles is dead.

Dad gives the note he found to Sheriff Benson, and tells him it was sitting on Niles Sunday suit he laid out neatly on his bed before changing into his work clothes. It read in large cursive writing,

Betsy, my darling, I love you with all my heart. You have made my life beautiful. I cannot let them take all we have worked for away from you. Don't come down to the sheds. Just call Sheriff Benson and have him come get my body. And tell Lars, this isn't his fault. It's mine.

Dad explains to the Sheriff his fear when Niles isn't at church with Betsy. He keeps saying, over and over, "if I'd only been five minutes earlier."

Dad takes off his blood-stained shirt and changes into one of Niles white-pressed Sunday shirts from his closet. Leaving his tie in the front seat of the car, he puts on his suit coat. My mother's strawberry pink Chanel suit is soaked in Niles blood. Dad asks me if I should change into something of Betsy's. I look at him and say, "No, Dad. I want to wear this down to the bank. I want them all to see what they have done to Niles. I want them to see what they've done to us."

He kisses me on my forehead, and shakes his head. "No, Rebekah," he says. "No more revenge. No more. This must stop. When we are done here, I want you to go straight home and burn those clothes." He hands me his bloody shirt, "burn this too."

History, once again, repeats itself.

I try to remember where I was that Friday, November 22, 1963, when John F. Kennedy was shot. I was eight years old, three years older than Eric is now. I just started the fourth grade at Malad Elementary that fall. Molly was in the third grade. We still lived in my great-grandfather's old house on North Main, the one Esther and Kenny moved into years later. I remember when Esther, who was in the seventh grade, got on the school bus with us: Molly on one side, me on the other. She put her arms around each of us as though she was our mother and told us a very sad thing happened. I said I knew, but Molly looked up into Esther's face and said, "what Esther? What?" Are we all going to die?" Esther assured us that we would be fine. I know Molly couldn't understand any of it, and I only remember how I felt— scared and sad.

I also remember feeling confused and angry when Lynn Severson climbed aboard the bus and with cheerleader zest, jumping up and down, clapping her hands announcing her delight. "Guess what? Guess what," she said. "The president has been shot. Isn't that the neatest?" And she sat down right behind us. Esther turned around and said, "Shut up, Lynn. He was our president." Lynn stuck her tongue out at Esther. I told Esther to ignore her.

Mom was sitting in front of the television when we walked in the house, her eyes were red, a rumpled white wad of handkerchief in her hand. "Oh, my," she said "This is terrible. Poor Jackie Kennedy. She is so young to be a widow. And those poor little children, Caroline and Little John John, losing their father this way."

Then she stood up and turned the television off, telling us it was too sad for us to watch. When I told Mom what Lynn said on the bus, Mom looked at Esther with a puzzled look on her face as if to ask, why in the world would Lynn say something like that? "She's the president of the Young Republicans Club," Esther explained. "She's always saying bad things about President Kennedy." Mom said that was no excuse for disrespecting our president.

So when someone mentioned to Mom that her suit looked similar to the one Jackie Kennedy wore on that day, I think Mom retired it out of respect for Jackie Kennedy, and not out of any fear of being ostracized by the conservative Republicans in Malad, who may have mistaken it as a sign of her being a staunch Kennedy supporter. I never heard my mother talk about politics, so that may be the way I wanted her to feel about it.

I also believe, thinking back on that incident, a child only does what their parents do, and it likely wasn't Lynn's fault she behaved so badly. I'm glad I stop and think about it on this Mother's Day morning. I don't need to parade Niles blood, spilt because of bullying and lies; either visually, or verbally. My children don't understand any of this and they only parrot my opinions, and my feelings, the way Lynn obviously did that day on the bus.

The coroner finishes his report, the ambulance leaves. Dan Evans zips Niles into the body bag and walks back up the hill, driving his large black suburban closer to the livestock shed. Evans's vehicle, the same one he used to pick up my mother's body six months earlier, is eerily similar to the black Suburbans the FDIC drove into Malad the previous Friday afternoon; the ones still parked in the bank parking lot.

Dan Evans drives around the shop and down the gravel drive to the corral gate. With the help of Dad, Kenny, and the Sheriff, they lift Niles body into the back of Evans's hearse while I stand with my hand over my mouth, muffling my cries.

Dad tells Kenny to drive me home to change my dress before the kids see me. He asks the Sheriff to take him back to the church where sacrament meeting is adjourning and people are streaming out into the warm spring sunshine. Women are carrying small potted plants of purple and gold pansies, gifts handed out as a token of thanks to mothers. My dad waits in the sheriff's car until he sees Betsy. When he gets out of the car and walks toward her, she reads his face the way he read hers earlier. She looks at the Sheriff's car and then at Dad, and she knows.

Esther walks out the door with Betsy, carrying Rosalyn, my boys trailing close behind her. When Esther sees Dad approaching, she immediately begins scanning the crowd, calling out for Scott. Molly's music is still streaming from the inside the church, the organ pipes echoing through the open windows as she plays the postlude music, "God be with you 'till we meet again. By his counsels guide, uphold you; With his sheep securely fold you. God be with you 'til we meet again."

"Scott," Esther is out of breath when she finally catches up to him. "Take Rosalyn and the boys to your house. I need to go with Betsy and Dad," She holds out Rosalyn to him and as he takes her. Esther leans in, squeezes Scott's arm, and kisses Rosalyn on the cheek, whispering, "Be good for Uncle Scott and Auntie Molly."

Chapter Sixteen: Rebekah

I smell the roast when I walk in the back door of Dad's house. It is heavenly, like Mom is there and will call out at any moment. When you miss someone, it is the smells that hang on the longest; the smell of bread baking, and of roasts slowly cooking. It calms my ache and makes it worse; first inhaling the aromas of pleasant memories, then exhaling of the sting of death—first my mother, and now Niles.

I turn off the oven, kick off my heels, and get a plastic garbage bag from under the kitchen sink. I put my father's blood-covered shirt and temple garment top inside. I head down the hall to my bathroom. Avoiding the mirror covering the entire wall over the double-sink vanity, I slowly begin unbuttoning the gold buttons covered with Niles blood.

 I am still undecided about what to do with Mom's suit. I take it off, along with my underwear, and stuff them into the bag, still plotting against Dad's will, and disregarding what I may be teaching my children. I so badly want to deliver it to the second story of the bank. I want to throw it down on someone's desk with a note to the FDIC; but my heart is sad and my adrenaline drained. I am exhausted.

I lean against the cool tile wall of the shower and let the water run over my hair and puffy face, swollen from tears. When Kenny dropped me off, he said he would stop by Molly and Scott's to tell them what happened. I am alone in the house, feeling the same aloneness I felt in Boise. I need to find my children. I can't imagine what they must be thinking. How confused they must have been when I left the church so suddenly with my father.

The phone is ringing when I get out of the shower and I hear the answering machine pick it up. My mother's voice still answers the phone, "You've reached the Helland's. We'd love to call you back, so leave your name and number."

"Hey Rebekah. It's Molly. I've got your kids at my house. I was just checking on you. Call me as soon as you get this."

I put on clean underwear, thick knee-high socks, pull on my wranglers, boots, and button my red and navy-blue plaid shirt. I call Molly. "I'm on my way over, honey. We'll talk when I get there."

"You don't need to bring a car seat for Rosalyn," she says, "Kenny left one here when he stopped by." Molly says, "love you sis, bye," and hangs up the phone.

I throw the bag with Mom's clothes, my underwear, and Dad's clothes into the bed of the pickup. I know Dad's garments are soaked in blood, but I have no idea what the protocol is for disposing of temple garments.

It is six miles from Dad's house in St. John to Molly and Scott's house. They live in an older two-bedroom stucco bungalow with an unfinished second-story attic with steep, narrow stairs to a sloped A-framed room the length of the house and twelve feet wide.

The floor and ceiling are finished with one-by-eight rough-cut lumber. Bobby has a twin bed at one end, with a small dresser next to it, and galvanized one-inch plumbing pipe Scott welded together to make a place to hang clothes. Molly made a curtain matching his bed spread with shower-curtain hoops to enclose the pipe frame, so it's like a closet; but Bobby always leaves the curtains open and the galvanized pipe exposed.

The kids love to go upstairs to play "Mother-May-I?" With a thirty-foot-long space to take scissor-steps, or giant-steps or, not so importantly, baby-steps, it's ideal. Molly put up a wooden expandable gate at the top of the stairs so Bobby wouldn't fall down the stairs when he sleep-walks at night. And it keeps Rosalyn from falling when they all play upstairs. I imagine they are all upstairs, or out in the yard on the tire swing hanging from the old elm tree.

When I pull into the side yard next to Molly's house, I don't see the kids. She comes to the back door of the utility room, formerly a screened-in porch Scott and Kenny enclosed and plumbed for Molly's washer and dryer. She waves for me to come inside. She hugs me when I get to the door. She is bare-footed and wearing a lose smock dress, like a Hawaiian muumuu. She whispers, "Rosalyn is asleep in Lindsay's room and the rest of the kids are playing out in the barn."

"Where's Scott?"

"He went over to his Mom's. She isn't feeling well and didn't go to church so I sent over a casserole I had in the freezer. Lester's hip is so bad he can't stand up. I think he's ready to have that replacement done, and the VA hospital in Salt Lake will do it for him for nothin'."

"Lester's a veteran?"

"Korea," she says. Pausing, she adds, "I saw you in Mom's pink suit this morning. You looked beautiful."

"Well," I say, "it's ruined."

"I heard," she says. "Kenny came by the house just after we got home from church. He told us what happened."

"Molly, is it okay if we don't talk about it? I'm sorry, but I just can't cry anymore. I can't think about it. I can't think about what Betsy's going through. And Dad…"

Molly is much shorter than me in her bare feet, especially since I'm wearing my cowboy boots. She put her arms around me, laying her head on my chest as though I'm her mother. She doesn't move for a long time.

"Thanks for going with Dad," she finally says, pulling away from me. "How is he?"

"Blaming himself." I sit down at Molly round oak kitchen table, wishing I didn't have to talk about it.

"Why? Why would he think this is his fault?"

"He thinks if he'd just gone over to Niles this morning and spent time with him he could have prevented it. But he thought Niles would come to church. We talked about it early this morning. I put a roast in the oven thinking we'd ask Niles and Betsy over for dinner after church. When Dad saw Betsy there, alone, he said he knew."

"What now?" She asks, getting me a glass of water, and sitting next to me. "What do we do now?"

We hear Scott's diesel truck pull into the yard. He enters through the back door, leans over and gives Molly a kiss on the top of her head.

"How's your mom?" Molly asks him.

"She's okay. Dad's the one who's hurtin'."

"Hey, Rebekah," he says, acknowledging me.

For as long as I've known Scott, he seems to cower around me. It's as though I'm going to tell Molly about the times he and Lance got drunk at the reservoir and I had to take care of them. I'd like to tell him I don't give a rip, and I'm not going to tell Molly, mostly because I don't care. Lance acts the same way. I'm a lot more upset with them for not stepping out of their fantasy world of playing cowboy and dairyman to see what it's doing to their wives and families.

"Sorry about Niles," he says. "I guess his boys will be coming back to Malad for the funeral?"

"I'm sure they will," I say.

Unsolicited, Scott offers, "I think Paul's in Chicago. He's some kind of big architect I heard your mom say a few years ago. I don't know about the older boys. I think one's in Utah somewhere and the other one teaches at a high school in Colorado."

I tell him that when Betsy came to the house after Mom died, she told me Paul is still in Chicago. She didn't say anything about the other two.

"Where are the kids?" Scott asks Molly, obviously wanting to change the subject.

"Rosalyn is sleeping and everyone else is out in the barn, playing. Would you go check on them for us?"

Scott gulps down a glass of water and leaves. I watch his shoulders droop as he slogs across the yard, like he's carrying a hundred-pound feed sack on his shoulders.

"Is Melanie pregnant?" I ask Molly as soon as he's gone.

"Yes," Molly's voice is quiet and doleful. She shakes her head.

"They really can't afford another baby right now." She is silent for a long time. "I know I shouldn't be saying things outside the bank,

116

but I suppose by now FDIC has taken over their loan, so it doesn't matter if I tell you. I'm not going to tell Mel, but things are going to get worse for them," she says.

"So, what's Lance doing about it?"

"That's the problem, he's not doing anything. He's buried his head in the sand. For months Melanie came to the bank by herself to talk to me and Dad. Dad restructured their loan three years in a row and loaned them more to keep operating. All the while, milk prices kept dropping and dropping, and Lance refused to sell the cows in the dairy buyout. I think that's when Melanie told him he had to figure out how to pay off the loan. She told me she was wasn't going to lay awake nights and worry about it anymore."

Molly likely doesn't realize she is shaking her head while she's talking. I sit quiet, not saying anything, taking sips of water to rehydrate my depleted body. I wonder if she knows she's talking as much about her own situation as she is Melanie and Lance's.

Molly interrupts my thoughts. "I know we're supposed to keep our hearts and our homes open to these new babies, but I just can't see how she's going to manage. I am so worried about her."

I'm not going to get into that conversation with my sister. I figure God expects us to do the right thing for the kids we already have, and not keep making more babies just for the sake of having them. I also realize I'm not able to judge. I managed to put my kids through a lot more suffering than Lance and Melanie ever would, with or without any money.

"Well, if you were her financial advisor, what would you tell her to do?"

"I'd tell her to figure out what they could pay, go get a loan at Farmer's Home and offer FDIC that amount of money to pay off the debt."

"And what do you suppose will happen if they ignore it?"

"FDIC will sell the cows. Mel and Lance lease the dairy, so there's no real estate for them to lose."

"And what do you suppose Lance will do if FDIC sells his dairy cows?"

"Oh, gosh, Rebekah. I can't even imagine what he might do. Go back to work at Thiokol, I suppose. But I know he'd flip out. He would absolutely lose it."

"Is he good at it?"

"Good at what? Losing the cows, or flipping out?" Molly chuckles.

"Good question," I smile. "I mean, is he good at being a dairyman? Does he get good milk tonnage? Does he produce good quality milk? How is his calf crop? Does he have replacement heifers? You know. All those things."

"Truth is," Molly says, "it's too darn cold in this valley to milk cows."

She says what I already know, but I want to listen to her reconfirm my theory.

"You need to be in Preston, or Cache Valley, but not Malad. This is a terrible place for a dairy. And they live even higher up in the hills than we are here. It's the reason Nelson's couldn't make it. They lost a third of their calves to scours and they were lucky to get fifty pounds a day from their milk cows. Melanie kept telling Dad they were getting sixty pounds a day, and it takes sixty-five to break even. But when I helped her with her cash flows, all her slips from the cheese plant averaged a whole lot less."

"So where are they hauling the milk to?"

Molly takes a deep breath. "Well, that's the other problem. Lance has the only dairy out here and they charge him a fortune to pick up the milk three times a week from Cache Valley."

I am sure it seems odd for two women to be talking farm cash flows, but it's what we both do, day in and day out. Dozens of them. It seems odd to me this same kind of conversation doesn't occur more frequently between Lance and Scott.

"Maybe we could help Melanie and Lance. Maybe Kenny and I could work something out with FDIC."

"I'll mention it to her," Molly says. "But my guess is Lance is going

118

to keep his head buried until the auction truck shows up to load his cows and haul them off."

"It's a shame," I say, "to be that stubborn." Like I have room to talk.

"Well," Molly whispers, as she looks over her shoulder to see if Scott's come back from the barn. "Scott and his dad aren't much different. They won't talk about it and I know our loan got picked up by FDIC too."

"Ah, Molly," I groan.

"Well, maybe it's not so bad. I've been talking to Richard in Pocatello at The Farmer's Home Administration. He's sent me the loan package to fill out. Now maybe we can make an offer to the FDIC, you know, like you and Kenny are doing with your clients."

"Can we help you?" I ask.

"No!" She is absolute in her answer.

"My husband and my father-in-law are Olson's, and that Welsh pride cripples them. It's bad enough I'm doing all the business for them. But I remind them it's what I do every day, so they said to just go ahead with it."

"What does Dad say?"

"That Lester is a stubborn man, which is the same reason he refuses to get a new hip."

The kids come running through the door with Scott behind them. Their loud voices wake Rosalyn. Scott offers to put the car seat into the back seat of my pickup and I take him up on it. I also take it as a hint for me to leave.

Eric hugs me and says, "Thanks for letting us come play with Bobby and Lindsay. We were having fun."

"Yah," Jason chimes in, "Me 'n Bobby, we were building forts out of hay bales in the barn."

"Bobby and I," I correct him, with a hug and tussle of his hair.

Well," I say to my boys, "you're probably starving. Go get in the truck. We have a pot roast waiting at home. I'll get Rosalyn." I look at Scott and Molly. "You guys hungry?"

"Sure," they both say at the same time. "We all came home from church and snacked on bread and applesauce and thought we'd fix something later," Molly says.

"Well, if you guys don't come help eat it, it's going to go to waste," I say.

"I wanted to go put flowers on Mom's grave anyway, and wish her Happy Mother's Day," Molly says.

Just as I am getting in the truck, I see the plastic bag in the bed. I hand it to Scott, pulling him aside." Go burn these in the burn barrel. Don't open it. It's the clothes Dad and I were wearing this morning. Just do it before you come over. Please."

He nods his head. I watch him in the rear-view mirror, walking around to the side of the barn where he burns trash and baling twine in an old fifty-gallon oil drum. Driving down the gravel drive, I turn north, toward St. John. I wish the pain I feel in my heart was in that bag of clothes, now turning to ashes.

"Where'd you go with Grandpa this morning?" Jason asks.

"Well, honey, it's sad news." I am quiet. I look both ways at the stop sign, then cross Samaria Road, continuing north. Brother Jenkins, the church janitor passes going the other direction and lets go of the steering wheel, momentarily, with his one remaining hand, and waves. I wonder if he even knows who I am.

"What? What's the sad news, Mom?" Gath pries.

"Well, Uncle Niles passed away this morning."

"Oh no! I'm sorry, Mom."

"I'm sorry too," I whisper. "Other than my father and Uncle Kenny, Uncle Niles is the finest man I've ever known."

"Except Dad," Eric says so unexpectedly it catches me completely off-guard. I didn't know how to respond. I glance at Jason who is sitting in the front seat with me.

"We're just talking about people who live in Malad, bud," Jason says to Eric who is in the back seat with Rosalyn.

"Oh," Eric mumbles.

120

Chapter Seventeen: Rebekah

Proverbs 22:7 *The rich ruleth over the poor, and the borrower [is] servant to the lender.*

I get to know Jack Whittaker, the FDIC Asset Manager, sooner than I thought I would. I learn his negotiating style on paper before I ever talk to him face-to-face, or over the phone. We secure a commitment from Farmer's Home Administration to loan sixty percent of the value of Ferron Hanson's farm and send the proposal over to the bank, in writing. It amounts to a seventy-five percent write-down on what Ferron owes the FDIC, most of which is an ungodly amount of accrued interest. What comes back to us is a response saying, in essence, no consideration is given to the value of his livestock or machinery. "Please resubmit the offer to account for the chattels." Signed by Jack Whittaker, FDIC Asset Manager.

"What machinery?" Ferron Hansen questions me when we meet. This time he is wearing a pressed flowery blue print western-cut shirt with matching blue patches on the elbows. "I have an old Massy Ferguson tractor that's broke down more than it runs. I have a grain drill that needs new drill shoes and plugs up half the time. The harrows are rusted," he says in his nasally tone. "The baler's a piece of shit!"

I put my fingers in my ears.

"Sorry Rebekah," he says.

Kenny is in my office these days more than his own. He sits in the chair beside his client and I sit behind my computer, entering and re-entering scenarios we print and attach to proposals—not just to the FDIC—but mostly to them.

Esther is in to the office nearly every day to answer the phone and handle clients at the front desk. We set up folding chairs for extra seating in the waiting room. Some clients go next door to Elsie's Café and drink coffee or Coca Cola while they wait. Esther, in her flat shoes and cotton dress, belted at the waist, and a matching scarf around her neck, runs, and I literally mean runs, next door calling for clients by name when it's their turn to see Kenny, or me, or both of us together. I offer to go, and she says, "no, no, no. That's my job. Besides, I need the exercise. I get tired of just sitting here."

Since Esther gave up her job of mothering my children, at her dismay, I now pay Melanie to watch my kids, though Jason says he and Grandpa are plenty capable, and likely are, but I'm not ready to put that responsibility on them.

Dad is still figuring out what he is supposed to do with his new, unattached life: First, no wife; now, no job, or best friend. He talks about taking a course in San Francisco and getting his securities license, maybe becoming a stock broker. He helps Betsy try to gather her life together. Kenny suggests Dad take her to his old law firm in Pocatello and have them settle Nile's estate. For one, Kenny doesn't have time to do it, and he thinks down the road he may have a conflict, which, as it turns out, he is right.

I tell Jason I asked Melanie to watch Rosalyn and Eric. It would be insulting to Jason to think I paid to have him babysat, so I tell him I am sending him along to help Melanie. I ask him to keep an eye out and not let the kids out in the dairy yard where Lance is feeding cows. I watch Lance in the mornings when I drop the kids off. He drives along the feed bunks, pulling the wagon as it grinds and spews feed into the mangers. I frown at the irresponsible way he careens around the corners of the corrals.

Melanie is usually outside hauling six or eight plastic calf bottles of formula replacement milk. She balances the wooden box filled with bottles on her now bulging stomach. I tell Jason and Eric to help her and I take Rosalyn inside the house where little Gracie is sitting with Erica at the breakfast table eating on slices of buttered toast. I wait for Melanie to come inside before I leave. "Those boys can feed those calves," I tell her.

In June, when we picked out Jason and Dylan's 4-H lambs, Molly asked if Bobby could have one too. I said sure, and Dad told me to take the money from Mom's account for payment. Jason and Dylan swamped out two pens for the lambs in the old barn at Lance and Melanie's dairy, the 'Old Nelson Place'.

It is a sturdy old barn with a gambrel roof, similar to the ones Lance talks about in Pennsylvania where he went on his church mission. It has a large hay loft, a line of small pens and old milk stalls of rough-cut lumber where they milked cows decades earlier. When the Nelsons built the new double herringbone dairy barn in the sixties, with automatic milking machines and a 500-gallon stainless steel holding tank, they abandoned the big old barn. A few years later, they abandoned the entire farm when they became financially insolvent. But the lovely old barn is a treasure, and a great place to house the new dairy calves with plenty of room for the boys' 4-H lambs.

A couple of weeks earlier, we weaned the lambs at Dad's Place. Lance and Scott came over with Bobby and Dylan riding in the truck bed, pulling Lance's livestock trailer, a heavy metal trailer, once laminated with ivory-colored paint, now rusting at the welded seams, and spattered with dried manure. Loose panels rattle with each bounced across the yard. Lance saw me shaking my head as he pushed hard on the brakes, sliding both truck and trailer to a stop in the gravel.

It was a sunny Saturday, chilly for first of June with visible breaths of air at first light. By eight, everyone showed up to work my small herd of Suffolk sheep. Bobby worked one gate, Dylan another while Lance, Scott, Jason, and I grabbed lambs, steering them one way, pushing the mothers another. The dust stirred as Scott and Lance complained, characteristically, about working with sheep. With the extra help, it was a good day to vaccinate and trim hooves. When I brought the idea up, they all grumbled. The sheep shearer arrived with his trailer and I traded him the wool for his labor. There isn't enough volume of wool for me to mess with. Selling the wool or having it cleaned for me to spin, is something I haven't done since leaving my old farm house in Lava.

I stood in the pen of wailing lambs, admiring their beautiful long, thin necks, and steely crow-black heads that make Suffolk sheep such a distinct breed. I pressed along their spine, spreading my hand across the flank of each lamb, looking for straight backs, and good teeth. I picked what I thought were the best three for our boys. Jason takes each by the head with both hands, cupping one under the chin, grabbing the jaw bone as his other hand cradles over the skull cap, just the way I taught him. One by one he walked each without a halter to Lance's trailer while Dylan gates the door. Jason is a natural.

Several families began arriving in trucks with livestock racks to select a lamb for their children's, 4-H or FFA project. I reminded them to bring halters to tie the lamb up, securing it so it won't fall during the ride and break a leg. Most of them remembered. I still had to loan a few from my lamb halter collection, with a promise they will be returned.

The bellowing mother sheep pushed against the fence, calling for their babies. The lambs cry back, the way I cried at Niles funeral.

"We take the dairy calves from their moms first day, getting it over with and they never know their gone," Lance said.

'Course, Lance. Isn't that the whole idea of extracting milk from cows?" I said, rhetorically, "we get the milk instead of the calf?"

"That was rude," Scott said, half in jest, half serious.

"I am joking," I said. "I advocate for sheep, and feel their pain when you take away their babies. But I do love your milk, Lance." I stop, thinking that didn't come out right. "I mean, I love your cow's milk," I murmured, blushing.

That's how it went the first two weeks of June. Every day we have our work cut out for us. Molly goes to work at the Fuller's new bank. Scott takes Lindsay and Bobby out to the fields with him and they help move sprinkler pipe after Kenny tells me to make out a check to Utah Power and Light from Mom's account to have their pumps turned on. I take my kids to the McDonald's Dairy at Daniels where they stay with Melanie for the day; Jason and Dylan helping Lance with chores, then working with their 4-H lambs; Grace and Rosalyn playing together; and Eric and Erica finding mischief to get into, though Melanie tries to keep them working on 'projects.'

Since I mostly drive the pickup I salvaged in the divorce settlement, I let Melanie take my minivan to haul kids around. On Monday mornings, Melanie heads into town for swimming lessons and Primary church classes in the afternoon. On Tuesdays, she drives to town to Relief Society family living classes. The older boys stay with Lance, and the younger kids stay in the nursery provided at church and play. On Wednesdays she is back in Malad for swimming lessons again. I tell her to fill up at Ballard's Oil and put it on my ticket since she is ferrying my kids around.

When I pick up the kids the first few evenings, Jason tells me Lance is kind of a butt-head. "Like Andy," he says, out of Eric's earshot, "but not as bad."

I tell him they are like everyone else in the valley. Times are tough and Lance has a lot on his mind. I don't tell him how bad it really is for Lance and Melanie. Kids don't need to know that kind of information, though they feel their parents' anguish when pray out loud for help to get them through, then pull themselves inward, suffocating the love their children crave from them.

Chapter Eighteen: Rebekah

The first day I am introduced to Jack Whittaker in person is on a Wednesday, the second week of June. I walk to the bank and ask Molly if she wants to go to Grandpa's for lunch. She is sitting at a desk in the open lobby. I suppose Clarence Fuller stationed her there to put her on display for borrowers to see the Helland girl is now working for the Fullers. She waves for me to come over to her desk.

"Want to go have some lentil soup with Grandpa?" I ask, looking around to see who is now occupying our bank.

"Sure, let me grab my purse."

We leave the bank out the back side door closest to Grandpa's back yard gate. As we open the door, Jack Whittaker is coming down the back-entry stairs. Molly and I look up at the same time. When he approaches the landing, he holds out his hand. "Molly Olson? Right?"

"Wow," she says, "what a memory. Gee, what's it been? Over a month now, right? Um, Jack Whitear, right?"

"Whittaker." He corrects her.

"Sorry. Jack Whittaker. This is my sister Rebekah." I think she doesn't say my last name because she can't think fast enough to remember.

At this moment, I wish Scott had not burned my mother's blood-stained suit. I wish I had it to dump it at his feet this very second. He must see that kind of vengeful look on my face.

"Yes," he says. "You work with Kenny Sorenson, your brother-in-law, right?"

"That's right," I say.

"Well, Rebekah, pleased to finally meet you." He holds out his hand.

When I don't extend my hand right away, Molly gets the same expression she did that morning of my senior year of when she found a wine bottle I hurled out my car window into the horse pasture. Her horse stepped on it, cutting his foot wide open. I look away from Molly, then look down, and reluctantly hold my hand out mumbling, "nice to meet you."

"You know," he offers, "we're less than two blocks apart. I don't think we need to send proposals back and forth by courier. Drop by anytime. Let's get these loans settled and off the books. All I need is solid justification."

"I can do that," I say. "And you feel free to do the same, Mr. Whittaker."

"Jack," he says.

Molly's face muscles relax, and she smiles at him and then at me. "Well then, we better get over to Grandpa's before the soup gets cold."

Jack opens the door for us and we walk out in front of him. He heads toward Elsie's Café. Halfway across the parking lot I yell, "Mr. Whittaker." He stops and turns around. "If you look up, you can see the tree house my grandpa and my dad built, up there in the apple tree that used to be right in the spot you are standing."

He looks up, then at me, puzzled.

"I just want you to include that in the damn value when you sell the bank to the Fullers," I holler. Then I turn and walk through the gate into Grandpa Thomas's back yard.

"I will," he calls out to my back. "I will remember to include it." I can't see his smile, but I can hear it in his voice.

Mrs. McMillan set the table for two. When she sees Molly, she quickly pulls a red straw placemat from the drawer, setting another place at the table.

"How nice of you girls to come and visit with your Grandpa," she says.

"Ah, McMilly," Grandpa says, "they only come over for a free lunch."

"And free advice," I say. "Don't forget that, Grandpa. I'm always looking for free advice along with the free lunch."

"So, who's your new boyfriend out there, Rebekah?"

"What new boyfriend?"

"That fella who walked out of the bank with you."

"What makes you think he's my boyfriend, Grandpa?"

"I can tell when some guy's sweet on you."

A high pitch wells in my throat. "Grandpa, do you know who he is? That's the FDIC jerk that shut down the bank. He's the one that harassed Niles until he…" I couldn't finish.

"No. No. Not Jack." Molly interrupts. "Jack's the one who helped me in the break room." Molly looks at me again with a silent message that clearly indicates she doesn't want Grandpa knowing she'd gone into insulin shock. "You're thinking of the other guy, Rebekah."

"You mean when you went into insulin shock," Grandpa says without looking up, his hand shaking as he spoons another small bite of lentil soup into his mouth. Then he says, without looking up, "Your dad told me. But I already figured it out when Scott came to the front door of the bank with the kids and handed that fellow a brown paper bag."

I figure Grandpa watched in the dark that night until Dad and Molly left the bank to go home. I'm certain if either one peered into the dark window they would have seen his silhouette sitting there in his chair.

"He's not the one that's the jerk?" I ask.

"No, Rebekah. He's the one who kneeled on the floor and gave me orange juice. You are talking about Benny something. I can't remember his last name."

"Oh. Well, I guess I'm sorry I was so rude to him."

"Which one is this?" Mrs. McMillian calls from the living room.

Molly and I rush to the living room, looking through the side window by Grandpa's perch. Grandpa is behind us.

"That's the one Molly keeps giving my oatmeal and raisin cookies to," Grandpa says.

"Ah, Grandpa," Molly touches his shoulder. "Sometimes when he goes outside by himself to smoke a cigarette, I feel sorry for him. He looks so lost."

Grandpa is often cynical about Mormons, and more often, cynical about people in general, which is likely where I get it from. "Their gonna kick you out of the church for fraternizing with a cigarette smoker," he says in jest.

Grandpa hadn't been to church for years, but Molly, bless her heart, never stops calling and asking if she can stop by and pick him up.

"Soon as they make me Bishop," Grandpa says to her. "Then I'll go."

"So who is he?" I ask, ignoring Grandpa and nodding toward the twenty-something young man nervously getting his nicotine fix.

"Will…something. I don't remember his last name. He's an intern for the FDIC," she says. "He's finishing his business degree at Stanford and is originally from Chicago. I told him the son of the board of trustees lives in Chicago and he was just in Malad for his father's funeral. He told me he felt terrible about Niles."

"I think he's the one who brings correspondence from the bank to our office," I say. "He seems like a nice kid."

Will apparently notices the four of us staring out the window at him because he quickly drops his cigarette into the butt can by the back door and goes inside.

***

Jack Whittaker darkens the door of my office two days later. Kenny and Esther are taking the rest of the afternoon to do some serious fishing at Deep Creek Reservoir. The idea, they said, was to spend some time together, alone, when they weren't completely exhausted.

A knock on my half-open door makes me jump. I look up. "Mr. Whittaker. What a surprise. Have a seat."

"Thanks," he says. "And, please, call me Jack."

Thinking back on it, the ease of launching into a conversation with Jack reminds me a lot of my relationship with Kenny. Within minutes we are talking like old high school classmates just bumping into each other after years of not being in touch. He tells me about getting his MBA at Berkley. I tell him I have several degrees in life, none of which I bothered to frame. He laughs.

We turn our discussion to insolvent accounts in general, and specifically agricultural accounts. He asks a lot of questions about how I develop my cash flows, indicating to me he doesn't know much about farming or ranching. I rummage through a pile on my desk and pull Ferron Hanson's file from the middle of the stack because Jack is familiar with the case. I set the printed excel cash flows along with the spread sheet of Hanson's five-year history, side by side.

"Look, Jack," I say, pointing at the bottom line, " this isn't rocket science." He looks offended.

"We follow the Farmer's Home Administration application guideline. We calculate the amount of money he can afford to pay on a mortgage payment, and still leave a twenty percent margin." I look at his face as he studies the pages.

"Where do you get the five-year history?"

"From Schedule F in his income tax returns," I say, flipping to that section of his file and showing him. Jack picks up the projected cash flow, and leans back in his chair to study it. "I wish your dad had done this before he loaned him the money." He doesn't look up. He knows he hit a nerve.

"Whoa," I say, "you just back that truck up." Jack sets the cash flow on the table, frowning at my expression.

"Of course my dad didn't do this," I say, pointing at the spread sheets, "nobody did. But he did loan Ferron Hanson money he could repay at six percent interest. Nobody could repay the bank at sixteen percent, or twenty percent."

"I understand that, but everyone can't always use that as an excuse."

He starts in about some tenured Berkley professor who wore the

131

same Harris Tweed jacket to a business management class Jack took to get his MBA. Jack says the Harris Tweed became significant to him because of his unwavering theory about feasibility and risk analysis. Jack, rather haughtily, says the business model of 'a wing and a prayer' would be considered the antithesis of academic theory. "And," he says, "after reading through the stacks of files, most farmers in southeast Idaho use the 'wing and a prayer' method."

I don't completely disagree with Jack, who has just insulted me by insulting my father and grandfather. And what's more, I don't tell him along with the frequently ill-conceived perception of business feasibility was a delusional belief in "The Will of The Almighty."

Truth be told, very few would have started farming in Oneida County, Idaho if they used the Berkley Model, and would have certainly been more faithful to their own beliefs had they followed the teachings of The Almighty, rather than using Him from time-to-time, for leveraging self-indulgence, irresponsibility, or stupidity. As a philosophical rule, it is best to recognize we are human first, and then we are saints. Not the other way around. A theory, of course, I kept mostly to myself. Well, maybe not mostly.

I read in Wallace Stegner's book about the hard lesson of my mother's predecessors traveling in the Martin and Willie Companies. In the fall of 1856 Franklin Richards stood at the Missouri River on the third of September. He espoused his belief it was 'The will of the Almighty' for nearly two thousand immigrants to begin the journey across the high mountain plains, three months late, placing them in the middle of Wyoming in late October.

And while Richards celebrated his belief that God would bring to them His choice blessings of 'good traveling weather', Richards was severely brought to task by Brigham Young when he was excommunicated for his folly. A much sounder reason, I thought, for being expelled from The Church than the one Bishop Fuller used to excommunicate me.

Whatever else I thought about him, Brigham Young seemed to have a clear, accurate view of how much these immigrants could expect the Lord to do about changing the laws of nature and held no such delusions.

There are many times in the year of 1986 I felt the same burden of rescuing victims, much like the hundreds of pioneers caught in the high mountain cold and snows that came in October near South Pass, who believed their autumn journey in 1856 was 'The Will of The Almighty."

"Do you know what Malad means?" Jack asks me out of the blue.

"Of course I do," I say.

He loosens his tie, and smiles at me with one side of his mouth.

"I can tell I don't have to explain," I say.

"No," he says. "You do have to explain. I know what *malade* means because I'm somewhat fluent in French. It means 'sick'. You need to tell me how this town got the name, 'Malad'."

So, I told him about the French fur trappers eating tainted meat of beavers they trapped, poisoned from the roots that grew along Deep Creek, "that creek, right behind the bank," I point southeasterly. I tell him how the French trappers defined much of our region. "Like the Tetons," I say. "Do I need to explain that one to you?"

Jack laughs, and I like his laugh. I like him. I like him much more than I want to. Not because he is muscular, or good looking, which he is, receding hairline and all, but because he is smart. And he is easy to talk to. No pompous arrogance, like I expected.

Chapter Nineteen: Jack

The first time I visit Idaho is the day we put the Idaho First Bank of Malad into receivership. By we, I mean the FDIC. I had been an employee of the Federal Deposit Insurance Corporation for nearly eleven years, and immediately prior to the Malad City job, I was promoted to Asset Manager. When I go to Malad City in May 1986, all I know is I have nothing to compare Malad City to, nor do I have any perceptions about what to anticipate.

I believe there is danger in knowing too little—or too much—about anything, or anyone, or any place. I know nothing about Malad City, Idaho, before I know everything. By summer's end, the initial professional isolation—and eventual unintended emotional exposure—almost buries me alive, before it eventually saves my life.

I originally confused Idaho with Iowa when my supervisor at FDIC regional headquarters, in San Jose, California, gave me the assignment. Truth is, I knew little about both places, so, at the time Sam Jackson hands me directives, it doesn't make much difference to me except I know Idaho is closer to where my parents and four-year-old daughter live.

I landed my job at the FDIC straight out of college in the 1970s. Activity at the FDIC was relatively quiet, which, as it turns, out, was the lull before the 1980s fire storm. By the end of 1985, I worked on several bank closures in Colorado, all urban banks, and predictable. They consisted of routine paperwork and bean-counting, that kind of thing. None of those bank closures were like the one I encounter at the Idaho First Bank of Malad City.

To make it easy to understand what we do at the FDIC, I will recite straight out of our handbook:

The FDIC and its employees have a tradition of distinguished public service. Six core values guide us in accomplishing our mission: Integrity; Competence; Teamwork; Effectiveness; Accountability;

and Fairness. We respect individual viewpoints and treat one another and our stakeholders with impartiality, dignity, and trust.

That's what the handbook says. That's not what we did in Malad City.

I don't have any background in agriculture, livestock, or farm cash flows and assets. I know something about horses since I spent my childhood riding the Saratoga foothills and the eastern slopes of the Santa Cruz Mountains facing San Jose. My mother grew up on a gentleman ranch north of San Francisco and cherished her horses. I am an only child who spent many days with my mother at horse stables. Our trails wander through vineyards and oak chaparral forests teeming with wildlife—a landscape much different from southeast Idaho.

I thank God that Rebekah became my confidant and my trusted friend who spent time teaching me. I believe what she did for me, in the end, was for the benefit of everyone—the FDIC, the communities of south Idaho, and the families who live there.

The mitigations we negotiated will allow farmers and ranchers the same chance to buy out their promissory note as anyone else trying to make a discounted acquisition in a depressed market. These kinds of pennies on the dollar buyouts are common for the FDIC. We generally bundle a bunch of bad loans and sell them in chunks to get them off our books as quickly as possible.

Rebekah, Kenny, and I manage to close out several underperforming accounts in July and August that would otherwise be bundled, with farm families' lives wrapped up inside, and sold to the highest bidder for between seven and ten percent of the total debt owed.

Back in April, when no other Asset Manager in the regional office volunteered to go to Idaho for this particular bank closure, I applied for the position. So did Benny Schnabel. It only makes matters worse when Benny ends up on the same job with me, believing in his own mind he has been selected to oversee the job, not me. It's not that I don't know what to expect from Benny. I've been on plenty of jobs with him—enough jobs to know he suffers from a severe egotistical disorder, now commonly referred to as

Narcissistic Personality Disorder, or NPD.

He is taller than me, about six-foot two, maybe three. I'm less than six feet by an inch and detest looking up at Benny when I talk to him. I make sure we are sitting across the desk from each other on an eye-to-eye level before discussing anything. He generally comes into my office without knocking. He pushes the door open and leans on the door frame until I invite him to sit down. He sits, then slouches down in his chair like he's settling in to watch a three-hour football game on television. Then he starts in.

"Stupid, ignorant bastards," he says the minute he's taken a sip of coffee. It's about anybody and everybody from debtors to desk clerks to supervisors. It doesn't much matter who he is talking about. Sometimes the adjectives change, or the order is different. Some days it is "ignorant morons," or "idiots." On the Malad job his favorite expression is, "just a bunch of mealy-mouthed Mormons," which I hear three or four times every single day. I can honestly say, I haven't met a Mormon in all of southeast Idaho I would described that way. I admire the tenacity of these folks, trying as hard as they do to make a life in such a god-forsaken place. They are good, hard-working people with honest intentions.

On the night I meet Molly Olson's husband, Scott, in front of the bank, I bring up the "mealy-mouthed Mormon" expression to the U.S. Marshal after Scott left.

"Dragons!" I remember saying out loud as Scott drives off in his truck, lifting his hand in a single wave goodbye.

"*What? What did you say?*" the Federal Marshal asks.

"Their Mascot," I say, my hands deep in my pockets looking toward the fading evening light on the western horizon, my nose and chin slightly upward to catch the tang of spring off the cooling mountainside. "You ever heard of anyone having dragons for their mascot?"

The Marshal shakes his head. "No sir."

"I would have thought they'd be Indians, or Bears, or Wolves. Maybe Miners. Malad Miners," I say. "The Malad Dragons. Huh." I say it without looking at the Marshal, more like I am talking to no one.

"You know, it always amazes me," I finally say, looking at him. "The things we never think about when we close down a bank. Everyone jokes about Malad being nothing but a bunch of 'mealy-mouthed Mormons.' But I think they are not defined as much by being Mormon as they are by being Welsh; and by the looks of that fellow, Scott, I certainly wouldn't call them mealy-mouthed."

I remember closing my eyes and pulling in a deep breath of the high mountain air. The crisp, clean smell of it revitalizes me. I push my hands deep into my pockets and touch the carved lines of the sterling silver dragon with a red ruby studded eye, attached to the money clip I keep in my right front pocket. I walk back into the bank, and lock the door behind me. Whatever I thought Malad City would be like, it certainly wasn't a community of Welsh folks iconized as Dragons.

***

August rain in San Jose, California is rare as frost—which is the reason the drizzle from the roof wakes me before my alarm goes off. The sheets are twisted around my torso and I give a yank, rolling over to look at the alarm clock. I lay on my back, arms raised and fingers locked cradling my head. I thought I'd miss Camila when she left me, but I don't. I miss my little girl, Stacy; especially the weekends I don't come home. But on weekends I don't make it home, Camila lets her spend those weekends with my folks. They call me almost every day at my temporary office in Malad City, Idaho. Stacy and I talk and blow kisses back and forth. She tells me about her horse-back ride with Grandma on the same trails I rode when I was her age. My mother taught her to ride. She brags on Stacy, "Even at three years old, she's more of a natural than you were."

Stacy looks a lot like my ex-wife, Camila. She has her Hispanic bone structure, her skin color, and dark hair; all the things attracting me to Camila when we met. She also has her mother's hot Spanish temper.

When I met Camila, she was working for the FDIC as an accountant, originally in Texas, where she is from. In 1982, FDIC assigned her to one of the Colorado bank closures with me. One evening we stayed late, working on accounts needing our attention and she asked me to dinner. She kept smiling as she watched me eat a Reuben sandwich. I asked if I had mustard on my face. She laughed, her white teeth glistening, her long thick black hair falling across her shoulder as she leaned over and wiped my mouth with her thumb, the palm of her hand grazing against my cheek momentarily. I believe I mistook my feelings of loneliness for love the moment I felt the touch of her skin against mine.

Camila is a smart woman, with impeccable taste in clothes. She was married, but he left her when her work kept her away from home for weeks at a time. She told me her ex-husband grew insanely jealous, and for good reason. Knowing this, I married her anyway. For a time, I was happy, I thought. I considered taking a job at my father's bank in San Jose to stay home when I found out we were having a baby. I don't remember why I stayed on with the FDIC. Perhaps it was the discovery of her hot temper; or her appetite for expensive clothing and furniture, or being tired of the exhaustive blame for her boredom.

The morning our daughter was born, the nurse brought Stacy to Camila's room at the Good Samaritan Hospital in San Jose. Camila was asleep. Sitting in the chair next to her bed, I remember being lost in watching shards of rain hit against the window and drizzling down the pane. I was supposed to be in Colorado on a bank closure. Sadly, for both us, I wanted to be there more than here. Or I thought I did until I held my daughter in my arms; her new-born ruddy face still swollen from her journey into the world and her coal black hair and tiny fingers clenching tight around my little finger. It changed me; but not enough to stay. Camila went back to work at the local FDIC office in San Jose and my mother happily volunteered to watch Stacy, essentially raising her, since we were both working irregular schedules.

I was separated from Camila for over a year when I accepted the Idaho assignment. I hadn't dated anyone else, nor did I care to be in another relationship. I was happy losing myself in my work and spending long weekends with Stacy, when I could. There is never a clear defining moment for me when it comes to love or relationships. Not until that Friday afternoon in May of 1986 when I lift Molly Olson's limp body onto my arm to feed her small drops of orange juice to bring her out of insulin shock.

I spent too long watching her face, her eyes flutter, feeling the flesh of her cheek against my hand as I steadied her. And when she opened her eyes and looked at me, my heart pounded in my chest so hard, I thought I was having an anxiety attack.

Every day since, I walk to the window in my second-story office, previously her father's office, and watch her walk across the parking lot and get into her rusting GMC. I watch her take cookies to Will, resisting the urge to descend the stairs just to run into her, briefly. I can't get her out of my head. I lose myself in her sway as she walks, or in her laugh as she stops to talk to someone in the parking lot. I have confusing emotions about Molly Olson, and I can't shake it. As the days of summer pass, it silently consumes me.

***

At quarter to seven I hear the cab honking from my driveway below to take me to the airport. Sliding on my tan golf rain jacket, I pick up my brief case and black leather bag of clean clothes for the week. Locking the house, I walk out into the rain, stepping over a worm stretched across the walkway. I hand my clothing bag to the driver and climb into the back seat—the windshield wipers still racing at full speed.

I don't spend every weekend in San Jose, but I need to go over several settlement proposals with the review committee. Flying from Salt Lake City to San Jose on Wednesday, I spend Thursday and Friday in committee meetings. The weekend is full. On Saturday, Mom, Stacy and I go to the horse stables. On Sunday I go church and brunch with my folks. In the afternoon Stacy and I take a swim in my pool. Camila drops by to pick up Stacy and we sit by the pool watching our daughter play in the water while we sip on ice tea.

"How is the bank closure in Malad going? And how is Benny doing? Is he hitting on all the women in the bank like he usually does?"

I tell her the receivership in Malad City is different than any we've done before. Then I answer her question about Benny. "The women are mostly older, married women," I say, not bringing up Molly Olson. "They're not his type. I have no idea what he does at night. I'm staying in Malad and he drives back to Pocatello every day to stay at the Quality Inn with the rest of the crew."

I wonder why she is suddenly so interested in Benny, but don't ask.

"You thinking about traveling again?" I ask.

"Thinking about it," she says.

"What will you do with Stacy?"

"Your mom said she'd take her."

I quietly crossed my fingers for Stacy's sake. My mother dotes on Stacy, and she seems to love her grandmother far more than either Camila or me.

The flight from San Jose back to Salt Lake lands on time. I am on first name basis with the Hertz rental car company attendants. I think about the cycle beginning all over again as I drive north on I-15 making the hundred-mile trek from the Salt Lake Airport to southern Idaho. I drive along the Wasatch front, through Ogden and Brigham City where fruit stands are full of fresh cherries and apricots and I stop to buy a bag full of each. "Peaches 'll be on in two weeks," the older man in coveralls says. I nod and say I'll be sure to stop by again.

Tremonton is the last significant town in Utah, driving north from Salt Lake City. It is where irrigated alfalfa fields begin to transition into an open sea of sagebrush. For the next ten miles, the dry silvery blanket sags between two hillsides where buckwheat grass and lupine bloom on the high lip of rocky ridges and Blue-flower vines break through the sediment left in the washouts. The arid stretch creates a natural buffer between these two waterless western states, redefining themselves by plumbing their parched valleys and the men loving their water more than their wives. I have heard more than one person make that remark at the local Café in Malad with a guffaw.

While I drive the interstate, I think about the farmer who keeps moving the sprinkler lines and turning on the pump day after day, knowing this is not going to be his land anymore. I learn two truisms about farmers in Oneida County, Idaho: Their big Welsh heads are thick as grasshoppers in wheat harvest, and hard as the alkali soil. If the crop is growing they're going to water it and if it's ripe, they are going to harvest it, regardless of who owns it.

At the Idaho-Utah border, a red and blue "Welcome to Idaho" billboard greets travelers as they enter the state, followed by a "Cecil Andrus for Governor" campaign sign. I try to remember the name. "Andrus." Oh, yes, Secretary of Interior under Jimmy Carter, and I think to myself a Democrat can't get elected in Idaho, though I remember he was the governor of Idaho before being called to Washington in the mid-seventies. Then it occurs to me the current governor, John Evans, is a Democrat; from Malad City, in fact. I met with him shortly after we arrived in May. A nice man, very concerned about the people of his valley.

Fifteen miles north of the state line, the wind becomes visual as the water arcs high into the atmosphere from the sprinkler heads, then disappears into thin air. Taking Exit 4 off the interstate, I turn left on the main arterial into Malad. The brittle crackling of the gravel in the parking lot announces my arrival. The 'Village Inn' sign is faded, but the thick plush grass under the long row of elm trees is brilliant green, and the petunias in the paint-peeled window boxes are a radiant red and white. It is the result of the healthy aquifer running deep beneath the surface; and the ambition of the widow caretaker who receives room and board from an absentee owner who left Malad when he couldn't sell the place.

I decide to stay at the Village Inn when we first arrive in May. Many nights I am the only guest in the place. Before going to the bank, I stop to drop off my bag. I pay in cash to get the weekly discount and pick up a key. The rest of the asset team, including Benny, stays in Pocatello and makes the hour-long drive to keep clear of the locals in Malad, they say, and to get a good bottle of wine with dinner.

Mrs. Howell is petite hard-boned woman. She startles me when she opens the door just as I am about to knock. Her worn jeans are clean pressed blue jeans and her flower print sleeveless blouse is covered with a bulky apron sporting two large pockets. Her sockless tennis shoes, bleached stark white, are beginning to fray around the edges. I often see her spare pair on a chair outside her room, drying in the sun.

"Morning–well, I guess it's almost lunch time. Well, anyways, hello there, Jack. Did ja have a nice weekend?"

The motel lobby is also Norma Howell's apartment; an over-sized room with a kitchen-living room, a small bedroom and a bath. I feel like an intruder, so I try to do business at the front step.

"Too short, but nice to see my daughter. I can't wait until this job's finished," I say as I pull the sterling silver money clip from my pants pocket. It reflects a glint of noon-day sun as I peel off a hundred-dollar bill and hand it to her. The gray-haired woman takes it with one hand, folds it around her gnarled middle finger and shoves it into the pocket of her red cotton apron.

"I wish you'd stay forever," she pulls out the bill and waves it, "but can't say I'd stay if I lived in California." Her raspy laughter causes her to hack as she runs her other hand through her cropped roan hair, bouncing like wheat stubble released from the weight of a combine header.

"Want a receipt?" She turns to go back into the room she keeps dark to repel the heat.

"I do. But not now. I'll get it from you later. I'm late getting down to the bank." I turn to go, not wanting to talk, and forgetting to get the room key.

"Ya know, Jack, I just want 'cha to know that Lars Helland wasn't a bad banker," she says to my back.

I turn and she's still fumbling with the money in her pocket. "Well, I guess that just came out wrong. If he'd been a good banker, he'd still have the bank. But what I meant to say was,…well, I guess he was just trying to help people stay on their farms and ranches."

I put on my dark glasses and slide my hands in my pockets, thinking a long time before answering.

"I think I know what you're trying to say, Norma. It's a hard thing for all of us, including me. I don't like taking away people's land, and livestock, and machinery. But if I don't do this job, someone else will." I try to be polite, but pragmatic.

"Well, I s'pose I know that. And I tell people you are a good man, but they sure do cuss the FDIC. When Niles Ogden shot himself after the FDIC started gunnin' for him, well, anyways, folks are saying the FDIC is just out to kill off everybody in Malad. Hell, it's killing all of this part of Idaho. Folks in Soda Springs, McCammon, Lava, Grace, Preston. They're all hurtin' real bad. "

I can see she is struggling, like she wants to say something else.

"The thing folks don't understand, Norma, is what kills a town is creating a loan portfolio heavy in one sector of the economy, like agricultural loans, and then not having any resources to loan out money to viable businesses."

I take off my sun glasses and continue. "We are just the insurance company who assures bank customers their deposits are secure, but I guess that doesn't help you understand why your neighbors are hurting. And I'm sorry for the Ogden family. Niles was a good bank board member," I pause, thinking about Niles reddening face that Saturday we interviewed the board of directors; the way his hands shook when Benny interrogated him, threatening to confiscate his property if they found any impropriety. I wish like hell I had intervened. I wish I had called Benny out and told him to back down. I wish I had pulled Niles aside and assured him those were idle threats. Unconsciously I shake my head, thinking about it.

"I will tell you this, Norma, I've read through a lot of confidential board minutes indicating if the rest of the board followed Niles Ogden's advice on a lot of these loans, the bank might have survived the downturn. But again, who knows?"

"Sorry I brought it up," she says. I can see a sudden feeling of conflict rubbing against the hundred-dollar bill in her pocket. Without speaking about it further, Norma Howell goes inside and shuts the door; then quickly opens it again. "'Bout forgot. Here's your room key." She holds out the green plastic tagged key stamped with a gold seven. I think about asking to use her phone to call my mother to let her know I made it back to Malad, but it is getting close to noon and I don't feel like talking about the human side of the bank any longer.

I unlock the door to my room where the meager furnishings consist of a double bed, a night stand with a lamp, and a two-drawer bureau with a vase of plastic purple lilacs just to the left of the mirror. No telephone, no radio, and no television. I hang up my clothes on the white painted iron rod attached to the cedar plank wall. I neatly store my underwear in a drawer with fresh butcher paper lining. I lock the door and walk to the café for some lunch.

I eat half the same Reuben sandwich I order every day at Elsie's Café across from the bank, sitting alone in a corner booth with a high-backed, badly worn, Naugahyde bench, hiding me from the rest of the lunch crowd. I ask the young, pallid-faced waitress to bag the rest for my dinner.

Opening the bank's back entry with my key, I climb the rear stairway keeping an eye out for Molly Olson, hoping to catch a glimpse, or just say "hello." The white sandwich bag goes in the bottom left-hand drawer. A framed picture of Stacy on her quarter horse sits on the desk, keeping me grounded. Walking to the window, I notice Molly's GMC isn't in the parking lot. I check my watch. It's close to one-thirty.

Like Rebekah and Molly's family, banking is my life. From boyhood to manhood I decisively follow in the footsteps of my father and grandfather. After I finished my MBA at Berkley in 1978 I went to work with FDIC in Colorado and bury myself in my job. Though times are slow, banks began crumbling in the early 1980s and I am the unmarried guy sent out to liquidate assets. I stare at Stacy's picture for a moment, trying to remember if I kissed her yesterday before she left with her mother.

Benny Schnabel jolts me out of my revere. "Good afternoon Mr. Whittaker. How was your weekend? Did you get in any golf?"

"Good golly, no. I was lucky to get my underwear washed."

"Did you hear we're shutting down three more in Colorado?"

"Not me. I told Sam Jackson I would take this one if they let me stay in San Jose for a while after we're finished here, so you guys are on your own. Now you can be Asset Manager." I smile at him and take two pencils and one pen from my desk drawer and place them next to the files I am ready to forge through. Benny's frown knits his brows together. I lean back in my chair and look over at the stack of files on his desk across the hall. Benny rests against the door frame holding his cup of coffee then, as always, sits in the seat across from me without being invited.

Benny wears heavily starched white shirts with his initials engraved on the breast pocket; Windsor knotted neckties, linen pants and leather slip-on shoes. I have worked with him on about half the bank closures over the past ten years. Camila told me she worked with him on several jobs before I came on board. It's no secret Benny drinks too much at night. It shows in his podgy, swollen face with red splotches, matching his tie.

"I hear Camila's planning on traveling again," he says, taking a sip of coffee to avoid looking at me.

"And you tell me this, because?"

"No reason. I thought she would have told you."

"What Camila does is her business. I don't ask."

I'm not going to give him the satisfaction of telling him Camila asked about him. Camila admitted once they dated before I met either one of them. I assumed it was just a fling for Benny, but I always suspected Benny meant more to Camila than the other way around. I honestly don't care, and it isn't a discussion for the office. Camila can be with anyone she pleases, including Benny, but the idea of my little girl being around him is an intolerable thought.

Everyone at the regional office knows about Benny's womanizing habit and his episodes at the cleaners every Saturday: dropping off underwear, shirts and pants, medium starch on the underwear and heavy starch on the shirts; and then picking up next week's supply.

I also know it is all Benny has going for himself. He left his second wife last year, the one he met in the bar in New Mexico at the Los Cruces bank closing. He said he told her his mistress was the FDIC

146

but she didn't believe him. I suppose Benny tries to milk it both ways: He dresses like a mafia boss to look like he is ready to ring your neck if you don't pay up and he brags it benefits him in other ways as well. I personally have a hard time imagining anyone wanting to cuddle up to Benny.

I start thumbing through the stack of files on my desk, taking inventory, trying to stay on task. "While I'm thinking about it, Benny, did we get the appraisal on the McDonald dairy in Daniels?"

"Nope. Not yet." Benny pauses. "I left two messages for Steve Black on his answering machine this morning. I'll try him again this afternoon. He is such a moron. No office hours and no secretary. I'm not sure why we give him these jobs."

I like Steve and I'm tired of Benny's insults. I come to his defense. "I think his wife comes in and types for him a couple of days a week. She's answered the phone a time or two when I've called."

"Well now, that's what I mean. He still uses his wife as his secretary, and an IBM Selectric typewriter, and it's 1986."

"Yes, but he's a reasonably good appraiser. It's just getting him to slow down enough to roll out the report."

"Well, maybe I'll try to call his wife and see if she knows where he is." Benny picks up his empty coffee cup, lifting his hand as a parting gesture, he walks out, closing my door behind him.

I check the window again, searching for Molly's vehicle. I think about walking over to see Rebekah and offer her the settlement decisions of the review committee in San Jose. I look up the street, but her truck isn't parked in its usual place. I know she'll be pleased with some of the results, but we still need to work out some details on a few others. It's always hard to justify not selling off livestock when they bring immediate capital. I use the same logic with the committee Rebekah used on me: I explain without cows, there is no operating capital to pay the mortgage the borrower is trying to get from another lender to pay us out; usually hardship money from Farmer's Home Administration. I received several calls from the congressman's office, from both D.C. and the Pocatello office, reminding me to tell the committee it is an election year. While we are a privately held corporation, we are still quasi-government and subject to political pressure.

"We're heading out for Pocatello, Jack," Benny pokes his face around the door frame. "See you in the morning."

"Wow, what time is it?" I look at my watch. It's nearly six thirty. "Did you get a hold of Steve?"

"I called three times and no answer. I quit leaving him messages after the second one."

"Man, I'd sure like to wrap that file up before we pack up." I stand and stretch. "I'll walk you guys out and get a cup of coffee or some ice tea. I need to get some air."

Benny, Will, and two others file down the stairway. I follow them out into the parking lot, telling them to drive careful and I'd see them bright and early tomorrow morning.

I can feel the slight cool of the desert at dusk as I close my eyes momentarily and take a deep breath. I smell the grain dust and the premature feel of fall in the air. Taking another deep breath, I look for traffic before crossing the street. The street is empty. There is no traffic in Malad, Idaho at six-thirty in the evening.

I peer through the window of Sorenson Law Office as I walk past. It's dark inside. I did not see anyone coming or going all day. The bell on the door rings as I enter Elsie's Café for the second time. I remember I still have the sandwich in my desk drawer I'll eat for dinner, so I sit at the counter to order something to drink. Besides, there is an old couple occupying my usual corner booth. This waitress is new, at least new to me. She is older than most who work here. She has hard, sad eyes, a sturdy frame and large hands speckled with brown sun spots and bulging veins, manifesting themselves when she sets down the ice tea I ordered. I assume she is supplementing income for a family short on cash to buy groceries and school clothes.

I take a sip of tea and reach down the counter to pick up the disheveled newspaper someone left there. It is Sunday's edition, but I thumb through it anyway, looking for names I might recognize. I look for bankruptcy filings and foreclosure notices, though we won't start filing foreclosures until we move files back to San Jose and turn them over to our legal department. After our hard work to find ways to keep the Malad Valley intact, I believe we've been successful in minimizing bankruptcies and liquidations.

When I see her picture on the second page of the local section of the newspaper, I quickly realize I am reading the obituary section. Her tiny porcelain-like face, the blond curly hair, the beautiful eyes, and the thin-lipped smile...

Grace Marie McDonald, daughter of Lance and Melanie McDonald, age two, died Thursday evening at Oneida County Hospital from injuries sustained on her family dairy Thursday afternoon. She was born in Malad, Oneida County, Idaho October 15, 1983. She is survived by a sister, Erica, and a brother, Dylan and her parents, Lance and Melanie. She is also survived by her maternal grandparents, Daniel and Lillian Johnson of McCammon, Idaho and her paternal grandmother, Leola McDonald of Malad. She is pre-deceased by her uncle, Jed McDonald, and grandfather, Charles McDonald. Funeral services will be held Tuesday at 2 o'clock PM at the Malad LDS Church. Interment follows the service at the St. John's Cemetery.

I am numb. I read it again. This is the dairy we sent Steve Black to appraise. Over the past two weeks, I tried to call Lance McDonald at least a half-dozen times. His wife said she'd have him call me back, but he never called. The last time I tried to call to let them know I was sending the appraiser out, the phone rang and rang. I asked Rebekah if she knew them.

"Of course, I know them," she says. "Melanie tends my kids. She's Molly's best friend. She's like another sister to me."

It occurs to me now why Molly wasn't at work this afternoon, nor Rebekah, for that matter.

The longer I stare at the face of the little child it reflects back the face of my own child, and I am sick inside. I asked Rebekah why she wasn't handling the McDonald's case and she shrugged. "He hasn't asked us," is all she said.

I told Rebekah she might suggest to his wife that they make some

149

attempt to settle with us. "Any kind of response or offer is better than ignoring it,"

When the waitress sets the check on the counter next to the newspaper I look up.

"You know her?"

"Gracie? Everybody knows Gracie."

"Do you know what happened?" I ask, pointing to the announcement in the newspaper.

"Yaw," she says with a Norwegian-Minnesota twang.

I look at her, waiting for a reply but her lip is shaking and the tears well up in her eyes. I think she is trying to tell me, but she can't talk. It suddenly occurs to me why Norma Howell started talking to me about the FDIC killing everyone off. I wonder why she didn't tell me about the little McDonald girl. I instantly realize, right or wrong, they all think I am killing them. Niles Ogden, and now Grace Marie McDonald.

I softly touch the woman's hand, stand up and pull the dragon money clip from my front pocket. I pull off a ten-dollar bill and lay it on the counter. Picking up the newspaper, I ask if I can keep it. She nods her head. I leave without getting my change.

Outside I watch the sun sink toward the western foothills, creating a moving mosaic of pink, lavender and deep plumb across the turquoise skyline as it quickly fades to an ominous gray. She is out there, I think. Little Grace Marie McDonald. I wipe a tear from the corner of my eye.

When I get back to my office I call Camila, and when she doesn't answer, I call my mother.

"Hi, Mom. Yes, the trip was fine. Have you seen Camila?"

"Yes," Mom says. "She called me this morning and said she has a meeting at the San Francisco office and asked if I would keep Stacy for a few days. I told her I'd keep her all week if she'd like."

I ask if I can talk to Stacy and Mom calls for her. "Honey, your daddy's on the phone. He wants to say 'hi'."

Her tiny voice yells out, "Daddy, daddy." I try to speak but my voice is like the lady at the cafe. Nothing comes out. I hold the phone against my chest, trying to gain composure. I pull in a deep breath and put the phone back to my ear. "Are you and Granny having fun?"

"I'm 'wimming in the pool like a duck, Daddy."

"You be careful, okay? I love you. I'll be home next week, okay?"

"Okay, Daddy. I luff you too, Daddy."

"I love you, angel," I say again, without thinking. I picture my little girl standing at the french doors leading to the pool, dripping water onto the terrazzo tile. "Let me talk to Grandma again, honey."

"Hi, again." My mother retrieves the phone.

"Well, I better let you go watch Stacy," I say to her, and hesitate. "Mom, don't let her in the pool alone. Stay out there with her, okay?"

"Quit worrying about us. Just get finished up so you can get home."

"Thanks, Mom. I'm glad she's with you."

"Me too, honey."

"Love you, Mom. Bye."

"Bye-bye, sweetheart."

I pick through the files on my desk until I find the Lance McDonald file. I open it and pull the stack of papers off the tines condensing the documents into an organized package. Meticulously, like excavating a cache of hidden ancient history I begin picking up each paper. I read the front, then carefully, deliberately turn it over, and continue to search for pieces of their file I previously missed.

This is the point in my life when everything changes. The lessons my Berkley professor pounded into me begin vanishing with the setting sun over the Idaho Mountains. The Harris Tweed jacket he wore every day begins unraveling as I read. How many children did they have? I guess I know, because I just read it in the newspaper. Now I want to know if they have a family dog. Where do they like to go for vacations, or do they even take vacations? What was

Grace's favorite bedtime story? Where are the answers to these questions? Have they always been here, sandwiched between the financial statement and the stack of chattel liens? I dangerously begin searching for the personal information that weakens people in my position.

The loan application doesn't say much about the McDonalds. Lance McDonald was born the year before me. He is married to Melanie McDonald and their application shows three dependents. The promissory note to Idaho First Bank of Malad City is for a hundred and fifty thousand dollars for operating capital. There are chattel liens on equipment and livestock for security. I gave Steve Black a photo copy of the same list in my file. No real estate, just dairy cows and equipment, I told Steve. The ledger indicates weekly payments from milk checks until about January. The McDonalds paid down their loan to less than thirty-five thousand dollars, but the twenty percent interest accrued back up to nearly sixty-thousand dollars of outstanding debt.

Then I find the memo I hadn't seen before, compressed between two ledgers. It describes a meeting between Melanie McDonald and Lars Helland. Melanie came in to talk to him in January, the date written in penciled handwriting was January 8, 1986. She was worried about her husband. He was becoming despondent and depressed over the bad milk prices. He refused to sign up for the dairy buyout program or sell off their replacement heifers. She didn't know what they were going to do. Lars reduced the interest on the note down to eighteen percent for another year with payments to start in October. His memo said they would be selling extra hay in the fall to pay the interest current on the note. Melanie would start substitute teaching at school again as soon as school started in September and she would send in her paycheck.

I close the file and lay my hand on top of it momentarily. No one at Berkley taught me how to value these kinds of assets, or how to reconcile the account of a family who is now minus one small child.

Sometime between eleven and mid-night I unlock the door to my motel room. Around 1 o'clock I finally fall asleep from exhaustion. The clap of thunder at 2 o'clock brings me straight up out of bed in a cold sweat. I finish the night in thirty-minute fits of sleep and wake before the alarm goes off. Standing in the shower, I let the pressurized water massage my back and neck. I don't want to wake Norma so I decide to walk the short few blocks to the bank, but I see her pull back the lace curtain and look out the window when I walk past. I pretend not to notice. Ballard's Service Station lights are turning on as I cross the street and walk west toward the bank, cutting across the parking lot between the bank and Molly's grandfather's house. As I'm fishing keys from my pocket, I notice the pickup parked next to the back door of the bank. The straw cowboy hat of the driver is visible from the rear. The window is rolled down and an elbow exposed. I decide it is too late to run.

"Mornin' Jack."

I move up the side of the truck slowly, and peer around the door frame.

"Steve! What on earth are you doing here at six o'clock in the morning?"

"Here's the McDonald report, but it's not quite what you were lookin' fer."

Steve's unshaven beard is heavy, his eyes bloodshot, his breath rank with alcohol.

"You wanna tell me what happened?" I take the manila envelope from his hand.

Steve waits what seems an eternity and his voice cracks as he begins to talk. "Lance was mad as hell I was there. Melanie was nice and the kids were friendly and I was takin' pictures of those little girls. Damn, they were cute. That blond angel with the kitty on her shoulder. You shoulda seen 'em, Jack. They just stole my heart." Steve lifts his hat, combs his fingers though his hair setting the straw cowboy hat back in place, as the tears trace the deep ruddy lines in his face, disappearing into his mustache.

"If I hadn't a been there, I don't think Lance would'a been so damn mad. He just wasn't thinkin' when he backed up the tractor without lookin'. God, Jack. He just screamed out, 'Melanie, I've run over the baby'." Steve grips the steering wheel with both hands trying to squeeze out the hurt until his knuckles turn white.

"Steve," I pull my motel room key from my pocket, "Here's my room key. Go over to the motel, take a shower and lay down for a while. You can't be out driving on the roads this way. Here, take it." I hold out the motel room key to him.

"Just give it to Mrs. Howell when you leave and I'll pick it up from her later. I don't even know why I bother using it. This is a good town. And these are good people who are just doing the best they can with what they got."

Steve takes the key quietly saying "thanks, pard'. I 'preciate it." It quickly becomes awkward. He looks away and we are both too uncomfortable to say anymore.

I pull the sterling-silver dragon money-clip from my pocket, ready to peel off money to pay him. "What do I owe you for the report?"

"Nothin'." He sniffs and wipes his nose with his thumb, rubbing it down his pant leg. "Just mail the picture to the McDonalds for me. It's the last one of their little gal, and they should have it." He fires up his diesel truck.

I put the manila envelope in my desk drawer without opening it, studying the stack of files on my desk, one by one, releasing the papers from the pressboard spines to read through them, front and back. In each one I find a handwritten note on the recognizable scratch paper, dated and signed by Lars Helland. The notes, I discover, are always handwritten on pieces of used typewriter paper, torn in two and the back side crossed out. I imagine the executive post-depression order going out from Molly and Rebekah's grandfather to his staff about saving used paper. I visualize a stack on the desk I now occupy, Lars Helland taking another half-sheet and writing as the borrower talks. Scratch paper reused by the heir, started by a thrifty old man trying to paper-mache the torn underbelly of a valley, dead on arrival a hundred years ago, until one small vein of water, after another, begins breathing life into it. I regret anything derogatory I said, or inferred, about Lars Helland. I particularly regret what I said to Rebekah in her office several weeks earlier.

I jump when I hear the crew from Pocatello coming up the back stairs and quickly put the documents back in place. I look at my watch. It is close to eight-thirty. I go to the window, thinking Molly won't be here again today, but she is. She looks up like she knows I'm here, but I know she can't see me through the tinted glass. She looks tired. I desperately want to go talk to her, to see if she is okay. My heart aches for her. I want to hold her and care for her the way she deserves to be cared for. I also know she loves her husband, and he loves her. I need to find a way to quell these aches I have for her. I know it ought to be Rebekah I should have these feelings for. She's single, beautiful, and more suited to my lifestyle. I enjoy working with her, talking to her, but I can never care about her the way I care about her sister.

I meet the crew as they come through the back stairway. "How was the trip from the big city?" I ask but don't wait for an answer. I catch Benny at the door when he walks in. He's wearing a fresh-starched shirt with a silk paisley tie and a light grey suit. I am wearing cotton Docker pants and a rayon polo shirt.

"Steve came by early this morning on his way to do the appraisals in Holbrook and Juniper." I say the names of the scab farming settlements to the west of Malad like they are suburbs of San Francisco.

"Did he bring the McDonald appraisal?" Benny's back is turned watching the intern fire up the coffee pot.

"Said he couldn't get to it right now." I look at the floor, uncomfortable in my lie, even though it is directed to Benny, the classic liar.

"What's his feeble excuse?" Benny asks, turning around to look at me.

"Said there's a problem with his typewriter and he'll have to mail me the report next week. I'll just pack up that file and take it back with me to San Jose."

"Sounds good to me," Benny shrugs. "We can't do anything with it now anyway. By the way, forgot to tell you yesterday about their girl getting run over."

"I read it in the paper last night. What a tragedy."

"Oh well, these people have so many kids...." Benny starts to say. I glare at him and he doesn't finish his sentence. If he had, I believe I would have punched him squarely in his refinished porcelain teeth. Instead, I defend the people I like to call "The Malad Dragons."

"Well, Benny," I say, "one thing I'll say about the people in this valley. They seem to wear their hardships like it's one more layer to wrap around their torn and weary souls. I have a feeling they handle these things a lot better than we would. I am beginning to think they live in cycles that forget the past; always believing tomorrow's going to be a better day. And us? Well, you know, Benny, we just live in a different culture where nobody really needs us the way their land and their livestock need them."

Will fills Benny's coffee cup and hands it over. I am tired of looking up at him.

"Come in my office for a minute," I say to him.

When he sits down across from my desk I ask him about Lester Olson's file. I hold up the file I took from his desk earlier. I know he isn't be happy about me rummaging through his work assignments, but I do it from time to time, not so much to remind him I am the boss, but to remind him that he isn't.

"Yup," he says, "Mr. Olson's coming in at 10 o'clock this morning. He says Farm Home's going to give him a hardship loan and take us out."

"Good. I'm going to let you handle it." I handed him the Olson folder and as he leaves, I stand up and slap him on the back. "And, Benny, when he talks to you, I want you to take off your tie, unbutton the top button on your shirt and ask him about his family. Ask him what kind of a dog he has, how many kids or grandkids he has, and if he's ever been on vacation. Write down everything he says on the back of this paper." I hand Benny a small pile of torn scratch paper. "It's an old banking trick. It takes them off guard and makes them think we care."

Benny looks at me, speechless. He turns, walks into his office dumping the paper I just handed him in the trash. I close the heavy solid oak door and lock it behind me. What I didn't know then, and would learn before the end of the day, is at that very moment, I just handed Benny Schnabel Molly Olson's entire life.

I lean back in my chair, pull open my desk drawer, and set the manila envelope on the desk in front of me. I pull the photos out of the packet and gently lay them out on my desk. The baby kitten sits across her tiny shoulders, the afternoon sun shines against her blonde curly baby hair, her sister standing next her. Then I pull out Steve's hand-written letter:

Dear Sirs, per your request I visited the McDonald Dairy Farm located at 14633 North Daniels Road, Malad, Idaho. I arrived at the farm at 4:30 PM Thursday afternoon. Lance McDonald was feeding dairy heifers with his Massy Ferguson tractor and Hollander feeder wagon, the ones you have listed as collateral. Melanie McDonald was lifting bales of hay into mangers feeding the nagging hungry Holsteins of varying ages, two to five years old, that you also have listed as collateral. Oh, and did I mention that Melanie McDonald is seven, maybe eight months pregnant? Their two-year old daughter was playing with the new orange and white barn kittens; the five-year old daughter was fussing about being hungry and the nine-maybe ten-year old boy was carrying large white plastic feeder bottles to bawling calves—calves that you also have a lien against. The boy stopped, and while juggling the bottles in his arms he asked me if I was going to take away his 4-H lamb, Flossy, 'cause he heard his dad tell his mom as much.

And that is all it said.

I take a piece of used scratch paper and begin writing, then pick up the phone and make some calls.

At noon, I look at the clock, realizing I haven't eaten breakfast. I close the McDonald file, fling my jacket over my arm, hiding the file under my coat and leave. Benny isn't in his office. As I walk past Will's office, I tell him to tell Benny I'd be out for the afternoon.

Norma Howell's door is open when I walk across the parking lot of the Village Inn. She pulls back the curtain at the kitchen window when she hears the crunch of my shoes in the gravel. I knock softly on her open door.

"Sorry to bother you," I say. "I just wondered if you know where the St. John Cemetery is?"

"Well, it's been a few years, but I know. My grandparents are buried there. Why?"

"If you don't mind taking a ride with me, could you just show me?"

"I suppose so. You're not gonna kill me for that hundred-dollar bill are ya?"

"No, no, no." I am shaking my head, chuckling. "I'd like to drive over for the interment of...ah..." I look away.

She looks down and sees the newspaper in my hand and says, "Oh. Yes. Okay. I gottcha."

Norma wipes her hands down her apron, and reaches into the front pocket, "Oh, and Steve said to tell you thanks for lettin' him use your room." She held out my room key.

"You know him?"

"Steve Black? His daughter's married to my grandson, Darrin. That's my oldest daughter's boy who took over our ranch out in Holbrook, twenty miles to the west 'a here after he graduated at the University of Idaho. I know you seen him drive in here a time or two a pullin' that old livestock trailer. Anyways, that Steve's a good guy and he raised a hard-working real sweet daughter."

"Did he say anything to you about what happened to the little McDonald girl?"

"Nope. Steve never talks much about anything. Didn't even say why he was in your room. He just told me to give you your key and said he was stopping by to have lunch with the kids on his way out to do some appraisals, so I told him to tell 'em hi for me. He left out'ta here 'bout 10 o'clock."

Norma Howell smiles as she covers the loaf of fresh bread using a clean white dish towel with faded embroidery of two Dutch kids on the torn corner.

158

"Well," she says, "I best change my clothes and put on a dress. Mormon women always wear dresses to church and funerals. I ain't one of 'em, but I better show a little respect."

"I can wait," I step inside the tiny kitchen and sit at the table.

"Did you eat lunch?"

"I'm not really very hungry," I lied for the second time in one day.

"Nonsense. I just baked bread. I can make you a tuna sandwich and grab some lemonade from the fridge. It'll take just a minute."

"Thanks. That's very kind of you."

"You best go and put on your suit and tie. You can change while I fix you some lunch. We should go to the service at the church first," she says. "Besides, Molly Olson plays music on that pipe organ that makes the angels sing. It's worth goin' just to hear her play."

My heart jumps. I raise my eyebrows and trying to keep my voice calm. "That is a good idea, Norma. I think I'd like to do that."

Chapter Twenty: **Melanie**

Lance and I are like everyone who dreams of building a life in Malad. Ours is Lance's dream, and I love Lance, so his dream becomes mine. More than anything, my dream is having babies, and lots of 'em. Lance's dream is having dairy cows, and lots of 'em.

Lance didn't grow up on a dairy, but I believe he fell fervently in love with the idea of being a dairy farmer over the span of time he tracked the rolling hills of Lancaster County, Pennsylvania serving on his two-year church mission in the mid-1970s.

I imagine on early mornings when he and his missionary companion would ride their bicycles down road-side lanes reserved for the Amish carts and horses, Lance would savor the green rolling hills sprinkled with red gambrel-roofed barns with immense white-washed feed silos attached to one end. He must have treasured the mild springs and Indian summer autumns; seasons rarely experienced in the harsh, wind-blown landscape of southeast Idaho. Delicate odors of fresh mown grass hay in May made him think of the headier aromas the windrows of alfalfa hay emits as cool air blankets the Malad Valley at dusk in mid-July; and somewhere between the two he became confused.

I suppose fanaticizing about this (and holding me close to him again) invigorated his growing passions without computing the facts. The average annual rain fall in Oneida County, Idaho is less than a quarter of the 40 to 50-plus inches of precipitation that falls each year in Lancaster County, Pennsylvania; not to mention a growing season that is thirty percent longer and soils producing three times as much hay tonnage without priming a pump to irrigate the crops. Lance cast off all the implications of predisposed failure (and he said as much in his letters to me) as wet blankets and a pessimistic attitude.

It's easy to mask these stark contrasts when the dream begins rooting deeper than the hardpan soils. Lance admires the way the Amish people are dedicated, humble, simple-mannered, and believe in so many of the same life-style values he tries to sell to them by telling them the story of the boy prophet who talked to God and Jesus in a grove of trees in Vermont; lessons he memorized from missionary lesson books. Lance believes the Amish outdid the Mormons on the concept of allowing their youth to sow their wild oats before settling down. They call it Rumsprina; a period when misbehaviors of their youth are overlooked. What Lance and I did before leaving for his mission leaves him guilt-laden and depressed; and what we didn't do leaves us both yearning for each other.

The Amish live a simple life in a beautiful place, causing Lance to fall in love with the idea of owning, and raising his children on, a dairy farm. He speculates without a single concept that demonstrates how he will carve out this life for us. He believes if he prays about it, the Lord will show him a way to have the dairy–and the girl who promised to wait for him while he goes on his church mission.

In May, almost eleven years to the day before the FDIC took over the bank where we borrowed money to grow his dream, I stand at Gate Eleven in the 'D' concourse at Salt Lake City airport with Lance's parents, Charles and Leola McDonald. Charles holds Leola's hand as the three of us wait for the Delta connector to taxi across the tarmac.

This is the last trip my soon-to-be in-laws make to welcome home a son from a church mission. Through the years, they watched as the airport continued to grow arms, and runways, and bigger planes powered with jet engines, since sending their oldest boy to serve in the London, England mission the year John Kennedy was elected (though they didn't voted for him).

They bid farewell to a total of four sons older than Lance, flying to scattered parts of the world to become Mormon Missionaries; and they bid a final farewell to one of their boys when he opted out of a church mission and went to Vietnam instead.

Their last trip to the Salt Lake Airport was to meet the Casualty Assistance Officer with the black arm-band who accompanied Jed McDonald's mangled and burnt body back to the United States. The McDonald family waited by the belly of the plane, the officer standing stiff as a board, saluting, as the box deplaned. They followed behind Evans's hearse along the old US 91 highway back to Malad, the American Flag draped over the pine coffin, neatly tucked around the corners.

Lance's parents dreaded the nightmare of traveling the new north-south Interstate 15 through the growing traffic of the Utah Wasatch Front. They called to ask if they could ride down with me, instead. I believe they relive the nightmare of following the hearse with the American Flag showing through the back window every time they drive to and from the Salt Lake City Airport.

As the mid-morning sun heats the airport corridor, and perhaps warmth generated from my own anticipation, I shed the thin light yellow cashmere cardigan I needed when we left Malad at sun-up. Lance catches me in his arms as he walks from the doorway, feeling the warm soft flesh of my toned arms. He buries his face into the curve of my neck, trembling with famished desire.

We set the wedding for June 30 in the Logan Temple in Utah. A simple wedding, quietly planned between us in the long letters he wrote to me on Mondays, and answered by me on the following Sunday, for nearly two years. Letters now carefully hidden at the bottom of my cedar hope chest full of hand-hemmed flour-sack dishtowels, crocheted table clothes and embroidered pillow cases edged in delicate white lace. The bundles of private communication contain apologies and regrets for touching and rubbing between us at the drive-in movie theater on those Saturday nights Lance drove all the way to Cache Valley without Molly and Scott, who usually accompanied us on out-of-town dates.

Yet the same desire pushes us to deliberately plan each detail toward solemnizing our passion by marrying as quickly as possible when Lance returns from his mission. We intentionally keep our distance between May and the end of June so, without looking down, we can each say to the Bishop Fuller, who holds the signatory pen of recommendation, we are clean and pure, worthy of passage through the doors of the Logan Temple where we will have our marriage solemnized for time and all eternity.

Three days before Lance returned, I finished my second year studying elementary education at the two-year Ricks College in

163

Rexburg. I lived at home during the summer, working afternoons at City Drug, dishing out ice cream cones and making malted milk shakes.

My mother came into the store one afternoon the last week of May and sat at the soda fountain. "Mel, honey," she says as she sets her black patent-leather purse on the counter, continuing to clutch it with both hands. "I can borrow some money to have a wedding reception for you and we can sew you a wedding dress. I'll even make your sister a bride's maid dress." My mother is a rigid woman whose round face is framed with stiff bouffant 'Revlon' brown hair. She bends her head to one side as though it is too heavy to hold up straight, waiting for me to answer.

"Want an ice cream cone, Mom?" I smile at her and she deliberately frowns back.

"Sorry, Mom. I know it's not the social norm, but Lance and I are saving every dime to start a dairy. We absolutely will not consider going into debt to have a wedding reception. We just want a little gathering with our families, and that's it." I lean on the counter, bend over and kiss my mother on the forehead. "Dad agrees with me. Ask him," I said. I picked up the terry cloth counter towel, rubbing it across the worn terrazzo counter top. "Now, let's not discuss it anymore, OK?"

"Well, at least let me help you rent a decent place to live. I can't stand the idea of you and Lance spending the summer living out of that old camper trailer in his parents yard."

"Mom. Please." It's the simultaneous sigh from both of us that makes my mother ask for one small scoop of chocolate ice cream in a dish.

After the June ceremony sealing our marriage, Lance drove us in my used Plymouth sedan to the Bluebird Café on Main Street in Logan, Utah to celebrate with our families; then we travel forty miles the opposite direction of Malad—through Logan Canyon—and stop at the top of the hill descending to Bear Lake. The lake is a large body of turquoise-blue water covering both sides of the Utah-Idaho border with the Wyoming border directly to the east. "It's the result of limestone deposits," I said, explaining the anomaly of the unusual color to Lance.

"How do you know everything, Mrs. McDonald?" Lance kissed me on the tip of my nose. He doesn't have to ask, because I continuously pass on to him the tidbits of knowledge I garnered from traveling with my father, a US Fish and Wildlife Ranger stationed in Malad and McCammon the past twenty years. As the oldest of two daughters, my father constantly espouses the rich history and geology of the region while I listen intently to his stories and dictum, savoring every bit.

The blue of the lake is a more deep bold blue than Lance remembered when he and his older brothers traveled with other Malad Boy Scouts to Bear Lake for camp outs. "I remember," he points across the lake, fidgeting with the new ring on his left hand as he talks, "when the Boy Scouts camped on that rocky bluff along the east shore. We put up our tents over there 'cuz tourists never liked that side. No beaches over there. We'd get the fires raging with old sage wood, then my brothers would start scaring the heck out of me and Scott Olson, telling us the Bear Lake Monster was going to come out of the lake and get us. Scott and I would lay awake all night in the pup tent we shared, too scared to go to sleep."

Lance and I decided to pay the cash to buy a motel room at The Garden City Motel to consummate our marriage in private. We spent the second night sharing a sleeping bag under the stars on North Shore Beach of Bear Lake, scaring each other with Bear Lake Monster and Grizzly Bear stories. We spent the rest of the summer in his parent's used camper trailer parked next to his parent's home on their small beef and grain farm on the east bench near the mouth of Deep Creek Canyon in the foothills northeast of Malad.

Lance's older brother helped him secure a job at Morton Thiokol west of Tremonton Utah, fifty miles southeast of Malad in the solid fuels rocket booster division; and I landed a full-time job at the local farm and feed store. We planned to use his paycheck to start buying dairy calves and saved the rest for a down payment on the dairy farm. We used my paycheck to buy the calf feed and medicine.

On Saturdays in the summer of 1977, we drove from Malad, east, through Deep Creek and Weston Canyons in the McDonald family's old International pickup truck with the bent front fender, pulling a manure crusted livestock trailer to purchase day-old dairy calves at the Preston Livestock Auction. I tethered my long brown hair with a piece of leather boot lace I found in the glove box to keep it from whipping in my face when Lance opened the truck window, inhaling the cool canyon air. I snuggled close to him; the gear shift protruding from the truck floor, sandwiched between my long slender legs. My arm draped across his back, letting my body fall hard against his as he sliced through the S-curves on the narrow canyon road.

The credit against my pay check from the Malad Mill and Grain was used to buy milk replacer powder and white square plastic milk bottles with terra cotta colored nipples, the size of large hot dogs. I loaded them, along with the powder, into the trunk and back seat of my car to haul home after work at night. The rear end of my '72 rust-pocked harvest-gold Plymouth fell under the weight. I drove at a crawl along the rutted dirt driveway up to the McDonald farmstead, trying not high center. The front of the car is elevated under the weight causing me to see the hood instead of the road. I stretched my neck out the side window, steadily straddling the deep tire ruts going uphill. Parking at the top of the driveway, I drug several fifty-pound brown paper bags sixty feet, grabbing the layered paper along each corner where the seam is reinforced and machine stitched.

With small beads of sweat forming on my brow and the back of my neck, I would heist the bags of replacement powder into the camper trailer and stack them on the bench by the table, leaving one perched against the cupboards to open and use. I poured the warm water heated on the propane gas stove into a big five-gallon plastic bucket, putting the metal thermometer making sure it is at least 112 degrees, adjusting for elevations over forty-five hundred feet. I added the supplement powder, stirring with a wire whip, trying not to spill it over the side. I held the plastic bottle over the sink as I poured in the mixture.

I did this exercise twenty-one times in the morning and twenty-one times in the evening, always thinking about Lance; wanting him to lean over, smile, and kiss me soft on the mouth when he came home late at night from Thiokol. I'd watch as he looked into the calf pens, seeing his calves growing into milking heifers, thanks to my diligence. I'd wait patiently each night, resting next to him, for a gentle bite on the tip of my ear, or a kiss to my neck, wanting to hear him say I am the answer to his prayers.

The bawling of hungry Holstein calves aroused me from daydreaming while stirring the mixture. They hadn't been fed since I left at seventy-thirty that morning, and it was after six. "Sorry, babies," I said. "I'm a comin'."

All the calves are on two feedings a day, except the four we bought three weeks earlier. I rummaged through the barn, finding strands of orange baling twine to tie around their necks, so I know which ones to corral and start on pellets.

Each day I talk through my routine methodically with Derrick Davis at the feed store until he scolds me to get to work. I put a sign at the front door of the store: "Need dairy barn, corrals and home to rent or buy." Lance's dad offered him the farmland on a crop-share lease starting the next year, but his parents want to stay in their house. There isn't a dairy barn within miles, and we have no money to build one, so Lance declined his dad's offer.

Everyone we approached told us Malad wasn't the place to start a dairy. The winters are too harsh and too long. Derrick Davis finally told me he heard about an older couple in Daniels, ten miles northwest of Malad, who were selling out their dairy cows and the place was going to be for sale. He suggested we might be able to rent it.

Derrick wrote the name on a torn piece of cardboard with the clumsy flat carpenter pencil he kept in his front shirt pocket. He scowled when I asked him how to get a bank loan. He told me to go talk to Lars Helland down at Idaho First. I said, "Oh, sure, Molly's dad. Sure. I didn't think of talking to him. Molly Helland's my best friend," I said.

In the early mornings of the first summer of our marriage, I would rise before sun-up, cook Lance farm-laid brown eggs, fry bacon from the pig they slaughtered and shared with the whole family, and toast thick cuts of home-made whole-wheat bread in the two-slice toaster my sister bought us as a wedding present. Then I would excuse myself to run to the barn and hang over the corral fence while I expelled the smells of bacon grease and milk supplement powder into the grass.

Lance watched me lean against the corner of the barn as the morning sun reddened, reflecting daylight off the corrugated tin roof. He saw my back bent over, heaving, again, and again. He would have to turn away as he began to retch. I would come back to the trailer to pack his lunch and make bottles for the calves before going to work at the feed store. He hugged me, asking what he could do to make me feel better. "It's what happens to women when they are pregnant," I said as I spread the grated cheese mixed with salad dressing on the homemade bread, wrapping it in waxed paper and laying it in the bottom of the brown paper bag with scrubbed carrots, and oatmeal raisin cookies. He never knew what to say to make it easier for me.

"Saw scours on one of the calves," he said one morning in late August when the nights turned nippy and the hot days blistered the paint off the camper trailer. "Got to catch that before it spreads. You better isolate that one and get some scours medicine today."

"Well, honey. Could you go out and catch it and put it in the barn for me?" I smiled at him a little sarcastically. My eyes were glazed over and my skin the color of the faded morning sky. The muscle spasms in my stomach kept me bent over.

"Oh, sweetheart. You gonna be okay?" He rubbed my back and left the trailer before I could answer the same way I did every day. I leaned over the sink watching through the small window as his tall lanky body ambled across the yard as though he had all day. The calves began to bawl and bunch for breakfast when they saw him coming. I could hear him talking to them. "Momma's comin'. Just be patient. She's a comin'." He patted their heads and let them suckle on his thumb before climbing into the pen. He tried pulling the scouring calf into the barn by the head. He finally tied a rope around the calf's neck and drug it like a stalled car in gear. I continued watching as the calf pulled away, and I knew if I'd fix a bottle and take it out, the calf would follow him straight into the barn. I smiled to myself instead.

"Crap, now I gotta change," Lance grumbled as he opened the door of the trailer and held out his arm soaked in mustard-colored calf feces.

"Lance, don't come in here!" I yelled at him. The wretched smell of calf diarrhea was permeating our trailer house as it heated up in the morning sun. I leaned over the sink ready to throw up again.

"Sorry." He closed the door and peeled off his shirt, exposing his white rayon, short-sleeved, scooped-necked temple garments, and hollered out to me, "throw me a clean shirt then, will ya?"

Before winter that year, I made a deal with Nelsons to rent their dairy in hopes of buying it someday. That is the year I gave birth to Dylan. The next year I lost a baby in my third month. Two years later, Erica was born. Grace Marie joined our family three years later. The spring Dylan turned two, Lance quit his job at Thiokol. That year we had twenty-five lactating heifers and he said there was no way he could do both. I continued to work at the feed store until Erica was born. After I quit, I worked twice as hard trying to help Lance make ends meet on the dairy.

***

On the last Thursday of July in 1986, we lost our precious Grace Marie. She would have been three years-old in October. On the first Tuesday of August, we lay her little body, crushed and broken, into a tiny coffin lined with pink satin and tell her goodbye until we meet again on the other side.

My faith is my Savior, and my Savior is my faith. I know my Redeemer lives because He breathes life into my every breath to keep me alive; to keep me moving with sufficient strength to buoy me up so I can take care of my broken husband, and our devastated children. My belief in this alone is the only way I can possibly get through each day.

While ironing Lance's shirt for the funeral I am lost in thought, and carelessly push the iron against my left hand, leaving a large red burn on my thumb. I run my hand under cold water, then finish the task. Lifting the white, freshly ironed shirt off the ironing board, I hold it out past my very pregnant stomach to my husband. His eyes are swollen, his nose red, and his hands shaking as he takes the shirt from me. I pull back my thick brown hair, lifting it up off my shoulders to cool my neck, saying with a tired whisper, "your tie and suit coat are lying on the bed."

Lance struggles to put his arms into the sleeves and I reach out and hold the shirt up for him to slide on. "What's Dylan going to wear?" he asks.

"He's a big boy," I say as I turn off the iron and unplug it, leaving it on the ironing board to cool. "He can figure it out."

"What about Erica?"

"Lance, sweetheart, you just worry about you. I sent a dress and shoes with Mom last night and she'll get Erica ready for the service. She said she'd meet us at the church. Now go polish your boots and make sure there's no dried cow manure caked to the bottom, okay hon?" As I stand on my tip-toes to kiss him on the forehead he clutches me, wrapping his arms around me, sobbing into my neck. His shoulders shake and his chest heaves, his shirt still unbuttoned.

"I'm sorry, Mel. I'm so sorry."

I stare stoically ahead through the laundry room window across the yard and watch as Scott Olson closes the dairy parlor door, gets in his truck, and drives away. I rub Lance's back with both hands without saying a word.

"Okay honey, we have got to go and do this," I finally say, and pull away. I button a couple of the buttons on his shirt, pat his chest and tell him I'll go see if Dylan is ready. "You go get your boots polished."

What I didn't say to Lance then, and will never say to him, is that he needs to stop blaming himself. He *does* need to blame himself, because it *is* his fault.

I made up my mind the Thursday evening of the accident, when I stood alone after lying Grace Marie's broken body onto the table at Evans Mortuary, I will not ever, ever blame him. But I also vowed I will never tell him not to blame himself. While I forgive him, I will never excuse him for recklessly and selfishly taking our daughter's life.

I climb the dark-stained wooden staircase of our turn-of-the century farmhouse, my swollen bare feet stepping up one-step-at-a-time, my hand holding tight onto the baluster handrail, pausing on every stair to garner strength for the next one.

It feels like a Sunday. The air is still. The house is eerily quiet. I gently knock on the door of my ten-year-old son's bedroom, calling out his name. "Dylan? Dylan, honey, are you ready to go?" I push open the cracked wood door when he doesn't answer. The room is tidy. His short-sleeved white Sunday shirt and black cotton dress pants are lying on the yarn-tied denim patch quilt I made for him a year after he got his own bed.

When he turned eight, and was baptized, I sewed appliqués of the twelve Mormon Temples onto twelve squares of the quilt and gave it back to him. A small denim braided rug matching the bed quilt hid deep scratches in the softwood pine floor where he kneels by his bed at night to pray. I used to sit on his bed next to him and listen. I remember the Sunday he was confirmed a member of The Church by his father, uncle, and two grandfathers. He told me I didn't have to come and listen to his prayers anymore. He said that since he was at the age of accountability, he would be responsible for asking God and Jesus to forgive him his sins on his own.

Under the single pane wood casement windows, four 1 x 10 rough-cut lumber planks held by gray cinder-blocks make a set of book-shelves. A wind-up black metal alarm clock with a white face and black numbers sits on the top shelf, its ticking piercing the morgue-like hush of the our home on the Tuesday we planned to drive to Pocatello and buy school clothes. Instead, we are attending our little Gracie Marie's funeral. On Dylan's dresser is a small box covered with black construction paper. "Book of Mormon" is written in gold lettering on the front, a slot in the top and a quote inked on the back "Money for My Mission."

I smooth out the wrinkled pants with the flat of my hand and walk to the bare paint-chipped windows, one still propped open with a 2 x 4 stud to let in the cool night air. I remove the prop and let the window slide across my fingers letting it down slow, trying to trap the left-over night-time chill still lingering in the room. I survey the empty farm yard below, holding the ghosts of Thursday's accident. I spot the family dog, a kind old Border Collie, standing at the closed barn door looking up, her black and white tail wagging. I retrace my steps to the laundry room, slip my feet into the loose flat-footed mud-caked shoes sitting at the back door to go find Dylan.

At the barn, I bend and pet the dog, "Hey, Jackie. How's my girl?" I lay my palm on the crown of Jackie's head and slowly follow the nap of the dog's fur along her spine, ending the gesture by gently petting her rump. Jackie looks up at me with sad, mournful eyes and whimpers. I dryly whisper back to her, "I know, girl. I know. It's as hard on you as the rest of us."

I take a deep breath and pull back the barn door, sliding it on the rusty iron rail. I push using both hands and my shoulder. The shards of morning sun light filter through holes in the metal roof, catching the roiling particles of hay dust. A rush of cool air against my flushed face feels refreshing. I silently thank the old barn for capturing and saving the best part of the early August mornings the same way I tried but couldn't seem to do as successfully in the old thin-walled house. I softly call out, "Dylan, you in here honey?"

"I'm getting water for Flossy and Bossy, Mom," he answers. I squint and walk down the center of the barn past pens made of the same rough cut lumber as the bookshelves in Dylan's room; pens now full of old feed buckets, used milking equipment Lance saves for parts. There are rolls of bailing twine we bought on sale at Cal-Ranch during the winter, stacked in the pens for summer haying.

In June, a month after FDIC shut down the bank, Lance, Dylan, and Rebekah's son, Jason, cleaned out the last two pens at the end of the barn to keep the boys' 4-H lambs. Dylan legitimately argued he could use his missionary savings money to buy the lamb and return twice as much to his bank after the livestock sale. I don't disagree since I have no way to pay for the lamb anyway, and I decide not to discuss it with Lance. Rebekah then offered to let Dylan pay her after the sale.

"Hey, Dylan. How's Flossy?" I say, just above a whisper, forcing out words as though they are the last bit of life left in me. I take hold of the top panel and peer over into the pen where my son is kneeling next to his lamb.

"She's doing pretty good, Mom." Dylan looks up at me, giving me a wistful smile. His little-man face is stained with tear tracks. I take a deep breath and begin shaking my head, trying to tell myself not to let go, not in front of him. I hold my breath. My lips begin quivering. I squeeze back the tears I have been avoiding. I bite my upper lip, sniff, and quickly wipe my nose and both cheeks at the same time. "Hey, little man. We have got to get ready to go."

"I know, Mom. I just wanted to say a prayer for Flossy, and for Dad, first." He ran his hand down the side of the black-faced lamb who is chewing on a mouthful of hay. He looks back up at me. "I don't want Flossy to die too, Mom." Dylan bends over, burying his face in the soft lanolin-soaked wool and begins to weep uncontrollably, his shoulders shaking, his wail muffled.

"Oh, honey. I know. But we talked about this before we took Flossy. Remember?"

I stand on the first plank and bend over to touch his sun-bleached hair. I run my hands through the thick mass, thinking the texture is course for a ten-year old boy. I pet his head the way I did our dog, Jackie. I know this isn't about saving the lamb. He has endured the rotations of farm livestock since the day he was born. It is about the boy carrying his father's guilt, feeling responsible for trying to save a life to replace the one we lost.

"Come on, son." I step off the slat of wood and open the panel for him to come out. I put my arm around his shoulder and pull him close to me "With the Lord's help, Dylan, we will all get through this. Your dad and I feel the comfort of your prayers on our family's behalf." I help him wire the pen gate and keep my arm around his shoulder as we descend the long dark passage to attend the funeral of his baby sister.

Chapter Twenty-One: **Melanie**

By one o'clock Lance, Dylan, Erica and I are standing at the head of the baby pearl rose casket lined with white satin in the Relief Society room of the Malad Church House for a final family viewing and a prayer. Grace Marie's favorite baby blanket has been washed and spread out beneath her; the frayed corner of the rayon binding she rubbed raw while sucking her thumb is carefully folded beneath her.

She is clothed in a white crepe dress with a pink sash, the bow tied in the front and the streamers carefully cascading down the three-quarter long skirt. On Easter Sunday I tied the bow in the back and Grace insisted I tie it in front where she could see it.

The bodice of my little Grace's dress is layered with a soft pink lace atop white bodice with a pink matching collar. It is the dress I sewed for her the end of March, the one that made her smile as she rubbed her hand down the front and said, "p'etty girl." The silver engraved heart necklace with a cursive G.M on the back lay at the small "v" of her tiny collarbone, crushed by the weight of the tractor tire. It is the necklace my mother gave to her to match the dress. Pink ribbons are pinned to each side of her blond, curled hair. She is truly an angel lying so serene, so beautiful, so painfully still. I gently graze my fingertips across her face, her skin the pale ashen color of the dry alkaline soil, scooped from the earth and piled next to her grave, waiting to entomb her.

I hear Molly playing the organ in the chapel. In my mind I see her setting her shoes off to the side of the organ bench, her long slender fingers pressing the keys, her feet pushing the pedals, changing the timbre and dynamics of the blending sounds that resonate through the church as she plays *"The Lord is my shepherd, I shall not want..."*

Scott quietly slips in the side door of the Relief Society room and moves through the small crowd to stand next to Lance and me. He places his large hands on each of our shoulders as he looks at Grace, bites his lower lip, and then he embraces us both.

***

On Thursday afternoon, the week prior, I was standing by the pen of yearling heifers with my pocket knife in my hand, slicing baler twine and spreading the sheaves of hay for the heifers to eat. Steve Black lifted another bale of hay and set it on the ledge for me to repeat the process, then he wrapped up the baler twine I'd cut off the bales and threw it into the old oil barrel to be burned. While we worked, he explained to me what I already knew.

When Steve walked into the feed yard earlier, Lance was on the tractor pulling the feed wagon, spewing silage out to the lactating cows. Lance knows Steve. We both went to high school with his younger sister and while Steve doesn't go to church, we run into him occasionally at football and basketball games. There isn't bad blood between Lance and Steve, but Lance chose to ignore him. I remember both of us looking up at Lance as he drove around the corner of the barn at a reckless speed.

"He doesn't need to be mad, Melanie. He's no different than five or six hundred or so other families in southeast Idaho," Steve said. "You want me to go talk to him?"

I told Steve it wouldn't do any good. I told him Lance wouldn't discuss the problems with the FDIC.

"OK," he said, "I'll finish my appraisal, Melanie, then you and Lance go down to the bank and talk to Jack Whittaker."

As he writes on his clipboard, he specifically said, "Don't talk to Benny. Talk to Jack. I know for a fact they'll write down the loan to whatever the cows and machinery are worth, and right now they're not worth much." Steve wrote Jack's name on a piece of paper, tore it off, folded it, and handed it to me.

"Melanie," he said, "this is important. Nobody's gonna shut you down. But you and Lance gotta go talk to 'em or I'll guarantee they will show up one day with a livestock trailer and flat-bed truck. They will have no choice."

I listened to what Steve told me. It was the same advice Molly and

Rebekah gave me. It was the same thing I tried to explain to Lance a dozen times. Then he'd mutter something about how hard he worked to build this dairy herd, and it would be over his dead body they'd take his dairy away from him.

And all I think of Thursday night, as the sun fades over the Curlew foothills on that last day of Grace Marie's life on this earth, is that it isn't Lance's dead body I am laying onto the stainless-steel table in the sterile room of Evans's Mortuary: A room where there are no pictures of Jesus sitting on a rock surrounded by children, or Winnie the Pooh, or books and toys strewn about the floor. It isn't Lance's chest that is still now. It's my baby, Grace Marie.

It's the same tiny chest I placed my hand on dozens of times in the middle of the night when she was croupy, or running a fever, or didn't wake up to eat when I thought she should have. The yard light from the dairy would shine through her window and I'd see the small crescent shape of her lashes. I'd lay my hand on her back and feel her take in tiny breathes, and let them out, sometimes slow and shallow; and sometimes in tiny heaves. But on this Thursday night, as I lay my hand on her stone-still chest, it is my worst nightmare.

I wonder if Grace is there in the room with me, aware of the grief moving through me like thick black oil, more real than the air I breath, or the dryness in my mouth, or the deafness to Molly knocking on the door, calling out my name, asking if it is okay if she comes in.

All I can do is wonder who committed this sin? Is it me, in my complacency of being a dutiful, loyal wife? And to whom does my first loyalty lie? Shouldn't it be to these babies who come out of my womb with their mouths open, waiting for me to feed them? Or is it Lance, in his determination to conquer, and then deny the reality that, like the Martin and Willie Handcart Companies leaving to cross Wyoming in late October, refusing to acknowledge the wisdom and common sense God gave us.

Or am I the one who made him believe it was always possible by feeding and caring for his dairy calves the way I have his children, finding the dairy we rented, meeting with the bank and arranging our financing. Wasn't this really all my fault? How was I any different than Laurie Hess who drives to Lucky's Tavern every night at half-past nine to retrieve her drunken husband and see to it he gets home? And how was Lance any different than Bud Hess who beats Laurie in his drunken stupor, and wakes the next morning to the bruises on her face he'd put there the night before?

Weren't these men of the priesthood supposed to care for their families? Why do Scott and Lance think it is acceptable in God's eyes to let their pride override their accountability to me and Molly and our children by facing their demons and slaying them instead of living in denial? And why does it become our fault when it doesn't happen the way they dreamed it would?

Molly arrives at the mortuary ten minutes after we'd gone from the hospital to the funeral home. She slips into the side door and knocks, calling out to me. Finally, she quietly opens the door and comes into the room where I stand over my child. She leans over Grace and kisses her little swollen cheeks and holds her hand on her face while she cries. Then she holds me until she feels the baby inside me kick. She pulls back, smiles through her blotched, red face and holds her hand against my stomach full of child and says, "You can't ever replace a child, but God finds ways to ease our pain." She didn't have to say any more. She came the moment I needed her and I was glad she was there to hold my hand.

The embalming room of the mortuary is stark, like an operating room. It is the room where the transformation from life to death occurs. Not just the death of my child, but the death of my duty of being Grace Marie's mother, which in many ways is the worst kind of pain to endure. It slowly smothers me in a shroud of unspeakable despair, making it hard for me to breath. It isn't imaginary or voluntary. It is as real as the life that is gone, and the new life I hold inside me.

***

Molly plays the song from the beginning again as Lance lifts Erica up to tell our Grace Marie goodbye. I reach in and straighten the bow on her dress, but I already told her goodbye and moved on. I look down at the floor when the lid is closed. I honestly don't remember a word of the family prayer, or who said it, before we file into the chapel behind the casket.

Molly plays the same song continuously until the procession is seated. She finishes the last measure, and lifts both hands from the keyboard. I recall watching Molly as she looks at the funeral service program and places the hymnal at the appropriate page then rests her hands in her lap. I look down at my bulging belly where my hands are resting. The burn on my left hand has blistered, the top layer of skin is festering. I rub it softly with my right thumb as I close my eyes for the opening prayer, and I wonder why I can't feel any pain.

Chapter Twenty-Two:　　　Rebekah

I select a light blue two-piece suit from my mother's closet to wear to Gracie's funeral. It looks much like the one Betsy Ogden wore on Mother's Day, but I chose the string of pearls instead of the scarf. I take Jason and Eric, and Molly's son, Bobby, to the funeral with me. Molly's mother-in-law, who is also watching Molly's youngest, agrees to watch Rosalyn.

Lester and Sarah Olson's house is a two-bedroom bungalow, not much bigger than Scott and Molly's but a good quality brick mansard-style, more like the one my Grandfather Thomas lives in. I called my grandfather earlier to see if he wanted to go to the funeral and he said his limit is two a year, unless, of course, the next one is his own. I hadn't felt like laughing the entire past week, but I laughed at Grandpa because I knew he meant to be funny, and he was.

Sarah Olson hands me a Corning-ware casserole dish with au gratin potatoes browned on top with melted cheese. I give Rosalyn a kiss goodbye. I closed the trap door inside me leading to Melanie's world, because I can't go there. I cried for her, and I held her when I went to her house on Friday. I did all of the things to show her my sympathy, but I can't put my feet into her shoes and walk in them. I cannot imagine the pain she feels, because I won't allow myself to.

"How is Melanie?" Sarah Olson asks me. "That dear, dear girl," she says, wiping her nose. The folds of skin in her face sag around her neck and chin, shaking as she talks, and the bags of skin hang from her arms. She is much shorter than me, stocky, with short gray hair, curled tight against her head from an over-active permanent solution administered at Shannon's every few months, I am guessing.

"She's in shock," I say. "I don't think it's hit her yet. When I last saw her on Sunday, she looked drained and anemic; talking to me in quiet whispers like it was all she had left in her."

"I can't say I don't know what she's going through," Sarah looked away from me, out the kitchen window, like she is talking to the empty gravel road that falls off the flat horizon to the west. I frown. I have no idea what she is talking about.

"I lost a baby to the sleeping sickness," her voice falters.

"Oh, Sarah," I say. "I had no idea."

"I don't talk about it," she says. "I just want Melanie to know that I know how she feels. I'll send her a note, not that it helps."

"It helps," I say. "She would like that, if you feel like you can share your story with her."

"Well, you run along now dear, or you'll be late," she says.

I tell Bobby to go get in the truck with Eric and Jason.

"Sarah," I say, "thanks for telling me."

She smiles a sad smile.

"I'll be back and pick up the kids and take them home with me," I say. "Molly said she has to leave right after the service to go to Pocatello for something or other and won't be able to make it to the cemetery or the dinner. She said Scott is going over to milk cows for Lance."

"I can keep them until Molly or Scott can pick them up," she says.

"It's okay. I'll likely just put them to bed at Dad's house if it's late," I tell her.

When I get to the church it is quarter to two. The parking lot is full. I park along the grassy ditch bank and tell Jason I need to drop off the potato casserole at the kitchen and need him to take Bobby and Eric and find us a seat.

The flat gray-colored hearse with matching vinyl roof and tinted windows is parked directly in front of the church in the same place it had been for my mother's service, and Niles Ogden's service. I walk around to the back door near the propane tank, where the hallway leads down to the kitchen. As I walk to the counter filled with plates of pies, homemade rolls, and casseroles, a stunningly beautiful Indian woman dressed in beaded regalia lays a pie on the counter next to my dish. I look at Verna Enders who was staring at the woman; then I look again.

"LaDona?"

"Rebekah?"

"Oh, my God," she says, then covers her mouth as Verna Enders frowns at the Lord's name being taken in vain, and corrects, "oops, I mean 'Oh my gosh'." She shrugs, looks at Sister Enders and mouths 'sorry'.

I grab my friend and hold her in my arms and sway as I laugh and cry.

"How long has it been?"

"Too long."

"Are you here with someone?"

"No."

"Can you come sit with me, or are you sitting with the family?"

"I've got to go sit with the family and I'm running late. I need to get down to the Relief Society room before they close the casket," she says, "but I'll catch up with you later."

I hold on to both of her hands. "It's so good to see you," I say. "I'll see you later," and I give her a slight kiss on the cheek.

LaDona Bearclaw was thirteen when she first came to Malad. The McDonalds, Lance's parents, fostered her under the Indian Foster Placement Program. It was rumored the program was restitution or reparation for the Battle at Bear River. It may have been their own way of healing by housing their children, and sending them to "white man" schools.

Though it was difficult for her to comprehend the teachings of the Mormon religion, being baptized was a prerequisite for placement. She struggled quietly with the concept that she was a descendent of Laman, who, as described to her by the missionaries, was a wicked Jew cursed by God. According to the teachings, Laman and his tribe had been cursed with dark skin for their iniquities, similar to the Africans, who were decedents of Cana. To be placed in an L.D.S. home under the church Indian Placement Program she either joined

183

the church or would be denied the program.

It was her wise and concerned mother who painfully encouraged her to lay aside her skepticism and take this opportunity to better herself. To the young skinny Sho Ban Indian girl it seemed a submission to accepting the belief her ancestors were Jews, a thought that provoked serious doubt and technically, she thought, was incongruent with her bone structure. In reality, these are arguments she wrestled with years later when she studied anthropology and archeology at University of Montana in Missoula.

She still acknowledges, although she has distanced herself from the religion itself, it gave her the opportunity to gain a relatively decent education in the Malad School system and garner an unexpected scholarship for higher learning and ultimately gaining her PhD and a teaching job at Idaho State University in Pocatello.

Over time, as LaDona spent each school year with the McDonald family in Malad, the Sho Ban Indian girl outgrew her pre-pubescent body, filling in her hips first, then growing plump bosoms, geometrically matching the rest of her body. Her nose is long and straight, her skin the color of light, rich, sinful chocolate, and her eyes round and black. She tried more than once to curl the coarse horse-like hair, and then receded to braiding it, though she learned to make a french braid in order to not make herself look so Indian in an all-white high school overwrought with polyester, big hair, and hairspray. On more than one occasion we commented on how much we are alike, similar height, similar course dark hair– thinking at times I may have been adopted and was, in truth, perhaps her sister.

LaDona used to spend many nights with me after late basketball games. We'd laid in bed together, talking into the early morning hours. She'd tell me how Lance once told her he loved her hair most when she parted it down the middle and let it cascade down her back, so she let him touch it from time to time when she wore it that way.

LaDona Bearclaw first loved Lance like a brother. It began on the day Lance's father set her battered tin suitcase on her bed in the main floor bedroom next to theirs, kindly welcoming her to their home then quietly closing the door to let her cry out her homesickness. She told me Lance heard her crying, so he shyly knocked on the bedroom door, then gently pushed it open, raised his hand straight in the air in front him and like an Indian chief said, "How." They both began to giggle.

She told me later, the last time she saw Lance was ten years ago, shortly after Dylan was born. I asked Lance if he has seen her or heard from her. I remember how much LaDona resented Lance dating Melanie in high school. LaDona was absent at their family wedding dinner in Logan. I was told she made the excuse she couldn't attend because of a conflict with finals at school, but I know different. She thoughtfully sent a white wedding ceremony blanket, the same one used to wrap around the shoulders of the Indian bride and groom when they take their marriage vows. It is a carefully woven blanket with all the same symbolism, ceremony, and covenants as Lance and Melanie took upon themselves in their own ritual in the Temple. What I know, that few other people know, is LaDona Bearclaw, a beautiful Indian woman of few words always secretly, passionately, loved this particular foster brother, and wished it could have been her, not Melanie, who lay beneath the blanket with him.

Chapter Twenty-Three: **Melanie**

The hearse, moving painfully slow, heads north, away from the Malad Ward church house. The line of vehicles following behind us travel along Old St. John Highway in the hot, dry wind of an August afternoon when farmers dressed in washed out polyester plaid Sunday suits would have otherwise been greasing combines or adjusting the tension on the baling twine knotters of their rebuilt worn-out balers.

Lance and I ride directly behind the hearse in the mortuary-owned family limousine with our two living children, Dylan and Erica, whose faces are drawn; and lips tight and pale. Lance holds my hand like a limp dishrag, his energy drained like he's been milked dry of regret, and grief, and blame, and tears. In the car with us are Lance's foster sister, LaDona Bearclaw, and my mother.

I remember LaDona from high school, but mostly because she and Rebekah were good friends; and some nights when I'd stay at Molly's house, she'd be there with Rebekah. When I was with Lance, or over at Lance's house she'd always disappear. She was quiet at school. She played on the basketball team the year Malad girls' team won the state tournament.

Behind us was a black Suburban, a type of highly over-used vehicle that summer of 1986 to transport the FDIC into Malad, and ferry dead bodies or pall bearers. My father occupies the front passenger seat, two of Lance's brothers and my sister's husband are in the center seat and Scott Olson and Lance's oldest brother are in the rear seat.

I watch Scott hanging back from the rest of the pall bearers after lifting the coffin into the hearse. He waits, looks around, then hesitantly climbs into the carrier with the others. I think now he must have been looking for Molly; wanting to talk to her before she left. I didn't know then, but would learn later that night, the reason she wasn't at the graveside service; or the meal at the church after the service.

Molly is closer to me than anyone, including my husband, my mother, and my sister. I allow her into the dark, private, places where I keep my secrets; a place similar to a furtive compartment beneath the bottom of my hope chest; a place I store my regrets like a treasure, keeping them for my day of reckoning. I share them only with Molly. Today, the day I visit the dark den of my past to account for the reasons the Lord has taken my child, my closest and dearest friend is not here to be with me, in my darkest hour of despair.

I can't imagine what is so important she would leave me to hold myself together without her by my side. I know, as I look at the balled-up tissue I hold in my hand, if she were here, she would have retrieved it and replaced it with a fresh one. No one else in this world would think to do that sort of thing for me; but Molly would have.

By late afternoon, the cultural hall of the Malad Ward Church is transformed into a dining hall with long rows of portable tables and folding chairs stored in the belly of the stage that lines the west wall. While we are at the cemetery, the Ward Boy Scouts are pulling out long carts on wheels stacked with tables and chairs and erecting the collapsed fixtures to create seating for the community funeral feast.

The cultural hall in a Mormon church house is the gymnasium, the dance ballroom, theater, and, because it always has an attached kitchen, serves as a dining hall, or a person could perhaps say, it is a community infirmary on the days the community gathers to prepare to move forward through sustenance and assuring one another there are brighter days ahead. Today is certainly one of those days. Based on the amount of people beginning to gather at the church after the dedication of Grace Marie's grave site, one can easily assume the prices of wheat and livestock are at a multi-decade low.

At the end of the food table is a galvanized ten-gallon thermos full of cold, heavily sugared Kool Aide. The children, mostly cousins to my children, have already revisited it twice or three times, gulping the cherry flavored sugar water, leaving a red ring along their upper lip, laughing at the looks of it on each other's face.

"Where's Molly?" I overhear Lance ask Scott, who is filling his plate with casserole, potatoes, ham, and a homemade dinner roll broken open and smeared with butter and strawberry jam. "I thought she'd be here." I watch as Lance's eyes dart around the room while he speaks to Scott. He should have known she would be with Scott, if she were here. Or, perhaps Lance is looking for his youngest daughter, forgetting, for a moment, we just left her to be buried at the St. John Cemetery.

I hear Scott tell Lance that Molly took the truck into Pokey to pick up a combine part before the John Deere dealer closes. "She said to give you and Mel her love." Which is what Scott knows she would have said if he had talked to her after the funeral. Lance looks hurt and Scott continues to account for her absence.

"And, well," he drawls it out, like any self-respecting man would, "she had to go meet with the Farm Home guy this afternoon to try and get the money to get FDIC off our back." I am silent. I watch as Scott looks down at his plate. I know how badly he wishes Molly were here, because he knows she would take Lance's arm and say to him, *we will all get through this together*. She would rub his back lightly, looking square into his eyes, and remind him about the promise of eternal families. She would be able to let Lance know, without saying it directly, that she forgives him for being so careless, so self-absorbed in his own anger. Something Scott isn't willing to do, and it hangs in the air between them, like a badly thrown football.

"Tell her thanks for the beautiful music," Lance says to Scott, in a sad, timid voice.

I can tell Lance wants Scott to look at him, but he doesn't. He stares at his full plate of uneaten food. "And thanks for the dedication prayer," Lance says, still waiting for Scott to look up and see the pain buried behind his eyes, and the ache lying in the bottom of his chest, stabbing at him like a dull hunting knife. I believe Scott doesn't want to tell his friend what Lance wants to hear; tell him it was just an accident, or say it wasn't his fault he carelessly put the tractor in reverse without looking behind him. Perhaps Lance wants him to excuse the accident by saying it was my fault for not watching her, or Steve Black's fault for distracting us.

Scott likely feels the same as I do. I wonder if Scott won't look at

Lance because he is afraid his eyes will divulge all this to him, but in a different, harsher way than Scott wants it said, especially today.

Scott and Lance built their relationship by learning to read each other's eyes. It started when they played football together in their early teenage years. Scott was the first-string quarterback on the Malad High School football team, and Lance was his primary receiver. If Lance missed a pass, Scott would remind him, when they got back to the huddle, to watch his eyes.

"Lance, just keep your eyes focused on my eyes. If you keep eye contact with me, you'll know where I'm going next."

It worked for them all the way to the Idaho State Champion semi-finals their senior year when, just once, Lance looked away from Scott and missed his cue.

And now, on the most difficult day of our lives, Scott is the one missing the cue. What Lance wants at this moment is the same thing I wanted from Molly. He wants his friend to set his plate of food down onto the table and put his arms around him and let him bury his face into his shoulder and comfort him. Instead, Scott continues to balance his plate with one hand, hold a cup of red Kool Aide in the other, while asking Lance if he needs him to go over to our place and milk the cows before picking up his kids from his mother. The indiscernible influx in Scott's voice makes the question seem so impersonal.

"That'd be nice." Lance sounds like a whimpering animal stricken ill from eating the poisoned roots of water hemlock.

Finally Scott looks at Lance. "I'll need to borrow your coveralls and chore boots then. I forgot to bring mine."

"They're on the back porch at the house." Lance says looking away from him. "You can just go on in and get them." They are awkwardly silent again.

"How's Jess going to get his 4-H lamb to the fair in the morning'?" I heard Scott ask, "Ya know, they got to be there at the livestock barn by eight o'clock for weigh in."

Lance shakes his head. "Dunno. Guess I'll worry about that

tomorrow," he says.

"I'll just eat, then and geta goin'." Scott pulls the folding chair away from the table to sit down. The rubber caps catch on the slick finish of the hardwood floor. The noise of the vibrating metal seat echoes through the hall now filling with women dressed in summer cotton dresses with short-sleeved jackets, mostly home-sewn. Long-faced men whose farm hats leave shocks of coarse hair standing permanently on end begin shedding their suit coats and ties. They unbutton their shirts at the collar, then roll their sleeves twice, exposing contrasting forearms browned from wind and sun, and hands with telling traces of grease tracks permeating the first thick layer of skin.

"I got Mom's car today," Scott says to Lance, setting his plate down, "or I'd just pick up those lambs tonight. I'll come back over to your place in the mornin' and do the milkin' again, if you need me to. I'll just load Bobby's lamb before I leave in the mornin' and stop by your place and pick up Jason and Dylan's lambs. I can run those into the fairgrounds. Anyways, I promised Rebekah I'd do that."

Scott sits down and tucks the paper napkin into the unbuttoned collar of his white Sunday shirt, likely trying to keep it clean to wear it again on Sunday. He finally looks up as Lance walks away. He takes a bite of casserole and I watch as Scott lifts his head again. It is as though he's ready now to throw Lance the football, seeming to search for the connection between them, seeming to want Lance to turn around. I watch Scott's frown deepen as Lance notably drops his shoulders and shoves his hands into his pockets as he walks away.

Heavy footed and sullen, Lance moves deliberately toward the table where his foster sister is sitting with Rebekah. I watch him look dolefully back at Scott sitting by himself at the far end of the cultural hall, both forearms resting on the edge of the table.

At the table where Rebekah and LaDona are sitting, Lance takes hold of the back of a folding chair to gain his equilibrium. His brooding face is twisted, looking as though his heart is being ripped apart by the gradual pull of a torture rack. Perhaps neither Scott nor I understand his hurt nor give Lance credit for his willingness to accept responsibility for what happened.

Scott wasn't there last Thursday afternoon and can not, in any way, comprehend what Lance felt as he scooped up the listless body of his little girl into his arms from the hardened ground. Scott could not possibly feel his grief or regret. Though we haven't talked about it since, I believe Lance hadn't gone to Scott for pity or forgiveness. He only wanted his friend to hold him briefly, like a brother would hold another brother, hoping he'd smother the painful hot coals still glowing inside his charred soul, like a burned-out log.

Chapter Twenty-Four: Jack

Norma Howell rode with me in my Hertz rental car from the motel to the church to attend the funeral service of Grace Marie McDonald. When I open the car door for her to get in, I realize the McDonald loan file is sitting in the front passenger seat. I grab the folder and move it to the back seat before she sits down. As we drive northwest on Bannock Street, Norma points, "Left there, where all the cars are turning."

Norma tells me if I park around back, she knows of a less conspicuous entrance to go in where we can sit in the back of the church. I know that's her comfort zone, and on this occasion, mine as well. When we arrive, I am stunned by the number of cars filling the parking lot; cars parked diagonal along the concrete curb that runs parallel to the sidewalk in front of the church, and more cars lining the ditch bank along the east side of the road across from the church. Behind the church is an empty pasture starting to fill with latecomers. Norma points to the open gate, indicating I should follow the truck now parking in the brittle, dry grass.

"We'll be lucky to get a seat," I say to Norma.

"Oh, they'll sit the overflow in the Relief Society room," she says. "They put a sound system in there for folks who come late or folks who need to take their crying babies out."

Norma is a wise woman who knows these people. She says, in her own rudimentary way, when times are hard, more people show up to a funeral than in good times. I can't say it exactly the way she did, so this is how I would translate it: it can be convincingly postulated the number of people at a funeral during grain harvest in Malad Valley is directly inverse to the price of wheat or cows in any given year. Despite the half-cut grain fields, the third crop of windrowed alfalfa hay waiting to be baled, the teeming crowd filing into the church on this Tuesday afternoon in August is massive.

"I can almost say for certain, Jack, in good times they find excuses to keep their combines and balers running, and in bad times they all show up. Like in nineteen seventy-seven, for instance," Norma said to me earlier, twisting her lace-hemmed linen hankie, "when little Emma Larson drown in the Liberty Canal and wheat was soaring past seven bucks a bushel, the church was half-empty."

I open the car door and hold out my hand to her. She takes it to hoist herself out of the car, though I am certain she barely weighs a hundred pounds, and could have handily gotten out of the car herself. I offer her my arm, and she takes it, holding on as we walk across the uneven ground toward the back of the church. The back door leads us into a large gymnasium with a stage on one side.

Rebekah is standing at the counter full of casserole dishes and pie plates that opens into a kitchen behind her. She is in deep conversation with a tall, stunning Native American woman dressed in a beaded leather dress. Rebekah doesn't see us. I let Norma lead me to the chapel room where I see Steve Black sitting in the back row. He is staring at the grey felt western hat he's holding, turning it around and around.

He looks up when I touch his shoulder. I shake his hand and let Norma sit down next to him, then I sit next to her at the end of the pew. Steve reaches across the back of the bench, putting his hand around Norma's shoulder, giving her a squeeze. Norma reaches over and touches his knee. When I look up, I see Molly, sitting on the organ bench, opening the music book in front of her. She is wearing a white dress with large black flowers and a short-sleeved black jacket. Her dark-blond hair is pulled back and bound at the base of her neck with a black scarf cascading down her back. Her face is a pale milky white, but I can almost visibly see the healing in her heart as she begins to play the prelude music. I don't have to take my eyes off her. I can sit and look at her hands moving across the keys, and no one will be the wiser, or judge me wrongly, though I know the thoughts in my heart are wrong. In nine days, when I leave Malad, I will try to put her out of my mind. But today I will take all of her in, knowing I will never be able to put her out of my heart. *The Lord is My Shepherd, I shall not want…*" the music echoes through the chapel.

We stand as the procession begins. I have no idea what Melanie and Lance look like. I'd read their file from beginning to end and shortly before noon, behind my closed, locked office door, earlier that day, I'd made the call to San Jose.

"Sam? Sam, it's Jack."

"Hey, Jack. How's it going up there?"

"Well, it's been better. Hey, Sam. We've got a special case up here I'd like to get an expedited approval on."

"What d'ya have?" I could envision him standing next to his desk having our conversation over the speaker on his phone, both hands on his hips, waiting to move on to the next fire he needed to put out. He is in his late forties, about my build and height, and smart. He doesn't like boondoggles. He doesn't usually wallow in regulation. He just wants things done right, and if it makes sense he wants to quickly resolve it, and move on.

"Well, I've got a dairy up here, the only one in Malad in our portfolio. The rest are in Preston area and a couple up in Grace. We don't have any real estate, only the cows and some old machinery. With this dairy buyout, the cows aren't worth much and they owe us about sixty thousand with the accrued interest."

"Ya, I'm with ya so far"

"Well, they had an accident on their farm last Thursday afternoon and their two-year old daughter was, 'um," I paused, looking out the window toward the mountains, catching my breath to finish, "Run over and killed…"

"Oh, dear God, Jack. How dreadful."

"Yes, well, it's really turned everything here in a tailspin and I've got someone who's willing to pay ten cents on the dollar, about six thousand to buy out their note."

"Well, I'd say that's a no brainer, Jack. I'd say go for it."

"Just wanted a second approval on it, Sam."

"You got it. And good luck with getting everything wrapped up there."

"Thanks, Sam."

"Benny behaving?"

"No problems so far outside the usual lousy attitude"

"Well, I'll keep my fingers crossed you won't have to leave town with some divorced bank teller crying her eyes out."

"None I know of. They're all good Mormon gals who won't give him a second look."

"Well, thank God for that."

"I'd say."

"Well, Jack, I guess I'll see you next week back here in civilization."

"Sounds good. I'll talk to you then."

The next call I make is to my father at San Jose Bank of Commerce.

"Bank of Commerce, John Whittaker's Office," Janet Devosio answered the phone.

"Hey, Janet. It's Jack. Is Dad in?"

"He is just leaving for lunch but I'll catch him."

""Hey, son. How's it going?" My father answers the phone, sounding out of breath.

"Good. Well, not so good, but that's a story for later. Dad, I need you to set up an account for me and transfer ten thousand into an account called Malad Livestock Holding Company, and put both of our names on the account."

I told my dad not to ask questions. I said I needed it available to me by that afternoon, and told him to wire certified funds to FDIC and I gave him the McDonald Account Number.

The funeral is shorter than I imagine and consists mostly of music. Kenny Sorenson gives the eulogy and a short consoling message to the congregation. Some little children sing a song I have never heard before, but I think about Stacy as they sing, *I am a child of God, and he has sent me here. Has given me an earthly home with parents kind and dear...* Molly moves from the organ to the piano to accompany the children while they sing. The piano music is softer, and does not drown out their voices.

After the funeral I drive Norma out to the cemetery. We follow the long procession of cars through the countryside, turning at mile intervals; first west, then north, then west, and then north again. I memorize the path as I go, looking for landmarks and road signs; remembering barns or houses to help me find my way back out to the cemetery after dark, not realizing it is the beginning of the New Moon. We are hushed as we drive past stubble fields, hay fields, and empty pastures where livestock will graze in the fall; information Rebekah taught me when we'd drive the countryside together making joint assessment about chattels and properties. Norma stares at the landscape like she is gathering nuggets of memories and I let her revere in her silence.

We are among the last to join the mourners at the small cemetery. We park and walk along the gravel road. I see Rebekah with her sons and Molly's son standing next to Lars Helland, who is standing by Kenny and Esther. I see Scott standing with the rest of the pall bearers. I scour faces in the crowd, looking for Molly, but I don't see her. Scott says a prayer and the crowd begins dispersing.

I consider walking over to Lance and Melanie to express my sorrow for their loss. I want to ask Lance why he hasn't called me back. If he was angry about Steve Black coming to take inventory of his cows and machinery and crops, he should have come in to see me when I first called in June.

I look at Melanie's face, cold and emotionless; Lance looks like he's been beaten up and thrown to the dogs for scrap meat. Their two children, Dylan and the younger girl—I don't recall her name—Erica, I think I'd read in the file. Dylan looks like he is carrying the weight of the family on his shoulders. He stands straight with a solemn face, his arm draped through his mother's during the graveside service. His tie is crooked and his shirt tail has come un-tucked from his pants that are an inch too short for his long legs. I haven't met him, but I know like him. I recall Steve Black's letter; him asking Steve if the FDIC was going to take his 4-H lamb. I don't know much about 4-H or FFA livestock programs, but it wasn't the first time the question had come up. There were several borrowers who came in to review their loan portfolio and ask if their son or daughter's 4-H or FFA animal was immune from the chattel lien on the UCC-1 filed with the Secretary of State. My answer is always been the same, "that depends on where they got the animal."

Norma and I wait for the crowd to leave. Rebekah sees me and walks over. "I'm surprised to see you here," she says in a chilled tone I don't think I deserve.

"Hey Norma, pretty shady company you're keeping there." She winks at Norma, and I am relieved to see her lighten up.

"Who, Jack? Shady?" Norma's voice raises an octave and I smile at her, curious to know what she's going to say next.

"Jack aint shady. He's just a California Catholic boy trying to warm up to all us Welsh Mormons in Idaho—you n' me excluded, Rebekah."

Rebekah laughs with a hushed respectable strain given the setting and then bends over and hugs Norma. Her features have a strong resemblance of the Welsh—dark hair, olive skin, strong thick bone structure. She is very different from both of her sisters.

"I'm surprised Molly isn't here," I say to Rebekah.

"I guess she had some important meeting in Pocatello with Farmer's Home Administration and needed to pick up combine parts for Scott," Rebekah says. "I can't imagine what would be so important she would have missed this. She said something to me as she was leaving the church about having until next week to come up with a payout to FDIC."

I frown. I have no idea what she is talking about.

"Did she say who told her that?"

"Nope," Rebekah says. "Are you handling the Olson's file?"

"Lester Olson?"

"Yes, and his son, Scott Olson. They're all on the same loan, according to Molly."

"I don't think I ever connected Molly and Scott with the Lester Olson file," I say to her. I knew she spelled her name Olson and the

Olsen on the file was spelled with an 'e'. Everything started filtering and sifting through my brain and the only thing I can think is I was stupid and careless. I suppose I naturally attached the Helland and Thomas name to Molly, but it never occurred to me that she was part of the Lester 'Olsen' Olson non-performing asset I turned over to Benny Schnabel.

Everything starts to jell. Benny met with Lester Olson that morning. He told me the Olson's are getting a loan from Farmers Home Administration; but half the people I am working with are getting hardship loans from Farm Home. I look at my watch. It's 4 o'clock straight up. I tell Norma, "if you want to go to the church dinner, maybe you could ride back with Rebekah. I need to get back to the bank before everyone leaves for the day."

"Sure," Rebekah says to me, then to Norma. "I'd be happy to give you a lift."

I don't pay attention to the route I take back into town, but follow a line of cars and trucks going the same direction. I pull into the parking lot of the bank at 4:10, key the back door for entry and run up the stairs. The entire second floor is empty.

"Will? Benny? Anybody here?" Cold silence.

"Damnit."

On my office door is a note Will scribbled and left taped there. "Benny wanted to go early so we left at 4. Will." I rip it off the door, read it, then wad it tight in my hand. I'm not sure what I should do. The door to Benny's office is closed but unlocked, which doesn't matter, I have a master key; something he didn't have.

The Olson file isn't there. I look through his office, then on Will's desk and find copies of balance sheets with Lester Olson's name on them, but it's the only name on them. I look through the stacks on the accountant's desk.

When I go downstairs and into the parking lot, Molly's grandfather is standing at the back wrought-iron gate.

"Mr. Thomas," I say.

"Jack," he says back, lifting his Benchley Fedora hat slightly from his blotched bald head, dappled with sweat. He holds onto his cane with the other hand.

"You didn't go to the funeral?" I ask.

"Nope. Been to funerals for my only daughter and my daughter's best friend's husband the past year and that's my limit, unless, of course, it's my own."

There is a swelling silence.

"You know," he says, "I couldn't help but notice somethin' odd today, which I do notice everything that goes on over here, day and night…" He pauses.

"Notice what?" I asked.

"This morning. I was sittin' in my chair there," he points his wooden cane toward the window he sits at every day, most all day long except when he goes out for his walk. I have observed him on several occasions when I stand by the window looking down at the people who come and go. Like clockwork, at precisely 4 o'clock every afternoon, he walks around the perimeter of the bank and goes back inside his house and sits back down in his chair by the window.

"Well," Mr. Thomas says, "I saw Lester Olson come at 10 o'clock, then leave about eleven. I saw Molly leave in her Gimmy about five minutes before Lester left, which I figured she was leaving to go get ready for the little McDonald girl's funeral, or maybe goin' down to the church to practice the organ, which she does every day on her noon hour except the days she comes to have lunch with me.

He pauses to cough, and catch his breath.

"Yes, I've seen her leave, and then come back" I admitted, wondering what his point is that he is unbearably slow getting to.

"Well, right after Molly drove away, then Lester left, and then that tall fella with curly hair that works for you, the one who dresses like a New York City mafia gangster and drives the other rental car, the big black Lincoln."

"Yes, Benny. Benny Schnabel."

"Well, he came out, got in his rental car about five minutes after

200

Molly came out, and he drove up Bannock Street, and I guess I think that's strange because the only time he gets in and out of that vehicle is when he comes from Pocatello in the morning and goes back to Pocatello at night."

I wonder how he knows so much. I suppose Rebekah, or maybe Molly tells him our routine. But then I remember the notes in his files, the notes he wrote so many years ago, and I know he is pretty tuned into what goes on around him. 'One savvy old man,' I heard Rebekah say about him, more than once.

"Then," Mr. Thomas continues, "about fifteen minutes later, he drives back into the parking lot and when he gets out of his car, he has this big Cheshire cat grin on his face that gave me the shivers an' left me shakin' my head. He's up to no good, I'm tellin' ya."

I think of how many times Benny Schnabel gave me the shivers. Almost every day. The old man pauses like he needs a good whiff of oxygen to finish.

"I don't know what he's up to, but he's up to no good," he says again, like he'd forgotten he'd already said it.

"Thanks, Mr. Thomas. I'll do some digging tomorrow and see what's going on."

"Well, the fact he left with your crew an hour or two earlier than usual should tell you somthin'," he says.

"Yes, well, that's an entirely different issue," I grumble. "I was pretty upset to come back and find they all left for the day. We're trying to get things packed up and out of here by next week."

I feel sorry for the old man. He sits and watches as his empire crumbles at his feet.

"You okay?" I ask him, watching his hands tremble.

"I'm fine," he says. "I'm going to go get myself ready for dinner." He turns away from me and takes deliberate, careful, steps to the back door of his house and disappears inside.

I suddenly realize how tired I am. I didn't sleep the night before. I think about driving back out to the cemetery while it's still light, just to make sure I remember the way, but decide to go back to my motel and lie down instead. I don't see any signs of Norma when I drive in and park. I assume she is still at the church participating in the funeral meal.

I lay down and before I've taken ten breaths, I fall into a deep sleep. I have no idea what time it is when the loud rap at my door wakes me. A male voice calls my name. I look around trying to gain perspective of where I am. I look at my watch. It's six-thirty. I fell into such a deep sleep, I lost myself. Without thinking, I jump up, trying to rub the sleep from my face with one hand as I reach for the door handle with the other. I had been warned about disgruntled borrowers who own rifles and shot guns, and stupidly open the door without looking out the window first.

Scott Olson is standing on the concrete pad at the threshold.

"Sorry to bother you," he says.

"Scott. What's up?" I'm still rubbing my cheek, trying to focus.

"It's Molly."

"What about her?" the panic hits me. If he's confronting me about my feelings for her, I'll deny it. I am leaving in a week and all I will take with me is my memory of this woman I found in a small Idaho town who I can't get out of my mind. But in life's cruel way, she is spoken for.

"Well," he says in a slow drawl, "I went to Dad's house after I milked Lance's cows to take Mom's car back to her? And I was going to have Dad give me a ride back to my place. That's when he told me somethin' weird was a goin' on."

"Your dad's Lester Olson, right?"

"Yup."

"What did he say?" I pull the door open and motion for Scott to come inside and have a seat.

"Well," he says, "He went to the bank this morning for his 10 o'clock appointment and Molly went upstairs to get the other FDIC guy, Benny something."

"Schnabel."

"Yah. Anyways, she asked him if he could come 'n meet with my dad downstairs 'cause he'd just had hip surgery and couldn't walk up the stairs."

"Right. I'm aware of that."

"Dad said he heard this guy Benny say something to Molly, like, 'You could just say you have to work late with the FDIC boss'. And she said something back, like, 'If I really wanted to go, I wouldn't need an excuse'. Then Molly helped Dad into Clarence Fuller's office to meet with the FDIC guy 'cause Clarence was gone for the day. Dad told me that Benny asked her to get him a cup of coffee and she told him no one on the first floor drinks coffee, so they don't have a coffee pot. Then Dad said she shrugged, smiled at my dad, and closed the door behind her."

"Yes," I say, wondering why it takes everyone in Malad such a long time to tell their story.

"Well, Dad told him that I was farming with him, and that we ran cows. He told him that I would'da' come to the meeting there at the bank except I was milking cows for Lance McDonald, who you know…"

"Yes, I know," I say, getting impatient.

"He asked Dad for a balance sheet and financial statement and Dad told him he'd given those to me and I gave them to Molly and she filled them out a couple of months ago, and gave them to that kid who works for you. Then Benny said to my dad in a real mean tone of voice, 'Well, I don't have them!'."

Dad said he looked at the file cover and told Benny that maybe they didn't know where to file it 'cause they have our name spelled wrong. "It's spelled O-N, not E-N."

"The fellow told my dad we have till Friday to get the debt paid off. Then he told Dad he'd go talk to Molly about it, and Dad told him not to bother Molly, that he'd take care of it."

"When Dad walked into the lobby he heard Benny ask the other gal who works with Molly where she went, and she told him to the church to practice the organ music for the funeral."

"After passing by the church on his way home, Dad said he turned right at the next corner and circled the block. He intended to go back and talk to Molly about the missing paper work but as he slowed to turn into the parking lot he saw Molly talking to Benny. He said he could see she was mad as hell, though Molly never gets mad. He said something was going on that's amiss, especially when Molly said she had to go to Pocatello after the funeral service. She'd never, ever leave Melanie like that."

It takes Scott about ten minutes to tell me the story. I am sitting on the bed, and he is straddling the iron-framed desk chair he'd turned around to sit down on.

"So, Molly's in Pocatello now?" I ask Scott.

"That's where she said she was going. But it don't make any sense."

It might not have made sense to him, but it is suddenly making perfect sense to me. I am wide awake now. I look at my watch again. It's 6:40.

"What vehicle did Molly take?"

"The pick-up. She is picking up combine parts for me."

"We need to go, Scott. I hate to tell you this, but I'm afraid there's trouble brewing. I know how Benny Schnabel operates and I'm afraid he's used his influence to try and trap Molly."

"Molly would never…"

"I know that Scott. And so do you. But she has no idea who he is and what he's capable of doing."

I stand up, grab my tan golf jacket. "*Let's go! Right now.*"

As I open the car door, I see the McDonald file lying on the back seat, face down and know it will have to wait. I ask Scott if he knows how to get to the Quality Inn in Pocatello.

Fifty minutes later, we pull off Pocatello Creek Exit, turn right, and right again into the Quality Inn parking lot. I tell Scott to stay in the car. I run inside and at the desk I ask the man to ring up Benny Schnabel's room.

"He's not in his room," he says.

"You know where he went?"

"I do, because he came down and asked me for directions to Remos. He's a pompous ass, isn't he? Said something about having a hot date tonight. I drew out a map for him."

I hold out my hand and shake his. "I'm Jack Whittaker, his supervisor with FDIC and I need to get in touch with him right away," I reach for my wallet to show him my ID card.

He waves it off and points west, "down Pocatello Creek Road that turns into Alameda to the second stop light, left to the next stop light, then right. It's one block west of Yellowstone Highway, looks like a medieval castle. You can't miss it."

I raise my hand to him as I run out the door. I jump into the running car and make a left out onto Pocatello Creek Road.

"He told me how to get to Remos, but I figured you'd know," I say to Scott as I put the car in gear. Scott points left and I drive into the sun, pulling down the visor to block the blinding rays.

The architecture of flat-lined cinderblock buildings, void of parapets or facades to mask their nothingness, line Yellowstone Highway and are less interesting, I think, than the lava carbuncles strewn along the river bottom of Marsh Valley. I am surprised at the unique restaurant to my right as I follow Scott's directions, turning west onto Cedar Street. The red-framed sign reads REMOS in front of a head-high grape arbor wall that camouflages the outdoor seating. Thick rolls of white canvas resting on overhead wooden stringers are tied like large rolled up flaps on circus tent doors ready to shelter patrons against frequent afternoon desert thunderstorms that usually break by 4 o'clock, if it happens at all. Something I observed during my time in Idaho.

Medieval crenellations top the turrets that frame the building at each corner, and seems incongruent. The summer-sun is positioned at the crown of the west mountain range as a calm evening breeze begins to consume the stifling hot August air.

When we pull into Remo's, Benny's rental car, a long black Lincoln Continental, is in the parking lot.

"Well, there's his car," I say, noting there are only about five other cars in the parking lot.

Scott and Molly's pickup isn't there and we both sigh a big relief though we were watching oncoming traffic along the interstate and didn't see her. Scott and I grew silent during those few stretches of the interstate the south-bound traffic is blocked by a wall of lava rock, both of us thinking we may have missed her. I am about to ask Scott if he wants me to go in and talk to Benny, but he is out of the car before I turn off the engine.

I hand the very thin, pinched-faced girl at the hostess podium inside the front door a twenty-dollar bill and ask her if she's seen Molly. "The lady is wearing a white dress with black print and her hair pulled back and tied with a black scarf." Scott looks at me when I described her so vividly and accurately.

"I saw her playing the organ at the funeral," I say. "She's wearing a dress like one my mother has," I lied. I doubt Scott noticed her hair tied back, or the black scarf cascading down her back. It wasn't the same dress she wore to work earlier. I could have described that one too, in finite detail, including the brown leather low-heeled shoes she was wearing. I guess at what Benny would be wearing and nailed it. I spent dozens of nights starting out with a cocktail from his velvet-lined traveling mini-bar in his motel room, then going to dinner clubs and bar lounges with him. It was always the same attire.

"They both left about fifteen minutes ago," she says.

"Did they leave together?" I asked.

"No, not really. She left and then he went out about a minute later. He was pretty intoxicated."

When we walk back outside I spot a kitchen chef standing near the back corner of the restaurant smoking a cigarette.

"Hey," I say.

"Hi, how's it goin," he says, taking a long drag.

"You see anyone leave here the past half hour in a red GMC dual-wheel pickup truck? A lady about five foot five..."

"Yea," he says, blowing smoke into the air, They left 'bout ten or fifteen minutes ago. She was climin' into her truck and the guy walking out behind her was tryin' to unlock his car over there," he pointed to the black Lincoln. "an' he was so wasted he couldn't even get the key in the lock." The kid takes another drag on his cigarette. "She keeps looking like she knows him, so I told her she shouldn't let him drive in that condition, that he'd kill somebody. I could tell she didn't wanna, but she told him to get into her truck and she'd take him to his motel."

Scott and I look at each other. "Damn!" I know my language is inappropriate, but I know somewhere Benny has her, and if she doesn't understand how to evade him, he'd have his way with her whether she wanted it or not. I am also worried she might go into insulin shock the way she did the night I first met her. She is completely out of her league. What league? Her world is so foreign to any place I have ever been. I look at Scott, thinking how trusting he is. I wonder why he doesn't look sick with worry, but realize he can't possibly comprehend the potential danger Molly is in. His world is so very different than mine. He worries about calving his beef cows and moving water lines, and operating combines and tractors and raising children. He worries about milking cows for his friend, while his friend is mourning the loss of a little girl. He is lucky he doesn't live in this kind of ugly world fraught with alcohol abuse, and people like Benny who believes preying on innocent women like Molly is acceptable behavior.

As I look to the right before leaving the parking lot of Remos I shield my eyes to see if any traffic is coming before pulling out. I honestly don't remember the drive between Remos and the Quality Inn convention center, a sprawling facility occupying a couple of acres of building and asphalt parking.

The parking lot is almost empty. It is eight o' five according to the clock on the dash. I don't stop at the lobby. I pull around back; and just as the sun is masked by the curvature of the earth, we both see the truck at the back corner of the parking lot. I look at Scott say, "I don't see anyone in there." The entire parking lot on the back side of the motel is completely empty.

"Why do you suppose it's parked back there?"

"Drive over there," Scott says.

I look at him. "You sure?"

"Molly would never, ever do anything against the teachings of the church," he says. "Never."

"No, Scott. I believe that. But even more, she wouldn't do anything to hurt you."

We jump out of my car like two detectives exiting a police car and at almost the same instant we hear Molly's cries for help. Muffled cries, desperate cries. *"Help me, help me. Somebody help me, please. God. Please!"*

I approach the truck on the passenger side. Scott goes around to the driver's side. I peer through the window. I see Molly's bare legs partially wrapped with torn panty hose. Her white dress with large black orchids is pushed up against her stomach. I see Benny grappling with her long-legged rayon underwear trying to remove it. It's one of those times that a split second feels like an hour. I can see her left hand flailing beneath the steering wheel, grappling with a large revolver that looks like a 38.

Scott yanks open the door and quickly puts his hand over hers, taking the gun out of her hand. Benny is on top of her, grunting and fumbling, pushing her face against the steering wheel. His pants and boxer shorts are down just far enough to expose his white buttocks. I know he is so lost in himself he has no idea he is banging the back of her head against the door handle, or that we were even there, or Molly has the barrel of a 38 pushed into his side.

I grab his hair and shirt, dragging him out of the truck before Scott can muster the gumption to pull the trigger. I know Scott isn't impulsive, and it would take him a bit of time to talk through something like that in his head before taking someone's life. I push Benny against the panel of the truck bed. *"Pull up your damn pants!"*

Scott lays the gun on the seat and holds Molly in his arms, wiping blood from her forehead and left temple with the large white handkerchief he pulls from his back pocket. Molly is tugging at her skirt, pulling it down, smoothing it with both hands.

"Scott, you stay here and I'll go call the police. Keep the gun on him if you want, but don't shoot him unless you have to!" I say it to hopefully put a little fear in Benny.

No, no. No police. Please, Scott, no police. I just want you to take me home. Please. Please. P-l-e-a-s-e, Scott. It comes out in sobs.

Scott picks up the hand gun from the seat of the truck. "I ott'a shoot the son-of-a-bitch right here n' now!"

"No, Scott. No! Please, please, please, just take me home. You'll end up in jail. It's not worth it. I'll be okay. It's okay. We can't do this to our kids. I can't do this for Daddy's sake. He's already been through too much. Nobody would understand what happened. He was drunk and the kid at the restaurant was right, I couldn't let him drive that way. He said he was sick. Going to throw up. He said to drive up here ...," her voice trails off and I don't hear what else she says. She puts her hands in her face, sobbing quietly. Scott consoles her as she tries to explain. The black mascara mixes with the blood as it runs down her face.

"He followed me to the church. He said he would foreclose if I didn't come meet him here. I thought he needed papers from Farm Home. I didn't know. I didn't know he would do this to me." Her words are deep, and painful.

Benny is leaning against the pickup, then he bends over to vomit and I step back. I walk around the truck, take hold of Molly's shoulders and look at her beaten face. I understand Scott's urge to take care of Benny, here and now.

"Molly, I'll take care of Benny. I can assure you Scott, and his parents, will not be foreclosed on. When I get back to San Jose next week, I'll personally oversee this. I'm fairly certain we'll be writing this one off. Scott, you better take Molly to the hospital and have her checked out." I pull my money clip from my pocket and peel off two hundred dollar bills and hold it out for him. He shakes his head.

"Don't need that," he says. "We'll take care of it." He puts the gun back under the seat where I assume they always keep it. He helps Molly up into the truck and she slides to the middle, still holding the handkerchief against her forehead. Scott gets in and shuts the door.

I walk back around the bed of the truck where Benny is still grabbing onto the truck bed for balance. I yank him by the arm across the parking lot. He jerks away and staggers on his own. I watch the Olson truck leave. Scott's arm is draped around Molly, and Molly has her head on his shoulder.

"Where's your room key?" I ask Benny. And like a boy who'd been caught with his pants down, he sullenly pulls a key chain out of his pocket and hands it to me. "Those the car keys too?," I ask him. He doesn't answer. I open the back door to the motel. I can tell he is sick with alcohol poisoning and I understand why when I see his room. His travel bar stands open. Two empty Latvian Vodka bottles sit next to a stainless steel decanter and dry vermouth.

I am shocked at the two-room suite. The parlor has a fireplace, a tall ceiling with crown moldings, padded window valances, and an adjoining terrazzo tile guest bath. The french doors to the bedroom are closed.

I don't know how to unleash my anger without jeopardizing my professional protocol. Instead, I rely on my professional training to walk through the process. The problem is, there is nothing in the handbook that covers behavior as egregious as what Benny did to Molly.

"My god, Benny, threatening foreclosure on her if she doesn't come to Pocatello and sleep with you?"

He slumps in the over-stuffed chair holding his forehead with his hand, eyes closed, saying nothing. He truly believes he has done nothing wrong.

It's part of Benny's personality disorder. He expects to be recognized as superior and special and has the right to take advantage of people he considers inferior or ignorant, which is how he views all women. He lacks the ability to own his indiscretions and bad behavior. It's the disorder that allows him to blame someone else for mistakes he makes, or believes in his own twisted mind his behavior is justified.

When I tell him there is a shuttle to Salt Lake City airport leaving early in the morning, and that he will be on it, and on the plane back to California, his mouth turns gray. The foul, ugly words start pouring out of him.

For the next five minutes, he defiles me and my family. He sneers at me while he tells me he's been living with Camila in the apartment I help pay for. He sees her on weekends. He's given up his apartment and moved in with her. I feel the blood rise from my stomach through my arms and clench my fists. If I had Scott's gun at that moment, I'd have shot him. In this life and the next, I will never allow my little girl near this animal. I'll see him in prison, or hell, first.

What I didn't understand then about his disorder is people like Benny have 'risk preferred behavior'. My statistics professor at Berkley explained these kinds of people are either going to be a Charles Manson or an Adolf Hitler, but in either case no single person can bring them down. It would take a coalition to thwart them; a police force, an army, or a judge and jury. People with these 'Risk Preferred' behaviors have no regard for following commands, rules or laws, or ethical protocol in general. They behave with a total and complete disregard for anyone but themselves by creating the world their passion dictates, regardless of who they destroy along their journey.

So when I tell Benny to go back to California the next day, I believe once he is sober he will feel regret and remorse; that he will be relieved Molly and Scott didn't bring assault, or rape charges against him. But I am wrong. When I tell him he no longer works for FDIC, I am wrong about that too. All I accomplish by sending him back to California early, is a one-week head start on me.

I take his rental car keys with me, and focus on regaining my composure. I take deep breaths as I walk the long corridor to the front desk in the lobby, trying to recall the steps for maintaining self-control in conflict management. Number one: Take deep breaths to move oxygen to your brain to help you think more clearly. Number Two: Pump your fists, not to hit someone but to pump blood through your system. Number Three: Focus on something good or something that makes you happy. I think of Stacy, and at first, it works. Then I think of Camila letting Benny move in with her and I get angrier.

Prayer, or some kind of meditation, I remember, is the last item on the list of ten behaviors to practice. I wondered at the time I memorized the list, why prayer isn't a higher priority.

I stop in the hallway next to the side entry door between the restrooms and the lobby and lean against the wall. In complete exhaustion, I lay my head back and close my eyes. Dear God, please take care of her. I stop myself. What am I doing talking to God about a woman I secretly care for. Worse yet, I have all these unsettling feelings about a woman who is married. I begin my plea again. Please, God, help Scott and Molly Olson get home safely. Help them heal. And help me get through this ordeal with a clear head. Before I open my eyes, I hear a voice.

"Jack. You Okay?"

I jerk my head up, followed by my body. Will is standing in the hallway of the motel, looking at me.

"Yes. Yes. I'm fine."

"What are you doin' here?"

I look down. "Well, actually, Will, everything's not okay. I was just going to the front desk to call your room. I had to stop and think a minute about how to handle a bad situation I've got on my hands."

"Sure, whatever you need. I was just out gettin' some dinner," Will says, like he thinks he needs to explain to me why he wasn't in his room. "I get tired of eating at the restaurant in the motel," he says. "There's a pretty good little Mexican restaurant a couple a miles southwest a here down by the University, but it's a hike. Walkin' that far makes me feel the pain in my lungs from smokin' those cancer sticks. I need to quit."

I tell him to wait there, I'll be back in a minute to pick him up. I don't want him asking why I parked in the back corner of an empty parking lot. I jog across the large field of asphalt and realize when I get to the car I left it running. I get in and drive to the west side of the building, where Will is waiting.

"It's Benny, isn't it?" he says when he gets in. I don't answer him. I just take another deep breath.

"What's he doing staying in the executive suite?" I ask as I pull out into the nearly empty street.

"He upgraded this afternoon when we got back from Malad. He paid the desk clerk cash, and said something about getting lucky tonight but we just ignored him like we usually do." Will pulls out a pack of filtered Camels from his pocket and lights one. He cracks the window and blows the smoke out.

"Did he happen to say who he was going to get lucky with?"

"Nope. Just said we were leavin' Malad early 'cause he had a hot date tonight. When I saw him drive out of the parking lot around 6 o'clock he was by himself."

"Do you know where he went this morning after he met with Lester Olson?"

"Nope. He just came bustin' into my office without knockin' like he always does, threw Olson's file on my desk and told me to send the file to foreclosure. He said we were liquidating. He said something about Olson's moving assets. I looked at the file and saw whose file it was and I said to him, 'this is Molly Olson's file, the lady who works downstairs' an' then he said he knows who Molly Olson is. Sure thought it was odd."

I pull into the parking lot at Remos, park the car, and turn off the engine. I roll down my window, breathing in the crisp night air. The parking lot is empty and the building is dark. The black Lincoln is now the only car in the parking lot besides mine. I hear crickets chirping in the vines enclosing the patio. Will finishes his cigarette, unrolls his window all the way, and flicks the butt into the parking lot.

"Shouldn't do that," I say. "Everything we do and everywhere we go, people watch us. They watch what we do, they take note of how we handle ourselves and they expect us to be better than everyone else in the world, like the FBI. For some reason, they always equate us to the FBI."

"You talking about Benny?"

"No, Will, I'm talking about you. You need to watch every move you make. Always. Benny got his job because his father was a big shot in the organization. He was liaison between the Feds and FDIC and carried a lot of weight ten years ago when Benny came on board. When Benny went to work for us, he had just been fired by a big San Francisco bank, so his father found him a job with us. My father knew about it because he knows Benny's father."

Will is quiet. We both sit as the night grows dark and the gray shadow of the new moon hangs large in the sky.

"Did your father get you your job here?"

"Nope," I say. "He suggested I should start here so I'll know what a bank is expected to do to never, ever get taken over by the FDIC. He said when he is sure I've figured it out, he'll hire me at his bank. I've been here over ten years and I'm thinking it's about time to make that move. This has been the most difficult bank closure I've ever been on, and I don't ever want to do another one like it."

Will is quiet for a space of time, then, in a low tone, like he is afraid to talk, he says, "You shouldn't liquidate the Olson's, you know. Molly Olson's the nicest lady I know. She brings me oatmeal and raisin cookies when I'd go outside to smoke. She asks me about school, and about my family. She is the only one of those Mormon women in the bank who even talks to me. I really, really like her, Jack. Her and her sister Rebekah, and their grandpa who lives next door."

"What in the world are you talking about, Will? We're not foreclosing on Olson's."

"I screwed up, Jack," he finally said to me. "I'm sorry."

I look at him, but can't see his face or the tear that drops down his cheek. I can only see him wipe it away with the back of his hand.

"Screwed up on what?"

"Well, she brought me their cash flow and financials about six weeks ago, and asked me to give them to you and then I couldn't ever find their file, I spose 'cause their name was spelled wrong, and then I completely forgot about 'em. When Benny said he was liquidatin' them I remembered the papers and I gave 'em to Benny and told him he ought to take a look at them before I send the file to legal. This afternoon, before we left, he glanced at them and threw them back on my desk and walked out."

"Will, that wasn't your fault. I had no idea until this afternoon Molly is Lester Olson's daughter-in-law and I asked Benny about the file early this morning after I'd found it buried in his desk drawer. I suppose you should have given me the paperwork she gave you, but this is not your fault. Besides, Benny doesn't have authority to send files to foreclosure or liquidation. That's all done by committee in San Jose. I don't even have that authority."

 Will seems surprised. "I didn't know that!" he says. "You know, Jack, when I told him he should at least look at the paperwork, he mocked me, 'Hey, college boy, I'm the reviewer of this file. Besides, if Molly has any brains she'll figure out what she needs to do to clear this up.' Then out of the blue, he wants the McDonald file."

I freeze. The McDonald file is in clear sight, less than three feet away. All he has to do is turn around, recognize the blue jacket and know it's one of ours. I don't dare glance back. "So what'd you tell him?

"That I gave it to you yesterday and it might be in your office."

Will lights another cigarette and hangs his head out the window to blow the smoke into the night air. He continuously flicks the butt, dropping live ashes onto the asphalt below while he talks.

"He asked where you were and I told him you left for the day. He tried your office door, but it was locked. He went into his office, then came back to me and acting all cocky and important, he asked for the Olson file back, said he'd changed his mind. That's when he said we were going to Pocatello early. Did you find my note on the office door?"

"I saw it. Thanks."

"Can I ask you what he did?"

"You can ask, but I can't tell you."

"Did you fire him?"

"Well, I told him he was fired, but I don't have the authority to do that either and I'm pretty sure he knows it. I have a feeling I'm not the first supervisor who's tried to get rid of him. All I can do is write up the report and send it to a grievance committee, just like everything else."

I have always believed committees are the safety net we use to justify conclusions that are less than optimal by the mere fact we are always dealing with high risk, non-performing assets to begin with. But committees, more often than not, are the bane of reasonable resolve. I know I need a final committee approval to close the McDonald file. I know Sam's endorsement on the deal was a preliminary okay, but it wasn't an official approval. And he didn't know it was me buying the note. I also know as long as the file is buried in a place no one can find it, it will never have to go through committee scrutiny. I wonder why Benny wanted to find the McDonald file. What did he know by noon he hadn't known at eight o'clock that morning? All I can think of is Lester Olson must have said something to make him want to find the file.

I am tired, and want to get back to Malad. I know before I retire for the night, I still need to find my way back to the St. John Cemetery. I hand Will the car keys to the Lincoln and tell him I'll see him first thing in the morning.

"Oh, Will, if you happen to run into Benny at the motel and he gives you any grief, just tell him there were two Pocatello City Police Officers in the lobby looking for someone who fits his description."

He laughs. "I will, boss."

"I'm not your boss," I whisper, as he walks away.

216

Chapter Twenty-Five: Melanie

After the sisters of the church feed us, we say our goodbyes to family, friends and neighbors. The trip home is veiled in silence.

Our two-story farmhouse, stifled by paralyzing grief on the morning of Grace Marie's funeral, is, by nightfall, muted by exhaustion and numbness as we force ourselves to breath. Holding left-over emotions deep inside a dangerously dark chasm, we pray they will eventually melt, or burn out, and be forgotten.

Lance slumps in his worn Barcalounger, the Book of Mormon open on his lap, as though he is still searching for an answer. His worn face tells me he has not yet reconciled his faith with the loss of our daughter.

Dylan changes his clothes and heads to the barn to feed and water the 4-H lambs. Erica gets out her potholder loom Lance made her for Christmas and is sitting on the living room floor, quietly wrapping strands of cloth around the nails as she weaves a blue and white pattern.

My feet are swollen to twice their normal size and they hurt. I have been bare-footed since we got home around six o'clock. We saw Scott leaving, but didn't get a chance to talk to him.

A long soak in the tub seems like a good escape. I fill the old cast-iron claw-foot bathtub with all the hot water there is in the tank, hoping to wash away my loss.

"Erica, you need to go to bed soon, OK?"

"I will, Mom. I'll finish this one, then I'll go."

I lean over and kiss her on the head. "Nice job, honey."

I ease myself into the tub, my muscles bulging to hold my weight. I am thankful for the strength I've garnered from bucking heavy hay bales. I lay back against the perfect slant of the old tub, close my eyes and drift. For a moment, everything feels like a bad dream that might go away if I just quiet my mind for a while.

I hear the back door slam shut, and boots dropping on the utility room floor. Dylan knocks on the bathroom door.

"Mom, how am I gonna get my lamb to the fair tomorrow?"

"Scott's coming to pick them up in the morning," I am fully awake now. "You need to set your alarm tonight so you're up on time to help get them loaded. And don't forget to take the buckets and some feed."

"I know, Mom. You don't need to worry. I just need to know how I am going to get there."

I can't say anything. He is such a fine boy; far too young to have to do all this by himself. I can't help wonder why he always comes to me. Why does he think I'm the one with all the answers?

"OK, honey. You best go to bed now."

"Good-night, Mom. Love you."

"Night Dylan. I love you too."

I soak until the water is cold. Unable to bend forward to reach the hot water faucet, I turn it on and off with my toes. Eventually, I lift my awkward body from the tub and put on a clean pair of temple garments. I pull my nightgown over my head, stretching it across my stomach.

I walk quietly to the living room. Lance has fallen asleep in his chair. I close the Book of Mormon, set it on the lamp table, and turn off the lamp.

I place my hand on his shoulder. "Let's go to bed."

"K. I'll be there soon," he whispers, rubbing his eyes.

I close the bedroom door and lay across the white woolen Indian Wedding Blanket Lance's foster sister, LaDona, gave us for a wedding present. It is as beautiful as the day I spread it on our bed nearly eleven years earlier. She didn't come to our wedding dinner in Logan, but sent the gift to Lance's mother to give to us. The letter she wrote to us is as precious as the blanket itself, and is bundled with my letters from Lance in my cedar chest. It reads:

This blanket represents the promise of your union. The tradition begins with two blue blankets, representing the couple's past lives, draped around the bride and groom. After a blessing by the Spiritual Leader, the couple sheds both blankets and then are enveloped in the embraces of their well-wishing relatives and covered by one white blanket. The singular white blanket represents unity, happiness, fulfillment and peace. The couple then shares their first marital kiss and embrace under the white blanket, and displays it thereafter in their new home.

She also wrote that the blanket was blessed by her tribal spiritual leader before she sent it.

The night is too hot to climb under the covers. I remain on top, asking the blanket to give me the strength to bring this new life into the world—this blanket that covered us when we conceived all our children. Had it failed us? Or had we failed it? I can't think about this any longer... I let the exhaustion take me.

I don't hear the knock at the back door. I don't hear Lance come into our bedroom. He lays his hand on my shoulder, rubbing it in a soft, circular motion.

"Mel," he whispers, "Mel, honey, you need to wake up."

I open my eyes, making out his profile sitting on the bed next to me, illuminated by yard light. I wonder if I'm dreaming. I can't remember where I am.

"What? What Lance? What's the matter?" I roll onto my back.

"It's Scott and Molly. They're here. Molly's been hurt. Scott said he needs you to help clean her up."

"What?" I try to sit up and can't. I hold out my hand to Lance and he pulls me up to a sitting position. I wait for a moment with both hands on the side of the bed, trying to get my balance.

"Grab my robe from the closet door, will you, please?" I hold out my hand to Lance and he helps me up. He holds the robe while I slip my arms into the sleeves. The tie barely reaches around my stomach. "What time is it?"

"Ten, maybe ten-fifteen," Lance says as he holds my arm, leading me to the kitchen.

219

"Are Dylan and Erica asleep?"

"Yes, they went to bed an hour or so ago."

I walk down the hall. Molly is sitting at the kitchen table, her head lying on her arm. Scott is standing behind, holding her shoulders with both his hands as though he is keeping her from falling off the chair.

"Oh Molly, Molly," I whisper. I sit next to her, putting my hand on her back and my face close to hers.

She raises her head. When she looks at me she lets out soft whimpers. The scrape across her forehead is superficial and the bleeding has stopped. There is a fresh bruise along the left side of her face and a scratch along her neck. She is bare-footed and her hair is disheveled. The left seam of her dress is ripped to her thigh and the front V is torn from nape of her neck to her breasts.

I know when I hold her chin in my cupped hand, examining her, the pain isn't in her wounded face, it is in her soul. It doesn't take a woman long to see this kind of pain in another woman. It's an open wound bleeding opaquely from one heart to another, much the way Molly saw my gaping wounds the night we stood over Grace Marie's limp body. As mothers and women, we feel, and smell, and see, and comprehend bodies having been defiled, or neglected, or abused. She doesn't have to tell me. I know. There is no way I could have known then who, or where, but I didn't need to know. No one needed to know.

I say, "Scott, carry Molly into the bedroom and lay her on our bed. Then I want you and Lance to go to your house and get her some clean clothes."

Scott picks her limp body up in his arms, carrying her to our room, and carefully lays her on the wedding blanket. I follow him. Lance is rattling dishes in the kitchen, trying to be busy. I suspect he doesn't know what else to do.

I close the bedroom door and take hold of Scott's arm. "Does she need insulin?"

"I asked her. She said she ate at seven, but we should check her blood sugar, I think."

"Where are your kids?"

"With Rebekah and Lars," he says. "I called from a pay phone at the McCammon Truck Stop and asked if they could stay the night." He is quiet. "Melanie, Molly doesn't want anyone to know. She wouldn't let us call the police, or take her to the hospital. You and Lance are the only ones we could think to come to."

"What do you mean, she wouldn't let *us* call the police? Who is *us*?"

"Me an' Jack, the FDIC guy who stays at Norma Howell's motel."

"Oh," is all I say. I don't want to know more. I need to take care of Molly. I'll let her tell me, if she wants to.

"Take Lance and go over to your house and get her clothes and some test strips. Get insulin and a syringe, just in case. Besides," I put my hand on his shoulder, "you and Lance need to talk. I'll take care of her, Scott. She's my dearest friend."

Scott looks at the floor. "We weren't here for you guys today," he says, putting his hands in his pockets. "Not the way we should have been, Mel," his voice cracks. "Now here we are asking you to help us on the night of your little Gracie's funeral. I'm sorry Mel, I don't know what to say, except I'm sorry."

I give Scott the best hug I can with my bulging stomach. Standing on my toes, I whisper in his ear, "Lance needs you to be his friend, Scott. Please let him in."

I hear the diesel truck start and watch the lights head down Daniels Road, going south. Molly is on her side, her fist against her forehead, her knees pulled up to her womb in a fetal position, like the baby laying inside me. It's as though she is trying to cover herself with the rest of herself.

"I'm sorry, Mel. I'm so sorry. We didn't know where else to go," she cries the words so quietly I can barely hear. I sit on the bed, then lay beside her, my stomach against her back. I drape my arm over her and put my face close to hers, whispering the way we used to when we'd spend nights together, uttering our dreams to each other.

221

Now, here we are, curled tight, trying to survive a hurt that burns deeper than any other—the death of a child and an assault to the womb bearing those beautiful babies.

"I'd be hurt if you hadn't come to me," I say. "Now let's get you out of those clothes and into the tub." I feel her very gently nod her head. The bathtub is the place a woman always goes to begin to heal. A bathtub full of fresh, pure water from the aquifer God put there to cleanse the offensive grit only we can feel. An immersion, or baptism of sorts.

I start the water and find the lavender bath salts my sister gave me for Christmas in the shelves over the commode. The smell of sweet incense fills the room as steam rises from the tub. I hold out my hands to Molly, and she takes them. I spend the next hour kneeling at the side of the tub, washing her back, her hair, gently wiping her face. We are quiet with only the sound of water wringing from the washcloth as I rinse, and wring it out, wash, and rinse again, as though it is a cleansing ritual. She doesn't offer to tell me what happened, and I don't ask. I warm the water again, and let her rest.

I get a brown paper grocery bag and line it with the newspaper someone handed me at the funeral with an article about Grace Marie's accident. I put her clothes inside; her defiled temple garments in the bottom, then her dress, and her torn bra. I wonder why the garment tops are torn at the 'V' in the neck where the delicate lace comes together, yet her bottoms are completely unscathed, though badly soiled in what I assumed to be a man's secretion. Then I wonder what happened to her panty hose.

I don't know the proper procedure for disposing of defiled temple garments, so I write all the information I know on sheet of paper I put inside, and write the date on the outside of the bag. I tie a white string around it and shove the paper bag into the bottom drawer of my paint-chipped dresser, thinking I'll find out how I should dispose of her temple garments later. Since Scott and Lance aren't back yet, I gather together the smallest clothes I own; a small purple and yellow-flowered cotton smock I sewed when Dylan was born. I open a new package of temple garments from the Beehive Distribution store I am saving to wear after the baby is born. I know the rules about allowing someone else to wear the sacred shroud, but I also know on this night, God expects me to do this for her.

I help her out of the tub, and wrap a line-dried towel around her. The hardened terrycloth is stiff from the harsh Idaho wind whipping it dry on the clothesline. I love the rejuvenating feel when I rub the sandpapered towels down my arms and legs. She smiles at me as she puts on the clean temple garments. I slip the smock over her head. She sits on the lid of the commode as I brush her hair, braiding it into a single weave down her back, stemming it off with the hair band from the small wicker basket of barrettes and hair trinkets I use for Erica and Grace. As I fish through the basket, I stop. I finger the yellow plastic butterfly barrettes I removed from Grace Marie's hair after the accident and close my eyes momentarily.

Molly looks up, sees my face, and embraces me. We let the pain and grief we both carry pass between us as we breath in the lingering smells of the lavender bath salts. We hear the truck pull into the yard. "I'll be okay," she says, giving me one more hug. "We'll both be okay. Thanks, Mel."

I want to tell her she is the blessing I needed tonight. I want to let her know she and Scott are a hidden blessing for both Lance and me. We needed them tonight as much as they needed us.

"Come on, Mol. I had Scott get your test strips and insulin. I want to make sure your blood sugar isn't too high." I run a light finger across the scrape on her forehead, then touch the darkening bruise on her face.

"I don't feel like it is," she says, taking hold of my hand and kissing it. "Thanks to you, I'm feeling better."

As I turn to leave, she takes hold of my arm. "I need to tell you. I went to meet the man from FDIC. The one I told you about who bullied Niles? Do you remember?" I nod. "It was him. He did this to me."

I shake my head. "You don't have to talk about it now." I hold her shoulders, peering into her eyes. "When you're ready. Tell me when you're ready." She nods.

Molly greets Scott in my smock with her wet, thick braid dripping down her front shoulder. He apologizes for taking so long to get back. He checks her blood sugar and we are surprised when it reads 110, so he takes it again to make sure. She says she'll take a shot when they get home, before she goes to bed.

The color has come back into Lance's face and he looks more calm, less stressed from the day's events. I take a hold of his hand, giving it a squeeze, and don't let go. I can tell Scott talked to him, giving him what he was begging for at the church. Had it only been seven hours ago? The clock on the kitchen wall sings out a short, single chime. It's eleven thirty. It feels like years between now and the time Lance walked away from Scott at the dinner. Now here we are, sitting around our kitchen table, staring at each other.

"Mel?" Molly finally breaks the silence. "Do you guys have any consecrated oil in your fridge?"

I look at Lance.

"We do," Lance says, squeezing my hand.

"Would you and Scott give me a blessing?" She is looking at Lance, but Scott answers.

"Of course, honey," Scott says.

"And Mel, too," she adds. "We both need a blessing."

"What do you want me to say?" Scott asks.

To be honest, I am disappointed he has to ask. I could have done it, if I had the authority. I know exactly what her heart is asking for. It is the dilemma these men of the Priesthood have. They are given the authority, but lack the insight of understanding the conception and bearing of our children, or the violation of the hallowed place these miracles of life take place—blind to the blistering anguish of losing them. My baby kicks. I put my hand on my stomach thinking how sad for them to never have the joy of this feeling from the inside.

"Let the spirit guide you, Scott," I tell him. "Just put yourself in Molly's shoes." I pause, looking down at her bare feet, and wonder where her shoes are.

224

Chapter Twenty-Six: Rebekah

I get up early, fix coffee, and drive to the cemetery. My coffee steams the window where I set the mug on the dash. I drive past the field of grazing ewes. I stand out in the early August morning light watching rays of sunshine bleed across the eastern horizon, mixing with lingering grain dust, and settling into a fog bank over the valley.

I stand first at Mom's grave, talking to her like I always do. I tell her about Gracie's funeral. I tell her about Molly going to Pocatello, skipping the graveside service and funeral dinner. She tells me to be quiet. She is trying to tell me something, but I don't understand what it is.

The fresh clay mound covering Gracie catches my attention. Pulling my jacket tight around me with one hand, my coffee cup in the other, I walk over to her grave and stare at the temporary grave marker.

Grace Marie McDonald.
b. October 14, 1983 d. July 31, 1986

Is Mom telling me to buy a head stone for Gracie? I think it's my head talking. I look over at Mom's stone and still my mind. I crouch down, my buttocks resting on my boot heels, leveling out the moist dirt of Grace Marie's grave like I am smoothing out the burial blanket now laying over her. A particle of blue is exposed as I move my hand back and forth. It looks like a file folder. I move more of the fresh dug soil away from the protrusion and pull it from beneath the mound. My hand trembles as I flip through the contents so familiar to me. UCC-1 filing against dairy cows; my father's hand-written notes; and Molly's computerized balance sheets. Across the promissory note is written in red ink, *Paid in Full*. Next to it are the initials *J.W.*

I empty the remains of my coffee cup on the dew-covered grass. Using it as a small trowel, I quickly dig away the top layer of soil, going deep enough to create a safe, long-term cache for the documents. I lay them inside the hollow and fill the hole. I feel I am violating her gravesite, and the law, but I know this is the sacrifice Gracie made for her family. It is important to bury it deep enough to keep the secret safe. I smooth it over and tamp it down, half whispering, half singing, "Amazing Grace…" Then I think, amazing Jack! I now know his hard shell has been cracked. I also know this likely means his time at the FDIC will be short.

I take my time getting home. I rinse out my coffee cup at the outside water hydrant. Dad is up, cooking a large pot of hot breakfast cereal. Before I ask, Dad offers to watch the kids. He says he'll drive them over to Betsy Ogden's with him to help pick tomatoes and corn.

"You want me to get us some?"

"Sure. I love fresh corn and tomatoes."

Scott calls at quarter to seven saying he needs to pick up Bobby and Jason. He says he's going pick them up first, then go get the 4-H lambs and Dylan at McDonald's and head to the fairgrounds.

"They're still asleep, but I'll get them up and have them ready," I say.

I tell Scott he can leave Lindsay with Grandpa. I ask if Molly was able to meet with the Farm Home lender. He hesitates, then tells me he needs to get going. He reminds me the lambs need to be weighed in at the fairgrounds by 9 o'clock.

When he called the night before he told me it had been a long day, and asked if I was okay with keeping the kids. I could hear traffic noise, mostly semi-trucks, in the background, and thought it was strange.

After I hung up the phone, Dad asks, "Where did Molly go after the service yesterday?"

"Pocatello."

"What for?" Dad stood, stirring the pot of oatmeal.

"I think she said she needed to pick up a baler or combine part for Scott at the John Deere dealer and then she said she was meeting with the Farmer's Home Administration loan officer. But after I thought about it, that didn't sound right because Richard's out on sick leave. Congressman Stallings' ag guy who works for him, told me Richard's got cancer and he's in treatment."

I look at Dad, knowing he also feels the full weight of these economic woes, like many of the lenders in the area. The affliction that sunk his bank is the same disease rotting the entire underbelly of the economic ship now sinking Idaho Agriculture. Like a poisoned aquifer, it filters into the lives of the bankers and loan officers as much as the borrowers. The vice-president of Production Credit Association in Blackfoot developed a severe case of Parkinson's Disease; there are reported cases of severe depression, and even a suicide by a banker in Idaho Falls. It's what makes Jack Whittaker bury a loan file in a dead girl's grave. It goes without saying, but I will say it again, the death of our dear friend, Niles Ogden, is undeniable evidence of the way the downturn affects everyone. Everyone, I think, except the Fullers.

"It certainly has been no easier on the lenders than the farmers and ranchers," is all Dad says.

After a quiet moment of reflection, Dad changes the subject. "I'll watch the whole brood as long as you need."

I tell him Scott is coming by to pick up the boys and I can send Esther out to help him.

"No, you guys only have this week and first of next to finish up with FDIC before they go back to San Jose. It'll be impossible to work with them after they leave Malad."

"Thanks for offering to help, Dad." I kiss him on the cheek. I think about how much our relationship has changed over the past eight months. He mellowed, and I let down the wall we built up between us over the years. Though, I admit, much of the netting of our lives has been formed by clinging to each other for emotional survival: he and I both missing Mom and Niles; Dad losing the bank—me losing another round of marriage. Now, the agony of losing little Gracie. We understand by our nature, we are survivors. He isn't the type of person who feels sorry for himself, and I'm not the type of person who wants to talk about it.

Dad created a regiment to keep himself busy every day. Even though his life changed, his character didn't. He fills his time helping Betsy rebuild her life. He spends time with Grandpa Thomas; and he took over the yard work at our house, as well as Betsy's. I figure it is his way of offering reparation to Betsy. Dad doesn't blame himself for losing the bank; but he does blame himself for losing Niles. No matter how many times Betsy tells him it was as much her fault for leaving him alone that morning, he places the blame squarely on his own shoulders—except for his silent contempt for Benny Schnabel.

After the accident at McDonalds Dairy, I agree to have Dad and Jason watch Eric and Rosalyn until school starts. I know as soon as FDIC leaves town, our workload will lighten up. Farmers are in harvest, which means a paycheck to them, easing their need for operating capital. If nothing else, they can take their receipts to the ASCS office and the government will front them money for their grain through Commodity Credit Corporation. It's a nice fallback for them, especially if the market's soft, and they're not wanting to sell. It's one of those government programs no one curses. Some of our clients stop by the law office to pay Kenny, after months of receiving legal services on a promise to pay when they harvest the wheat.

Esther says when the boys are back in school, she wants to take Rosalyn again during the day. I don't want to take my kids back out to Melanie, but I don't want to hurt her feelings either. I decide to tell her she has enough going on in her life, and besides, she needs to get ready for her new baby who is due mid-September, not to mention getting Dylan and Erica ready for school. It occurs to me Lance will likely continue to live in his world, oblivious to reality, the same way he was before the accident. When no one calls on him to pay up or to pick up his livestock and machinery, he'll dismiss it without wondering why. If anyone pursues it, it will be Melanie. Though Molly told me Melanie vowed she will no longer be Lance's facilitator. I wonder how Lance and Melanie will find out about the buried file, or discover their note has been written off by Jack Whittaker. Then I think perhaps it's okay if they never find out.

When I see Jack walk past the office later that Wednesday morning, the day after Grace Marie McDonald is laid to rest, I tell Esther I'll be right back.

"He's sure a looker," Esther says.

I glance over my shoulder and wink at her. "He's not my type,"

I tell her Francis Jenkins is coming by to review some cash flows. "Just have him sit down and I'll be right back," I head to the café.

Elsie's is empty except for late-morning coffee drinkers with nowhere else to go but home where their wives wait for lawns to be mowed, or ripening vegetables to be harvested and preserved.

It's opening day of the Oneida County Fair. Even though my father spent the last few months tending Mom's flower garden, he refuses to enter any of her prize roses in the fair the way she used to. I tell him it will honor her. He tells me to mind myself.

I work early mornings and Saturdays with Jason, Dylan, and Bobby to get their lambs finished with the precise grain mixture. Despite several arguments with Scott and Lance about what to feed them, I win out. I am not a novice at this stuff. I know what I'm doing.

"They're not dairy cows, and they're not feed cattle," I argue. "They are fat lambs, and if you get the mix too hot, or too starchy, you'll be milkin' em, not eatin' em." Which is precisely the reason I want to talk to Jack.

The bell on the door jingles when I enter and Vickie Thompson points toward the back of the café. I nod my head and smile at her.

"Hey," I say, as I slip into the booth across from Jack. He looks like he's been beat up. His hands are wrapped around his coffee cup and his eyes fall to the table when I sit down. Vickie brings me a cup of coffee and leaves us alone to talk.

"You okay?" I ask him.

"Not really."

"We have to move forward, Jack. People in Malad understand hardship. Not that we like it, or thrive on it. We just understand it enough to know moving past these things is the only sustainable way we can survive here."

Jack looks up at me and I see he is enduring something far beyond hardship. I honestly don't know what to say. I don't feel sorry for

229

him; I know him well enough by now to know he'll figure it out. But the agony of watching him makes me look away as I take a sip of coffee, trying to gather myself.

"When are you leaving?

"Next week."

"I saw you walk by the office, so I came in to buy you coffee."

"Thanks." He smiles, but when he blinks, his eyes close and open like sludge moving, as though he deliberately has to force his eyelids open again.

"You flying to California this weekend?"

"No," he speaks in a hoarse whisper. "I'm going to finish boxing up files. The truck is being delivered next Tuesday, and by Wednesday, we're gone from here for good."

"I'll miss you," I say, putting my hand on his.

He takes my hand in both of his and looks at me with a kindness I have only known in very few men—the one married to my sister, Esther; my father; and Niles Ogden. I know this is the way I love Jack. He is such a dear friend to me. It will be hard to see him go.

"Actually, I came over to ask you to go to the fair with me if you're not going home this weekend."

"Sounds like it would be a nice relief to foreclosures and funerals," he says.

"Good. I'll pick you up Saturday morning at eight. We'll be just in time to catch the tail end of the Boy Scouts' pancake breakfast. The 4-H Round Robin competition begins at nine o'clock and the livestock sale begins at eleven. I'll drop Jason off to feed and water his lamb, and then I'll stop over to the motel and pick you up."

"What should I wear?"

"Surprise me," I say, as I get up.

"I got this," he says, picking up the tab Vickie left on the table.

"Good thing." I say. "I forgot my wallet."

He smiles as he pulls out the money clip.

230

"That's my high school mascot," I say, looking at the dragon-head clip with the ruby eye that glints under the florescent light. "You know, I've coveted your money clip since I first saw it."

"I know. That's one of the first things I learned about Malad after I got here. I've noticed a lot of people eyeing it," he says. "My grandfather gave it to me when I graduated from high school."

"Don't suppose you'll leave it here, then."

"Not unless I'm here with it."

"I'll go for that." I brush off my blue jeans. I gave up my mother's wardrobe as work attire and migrated back to my cowboy boots, wranglers and sleeveless button-up blouses.

"Where can I find clothes like those?" Jack waves his hand up and down from my feet to my waist.

"At The Merc."

He raises his eyebrows, purses his lips, and nods approvingly as he looks.

"These are mine," I say. "You'll have to get your own."

He laughs heartily. We all need to laugh that way, I think.

"Hey, Mr. FDIC nice guy, don't forget to take Benny with you when you leave town."

He doesn't just frown, he turns icy cold and grimaces hard enough his brow furrows.

"Benny left this morning," he says in a way I don't ask why.

Chapter Twenty-Seven: Rebekah

Jack opens the door of his motel room at ten minutes before 8 o'clock on Saturday morning when he hears my truck drive in. I smile with a quiet chuckle. Norma Howell is standing at the threshold of her cottage with a smile as big as a banana. Jack saunters across the gravel parking lot toward my pickup. He is wearing a cream-colored straw cowboy hat, Levies—a disappointment to a die-hard Wrangler girl, but not all that bad—and a new pair of cowboy boots.

"Hey, cowboy, got your money clip?" I laugh. I look at Norma. "You had something to do with this, didn't you? She just keeps grinning.

"I'm gonna miss him," Norma says.

"We all will."

"He's a good catch, ya know."

"Not fishin', Norma. Though in that outfit it's sure temptin."

She laughs. "Hell, I'm tempted," she says.

"You helped him buy those clothes, didn't you?"

"Sure I did. Why da ya think he looks so good."

He is still wearing his polo shirt, but it's tucked in and the new leather belt shows off his trim waist and hips.

"Let's go, cowboy," I say, "hot cakes are gettin' cold."

"You kids have fun," Norma yells out.

Eric and Rosalyn are in the back seat. Jack reaches across the seat and shakes Eric's hand as he introduces himself.

"Beautiful kids," he says. "But, then they have a beautiful mom."

"Don't make me blush, Jack. You know, the meaner you are, the better I like you."

"I could have guessed that's how it works with you," he says as he buckles his seat belt.

When we park, he jumps out, opens the back door and un-belts Rosalyn from her car seat. He carries her as we walk across the grass toward the pavilion where the Boy Scouts are serving up hot cakes for their annual fundraiser.

"She can walk," I tell him.

"Is it okay if I carry her?"

"Sure." I shrugged. "She loves it."

"I'll be glad to get back to my daughter," he says. "I sure miss her."

I tell Jack to have a seat with the kids and I'll get the hot cakes. I see him reaching for his money clip and I hold up my hand. "My treat," I say. "I remembered my wallet this time."

I rush everyone to finish. We dump our paper plates in the trash and I wait for Jack. He is just standing there watching the boys in their mud-green uniforms and neckerchiefs ladling out batter while other boys turn the pancake over with a spatula, still others clear tables, wiping up spilt maple syrup. He seems mesmerized by this anomaly of youthful production.

"Come on, Jack. We're going to be late."

"I just can't believe how these kids work," he says as we leave the old post and beam framed building clad in rusting corrugated metal.

"I suppose I've been in California too long, seen too many long-haired, drugged-out kids with nothing to do. This is a real treat to watch these kids. They actually know how to work, and they can't be much older than twelve or thirteen."

"These are the boys who didn't have a 4-H or FFA livestock project. The rest are in the livestock barns getting ready to sell their animals after the Round Robin competition," I tell him.

While we sit in the bleachers, I explain to Jack how the Round Robin competition works. The showmanship winner in each livestock category competes to show in each of the other categories. Jason is required to show a beef, a hog, a chicken, a goat, a rabbit, and a horse. Dad worked with him for days using Mom's horse she gave to Lindsay before she died, and one of Scott's beef cows. Betsy taught him how to show a chicken and a rabbit. He either guessed how to show a pig, or asked one of the FFA kids in the barn how it was done. He watched several of the competitions to hone his skills at showing goats, though he said it's just like showing a sheep.

While Dylan and Bobby both receive blue ribbons for showmanship, Jason is older and more experienced. He spent hours teaching his younger cousins how to hold the head of their lamb, how to stretch out the neck, set the feet, and how to stand back, smile at the judges, then move confidently around the lamb, never putting himself between the judge and the lamb.

I explain all this to Jack as we sit next to each other, Rosalyn content to sit quiet, leaning against his chest, sucking her thumb. Eric climbs off the bleachers and is playing underneath with a couple of his grade school friends. We watch Jason confidently move through each category. He is showing the horse when I see Molly and Scott at the arena doorway, looking for a place to sit.

"Hey," I blurt out, "There's Scott and Molly." I stand and wave at them, and they wave back. As they walk toward us, Jack clears his throat and nervously looks away. Jason finishes his competition and is leaving the arena. I stand up to hold out my hand to Lindsay, helping her up the bleachers.

"Shoot, we missed it," Scott said. "We were trying to hurry. We got here just before they shut off the grills and barely got fed. Bobby and Dylan ran over to feed their lambs."

"Oh, I hope they don't feed them too much," I say." They don't want them pooping in the sale ring."

Jack hands Rosalyn to me, stands up, and shakes Scott's hand. I watch as Scott puts his other hand on Jack's arm and I watch their eyes meet. I think it's odd how familiar they seemed to be with each other. I sit next to Molly and put my arm around her.

"Oh, honey," I moan, looking at her face. "How'd you do that?" I put my fingertips lightly on the scrape across her face and the bruise on her cheek.

"Oh. That! I was helping the guy load up the combine parts and I forgot to duck. Stupid me," she says.

I took her chin into my hand and turn her face toward me to have a closer look.

"Oh, Molly, it looks like it hurts."

"I've had worse," she says."Oh, look, they're announcing the Round Robin Grand Champion," Molly forces me to look away from her.

"Round Robin Grand Champion," echoed through the PA system, "For 1986 is Jason Udall." The crowd is small, mostly parents of the participants. I jump to my feet and holler. I put my two little fingers to my lips and let out a whistle. Jack turns, surprised, then grins. I see him turn to look at Molly and when he does, it is as though he's committed the sin of Lot's wife who turned to look back at the place she was leaving. It is at this very moment I know how he feels about her. Not that he is sinful, but I know if he turns to look at her too long, he will never leave. His face turns as ashen as salt, his eyes full of wanting, and when she looks at Jack and smiles, he quickly puts his head down and turns away.

In my elation and trying to quell the awkward moment for Jack, I hug Molly. Scott is now holding Rosalyn. I quickly descend from the bleachers to greet Jason as he leaves the arena. "Nice job, son." The tail of his white shirt I'd ironed that morning is pulled out in back and his green scarf is twisted. His hair is mussed a little but he is bearing a broad, beautiful smile, warming me to my core.

As we walk out of the show ring, the rest of the family joins us. He holds out his purple ribbon to Scott, and then to Molly. Molly hugs him. "Nice job, Jason."

I introduce Jason to Jack, and while I fear he might shy away from Jack, thinking Jack might be his next father, he holds out his hand and shakes Jack's hand. "Nice to meet, you, sir," he says.

I smile. I am so proud of him and I am happy he is in such a great place with so many people who love him.

"Where's Esther, Kenny, and Dad?" Molly asks.

"Gone camping this weekend. They decided to drive up to Island Park and go fishing. They took Dad with them."

236

"Mom, come help me hang it above my pen with the other one," Jason says.

"Actually," I put my hand on Jason's shoulder, "we need to take the one that's hanging up in your pen, down, so you can drape them over your lamb in the sale ring. He's gonna look great with two grand champion ribbons hanging on his back."

"Come on," I say to my family and Jack, "let's go help the boys get ready for the livestock sale."

"Mom, does this mean I get to sell first?" Jason asks me.

"Yup, it sure does.,"

"Awesome."

We walk through the side door into the beef barn, then through the pig barn, the smells changing to a distinct pungent odor with a lingering smell of alfalfa hay. Young people are busy swamping out pens with pitchforks, pushing wheelbarrows and carrying water buckets hitting against their leg as they hoist them along, spilling water down pant legs and in the dirt alleys between the pens, creating small trails of mud.

The sheep barn is the farthest to the north. Dylan has the grooming card and is tapping the wool on his lamb the way Jason showed him. Bobby is shining the black face with a rag, then dipping it into a can of black show polish and shining the hooves. Jack stands back watching them. He walks well in his cowboy boots. I suppose he watched enough Malad cowboys ambling down the street that he picked up the soft slog and amble walk with style.

Jack stops at Bobby's pen first. He leans over the gate and watches him polishing his lamb's hooves; then he looks at me, "is that legal?"

"Sure. Don't you polish your shoes?"

Bobby looks up at him and smiles. "You Aunt Rebekah's new boyfriend?"

"Bobby!" Molly says from behind me.

"No, it's okay," Jack says, turning to look at Molly. "It's a fair question."

237

"Well, son," he says, "It's like this. I would be, but your Aunt Rebekah told me she's gonna wait for some rich oil man to move into Malad. She won't have nothin' to do with me," he says with a teasing grin. "Can't say I haven't tried."

"Ah, too bad," Bobby says. "Aunt Rebekah would be a fine catch for you."

"Bobby Olson, what's gotten into you?" Molly is standing over him.

"Nothin' Mom. I heard you tell that to Dad."

"Ah, you guys are so sweet," I say. "You're always looking after your poor old Aunt Rebekah."

I turn around to look at Jack and he's moved down to Dylan's pen. He is having a serious conversation with him. He leans in, his hand on Dylan's shoulder, and he points and nods his head as Dylan talks. He looks genuinely interested as Dylan explains to him how to judge a lamb. I stop to listen. It amazes me how Dylan paid attention to me and Jason; how he is parroting everything I said to him about a good quality ewe lamb.

"I was hopin' I could keep her," I hear Dylan say. "You know, for breein' stock. Maybe start a small farm flock like Jason's mom has. I think I could feed her out for a year; then turn her in with Rebekah's, I mean Sister Udall's, ewes to have her bred. It's a shame to send a good little ewe lamb like her to slaughter." Jack turns, raises his eyebrows and smiles at me when Dylan calls me Sister Udall. I hear Dylan's voice grow quiet, and his voice quivers ever so slightly as he explains his dilemma.

"Who says you can't keep her?" Jack asks.

"My mom," he says. "Well, that's against the rules," Dylan says. "Mom said I agreed to let Flossy go when I got her, and besides, I still owe Rebekah, I mean Sister Udall, the money for the lamb. So, whoever buys her gets to say what happens to the lamb. Most people send them over to Riches'."

"Dylan," I interrupt, "it's Rebekah. Not Sister Udall."

"Who are Riches'?" Jack asks, ignoring me.

"The meat packing plant."

238

"Oh, *those* Riches'," Jack responds like he recognizes the name. I figure by the way he said it, the small meat packing plant must be in the stack of files Fullers turned over to FDIC. Monte Rich hadn't been in to see Kenny, but like Lance and Scott, a lot of people figure if they ignore the FDIC, they will go away.

I check my watch. "Hey guys, sheep sell first, and Jason gets number one spot. Let's go."

Jack scoops Rosalyn up in his arms and holds out his hand for Eric. "I'm good," Eric tells him, refusing to give Jack his hand. But Lindsay quickly releases her hand from her mother's and runs up beside Jack and offers him hers. Molly turns and looks at me, smiling, like I'd found a good man. I frown at her and shake my head as if to say, "aint gonna happen."

I think, as they walk away from me—Jack following behind Molly—how tired she looks. I worry her diabetes has taken a turn for the worse, especially with everything that's been going on this summer. I'll go talk to her tomorrow, I think. After she gets home from church, I'll spend some time with her.

The seats around the arena are filling. Ballard Oil, Malad Mill and Feed, and even Clarence Fuller is there. He sees Jack Whittaker walk in with us and quickly looks away. It reminds me of the day in church when his brother watched as I passed up the sacrament, then quickly looked away. I worry Molly might be the next Helland called in and rebuked by the Fullers. I know in my heart Clarence takes what he can get from her and will turn her loose when he is finished. It was a mistake in the beginning for her to stay. I detest them, so I can't bear the thought of her helping them out.

"Hey guys," I say, "I'm going to get a bidding card."

"Ah, good idea," says Jack. "Where do we get one?"

Scott holds out his hands to take Rosalyn from Jack, and Jack follows me to the front of the building where Betsy is volunteering. She is taking information, and handing out bidding numbers. I know it's going to be awkward to introduce her to Jack, so I don't. I direct Jack to Jewel Fisher, the other table attendant. I say, "Jewel, this gentleman needs a bidding card, can you take care of him?" Then I leave Jewel to take care of Jack while I walk to Betsy's station.

"Who's your new friend?" Betsy whispers as she looks down the table at Jack.

"Jack Whittaker." I offer her nothing more. I know she recognizes the name. She looks over at him like she's staring down her husband's killer. I want to tell her he's not the one, but I can't. A cold silence hangs between us for an uncomfortable moment before she asks me where my dad is today. I think she's surprised he isn't here for the sale. It's the first one he's missed in thirty-five years. He is always the top supporter of the auction, and usually buys the grand champion steer or lamb; or sometimes both. Fullers have never been as generous to these kids as my father and grandfather have been.

There are too many painful things to think about at this moment. There I am, escorting the FDIC Asset Manager around the fair, four days after Gracie's funeral; I'm requesting a bidding card from the woman whose husband took his life because of an errant FDIC officer; and the ex-bank president who's been the number one 4-H livestock sale supporter has gone fishing on the year these kids need money more than ever. I lean over the table and put my lips next to Betsy's ear, "I'll see what I can do to get him to pony up a little cash for these kids." I stand up and give her a mischievous grin. She finally smiles back, but it isn't warm or friendly, and I don't blame her. "Put my number under Kenny Sorenson Law Office, will you Betsy?"

"No problem," she says. "I know he's good for it."

The feedback from sound system echoes, then makes a loud buzzing noise. The auctioneer adjusts the system, and tests it again. Fred Harley's voice is meant to call a sale, and like most staples in the valley, he is the voice we know when an auction is held.

Jack and I sit down just as Jason leads his lamb into the ring. Fred Harley's booming voice doesn't need a PA system, so when amplified, it's deafening.

"Ladies and Gentlemen, we have a fine young fellow with two grand champion ribbons." Jason fastened the large round medallions trimmed with ribbon streamers to each side of the halter. Smart display, I think.

"Jason Udall is the son of Rebekah Udall," Fred says. Then he pauses. I know he doesn't know what to say. He has no idea who Jason's dad is and the silence is twice as deafening as his thundering voice. Jason finishes his first circle around the ring and stops at the auctioneer's stand. Fred leans over the podium while Jason says something to him and Fred nods his head.

"The son of Rebekah and Andy Udall," Fred finally says. I see Eric look up and smile when he hears his father's name. I know Jason did it for his little brother's sake.

"So, let's start this sale with some support from you good Malad folks," Fred begins chanting, like he's warming up to begin his bidding banter.

Malad Mill and Feed started it at a dollar. Someone from the far side raises a bid card, and the auction spotter yells out "yep" as his arm flies into the air, then the spotter's arm on the other side of the arena yells out "yep," as the auctioneer announces the bid at two dollars. Back and forth it goes, "two twenty-five," Fred yells, "two fifty," and then Fred Harley yells "sold for three dollars a pound."

Even though the grand champion always brings top dollar, it is a ridiculously high price, I think. I clap my hands along with the crowd until Fred Harley yells out, "and the buyer is number sixty-seven," and he pauses, running his finger down his buyer list, "Clarence Fuller, Malad Community Bank." The room grows still as Clarence crawls over the benches to claim his prize.

I know his prize wasn't the lamb, or Jason, but the glory of buying out the Helland's one more time, putting us on public display with the photo he'll hang behind his desk in Lars Helland's bank, with his arm around Lars Helland's grandson. I look at Molly and frown. She looks at me and shrugs. Jack taps me on the arm. "Hey," he says, "they're asking for you." I look up. Jason is beckoning for me to come over where Clarence is standing with him. I stand up and nearly tumble down the bleachers. Jack catches me before I fall on my face. As I approach Jason he says, pointing at Clarence, "he wants you in the picture with us."

"Here, Rebekah, over on this side of me," Clarence says, positioning himself in the middle.

I stand uncomfortably close to him. He puts one arm around me and one around Jason, and as the flash goes off, I leaned into him, putting my lips against his ear, and I say, "you are a sorry son-of-a- bitch."

Clarence jerks his head back and stares at me. I smile at him, shake his hand, pat Jason on the back, and say, "Congratulations son." I take large strides back across the arena with a smile on my face. Clarence climbs up and perches himself on his bench, glaring at me from across the sale barn. I think I might regret what I said to him later, but not today. At this moment, I taste the blood of sweet revenge.

Bobby is number five to sell, and Dylan is right behind him. Malad Feed and Mill buys the second lamb at a dollar-fifty a pound. I write down the results as Fred announces the sale price and the buyer's name. The third lamb sells for a dollar sixty-five and the buyer is Evans Mercantile; the fourth is purchased by Ballad Oil at a dollar and a quarter a pound.

Malad Feed and Mill starts Bobby's lamb at a dollar. I see Clarence hold up his card at a dollar twenty-five. The bidding war warms up and Malad Feed and Mill backs out at two dollars. When Fred says two seventy-five I raise my card and the spotter yells "yep" as Fred Harley finishes saying "going twice with his hammer in the air to finalize the sale. Clarence bids three dollars and I bid three twenty-five. Clarence bids it up another twenty-five cents. I catch the spotter's eye and put up my left hand spreading out four fingers and my thumb and wave my card with the other, my eyebrow going up as I continue to stare at my spotter. The spotter on the other side of the arena says, "six dollars." "Seven," I say. The other spotter yells, "eight." I hold up both my hands. Fred Harley says Ten Dollars, and he didn't give Clarence another chance. He yells, "sold to," and I hold up the card, number forty-seven. He looks at his list. "Sold to Kenneth Sorenson Law Office," he bellows.

This time the crowd doesn't clap as Clarence crawls down from the bleachers and leaves the sale barn, red-faced and grimacing. There are obvious groans and murmurs as he stomps out. Jack takes hold of my hand to steady me as I climb down to have my picture taken with Bobby. "Not sure if that was worth it," Jack says as he let go of my hand. The Welch people are a proud people and the Thomas part of me isn't going to let a Fuller hang two photos in his bank with Helland grandchildren being displayed like trophy mounts. But, in the end, pride isn't a winning number. It's something I chastise Scott and Lance for, and think I am exempt. Eventually, contrition will be my Gethsemane.

"Whoa, Aunt Rebekah," Bobby is grinning like a champion. "I'm rich," he says.

I put my arm around him and as I smile into the camera for a second time, "don't forget, you still owe me for the lamb, buster."

Fred Harley introduces Dylan as he enters the sale ring; his ewe lamb following him like a pet dog. Dylan takes the halter off the lamb, and she continues to follow him as he walks in circles around the sale ring. People whisper, and laugh, and coo. I hear Fred Harley's voice drop to a respectful quiet tone as he says, "Dylan McDonald, son of," and he pauses before he can say the names of Dylan's parents. "Lance and Melanie McDonald," Fred finally chokes out.

A young child doesn't die in a small community like Malad without taking a part of all of us with her, and Fred Harley is no exception. The bidding starts on Dylan's lamb by the time I am back in my seat. I sit between Molly and Jack. Molly is holding Rosalyn and I take her, holding her in my lap and watch as the crowd rallies. The spotters are having a hard time keeping up with all the bidders. As the price goes past five dollars, several bidders drop out.

At six dollars, I see Jack raise his card and the spotter yells, "yep," as he points at Jack. There are two more "yeps" from the spotter across the arena. Dylan walks his ewe lamp around the ring again and again. Jack raises his card one more time when the bid hits seven-fifty. The bidding slows, and Jack puts up his card again to signal another hike to eight dollars. Fred Harley yells "sold to bidder number," he pauses, "bidder number forty-eight." He looks down

243

his list for a name. I wondered if he'd bid for FDIC. "Whittaker Livestock," Fred finally says, looking back up at Jack as though he should know him. Scott, Molly and I all look at Jack at the same time. He smiles at us. "I'm going into business with Dylan," he says. "That ewe lamb is my first investment."

"Well," I look at Jack, "you'll go broke in a hurry if you pay that price for all your breeding stock."

"Says the ten-dollar bidder to the eight-dollar bidder," Jack teases.

But the truth is, it doesn't really matter how much either of us paid. I bought Bobby's lamb out of bitterness and hate. I refused to let Fuller's publicly humiliate the Thomas and Helland family one more time; and Jack bought Dylan's lamb out of kindness and love in an attempt to keep a young boy from feeling the pain of losing a young creature he cared for and grew attached to only days after losing his baby sister.

As the months pass, my inability to shed the cynicism I feel toward the Fullers has mutated into my own self-loathing and inability to move to a better place in my life. Molly's and Esther's gift to forgive and love unconditionally leave them morally and spiritually healthier and happier people. I never hear my father or Kenny say anything contrary about the Fullers. On occasion, I can get my grandfather to engage in a Fuller bashing conversation with me; but when I tell him what I said to Clarence Fuller at the junior livestock auction, he is disappointed in me.

The torturous part about refusing to part from this burden is the way it darkens my perceptions about everything and everyone. Nevertheless, I continue to hold on to it like a wet blanket that clings to me until it becomes my own flesh, poisoning my life much the same way the wild parsnip or meadow fennel poisoned the beaver and muskrat meat, making the French trappers so deathly ill.

Jack climbs down and walks across the arena to have his picture taken with Dylan. He holds out his hand to Dylan, and shakes it. When he comes back he leans over to Scott and asks, "can you haul the lamb back to the McDonald farm for us? That one's not going to slaughter."

"Well then," I tell Scott, "haul Bobby's out there too. Whittaker and McDonald Livestock Company might as well start with a flock of two very nice Suffolk ewe lambs. I don't want Flossy getting lonely."

We write down prices and buyers names on the next eight lambs, none of which go over two dollars a pound. Jason, Bobby, and Dylan put their lambs back in the pens, water them and join us. We all agree it's about time to retreat to the midway for the rest of the afternoon and have some fun.

"Hey," I put my arm around Molly before we get up to leave the sale barn, "I'm going to cook a roast in the morning and I have a bunch of fresh tomatoes and corn from Betsy's garden. If you guys will stop by Dad's and take Jason and Eric to church, I'll bring it over to your house and have dinner ready when you get home. "

"Sounds great to me," Molly says. Then Molly leans over me and touches Jack's arm. Her hand is like an electric shock. He jumps.

"Sorry, didn't mean to scare you. Hey, would you like to come out to our place for Sunday dinner tomorrow? Rebekah's cooking."

"Well." He pauses a long time. "I've got to work at the bank for a while. I need to start organizing files to get them ready to ship."

"You've gotta eat somewhere," Molly says." And the café's closed tomorrow."

"I'm not sure how to get to your place."

"It's easy. Just head west like you're going to Holbrook, then at the St. John Road, turn left, and we're about half mile south."

"Doesn't anyone around here use addresses?"

"Kind of. Our mail box has RR 4 Box 9 painted on the side, if that helps."

"I'll just look for your GMC," he says.

I know Molly is thinking she is baiting Jack to fall for me because I'm single, and happen to be a good cook; but I also know if Jack agrees to come out, it won't be to eat my cooking. He has obviously been smitten by my sister. I wonder if it's a good idea for him to be there. Then I decide in three more days it won't make much difference. He'll be gone for good.

CHAPTER TWENTY-SIX—REBEKAH

I telephone Molly early Sunday morning.

"Hey, little sister," I say in a quiet, almost whisper, hoping I'm not disturbing her too early. "How are you feeling this morning?"

"Better. Bobby was on cloud nine last night and didn't want to go to bed. He got a piece of paper and pencil and kept figuring up what he is going to spend all his money on. Ten percent for tithing, two hundred dollars for his missionary fund, a hundred and fifty to pay you for the lamb, fifty for his dad to pay for feed. It was really heartwarming. He even said he was going to help buy Lindsay's school clothes."

"What a kid. Just don't tell him he has Clarence Fuller to thank. Oh, and ask him not to tell Uncle Kenny until I have a chance to explain. I have a feeling he might be taking it out of my paycheck."

"Rebekah," she lowers her voice," Clarence is just a sad old man who doesn't know anything about getting along with people. He just does the best he knows how."

"You know he's younger than Dad, right?"

"No way!"

"Three years younger. Dad told me. And President Fuller is the same age as Dad," I tell her.

"Well, banking sure hasn't been his friend, then, 'cause he looks ten years older."

"Sweetheart," I say, "Since Dad and Clarence have both been bankers all their life, it's obviously not the banking. He's just an obnoxious, vindictive human being."

"Well, Rebekah," she says, "we should take a lesson from Clarence if we don't want to look like old hags in our fifties."

That stopped me from saying any more, but Molly wasn't finished.

"Besides," she says, "it's like Gandhi's saying, 'an eye for an eye leaves the whole world blind."

I know she is talking about a lot more than me trying to gouge out Clarence Fuller's eyes at the livestock sale the day before; I just didn't know then what she was referring to.

I told her to go ahead and get ready for church and I'd bring the boys over to her house with me when I brought the meat and vegetables. That way she wouldn't have to come all the way out to St. John to pick them up for Sunday School.

It is the second Sunday of August. The day starts out warm and only gets warmer. I pull into Molly's yard at 9 o'clock with the boys bathed and dressed in their Sunday clothes. Scott left early for Priesthood meeting, and Molly wants to get there early enough to practice the organ before church. The noisy brood loads into her Gimmy and as she leaves with a trail of dust following her down the driveway. The house is quiet. Rosalyn plays in the living room while I load the pot roast with seasoning, carrots, celery and a little Worchester sauce, wishing for a nice red basting wine. I scrub the potatoes and shuck the corn, leaving them soaking in cold water. I make a large coleslaw salad and put it in the fridge. At eleven-thirty, I hear a vehicle come into the yard and look out the window. It's Jack. He is early.

He is heading for the front of the house when I open the utility room door and hold it open for him. He is carrying a pie, carefully balancing it with both hands as he walks, acting as though it might slosh over the edges.

"You brought desert, I see. Nice."

"Norma baked it yesterday and brought it over to me. Rhubarb and strawberry pie is what she said it is. I've never had Rhubarb pie."

"Well, Jack," I say, taking it from him, "you haven't lived until you've had strawberry-rhubarb pie."

He looks around, nodding his head. Rosalyn hears his voice and runs to the kitchen with her arms out. He laughs, scooping her up with a bear hug.

"How's my little princess?" She holds up her face for a kiss and he gives her a smooch on her cheek.

"I'm gonna miss you guys when I go," he says, setting Rosalyn back down. She smiles at Jack, and runs back to the living room to play.

"I think the feeling's mutual. Did you get your files packed up and ready to go?"

"Close." He pulls out a chair from the round oak table and sits down.

"I'd offer you coffee, but Molly doesn't keep any. About all I've got to give you is water, or milk from the McDonald dairy."

"I'll take a glass of water," he says. "Nothing wrong with drinking this good Idaho water."

"Smells wonderful in here," Jack says putting down his glass. He eyes Molly's charming kitchen with ceramic roosters, and little knick-knack shelves she painted with appliqués. He looks up at the antique kitchen utensils and enamel-baked dishes she found in the barn are arranged on top of the kitchen cupboards. Her entire home looks clean, crisp and warm. She dresses the same way. She is like our mother in so many ways.

Jack gets up, walks to the hallway, and looks close at the picture of Molly barrel racing on her Paint quarter horse.

"Molly rides?"

"Molly came out of the womb looking for a horse to ride," I tell Jack. "That's Thomas, her favorite." I point to the picture. "He's out in the pasture. I'll bet he's getting close to seventeen years old. Grandpa Thomas bought him for her when she was fifteen, so she named him Thomas. She still rides him, but doesn't push him. She won three regional barrel-racing contests on him, then quit racing after she got married."

"That's a shame. When it gets into your blood, it never leaves."

"You ride?" I keep washing dishes at the sink, talking over the shoulder that's holding the damp dish towel.

"My mother put me on a horse almost before I could walk," he says. "Her father owned a big ranch north of San Francisco, and when she married Dad, she brought her horse to San Jose, then bought three more. She lost her favorite horse a few years ago, but still keeps about four horses at the stables outside of town. I still go riding with

Mom and Stacy when I can. Mom has Stacy in some English riding classes."

"You know, Jack," I was cautious about broaching the subject, "there are a few things I want you to know before Molly and Scott get home. I turn around and lean against the sink. He looks at me like I stabbed him with my paring knife. "What?" he asks.

"You need to know Molly thinks she's playing match-maker between the two of us."

"Well, I kind of guessed that," he says.

"And I know you played along to spend time with her before you go."

He is dead silent. I can see the rigid, pragmatic side of him fighting with a tender and vulnerable human side, far too underexposed. I realized after I found the McDonald's file at Gracie's grave, how truly susceptible he's become and I want to catch him before he exposes too much of his human side too soon.

I am guessing he is either letting down because he is near the end of this journey to Idaho and doesn't need to keep up the federal agent guise; or when the shell he lives in cracked open, he didn't realize he is still liquid inside. He is not ready to shed his casing just yet. He needs to go back to California and let those tender under-exposed parts inside him solidify before the shell he's lived inside his entire adult life completely falls away.

"I thought about not coming today," he finally says. "Did she tell you what happened to her last Tuesday night?"

"No. Well, yes. She told me she got hit in the head when she was helping the kid at the store load the combine parts. But I know she is covering something. I didn't press it, though. Do you know what happened?"

"I promised I wouldn't say anything. Or I should say, she asked that it be left alone, and I assumed that meant she didn't want Scott or me to bring it up. Not ever. Not to anyone."

I look at him. "You know, Jack, I knew something was wrong when Scott called Tuesday night to see if they could leave the kids with

Dad and me. I had no idea what it was, but I knew. And the next morning, when I went to my mother's grave to visit, she was trying to tell me something. She kept trying to tell me to take care of Molly. At first I thought she was trying to tell me to buy a headstone for Gracie's grave."

I look at Jack and he is staring out the window toward the road.

"What time are they getting home?" he asks. I ignore him.

"You can tell me you don't want to have this conversation if you want, Jack, and I'll shut up, but you need to know that I know two things: I know you love Molly; and I know you buried McDonald's file in Gracie's grave.

His face burns red. "Maybe I should go. This isn't a good idea for me to be here."

"No, Jack. You need to stay. She'd be hurt if you left."

"Did she tell you about Benny?"

"No. What about Benny?"

"She didn't say anything to you about what happened in Pocatello?"

"You mean Tuesday night?"

He nodded his head.

"No."

Jack sits down at the table and motions for me to sit with him. He reaches across the table and takes ahold of my hands. Without looking up, he starts talking.

"Rebekah, you and I have shared a lot this summer and we haven't always agreed on everything. You know, and I know, there is nothing between us except a friendship I hope will go on forever. I consider you as one of the best friends I've ever..."

I interrupt. "People who call me their best friend, Jack, usually don't have very many friends." His face stays stone gray. While I'd said it in jest, I grew more serious. "I guess what I am trying to say is the best part about having these kinds of friendships, Jack, is people who feel that way about each other don't have say it, or say it more than once."

He squeezes my hands and shakes his head like he is trying to make all of this go away.

"You have helped me face my feelings and my fears. I have denied that I love her. Now I know I do love her more than I've loved any woman and I can't explain why, or how. I felt it the moment I lifted her head that night she went into insulin shock at the bank, but I didn't know what it was. There was some force at work when I held her in my arms trying to revive her. I can't make it go away. But I'll go away, and I won't be back and I'll try not to think about it."

I am shocked at his raw, open, confession of how he feels about my sister. "What happened to her, Jack?" I lift his chin until his eyes meet mine. "what happened to my sister Tuesday night?"

"You know who Benny Schnabel is?"

I nod. "Don't like him," I say. "He's an ass. But you said Wednesday morning he went back to California."

"On Tuesday morning after he met with Scott's dad, he drove over to the church where Molly was practicing her music for the funeral and told her he was foreclosing on her father-in-law and her husband unless she met him in Pocatello Tuesday night."

"What did she think he was going to do?" I ask.

"Well, Rebekah. I can tell you if she'd been you, or at least confided in you before she went, you would have known it was a scam, or a snare. But she didn't. She didn't tell anyone, except Scott. She told him she was going to see the Farm Home loan officer and he asked her to get combine parts while she was there. That's all anyone knew. It was Scott's dad who saw Benny in the church parking lot talking to her that tipped off Scott. Scott came to my motel room about 6:30 Tuesday night after he milked the McDonald's cows. As soon as he told me, I knew what Benny was up to. He tries this everywhere we go. Most women know the game, but Molly was an innocent victim."

I sit in silence, shaking my head, not sure who to be angry at. Jack looks at me. I tell him she told me she was going to meet with the Farm Home guy, because she wanted me to watch her kids. I am furious she didn't confide in me about any of the rest, and I told Jack so.

"Rebekah, I wasn't going to tell you because I knew you'd react like this. So stop it. Stop being angry and think. She doesn't want anyone to know. I'd bet a million dollars you are holding the same kind of secret from her."

I jerk my head up, narrow my eyes, and stare at him.

"Bingo," he said.

"Bet you think you're the smartest guy in the world, don't you?"

"No, I just know people, and I've gotten to know you pretty well. You're not mad at Clarence Fuller, you're mad at his brother for some reason."

"How dare you…"

"Stop, Rebekah. You are the one who brought all this up. You are the one who called me out."

"President Fuller has nothing to do with this conversation. What do you even know about him, anyway."

"Remember when I was sitting in your office and I told you he stopped in to see me about wanting to buy the McFerron farm?"

"Yes. And I told you if you sold their farm to him for pennies on the dollar without giving them a chance at it first, you and him both are going to hell."

"Well, that's not exactly what you said," Jack whispered. "You said I was going to hell if I didn't give McFerron's a chance to buy it. President Fuller is going to hell anyway as far as you are concerned."

"So what," I said, "he *is* going to hell. I'll guarantee you he is."

I heard Rosalyn in the living room. "Hell, hell, hell."

"*Rosalyn*! You're not supposed to say that," I yell.

"No, no, no." she says.

"That's right Rosalyn." I smile and shake my head. I hate having to clean up my act for my kid's sake.

"You're a good mom, Rebekah. Don't let anyone tell you any

different. I watch my ex-wife with Stacy and it makes me sad. I'm relieved when she drops Stacy off at my mother's. But she leaves her there for days on end, which is great for my daughter, but Camila never even bothers to call."

That's all he said. He tells me he really can't say anymore and I promise him it is our secret. The McDonald file and Molly will be our secret. He stands up, holds out his hands and pulls me out of the chair. Putting his arms around me, we hug long with understanding. I smell his cologne, the shower-fresh soap, his shampoo, and for a moment I feel a carnal hunger for him. It's a fleeting whim, a natural impulse from a brief amplification of hormones that quickly pass. I know his heart pines for my sister. And I know he will go back to California aching for someone he can never have. I feel bad for him. He deserves to have today with her. I pat his back, and give him a kiss on the cheek. It is lust I feel in my heat of passion, and that is a sin. It is love he feels in his heart for my married sister, and there's a big difference between the two.

"You know, Jack, you piss me off that you read me so well."

He smiles.

"So do you," he said. "Piss me off."

He helps move the oak table outside onto the lawn under the large elm. We pull it apart, put in two leaves and cover it with Molly's red-checkered table cloth with matching napkins. The early afternoon breeze teases the cloth, whipping at the corners and quivers the elm leaves overhead, their silvery coating of sap shimmering in the sunlight. Jack and I set the table, move chairs around and place a large pitcher of cold lemonade in the center.

While I am in the cellar getting extra folding chairs, Jack goes into Molly's garden and picks several sprigs of fresh mint, washes them under the water hydrant and puts them in the pitcher, with a small sprig in each glass he fills with ice. He picks a bowl of strawberries and cuts them up into the lemonade. It's like a scene from "The Great Gatsby" I think, him trying to pander to Molly as though he might win her over. I picture him turning to me, like Robert Redford to Sam Waterston and saying something like, "what do you think,

Old Sport? That makes a nice touch, now, don't you think?"

It is a nice touch, and is something Scott would never have thought of doing, not that it is Scott's fault. It's certainly the kind of thing Molly deserves. While I am sick in my heart, learning what Benny did to Molly, I know Jack is just as sick and angry, but handles these kinds of things so much better than me. Like the day before at the livestock sale, he looked for ways to heal, not ways to stew and flounder in the anguish. More than anything, I wonder how Scott is taking it. I hadn't garnered a clue from his behavior at the fair the day before. He seemed ambivalent, almost oblivious.

Scott pulls in with the boys riding in the back of the truck; Molly behind him with Lindsay in the front seat. What a great sight, to see this family coming home from church, happy, laughing, cajoling. I'm glad Jack is here. Where in San Jose can he see this? A brood of farm boys bailing from the back of a farm truck arriving home from church; a beautiful blond lady with her hair cascading down her back, climbing from an over-sized, rusted-out Gimmy four-wheel drive carrying a stack of music, her husband helping her to the ground, though it is unusual for Scott to be so attentive to Molly. Maybe her experience in Pocatello enlightened him after all, and I'm not giving him the credit he deserves.

A long table under the elm spreads out to feed the crew of hungry people coming together to feast on the high plateau of a wind-swept desert; a plateau that offered her own table-top to these Welsh people to live on, plant in, and on this Sunday, partake of the fruits of their labor. I don't bother telling Jack he is eating beef owned by his employer, the FDIC.

Everyone lavishes themselves with roast beef, mashed potatoes, salad; and Betsy's rendering of fresh corn on the cob and sliced beefy red tomatoes. I am sorry Betsy and Dad aren't here to help indulge in the feast they helped create. We all agree to save the pie for later.

It isn't far from the dining chairs to the cool grass. Jack and I stack plates and carry and them to the kitchen, leaving them to soak in the sink. We lean against the elm while Scott and Molly lay on a blanket on the grass, his arm around her, tight at first, then falling away as he falls into a deep sleep. She remains still, her eyes staring into space. The kids are in the barn playing, and Rosalyn is asleep next to Molly. Jack gently picks her up, takes her into the house, and puts her on Lindsay's bed to nap. I smile when he returns.

"You ride?" Jack asks me, like we'd never had this conversation.

"Some," I say. "Mostly when I used to go hunting with my ex-husband."

Molly raises her head. "Do you ride, Jack?"

"Since he was a baby," I say.

"Well, almost," Jack intervened, "My mother put me on a horse when I was two and left me there."

Molly sits up. "You want to go for a ride?"

"I'd love to," he answers almost too quickly. "You want to go, Rebekah?" Jack asks me.

"Naw, you two go. I'll wash the dishes. Maybe Scott wants to go."

"I think he just wants to rest," says Molly. "He's been on a horse every day this week moving cows to an allotment up Wood Canyon."

"Why don't you guys ride up to Indian Head Ridge," I tell Molly. "Jack can see the whole FDIC kingdom from up there. Maybe the boys and Lindsay want to ride up with you."

"Are you being snide?" Jack looks at me, his mouth turned down.

"I'm actually quite serious," I say.

"I'll go change my clothes," Molly says. She jumps up with excitement, running to the house in her stocking feet. This will be good for her, I think. It will be good for both of them.

"Rebekah," she yells back at me, "go out to the barn and see if the kids want to go."

When Molly returns, Jack jumps to his feet. I watch them walk to the barn together, Molly in her faded jeans, worn boots and beat-up straw cowboy hat. She is wearing one of Scott's long-sleeved shirts over her t-shirt; I'm guessing to hide her bruised arms just like the

256

long sleeve dress she wore to church this morning in the blistering heat. Jack walks with his hands in his pockets, reminding himself, I conjecture, he isn't allowed to touch her. But, he gently touches her back when he holds out the door for her, then quickly pulls it away. I hear Molly's thin, feathery voice say, "Anyone goin' with us?"

Jason releases the metal gate to the horse pasture and lets Bobby and Eric through, latching it again behind them. With halters hanging over their arms, they shake a bucket of oats, luring Molly's horse, who is an easy catch. Bobby's horse, Cobalt, is a cross thoroughbred. He is younger, and more difficult to halter, but he comes as soon as he is called. Cobalt is all black except for the white heart on his forehead. He was rescued at auction, just one step away from what we call "the glue factory".

Scott did not agree to the purchase of $105, but Molly bought the horse anyway. She broke her "divine intervention" for Bobby to ride.

Mom gave Lindsay her old sorrel horse, Cadre, when Mom got too sick to ride. Scott called her Cadaver to get Molly's goat, which it usually did. Molly would give Scott a punch in his arm and say "she's not a cadaver; she's still got lots of life left in her." Scott quit calling the horse that after Mom died.

Nobody rides Scott's horse, except Scott. He's a high-spirited gelding Scott bought as a colt from a rancher in Arbon Valley and broke himself. Nobody but Scott *can* ride him. He whinnies as the boys lead the three horses from the pasture, objecting to being left alone.

Lindsay decides to keep me company and help do dishes. Jason and Eric ride on Lindsay's horse, and Bobby rides behind his mother on Thomas. Jack rides Cobalt. I think Molly is glad the boys are going with her and Jack. It's obvious to me she wants to go riding in the hills.

The drainages in the Elkhorn Range are where she always goes to find herself when she feels lost. Today she will find Mom and Gracie in the canyon of quaking aspen and lodge pole pine; and perhaps she will find her innocent self, the woman who only knows goodness and purity; the one who scratched a heart into the skin of a quaking aspen tree with the initials SO/ML when she was sixteen years old. Someday she will find that tree and try to believe nothing inside her has changed through the years, except the layers growing around a solid core belief that "all is well, all is well".

I watch the horses canter down the lane, the boys' heads bobbing up and down while Jack and Molly both move with the gait of their horses. They are lovely to watch. Scott stirs, mumbles something, then turns over and goes back to sleep. I put my arm around Lindsey's small, thin shoulders and we walk into the house.

"Is that your new boyfriend, Aunt Rebekah?" she asks in a sweet, quiet voice.

"Naw," I say. "I think your mom wants him to be, but he's too nice for me."

Molly, Jack, and the boys are still gone two hours later when Scott wakes. Lindsay and I are playing a game of Chess. Rosalyn wants to pick up pieces and move them around, or put them on the floor, so I give up my place to Scott and play with Rosalyn on the floor.

"Where'd you say they went?" Scott asks after he lets Lindsay beat him.

"Check," she giggles.

"Ya got me, sis," he says. "Want to go again?"

"It's okay, Dad, I'm going to practice the piano."

"Good girl," Scott gives her a pat on her cheek.

I never did answer Scott's question.

Lindsay and Rosalyn sit on the piano bench together. Lindsay tries to teach Rosalyn to play "Mary had a Little Lamb," singing while she plays. Rosalyn wants to pound on the keys. Lindsay is patient, and soon she has Rosalyn playing with one finger, instead of both hands.

"That's impressive," I say to Scott.

"Takes after her mother," he says.

"Here, let's go get the table," I point to the elm tree where the table

258

still sits with the table cloth blown halfway off. The empty pitcher with strawberries and mint leaves floating in melting ice keep it from blowing away.

"He's really a great guy, Rebekah," Scott says.

"Who?"

"Jack."

"I know he is."

"No, I really mean it. I know him better than you think I do."

"Scott. I've been married twice. The first one died from driving drunk and rolling his truck, and the second one died inside, then took it out on me and my kids because of a war we had no business fighting. Do you really think I'm interested in trying this again?"

"I don't even think he drinks, Rebekah."

I shake my head. Why does he think drinking is the problem? It's the symptom, not the problem." Then I feel bad for chastising Scott. "Honest, Scott, that's not the point. I don't think I'm suited to marriage, and it sure isn't suited to me. I'm just going to give it a rest for a while." I pull on my end of the table while he tugs on his. He lifts out the heavy oak table extensions and leans them against the tree, and we push the table together in a perfect circle.

"But, if I were to start looking, he'd be a good choice," I confess. "He's my friend, Scott. I do consider him my good friend and I hope that never changes. You're right. He's a good guy." And for some reason I add, "and so are you." Then wish I hadn't.

"What's that supposed to mean?" he asks.

"That I consider you my friend too, I guess. I don't know. You and Jack are both good guys."

Scott holds the screen door open with his hip and we finagle the table into the house. We each take a table leaf and put them back under their bed. I put the large table cloth and matching napkins in the washing machine. Scott moves all the chairs back inside and puts the extra folding chairs back down in the cellar beneath the house, more of a dirt cave than a basement.

"Ah, it's nice and cool down there," he says as he emerges out of the dark, steep stairway. The clock in the living room chimes four times.

"Did you tell me where they went?"

"Up to Indian Head Peak."

"What time did they go?"

"About one thirty."

Scott looks up the lane. "They won't be back for another hour." He's made that ride enough times to know how long it takes.

We both sit at the table in silence and I want to ask him about what happened Tuesday night, but I promised Jack it would be our secret, so I don't.

"How are Lance and Melanie doing?" I ask. "I meant to ask Molly if we should have them over today, and then forgot. Were they at church?"

"Yah. I went over and helped Lance milk and feed cows this morning and he said he couldn't make it to Priesthood meeting but he brought Melanie and the kids to sacrament meeting. It's just gonna take some time. Maybe havin' the new baby will help."

"I suppose Dylan's happy about being able to keep his lamb."

"He is, but not as happy as Mel. She told me she prepared him to give it up. When I drove in with those two lambs yesterday, she was laughin' and cryin' at the same time."

"Well, I better talk to Dylan about putting together some kind of plan for breeding those ewes next year and starting his flock."

"See, Rebekah, that's what I'm talkin' about. That was really nice of Jack to do that for Dylan. I'm sure he has no intention of starting a livestock operation in Malad, Idaho. For a while I thought he was in cahoots with Leon Fuller."

"President Fuller?"

"Molly told me he is comin' in almost every day to see Jack or that other FDIC guy."

I don't ask Scott who the 'other guy' is. I know. And I know Scott knows his name, but refuses to say it, which is fine. I already decide I'm not going there.

"Did Molly say whose places he is trying to buy?"

"I'm not supposed to say."

"Come on, Scott. I'm not going to say anything. Besides, I'll almost bet when Jack leaves on Wednesday, Fullers are going to be done with Molly anyway, and let her go."

I think I am telling him this because I know there will be repercussions for my little encounter with Clarence. I am hoping Scott won't bring it up; I don't want to talk about the reason I bought Bobby's lamb for such an outrageous price.

"I think Molly's already prepared to be let go," Scott says. "She stayed on mostly for the health insurance. We talked about it," Scott says, like it was something married people don't usually talk about. "I haven't told her yet, but two weeks ago, I put my application into Morton Thiokol."

I am shocked, and he sees the surprised look in my face. It's the one thing I can never do very well; hide my feelings from my face.

"It's time for me to accept the fact this ranch is never going to support two families and I can't ask my wife to subsidize it any longer. It was okay so long as she was working for your dad, and she loved going in and working every day." Scott wipes at a water spot on the dark stained wood of the table top as though he can polish it out with his hand.

"But she's not happy working for Fullers. Besides, everything's changed."

"What's changed?"

Scott stutters. "I mean, Fullers taking over, and well, other stuff."

"You heard anything from Thiokol yet?"

"Yea," he says real slow. "I go in for an interview next week."

"That's great, Scott."

"I guess. It'll be different, that's for sure."

"Well, if Molly wants, she can just quit and I'll pay her to watch Rosalyn. Or she could come in and work with me and Kenny. We've got lots of work she could help us with."

I decide not to press Scott about whose farms Fuller is trying to buy. Jack already told me about a few of them, and the more I know, the more it feeds the ugly, hungry, monster inside me.

At four-thirty I hear the riders coming down the lane. I pat Scott on the hand. "Everything's going to be okay, Scott. It's going to be fine. You're going to be fine. And good luck next week. I hope the job works out. You'll be good at whatever they ask you to do."

"Well," he says, "I hope it makes me feel like a man again. Taking care of my family like I should."

"Scott. You have always taken care of your family." I didn't tell him the rest of what I want to—that he should have been paying more attention to the financial reality instead of making Molly handle it all.

"I spose," he says, "but some days are harder than others. I just thank my Heavenly Father my wife loves to play music. It is such a blessing to me. When times get overbearing and I walk up that back walk and hear her playing the piano—like the other night I had a hard day when the combine broke down; then I went over and milked cows for Lance, and I thought I couldn't take another step. As soon as I step out of the pickup, I hear "I Know My Redeemer Lives," through the open windows and I stood there and soaked in the comfort. All my burdens just seemed to lift. I don't know what I'd do without her music."

"Mom, mom," Eric comes busting through the back door yelling. "Jason killed a rattle snake!"

"What?"

"Yea, up Secret Canyon. It was huge. We got the tail an' it's got six rattles on it."

I look at Scott. "Well, it never ends," I say. "Let's go see what happened."

Chapter Twenty-Eight: Rebekah

On Tuesday morning I drop Rosalyn off to stay with Esther who is canning the rainbow and brown trout she, Kenny, and Dad caught in Island Park.

"Did you go into the Park?" I ask, meaning Yellowstone Park.

"No, we just camped down at Last Chance and fished the South Fork. Fantastic fly fishing. Dad tied new dry flies last week. They were great."

"You guys missed church then?"

"No, they've got a service at Mack's Inn. We went to the morning service and then headed for home."

"How was the livestock sale?" Esther asks while she screws on the cap and sets the Mason jars into the rack, then lifts the rack into the hot water. She twists the pressure cooker lid into place, increasing the heat and looks at me, still waiting for an answer.

"Well, I don't dare tell Kenny what happened. I got a bidder card for Sorenson Law Office and bought Bobby's lamb."

"I actually think he knows," Esther says in a whisper as she leans to check the pressure gauge.

"Does he know what I paid for it?" I pick up a slice of bread and chews on it nervously, glancing at her face.

"Well," her tiny voice makes a long influx, "I'll let you talk to him. He's at the office."

"Is he mad?"

"Not about the money. But I should warn you that he's not happy."

"Oh, oh."

I hug Esther, "Love you, sis. I'll be back at 5 o'clock to pick up Rosalyn."

I park along Main Street in my usual spot, but walk down the alley and let myself in the back door. I go to my office and quietly shut the door. I pull out Sven's file and write a response to the letter I received from San Jose FDIC committee, sign it Kenneth Sorenson, P.A., printed it out, and set it on top of Sven's file. I pull out another file and start revising the cash flow when Kenny knocks, then opens the door. I look up. His tall lanky body seems more like a shadow than his real self. The dark moves into his brow and eyes, and for all the years I have known him, I have no idea until now how long his face can be when he isn't smiling.

I hold out Sven's file with the letter as though it's a peace offering. He takes it without looking at it, sits across from me, and looks me square in the eye.

"Who told you?" I ask.

"Clarence called me." He is quiet. So am I. Finally he says, "Did you really say that to him, Rebekah?"

I wasn't sure what Clarence thought I said and I thought if it wasn't as bad as what I did say, I wasn't going to admit it. But I don't have the courage to ask Kenny. Besides, I have every reason in the world to say what I did. I wonder why Kenny can't understand. But I'm not going to lie to him.

"Why would you call him a sorry son-of-a-bitch? Especially after he bought your son's lamb?" I can't say a word. "You don't just represent the Helland family, Rebekah, you represent this office. Not just my law office, it's *our* law office. It's just so unprofessional, Rebekah, not to mention childish, out of control behavior."

Then he asks the worst question of all.

"Was it worth it?"

I look down, and while I don't lie, I change the subject.

"Do you want me to apologize to him? If you do, I will."

Kenny doesn't answer my question. He looks me straight in the eye and asks me again, more stern than before.

"I want to know if you think it was worth it?"

"What? What I said to him after he bought Jason's lamb? Or me buying Bobby's lamb?"

"Both,"

"I guess that depends," I say.

"On what?"

I look at Kenny and put my hands up into a time-out signal. "I need a minute to think."

"Oh Lord," Kenny looks up at the ceiling, "You have answered my prayers. Rebekah is taking a time out to think before she talks."

I start to laugh. I start slow with a chuckle, and keep on laughing. I lean over, lay my head on my arm, and laugh so hard I start to cry. When I catch my breath, wiping away my tears, I look up and ask Kenny if he is going to fire me.

"Of course I'm not going to fire you," he says, pulling out a tissue from the box on my desk.

"Then, yes, Kenny," I say, looking into his eyes, "it was worth it."

"What if Clarence fires Molly."

"He's going to do that anyway."

"What makes you think that?"

"I've always known that. And Scott told me yesterday he and Molly are expecting it will happen. I told her last May that Clarence would take what he wanted from her, and when he didn't need her any longer, he'd throw her out the door. I couldn't stand the thought of him putting two photos on the wall with Lars Helland's daughters and grandsons, like some kind of trophy."

When my tears change from laughter to pain and anger, I can't believe the pent-up emotion escaping out of me. And it isn't Clarence Fuller, or his arrogant brother, Leon Fuller. It's Molly I'm crying for. I want to tell Kenny so badly I can't bear it. I know he'd understand if I told him. But I promised Jack I wouldn't say anything. I also know without client privilege, he is bound by law to do certain things. I'm not sure what they are, or what he might be inclined to do if he knows.

"I'm sorry, Kenny. I'm sorry I shamed our office. But I'm not sorry for saying it. And I'm not sorry I bought Bobby's lamb to keep Clarence from getting it."

"Well," he says, "that's exactly what I'm going to tell Clarence."

"Okay then," I say. "I'll get back to work." I am proud of the honesty he models, yet I wonder if he will say it to Clarence exactly the way I said it to him.

"You are a tough one, Rebekah," he says as he picks up Sven's file and leaves. I spend time in the bathroom with cold paper towels against my eyes to get the swelling down. It takes me until noon to finish the cash flow report I have struggled with since last week. I stop at the bank to get Molly for lunch. Sarah Evans tells me Molly is meeting with Mr. Fuller.

"Will you tell her I'm having lunch with Grandpa? Tell her to come over when she comes out."

"I will, Rebekah," she says.

Fifteen minutes later, Molly comes through Grandpa's back door. Grandpa doesn't look up from his beef stew. He just says, "Fuller give you the pink slip?"

"What's a pink slip?"

"The door. Canned. Fired." He chews on the meat in small chomps with his front teeth, trying to break it up.

"He said he needs to downsize. He said now that FDIC is leaving he only needs two secretaries."

"Good, he can pay you unemployment," Grandpa says.

"What's unemployment?" Molly asks.

"I'll tell you later," I say to Molly.

"The bastard!" Grandpa mutters. Molly's eyes grow wide when he says it, but I love it, and I give Grandpa a smile of approval.

"It's okay, Grandpa. I was thinking about quitting anyway," Molly tells him.

"How did you get that bruise on your cheek?" he asks.

Molly looks at me like she can't explain it again. Everyone is asking.

266

People are joking about Scott being mean to her. She is mostly tired, I know, of telling the lie, more than anything else.

"She forgot to duck, Grandpa," I say. "Some kid loading the cutter bar into the pickup turned around and wacked her in the face."

Molly looks at me, surprised. She knows I just embellished her story and it seems to unsettle her.

I change the subject. "I'll pay you to watch Rosalyn for me?"

"That would be great."

"Or maybe you could come in and help me and Kenny."

"I think I'm going to start teaching piano lessons," she says.

"I don't know why you stayed on working for that…"

I break in. "For the insurance, Grandpa. She stayed on for the health insurance."

"Oh." Is all he says.

Chapter Twenty-Nine: Jack

I leave Malad and the Land of Dragons on the second Wednesday of August, 1986. I hire boys the same age as Will, some a few years younger, to carry boxes from the second story of the bank into a U-Haul truck. I decide to drive the files to California myself.

I study the map and talk to a couple of ranchers at the café. They tell me if I want to brave it, I can head west from Snowville, down through Montello, Nevada; but if I get lost, no one will ever find me. They warn me I may end up living the rest of my life out there in a polygamist colony. I am tempted to go that way just to have a look.

Will agrees to ride with me to keep me company, so long as I agree to take highways and interstates. The other two accountants take the two rental cars back to Salt Lake and fly home. It is eleven-thirty when the truck is finally loaded and ready to go.

"Hey, Will, run up to my motel and ask Norma Howell if she wants to come have lunch with us. I'll go see if Molly and Rebekah want to join us. "

"Sure, boss."

"I'm not your boss," I say. "But go do it anyway."

I move Will's suitcase and my leather travel bag and clothes bag from the front seat to the back, pull down the back metal rolling door, and lock the cargo with a heavy paddle lock I purchased from the U-Haul company. Nice way to make a little more profit, I think. I bought the biggest one they had—guaranteed to resist cutters and hackers. "Just don't lose that key," the bulky man with a day-old beard and stained tan uniform said, lifting and resetting his cap twice for good measure. "You have to get the company to come out and take the truck apart with a cuttin' torch if you lose that key." I double check my pocket before sliding the hasp of the paddle-lock into the hole, letting the lock engage with a click.

Will jogs up the street toward the Village Inn. I look toward the window where Molly's grandfather usually sits while observing the life that flows in and out of his old bank, but he is gone. Perhaps he's eating lunch early.

I open the same front door I entered fourteen weeks earlier. I search for Molly. Her desk is cleared off. I ask Sarah Evans if she knows where Molly is. She looks at me with wide eyes, the same way Molly looked at us the afternoon of May 11; stunned, unsure of what to say, or not say. She shakes her head, looking like she is about to cry.

"Molly doesn't work here anymore."

"Why?" I asked.

"Mr. Fuller let her go. Said since you were leavin' he didn't need her any longer."

"Thanks Sarah," I say to her. "We're taking off. I just came in to say 'goodbye'.

"K. Well, bye then," the girl who looks hardly a day over 18 replies. She stands and timidly holds out her hand. I take hold and shake, trying not to scare her. I give her a smile, and leave.

I walk to the Sorenson law office, next to Elsie's café, and the door is locked. I peer through the window. No one is at the front desk.

In the café, Vickie Thompson is wiping off the lunch counter.

"Have you seen Kenny or Rebekah around today?"

"Nope. I think Kenny's in court today. Rebekah came in this morning, but left about half hour ago in her truck headin' toward St. John."

Norma arrives in her old, red, sixty-eight Ford Galaxy with the scaling black vinyl roof. Will is in the front seat with her. He opens her door for her and they walk across the street. Norma sits next to me, across from Will, in the booth I occupied nearly every day for the past hundred days. The café is mostly empty.

"Where's everybody today?" I ask Vickie.

"Finishing up harvest," she says, smiling at me. "This week's likely gonna be the last of it, long as it don't rain." Vickie holds up her order pad and I assume the next thing she's going to ask is "What can I git cha? But she says, "these guys are sure anxious to get some money. Nobody's been paid this summer. Fertilizer guys, seed guys, Ballard's Oil, hired help, grocery store, not nobody."

I don't tell her FDIC is also on the list; anything left over is our money. There have been a lot of legal arguments about it. If we didn't take a lien on the 86 crop, is it ours, or someone else's? Lots of local distributors and business people filed against this year's crops. Kenny saw to it. Regardless, it would be a process beyond my job description to follow the money trail, making sure the last drops of what is left come to us, rather than to the farmer to feed his family, or keep the electricity on.

Norma orders a chicken fried steak. Will orders a double cheeseburger and fries. I order my favorite Rueben sandwich, half on my plate and half in a white paper bag to take with me to eat on the road, though I know by nightfall we will likely want to stop somewhere in Nevada and eat. I only think of getting home to Stacy, making sure she's not anywhere near Benny Schnabel.

As we finish lunch, I realize I don't have a present to take home to Stacy. "Say, Norma, would you go to the Merc with me and help me pick out some boots and jeans for my little girl before I go?"

"Sure, Jack. That'd be a nice thing to buy her and you can leave just a little more of your money here in our community." She laughs.

We finish our shopping. I hug Norma when I tell her goodbye. I unlock the back of the truck. I put the brown satchel with Stacy's new blue jeans and shirt, tied with white string, along with the cowboy boot box, also tied with white string, into the back. I pull down the rolling door, and bolt it shut again. I look up and down the street. I decide it's best to leave without saying goodbye. Our horse ride on Sunday to Indian Head Ridge will be all I have to remember her by, but it is enough.

***

After sundown, the semi-truck lights come at me like mortar shells. If nothing else, it keeps me alert. Between Lovelock and Reno, Nevada, I open my window and let the cold nighttime desert air hit my face. Will is asleep, his head bouncing off the passenger window as the shocks of the truck jolt on every frost-heave and heat track in the asphalt. With the gas pedal pressed against the floor, I push it past 65 MPH, even though the speed limit posted on the side of the truck is 55 MPH. I am surprised at the number of rules and laws I am suddenly breaking. My comportment of low-risk behavior has suddenly gone rogue.

In that long night across Nevada, I make up my mind I'll work through these files and give the people in Malad as good of a chance as anyone else to buy their notes and stay on their farms. I'll personally carry the Olson file to committee with a write-up on what happened. I'll recommend they cancel Olson's debt in exchange for an agreement with Molly to not press charges against FDIC. I don't think about how I will handle the legal aspect, which is very different than the passion of being there, dragging Benny off her beaten and bruised body. It is somewhere out on that long drive across the Nevada desert I suddenly realize I don't know where the Olson file is.

"*Will? Will? Will!*" I hit him in the arm.

"What? What Jack? What's wrong?

"Will, where's Olson's file? After Benny gave it to you, what did you do with it?"

Will moans, still not completely awake. He rubs his hair, and then his eyes.

"Um. Let me think." He is quiet, still trying to get his mind awake. "Let's see, he came back in and asked me for it before we left for Pocatello."

"Did he have it with him when you guys left for Pocatello?"

"I don't know. I didn't see it. But he had his brief case with him."

"Did we pack it? Is it in the truck?"

"I don't remember, Jack. I just packed everything up, but I didn't specifically look for it."

"Did you see it?"

"No. But I guess I thought he'd given it to the accountants."

"Shit."

"What?"

"Benny had it with him. I bet he took it back to California. That's not good, Will."

As we ascend out of Reno into the high Sierra Mountains it's too late. Benny had already created his story, a fantasy he concocted by the next morning when he left Pocatello, and he sold it hook, line and sinker.

On the Wednesday I loaded up and drove the U-Haul truck out of the bank parking lot in Malad, Benny had already made himself look like a hero. He leveraged the Olson's by personally negotiating a written offer from Leon Fuller to buy the Olson ranch. By the time I drove the U-Haul truck into the parking lot of the Federal Deposit Insurance Office in San Jose at 7 o'clock Thursday morning, a week and a day after I sent Benny home, he already won the battle. He finished destroying Molly Olson, and sunk my ship in the process. While I was swooning over her as she rode on her Paint horse on Indian Head Ridge above Malad, Benny was in California, making fools out of both of us.

Will's mother and my mother are waiting in the parking lot to retrieve two exhausted travelers. We take our travel bags and Stacy's gifts from the back of the truck, lock it back up, and my mother drives me home to shower and get my car. By 10 o'clock I am back, sitting in Sam's office.

"What did Benny tell you?" I ask Sam who is walking in circles around the room until I ask him if he will please sit down.

"He said he got a little drunk and got into it with you. Said he took a swipe at you, and you ducked. He said you got mad, fired him and sent him home."

"I wish it would have been that way, Sam," I say.

"Well, he's already signed a disciplinary agreement and the committee approved it."

"Sam, that is not what he did. I didn't call you and tell you because I knew I'd be back. I told Benny not to come in."

"So, what'd he do?"

"He raped Molly Olson, or at least he tried to."

"What the hell are you talking about?" Sam is back on his feet.

"He told her he was foreclosing on her unless she came to Pocatello to negotiate a settlement."

Sam stared at me.

"He had their file with him didn't he?"

"Yes."

"Why do you think that is the only file he carried home with him?"

"I don't know."

"Molly Olson's father-in-law told her husband, Scott…" I stop. There is no way I am going to be able to tell him this story.

"Oh dear god, Sam. I don't even know how to cover everything. I'm just going to write it up and file it. But I will tell you this: Scott Olson and I pulled him off her after he attacked her, and bloodied her up."

"Did she file charges?"

"No. She begged us not to call the police. She has kids. Malad's a small town. She's a good Mormon woman. Molly Olson had no idea what Benny was baiting her into. Hell, Sam, you know Benny. You know he does this kind of thing every chance he gets."

"Jack, this is a big problem."

I am quiet and stare out the window.

"I suppose you have the McDonald file with you," Sam finally says.

I look at him, and I lied. "I'm sure it's in the truck," I tell him. "Why?"

"Benny said there are some issues with that case we need to pay attention to."

"I called you on that one, Sam. The note's been paid off."

"Well, committee's still got to act on it. We'll look at it when we get the truck unloaded and get the files organized."

274

"So what are you doing with Olson's file?"

"Well, if we don't take Fuller's offer, it's going to foreclosure. That's what the committee ruled, Jack. Benny's personally handling it."

And that's what I mean about dealing with guys like Benny. It happened exactly the way I thought it would somewhere out there in the middle of the night as I drove across Nevada. He not only convinced Sam and the committee in San Jose of his lies, but convinced himself all his lies are true.

I stand and stare at Sam. I am tired. I've been up for forty-eight hours, loaded the truck and drove all night. I should have gone home and slept before I said or did anything I'd regret, but I didn't.

"Sam, you and I have worked together for nearly eleven years. You have fielded more complaints about Benny's abuse and misbehaviors than anyone on this team. He bullied the chairman of the board at the Malad bank until Niles took his own life. He beat and raped Molly Olson. You can ignore it if you want, but I swear to God, if you get a law suit filed against you, Sam, I'm plaintiff's witness, not yours."

I walk out with the keys to the U-Haul in my pocket. In my office, I look up rendering plants in the yellow pages. I grab the plastic garbage sack from my waste basket and stuff it in my pocket.

From the San Jose FDIC office, I drive to an animal shelter on the edge of town. There are three fresh cat carcasses in the rendering bucket. I put one in a plastic garbage bag, put it in my trunk and drive back to the parking lot. I unlock the back of the truck, throw the dead cat inside, lay the keys inside the back of the truck, and pull down the roll-up door. I put the "fool-proof" lock back in place, thinking about what the man said when he sold it to me. I think about what a fool I'd been. I listen as the hasp clicks into place. I climb into my car, drive home and sleep for the next twenty-four hours before going to spend the rest of the week with my daughter.

On Monday, I meet with my attorney. I have him write a full disclosure to FDIC and have it served. In the affidavit it states, in part, that I turned the truck keys over to Benny Schnabel, since he was second in command on the Malad bank closure, and I left him in charge of the files.

I sign the affidavit laying out the entire events of the fourteen weeks in Malad. I wrote them in detail from the beginning to the end, and included every element, except one. I did not say in the affidavit I buried the McDonald file in Grace Marie McDonald's grave. I say only that I offered the settlement to Sam, and he agreed to accept it. The money was deposited against that account, and I marked the note "paid in full".

The second legal action I take is filing for full custody of Stacy. I ask my father if there is a position open at his bank. He said there has always been a job there for me, and wondered why it took me so long to ask.

I live in my own agony and my own peace every day. I left part of my heart in Malad, and the rest is here in San Jose with my daughter and my parents. I enroll Stacy in pre-school the first of September, and by mid-September Camila is silent. I suspect it has a lot to do with Benny's influence, or she is out on a job and hasn't been served. I did not receive a response from FDIC, either.

I drop Stacy off at pre-school every morning at 8:30 before going to work at the bank, and Mom picks her up at noon. She keeps her until I pick her up at five. Mom, Dad, and I eat dinner together, then Stacy and I spend the evening together at home. It's a relief, to have her here with me; and to be home for more than three days at a time.

I don't hear from Rebekah, but I hadn't expected to. I didn't give anyone my home phone number. I know she was corresponding with committee chairs in San Jose on loan settlement agreements before I left Malad, so she likely knows by now I resigned. My home telephone and address are unlisted for obvious reasons.

In the evenings, I lay the ash-gray Steiff teddy bear in Stacy's arms while I brush out her hair, then braid it to keep it from tangling while she sleeps. My mother showed me, and then made me practice the braid over, and over, until I got it right. "I know it's not a man thing, but you need to learn it," she said to me with a wink. Then she would take the band off, and make me do it again.

I read a chapter out-loud from one of Stacy's favorite Beatrice Potter books, saving our place for the next night. I turn on the CD player to let soft blues lull her to sleep. I kiss her goodnight and go to the pool, leaving her bedroom window open, listening in case she calls for me. I feel the rhythm of the music, as much as I hear it, while I swim slow laps up and down the pool. Relaxed, I sit on the edge staring into the rippling water, backlit with lights shining from the bottom of the pool.

It's not healthy to reflect on things from the past, I keep telling myself. I know I should call Rebekah, but what will I say? That I'd been stupid enough to let Benny get the upper hand? Worse yet, I have no idea what I can possibly say to Molly. I completely failed her. I spoke in the passion of the moment. I had no authority to make the promise I made to her.

In the larger scheme of things, Benny always had more power than me. He knows how the system works, while I operate on the premises that right prevails. It is best to move on, and put it all behind me. I lay back in my lounge-chair and look at the sky. I try to see the stars I saw at night in Malad; sharp, and crisp, and brilliant; but they are diluted by the millions of lights around me. I can hardly make them out, confusing the light of an airplane with what I think is a star.

I fall asleep, waking when the music stops. This is the worst time of day. Too much time to think. Too much time to remember what she looks like; smiling at me from the back of her Paint horse as she talks, and points, and shows me her world. How my heart aches for this woman I can never have.

Chapter Thirty: Rebekah

Scott started work at Morton Thiokol the week after Jack left. He came to me and told me personally, but he said the health insurance wasn't going to cover Molly's pre-existing conditions, which means it doesn't cover her diabetes. I tell him if he can manage to find a little money, I'll take some funds out of our mother's trust, but we need to find her a different doctor. Molly seems healthier since she's been home, away from the constant pressure of trying to prove to Clarence Fuller the Helland family is at least as competent as he is, if not more. She cans the beans and tomatoes from her garden. She drives to Brigham City with Esther and picks six bushels of peaches, canning two for herself, one for me, one for Esther, and two for Melanie.

Dad asks Betsy to help him find Molly a new doctor. Betsy calls some friends in Salt Lake and finds a doctor at University of Utah Medical clinic who is reportedly world-renown in Type I Diabetes research. Dad makes an appointment and he and Betsy take Molly down for an office visit. They changed her diet, have her eat at precise intervals, and despite her small frame, she has to exercise every morning. It all seems to be have a positive effect on her.

Melanie and Lance have a new baby girl the fifteenth of September; seven pounds and two ounces. Her spirit is everything we all hunger for; so much life in such a tiny body. She possesses a soul much different than her sister who just left us. She seems to be an old soul, one who has been through many bodies and different forms of life. Of course, I don't say this to Melanie. I just think it as I hold the child who stares back at me with an energy of encompassing knowledge and wisdom beyond explanation.

Molly stays with Melanie while she's in the hospital during labor, and spends the next week helping Melanie at home. I take Jason over to the McDonalds before and after school to help Dylan feed the bottle calves, and hay the heifers. I take my minivan back from Melanie and bus kids around. Esther keeps Rosalyn while I take all the boys, Erica, and Lindsay out to Daniels to the dairy after school.

After dinner, Molly drives Jason home and she goes home to fix dinner for Scott. Both Molly and Mel seem to be rejuvenated by the new life of this baby girl Melanie names Lillian Grace. Lillian, after Melanie's mother and, well, you know. There is a lot of talk about the wisdom of naming the new baby after the one who just died, but Melanie knows her own mind and has a strong resolve; a trait I admire her for. Whatever her reason, I respect it. We all call the new baby Lil Grace, something Dylan started.

By the end of September, Molly falls into an unexplained slump and spends more time in bed than she does out of bed. Esther is watching Rosalyn again and takes her to Molly's house, spending most of the day caring for both of them. Bishop Williams called someone else to play the music at church. It is so different, according to Kenny and Esther. Esther says it is as though someone let the air out of the organ pipes. "Absolutely no one breathes life into those old brass pipes the way Molly does," someone said to me at the grocery store.

Scott takes their kids, and mine, to church the next two Sundays, while Molly stays home. I drive over and cook dinner for them. Dad and Betsy come after church with Kenny and Esther, and we move the table into the living room, adding folding chairs and use the piano bench for the kids. All these people rally around her, but nothing seems to help.

The second Sunday morning in October I drive to the cemetery, coffee cup in hand, stopping at the upper pasture to check the water trough. I break a thin crust of ice forming on top. I figure six more weeks and I'll have to bring the ewes back to the corrals at the house.

It's been a year since I left Andy. A year ago, I could not possibly predict how the events over the next twelve months would change our lives.

A hard frost sends a shock of cold through the quaking aspen, turning them a heart-gripping gold. Fall always manifests itself in the most brilliant colors, but last such a short time. In those few days between green and gray, I embrace the beauty, and then let go, savoring the memory. The glimpse of splendor and energy God shares so briefly, reminds me there will be life after death, and spring will come again. Like Gracie, I think. So powerful, so young, giving me joy every day I interacted with her, impacting me with the same kind joy the fall season gives me. I kiss the palm of my hand, bend over and touch her grave as I walk by, whispering, "Good morning, princess. You have a beautiful baby sister, but you likely know that. You picked out a good one for us." The recently set granite stone is a milky-white monument with a lamb engraved above her name. Melanie's mother and sister pitched in to help pay for it.

I stop at my mother's grave and take deep, focused, breaths. "Help me Mom. Help me know what to do to help her." The tears sting my cheeks as they fall.

I scan the panorama of the valley and my eyes pause on the mountains. The heat of the morning sun is gathering warmth when it hits me. Mom is standing next to me. "Take her to the mountains," she is saying. "Saddle up the horses, and go to the hills." It could not have been any more clear. I say out loud, "Ok, Mom. I hear you. I'll do it. I'll do it."

Back at the house, I get the kids ready for church. Dad takes them with him. Esther likes to take Rosalyn to the children's Sunday School, and she likes to go. I tell Dad I need to spend the morning with Molly. He acts like I've have found a new excuse not to go to church with him, but he nods his head in agreement.

When I get to Molly's house, she is alone, playing the piano. I slide onto the bench next to her and put my arm around her. As she lifts her arms to hug me, her shirt rises above her waist and I touch the bare skin of her back. I immediately wonder why she isn't wearing her temple garments.

I'm sure she notices the shock on my face. I clear my throat. "Hey, Mol, if I take the day off tomorrow, you want to take the horses up the canyon?"

"I s'pose we could do that," she says. "I was thinking of going up and moving the cows down next week. Scott is off work on Saturday and Sunday but they are supposed to come off the BLM allotment before Friday, or we'll get fined. I just didn't know if I could do it by myself." She talks slower than normal, like everything inside her is sludge. She smiles at me, but there is no light in her eyes. There is no doubt in my mind she is suffering from a severe case of depression; I just don't know why. I am pretty sure it's connected to the incident in Pocatello. I just don't know how to fix it.

"Tell you what," I say. "Let's call Mel and have her go with us. The three of us will go get those cows. Tomorrow."

"What about Lil Grace?"

"Esther can take her. If we call Mel today, she can pump enough milk to get Lil Grace through the day. Come on, Mol, it's a great idea. I'll call Easterday's and have two trucks at the corrals by four tomorrow afternoon to load up the cows."

"You are somthin' Rebekah. You just think you can do any doggone thing you put your mind to."

"Well, I can." I say, "But this isn't my idea."

"Really? Well whose idea is it then?"

"Mom's."

"Oh. And she told you to come get me and go round up the cows?"

"No. She told me to load up the horses and take you to the hills. I just figured we might as well round up the cows while we're up there."

Molly releases a deep, warm laugh, slowly settling to a brooding, quiet smile. I think it's the first time it occurs to her that Mom is here. Everywhere. She has always been here and there is nothing Mom doesn't know about her. She is not now, nor has she ever been alone. Mom knows they are losing the ranch. She knows about the incident with Benny, about losing her job at the bank; and she knows the reason the music is silent. She knows why Molly stopped going to church.

"Let's go," Molly finally says. "Soon as church is out, I'll call Mel. We all need to go."

"Okay," I say. "I'll get the food packed. I'll be here at five tomorrow morning and we can load the horses.

"If we can take your truck, we can use my horse trailer. Scott needs our truck to get to work." I watch her face brighten as she starts thinking through our scheme.

"No problem," I say. "I'm sure my truck tow fits your trailer hitch. If not, we'll take the one off your truck before Scott leaves tomorrow."

"We can pick up Mel on our way in the morning," Molly says as she looks out the kitchen window, first peering right, then left. I'm not sure who or what she is looking for. Answers, maybe. "I'm sure Lance can take care of Lil Grace 'til Esther gets there," she says.

I feel the slightest glimmer of warmth, like an ember still glowing inside a dirt-smothered campfire. I hug her for a long, long time.

CHAPTER TWENTY-NINE—REBEKAH

The sky breaks gray the next morning, much like the October morning I drove away from Lava Hot Springs, fleeing from my second failed marriage. On this morning, I am on a different journey. A journey to find the chokehold smothering my sister's soul, and repair, if I can, whatever is broken inside her. It is something I am more passionate about than pruning the strangling vines bunging my own existence.

The mercury dips to fifteen degrees before sunrise, and is up to about twenty-five when I pull into Molly's yard, according to the old Malad Mill and Feed metal thermometer on the side of her barn.

Dust roils down the road as I pull in. I assume it's Scott leaving for Thiokol. The food is packed in a way we can easily load it into saddle bags. I have three of Dad's orange hunting jackets along with his 240 Remington inside the leather scabbard and an extra canteen of water.

Dad asks again if he can go and I tell him Mom said nothing about taking him along, so the answer is "no". I remind him I need him to get the boys on the school bus and watch Rosalyn since Esther will have her hands full with Lil Grace. I ask him to be sure the sheep are watered. I remind him he has plenty to do around the place. I know he desperately wants to be with us, high on the ridge, maybe look for a deer. He bought his tag from Idaho Fish and Game, but hasn't been hunting yet.

"Where's Bobby and Lindsay this morning?" he asks before I leave.

"They spent the night with Scott's Mom and Dad. They'll get on the bus there."

"Well okay. Did you get a hold of Easterday's?"

"Yes, Dad." I sound a bit snarky, almost like I am seventeen again. He is only trying to help. I scold myself and let my voice mellow. "They said they'll have the trucks at the corrals by four." I give him a kiss on his cheek.

"I guess I've got to let you girls prove you can do this by yourself."

"We're not trying to prove anything, Dad. Of course we can do it. That isn't the point. And if we miss a few cows, you and Kenny can go up with Scott on Saturday and ferret them out while you look for your deer."

"Ah, good idea." He is finally satisfied he hasn't been left out.

"Come on Freddy," I call to our border collie. "You get to go herd cows today." His tongue is hanging out as he jumps into the truck bed.

Scott saddled up three horses, loading them in the trailer before he left for work. All we need to do is hitch up. He left his towing ball on the trailer hitch, but the one I have works. By five-thirty Molly and I are ready to head to Daniels. Molly looks marvelous in the old straw hat she wore when she took Jack riding. She has on her Carhartt coat and we both put on our long-legged wool underwear. Most of all, she is wearing a beautiful smile on her face.

"Thanks for doing this, Rebekah,"

"I'm happy you agreed to go, Mol. I sure wish I could figure these things out on my own without Mom having to tell me." I let down the tailgate for Molly's Blue Heeler to join Freddy.

"But isn't it nice you are the one who gets to communicate with her."

I must have twisted my face.

"I talk to her all the time, Rebekah. But she doesn't talk to me the way she talks to you. I ask her what I should do, how to fix things, but it's always quiet. Then you come along and tell me Mom wants you to take me to the canyon. Why does she talk to you, and not to me."

"I don't always listen to her, Molly. Sometimes I stand by her grave and I talk and talk without listening. But yesterday morning, I knew she was telling me to be quiet and listen to her—to look around, to let the answers come from the mother of all life. That's when it hit me I knew that moment this is what we need to do."

When we pull into McDonalds yard, the amped up yard light is still shining as the day breaks over the east hills. Kenny and Esther's car is parked next to the house.

286

"I knew it. I knew she'd be here at the crack of dawn. You're not going to keep her away from the chance to take care of a new baby," I say to Molly.

Mel is in the house loading bottles full of pumped breast milk. She chuckles, "I produce more milk than those darn cows out there. If they gave as much milk as I do, we'd be rich." We all laugh. Those are the kinds of things Melanie always says. To some it may seem a little crass for a Mormon woman to say, but we are Mel's family. She is real, and I love her all the more for it.

She hands her new bundle of joy to Esther. Kenny put the car seat in the back, but Esther won't let go of Lil Grace, and insists on holding her while Kenny drives.

I hear the radio blaring from the barn. Lance is up and putting the first bunch of cows through their morning milking. He pauses to walk us out to the truck, and opens the back door for Melanie. With her cowboy boots and long legs, she steps in easily. She looks authentic in her wranglers, boots, and hunting jacket. "Go get the kids up," she says to Lance. "Erica can fix breakfast for you guys while Dylan gets the calves fed. You guys will be fine."

"You want Jackie to go with you?"

"I think two dogs are enough," I tell her. "Lance can keep her here to help move the cows into the milk parlor."

"Let's go Rebekah," Melanie taps me on the shoulder, "before Lance figures out he can't get along without me."

"Ha!" Lance snorts, and shuts the door. The problem is, he knows she's right. I look in the rear-view mirror and watch her blow him a kiss.

As we drive north on West Daniels Road, the sun is still hiding behind the east side of East Elkhorn Mountain Range. About eight miles up, we turn left, toward the Pleasantview Hills, cross the Little Malad River, and drive up West Elkhorn Canyon for a couple of miles to the BLM corrals, and park. The sun edges itself up, glinting off the aluminum trailer as we unload the horses, and load up our gear. The morning frost steams off the wilted grass in the clearing.

"The cows are going to be over toward Wood Canyon," Molly says, pointing to the west. "We can head up this draw and start circling around to move them down."

"Ladies," I say, as I mount Bobby's horse, Cobalt, and take a deep breath, "please tell me why we don't do this more often." I pat Cobalt on the side of his neck, and say, "come on boy, take me to those cows."

Molly takes the lead, Mel is behind her, and I follow. The dogs circle around us. The drainage is easy to follow. It's been years since I've been up here. Molly lives in these hills. She's been riding them since she was a teenager. They have summered cows here on their BLM allotment for the past ten years. This is a second home to her.

We ride a couple of miles toward the Wood Canyon Spring where the cows generally water. Molly says most of them will be near there. The Wood Canyon drainage runs west from Sheep Creek, over on the Curlew National Grasslands side of the Pleasantview Range.

"Howells likely took their sheep off a few weeks ago," Molly says. "We should have been up here sooner, but Scott's been so busy."

"They're fine, Molly. It was a late frost this year. There's been good feed." I tell her.

The sun is brilliant, the sky a bright fall blue, and the aspen trees are a vivid gold. The breeze flutters the leaves picking up the sun's glint. It could not be more glorious. The hillsides are dotted with lodge pole pine and conifers, interspersed with junipers and cedars.

We stop in a clearing for Molly's stabilizing mid-morning snack. When the skies clear, the sunshine warms us enough to shed our heavy coats and they become small lap blankets to sit on in the grass. Molly walks through the trees to find a place 'to go'.

Within moments after she leaves us, Molly begins to scream. Mel and I look up, then at each other. "I found it!. Rebekah!. Mel!. I found it, I found it!"

Mel is pumping milk from her bulging and sore breasts. I jump up and hold out a hand to help her up. She beats me to the tree where

Molly is standing, now rubbing her fingers over the scar long etched into the tree.

"Oh, my gosh," she says "I've looked for this tree for twelve years. This is amazing." Molly looks at me grinning. "I think you did talk to Mom."

I could never understand why it was so important for Molly to find the tree. What happened here? I have no idea, but I think Mel does.

She keeps rubbing the heart with MH and SO inside. – "Molly Helland loves Scott Olson," she said.

"Did you carve it, or Scott?"

"I started carving it. Then Scott finished," she said.

By the way she looks at Melanie, I know Mel knows this story, or at least some of it, and I am about to learn it.

"Scott and I rode our horses up here when we were seniors in high school. I packed a lunch, and we brought a blanket. We ate, and laughed, and we laid down. He put his arm around me and we started kissing, and then, well, you know, one thing led to another, and it was real hard for both of us to stop, but he was the one who rolled off me and said, 'I can't, Molly. We can't do this until we're married'. Molly pauses. "He said he respected me and loved me too much to do 'it'."

She looks at me. "I would have done it, Rebekah. I would have. I deserve to be ex-communicated from the church."

It feels like a spear pierced my heart. I stare at her. What in the hell is she talking about? She starts to cry, laying her forehead on her arm against the tree, her shoulders shaking, then cries out loud.

"Molly, please tell me what's going on. What in the world are you talking about?"

Melanie's face is sober when she looks at me, then at Molly. "Let's sit down," she says. "Somebody needs to start talking." She puts her arm around Molly, leading her to where we'd laid out our coats. I hand her a sandwich, "first things first. You have to eat something before we talk." I give her a bottle of juice. She takes a bite, then a sip of juice.

"You were ex-communicated, Molly? For what?"

Molly takes a deep breath. "I'm not saying it was the right thing to do," she says, "but I'm just saying maybe I deserve it."

Her blue heeler lay down next to her and she strokes him as she talks. She eats a few more bites of the sandwich, then breaks off a piece and feeds it to her dog. He occasionally looks up at her with his one blue eye, giving her his sympathy, and begging for more food at the same time. She tells us the story; some I already know.

If I despised Leon Fuller before now, it morphs into a mountain of hate by the time Molly finishes. I confess I know what happened in Pocatello with Benny. I admit to her Jack told me under the strict promise of confidentiality, that Jack thought I should know before he left. "He wanted to me to keep an eye on you," I tell her. But I don't tell Melanie about the file Jack buried in Gracie's grave the night of her funeral.

Molly confesses she knew Leon Fuller was working on buying out several of the farms from FDIC, because she put together the paper for the bank. She saw the purchase agreement with FDIC on Bishop Williams's place, and it made her sick to think President Fuller would buy it out from under him. Molly tells us she visited with Bishop Williams about it, and told him she would help get some financing through Farmer's Home. She told Bishop Williams he should be able to pay the same price as Leon Fuller's offer. She advised him he should go talk to Kenny.

"Maybe I shouldn't have done that," Molly confesses. "I know I was out of line, but I just couldn't stand the thought of them losing their place if they didn't have to." I look at her and wonder how such a tiny body can brood over all these problems, all the while thinking it's her job to fix it. I understand the feeling, because it's how I feel every day I wake up and think about the stacks of files sitting on my desk—and on the floor behind my desk.

"Do you think that's why Clarence let you go? Well, besides what I said to him at the livestock sale."

"What'd you say to him?"

"I'm not going into to it right now. That's a whole other thing. I just

290

figured he'd fired you for what I called him."

I wanted to say a lot of nasty things about Clarence and Leon Fuller. That they are greedy, self-serving, pious, jerks; but my mother intervenes, telling me to be still. She reminds me we are here for Molly to heal, not for me to espouse my opinions about the Fullers.

"So, Bishop Williams didn't excommunicate you?" I asked.

"No. It was President Fuller. He called me after Clarence let me go at the bank and asked me to come by his church office to visit."

"Boy, I remember those days," I say out loud without thinking.

"What are you talking about?" Molly asked

"Finish your story, and then I'll tell you."

"The incident with Benny Schnabel in Pocatello?"

"Yes."

Melanie sits quietly, pumping her breasts, filling half a bottle.

"President Fuller said Benny Schnabel called him about some business and in their conversation, he told President Fuller that I gave him sexual favors in exchange for writing off our loan."

My jaw drops. "What did you say?"

"I told him the truth. I told him what happened. And he said when a woman allows herself to be in that situation, she is as guilty as if she willingly furnished herself to him."

I am hot with anger. What arrogance. What foolish garbage. I am shaking my head, wanting to spew the horrible taste in my mouth; but Mom has a hold of my tongue. Believe it or not, I let Molly keep talking.

I look at Melanie. She seems calm; but deeply hurt. She looks as though someone has a hold of her heart and is squeezing, the way she is squeezing the milk from her breasts. "Mol, hon, you need to finish telling us what happened. I think it's important for you to get this out."

I didn't know Molly and Scott went to Melanie and Lance the night of Grace's funeral, so, at the time, I think it's strange Melanie is so calm. I know it is hard for her to reconcile Molly being excommunicated from the church for being raped. She lives and breathes the Mormon Church and its doctrine. She believes with all her heart the decisions made by the brethren of the church are under the direction of divine revelation and intervention.

It becomes more complex when a leader like Leon Fuller shares some of same personality traits as Benny Schnabel.

"Well, there's not much more to tell. President Fuller called a court with the High Council. He notified me, but I didn't go. I couldn't face all those men; men I've known all my life. Men I see every day in the bank. How can I answer such private and personal questions to fifteen men staring at me, asking me such things; horrible things? I just couldn't do it. I couldn't." She sobs while Melanie holds her.

Who does this? What God creates a system like this? This woman who plays their music for ten years, as faithful as the pipes anchored against those walls; as faithful as the walls themselves. All of them, sitting there in judgment of this sweet woman who suffers from a life-threatening illness every day, works like a dog to keep her family fed, tries to keep the wolves from taking her husband's ranch, is raped by the alpha wolf. Didn't any of them stand up and question the validity of this story? Didn't any of them say, 'there is something wrong here. Molly Olson would never, ever do this.' Why would they believe a stranger who came into our town, threatened my father, and then badgered Niles Ogden until he shot himself. Many of them know who Benny is and how he works. They told me personally what an insulting man he is. I am so angry and bewildered, my mind spins. I don't know what to do or say. I move to the other side of Molly and hold her.

How can I not say anything to these men who are as desperate to save their ranches as my sister? How can I not ask them how they make this kind of judgment like they are gods? I know these men. Many of them are clients of Kenny and sat across from my desk, having to expose the most painful parts of their own lives, admit their own failures as farmers and ranchers. Like Molly, they know it isn't their fault, and yet they are having to pay the price. How can they sit together and allow Leon Fuller to administer this kind of injustice?

It takes me a very long time to understand how good, decent men with kind, loving hearts can be controlled and influenced by someone like Leon Fuller. But it happens, from time to time, and as I listen to Molly, I hate them all. But, before we can heal, I learn why I have to forgive them, and why I even have to forgive President Fuller. Christ didn't tell us to love our enemies for their sake.

I think the communication got messed up when somebody wrote the handbook for Mormon Bishops and Stake Presidents. When someone stumbles, and falls, and are drowning in the abyss of guilt and shame, they are looking for a hand to pull them up and save them from drowning. A Savior holds out his hand to that one lost sheep, or the apostle taking a misstep and losing faith as he walks on water. He embraces them, and carries them gently back into the flock; he doesn't kick their ass out the door, like Fuller did to me and Molly. Granted, that one lost sheep may need to be put into a separate pen for a while to heal from the wounds sustained from the wolves, but what Molly tells me is hard to wrap my brain around. It isn't anything close to what I'd read in the Bible–or even the Book of Mormon, for that matter.

Molly says they wrote the official letter, and it came in the mail. "I can't go out in public now," she says. "I can't look at people. All the high councilmen are people I know. I didn't press charges against Benny Schnabel because I didn't want to go through what I'm going through now," she says in a soft whine. "The worst part is the letter said I would longer be the Ward Organist. And they took away the one place I could go to find my respite and my peace. They took my temple recommend and told me I couldn't wear my garments," she cries.

"So, they just throw you out? A guy rapes you and you're excommunicated just like that?"

"Well, maybe it's punishment for what I did here, with Scott. Something I've never paid for."

"I know what Molly means," Melanie says to me, like I am the high court on these matters, here in the mountains above Malad.

"You know, when Gracie was killed? I thought it was because of what Lance and I did before he went on his mission."

"You had sex with him?" I asked, raising my eyebrows, I'm sure with a shocked look on my face.

"No, just touching, hugging, you know, that kind of thing."

"Listen to me." My fists bang the ground like pounding a gavel. "And, this isn't Rebekah talking to you right now. It's Mom talking through me and she's up there with God, so, you need to believe what I'm saying to you."

Melanie and Molly just stare at me as I continue with fierce resolve. "God does not, and I mean this, He does not punish us for succumbing to what is natural in the environment of love. There are rules, but they are there for us like the fences I put around my herd of sheep. I do not know how you two got these crazy ideas into your head, but get them out. What President Fuller did to you, Molly and me is unadulterated sin. What was forced on us was a sin. What you and Scott did was not a sin. What Mel and Lance did was not a sin. You both hit the fence and stayed inside. The barbed wire stung a little when you rubbed against it, but it's supposed to. Come on guys. Get this into perspective. Raw lust is a sin. Sexual assault is a sin. Love is not a sin. Not today, not tomorrow, not ever. Benny Schnabel sinned. Michael sinned. Leon Fuller sinned. WE DID NOT commit a sin! Not for what Molly or I were excommunicated for.

Molly and Melanie are speechless.

"Rebekah, when were you excommunicated?"

I can't answer Molly. When I think about having to tell the story again I can only cry, wiping my hand down my face and over my mouth, muffling my pain. My chest heaves, and I pierce my lips trying to keep everything contained. I close my eyes. It is impossible to talk. I had no idea the pain is still this close to the surface. Molly holds me tight, giving the time I need to recover my composure. I tell them the same story I told Kenny on Thanksgiving two years ago.

"We don't go to the Bishop to confess because he needs to know

294

everything we've done," I say. "We go to cleanse our own heart if it needs cleansing in order for us to feel we can start in a new clean place to move forward. I figured I was making it right by marrying Michael, which only made it worse. Confession is for you, not God, or the Bishop, or Stake President." I tell them.

"Molly, Mel, the plan isn't for us to go through life being perfect. That would make us crazy and depressed all the time. The plan is for Christ to atone for our sins so we don't have to carry the burden. But having someone force us to believe we are soiled and ruined, and we must pay with our bodies, our hearts, and our children for a crime committed against us is just wrong."

I think about a leg or arm being severed, and the length of time it takes for the blood vessels to close off and the nerve endings to die. But isn't the first thing we do is try to save the limb, rather than cutting it off? And shouldn't it also be true regarding our membership in this church? I also know while I once thrived on the spiritual circulation of this religion, being fitted now with a prosthetic membership would never graft. Not because the wounds are too deep, or the resentment too strong, but the fear of going through the pain of being cut off all over again is too great.

I also know it isn't too late for my sister. This church is far too important to her. It is as much a part of her as the air she breathes. I know because I've watched her physically dying these past weeks as she suffers her spiritual loss. She is far deeper entrenched than I ever was. She has invested her entire spiritual capital in the beliefs she holds. I know, on this mountain above Malad, I will go forward and do whatever it takes to keep the blood vessels to her soul flowing and the nerve endings alive until we can have her soul reattached. If not, I know she will surely die.

"You know what, guys," I say, "we're going to get through this. We're going to talk to Kenny and ask him what to do, and I know he'll help you get your membership back, Molly."

"What about you?" Molly asked me.

"Mol, your life is the church. Mine isn't. I've gone beyond it and I don't think I could ever go back. You and Mel have made it your life and I think it's important for you to find a way to get this straightened out. I'm not talking revenge against Fuller. I'm just saying they got it wrong and you need an advocate to get the record straight."

"But Rebekah, somebody needs to make it right for you."

"I'm fine, Molly. I'm fine. If we get you fixed up, it will be restitution enough for me. I promise. As soon as we get back, Mol, we're talking to Kenny, okay?"

"Okay. We will, I promise. But you need to be with me."

"I'll never leave your side," I say as I pull her close to me. "Never."

"Now, ladies, we got some cows to round up."

I looked at my watch. "Holy cow, speaking of cows, it's almost noon and we have to move an entire herd down to the corrals by four. Now we're going to need a miracle." I look up, hoping Mom is listening.

We pick up our gear and shake off the dead grass and soil from our coats. We mount up and ride over the top and down toward Wood Canyon watering troughs. We hadn't gone half-a-mile when we run into Melanie's neighbors, Bob Elston, and his two sons. There is another fellow with them I've never seen before.

"Hey, Brother Elston." Melanie says.

"Hi, Melanie. Molly. Rebekah. What are you girls doing way up here?"

"Roundin' up Olson's cows," Melanie says.

"What are you folks doing?" Melanie asks. I see the way she suddenly turns cold eyeing Bob Elston. Then I figure it out. He's on the Malad Stake High Council.

"Trying to find a deer," he is talking to me now, so I engage in his conversation to be polite. "Rebekah, this is Dan Williams out of Ogden. He's our CPA." He introduces us to a man dressed in high fashion hunting gear straight out of Filson catalog, riding on an expensive quarter horse.

"Find anything?" I ask.

"Nope. We been up here since before dawn. We were just talking about going back down," Bob Elston says.

"I hear Scott's workin' over at Thiokol," Bob says to Molly, but she doesn't answer him.

I clear my throat. "Yea," I finally say to break the silence. "We have to get these cows off the allotment by Friday so Melanie volunteered to come help us today."

"Molly, why in the world didn't you call us? We'd a had the whole Elder's Quorum up her to get these cows down to the ranch for you."

Molly stares at him until he turns away. He doesn't look back at her, but she doesn't quit staring, not saying a word, just staring.

"Well," Melanie finally says, "you can help us now."

"Sister McDonald? Didn't you just have a baby?" one of the younger Elston boys asks.

"I did, John," she says, smiling sweetly at him, "about a month ago. And that's why we need to hurry up and get these cows out of the canyons so my baby doesn't go without her dinner tonight."

"Esther's watching the new baby for Melanie today" I explain, not wanting them to think she left Lil Grace with Lance to tend. Though I'm not sure why I wanted them to know that. "Easterday's gonna have the trucks at the corrals by four."

Bob Elston doesn't say another word to us. He hollers at his two sons, "You guys know where we saw Olson's cows this mornin'? Down there by the troughs at the spring? Come on, let's get a goin." They turn their horses and give them free rein to move quickly toward Wood Canyon. In four and a half hours, the seven of us on horseback and our two dogs round up and move two hundred and fifty mother cows and their calves three miles. An impossible feat for most. The cows move like they know the routine from the year before, their calves following best they can. The dogs herd from the sides and we corral the cows and calves just as the semi-trucks pull double decked trailers up to the chutes.

We load the horses into the trailer while the semi drivers load the cows. They move out ahead of us, heading south towards Olson's ranch, where Lester said he would intercept and unload if Scott wasn't home from work.

I reach out and shake Bob Elston's hand, telling him thanks. As he grabs hold of my hand, I maintain a firm grip and hold on. I check to see where Molly is. "I'm not sure how, but the high council got it wrong, Bob. You need to know that. I need you to help make it right before this kills her. Can you help her do that?"

He is puzzled for a moment, then it registers and he pumps my arm. "I will do whatever I can, Rebekah."

I continue to hang on to him. I look at the deep ruddy lines of his weathered skin. Under his protruding brow, his eyes are set deep. I know he is a good man. He reminds me a lot of Niles. "You're a good man, Bob."

I don't just mean thank you for helping us move the cows down, but thank you for being a good person, and trying to make things right for Molly. But I only say this to him in the way that I look at him and hope he gets the message.

"No problem," he says. "Glad we can help." And I knew he wasn't just talking about helping round up cows, either. I suppose, like everyone else, he misses Molly's music.

I send a silent message to Mom as Molly and Melanie climb into the truck, "Thanks, Mom. You sent us some good help today."

On the way toward Malad, I watch Molly looking out the window toward the setting sun. I hear her humming the song 'Come, Come Ye Saints.' She looks at me and smiles, singing the words softly, "All is well. All is well".

Chapter Thirty-One: Jack

The days grow shorter, and then longer. December passes, cooling the dry hillsides outside San Jose. By January, the hills are starting to green again. I continue holding the memories of my summer in Malad close enough to feel her smiling eyes and the touch of her skin, but obscure enough to forget the sadness of death and the personal devastation of so many good, hardworking families. Everything I learned at Berkley was text book, and I applied my knowledge to every other bank closure I was assigned; until I was called to close down the bank in Malad, Idaho.

I admit working for the FDIC is an exhilarating lifestyle. I find it difficult to adjust to a more sedate, predictable existence. For instance, I'm forced to wear white shirts, suits, and paisley ties every day, instead of wearing that kind of professional attire only on the days FDIC closes down banks. I settle into a relatively uneventful, but enjoyable, routine of parenting. I'm offered the position of Junior Commercial Loan Officer at the bank my father holds a majority interest in.

When Camila finally calls my attorney, asking if she can arrange to see Stacy, I agree to meet with a family arbitrator. My intention is not to prevent Stacy from seeing her mother, but I will not, under any circumstances, allow her to be any place Benny Schnabel is, particularly since I now know he lives with my ex-wife. I agree to let Camila spend at least one weekend a month with Stacy, so I arrange to stay with my parents, letting her stay at my house, formerly 'our house'. It has worked well the past two months. There is no news from Idaho, though I don't expect Rebekah to call. Until January, no one tries to contact me from FDIC. It's my former boss, Sam Jackson who finally calls the end of January, almost six months after I resigned.

"Mr. Whittaker, line two," Janet Devosio says. "It's Sam Jackson, FDIC."

I take a deep breath and pick up the phone, trying to guess what he wants "Hey, Sam. How's it going over there?"

"Same battles, different day," he says. "You got time for lunch? I need to visit with you."

I think of the U-Haul truck, but they would have resolved that months ago. "Sure, Sam. Where do you want to meet?"

"How about John's Restaurant, on Lincoln?"

"That'll be great. I haven't had good Greek food for ages."

"Thanks Jack," Sam says, in a sincere tone, seeming a little out of character.

"You buying?"

"Spoken like a true banker," he laughs. "I called you so I guess that means I'm buying. See you at noon." After he hangs up, I continue holding the phone in my hand, resting my knuckles against my chin. I wonder how much I should say, or if I should say anything to him without the advice of my attorney.

Janet Devosio, often more like a mother than a secretary, stops typing and stares at me until I realize I'm still holding the phone.

"I'm going to lunch, Janet," I say.

She looks at her watch, and then I look at mine.

It's ten-thirty. "I mean I'm leaving to go to lunch in an hour."

I pick up the loan application I'm working on. It's hard to focus. I shuffle papers until eleven and go find my father.

"Sam Jackson called me this morning," I say, as I close the door to his office. I take a seat in one of the two leather chairs facing his desk. "He wants to have lunch, says he wants to talk to me," I look at Dad, searching for certain clues in his constant, stoic face.

"Well, go have lunch with him and listen, maybe take a few notes, and tell him you'll get back to him if he asks questions you're uncomfortable answering."

Dad always has a simple answer to everything. I suppose over the years, I learned more from him than I ever learned at Berkley. Stopping to sort out the amalgamation of information I accumulated through the years, I have to say Dad's advice provided the armor, of sorts, and my college education filled in the chinks. My boots on the ground education at FDIC in asset management taught me all the things not to do in the banking world.

I confess, after a decade of working at FDIC, and moving up the ladder to Asset Manager, my prominence has been unquestionably deflated by taking a job as junior loan officer at a regional bank. I just naturally assumed after working at the FDIC this long, my rapport with my father would evolve into a contemporary relationship. Though, I admit, the fact that it hasn't isn't his fault.

"Is it okay with you if I leave a little early for lunch?" I ask.

"Jack" he says, his eyebrows down and a deep frown on his face, "you don't have to ask."

John's is a nice Greek restaurant. It's been a staple in Greek cuisine for twenty years in San Jose. Their tables are covered with white linen tablecloths and napkins, topped with small cut crystal vases of fresh flowers. They have the finest assortment of wine and beer. It strikes me, as I walk into the noon-time darkness, what a stark contrast this is to Elsie's café in Malad. The maître d' recognizes me and I hold up my fingers signaling a table for two. He waves to me and I point toward the end of the restaurant. It is always my preference to sit in the corner.

"I'll just have a cup of tea," I say to the gentleman I recognize, but can't remember his name. "I'm waiting for Sam Jackson."

"Ah, yes, Sam," he says, with an accent.

I think about a lot of things Sam might want to discuss. Maybe he wants me to come back to work. It is certainly tempting. I'm beginning to understand what Camila went through after she quit. My job at FDIC was a natural high. I thought problem-solving is what gave me that surge; but after having been away from it, I'm convinced the thrill is controlling the outcome. I know it will be hard for me to say 'no' to Sam, if he asks.

Sam is five minutes late. I stand and shake his hand. He is dressed in my favorite work clothes: a pair of Docker pants, long-sleeved cotton plaid shirt, no tie. He looks tired; his face is drawn. He orders a tall double gin and tonic. I must have raised my eyebrows because he says he earned it, or something similar.

We talk through the family talk. He asks about Stacy and I ask about his daughter who is now in college at Stanford. I tell him our summer intern at Malad is a senior at Stanford. I write down his name on the back of my business card and tell Sam he should have his daughter look him up. "He's the best employee I had on that job," I tell him. Sam confesses he doesn't remember Will.

He asks me how I like my job, and I lie. I wonder how many more I have to tell before we finish eating. Then he says he needs to get down to the business at hand, an expression he always liked to use. This time he means it.

"Benny's been charged with battery and sexual assault ," he says.

I am speechless. I watch as Sam takes a long drink to swallow the words back down to a place he can dilute them with alcohol.

"Molly Olson?"

"Yup." He takes another drink.

"I don't know what to say," I tell him, "except I know he's guilty. I drug him off her, remember, Sam?"

"I'm sure you'll get subpoenaed to testify."

"Well," I tell him, "Scott Olson was there too. I'm sure he'll be testifying as well."

"Scott Olson's dead."

I'm not sure if I can explain what that moment felt like to me. The news about Benny was a shock, though admittedly, a pleasant one. The instant Sam tells me Scott Olson is dead, it is as though I've been hit in the chest with a bolt of lightning; the kind of lightening that strikes on hot July afternoons at the foothills of Elkhorn Ridge in Oneida County, Idaho, just before a hail storm. My hand starts to shake when I lift my glass of water. I don't know what to say.

"How did you find out?" I ask. I wonder if he talked to Molly. I am sick inside. "Who told you?"

"Well, Jack," he stops, shakes the ice in the glass and finishes the drink. "I just got back from Malad, Idaho yesterday."

"What in the world were you doing in Malad?"

"Talking to Kenneth Sorenson. He's filed a joint law suit against us for five million dollars. Molly Helland Olson and Betsy Ogden are the plaintiffs. And Molly filed a complaint in Bannock County, Idaho through the Pocatello Police Department against Benny. Her complaint says he beat her and sexually assaulted her."

The waiter places large white plates filled with lamb shank and lamb chops in front of us. I pick up a lamb chop with my fingers, something Rebekah told me was acceptable, according to Emily Post. I take a bite and chew a long time, like I am chewing on everything Sam just told me.

"How did Scott die?" I am finally able to ask.

"Explosion at Morton Thiokol. Four days after Christmas. They were fueling an MX Rocket, something sparked and it killed five employees, and Scott Olson was one of them." And he almost doesn't take a breath before he says "That Kenneth Sorenson is a nice fellow, isn't he?"

"I told you he is, Sam. I told you in committee meetings every time I brought back offers from his clients. He is a good man to work with, but I sure wouldn't want to piss him off." I pick up another lamb chop, look at it and set it back down. I cannot believe Scott Olson is dead.

"I should just let you read the complaint. It's pretty damming. "

"Well, if it involves me, I think you should let me read it."

"There's nothing about you in there except you told the Olson's the FDIC would write off their loan to compensate for Benny's actions against Molly. It's all about Benny from start to finish. That he was going to let Molly Olson die of insulin shock, and he bullied Niles Ogden until Niles shot himself. That he tried to rape Molly Olson after she gave him a ride back to his motel because he was too drunk to drive."

"And which part don't you believe, Sam?" I ask. "Benny held Molly's father at gun point to keep him from going to help her.

When the intern, Will, finally found me that night, I went to the break room and found some orange juice and we were lucky it brought her out of her comatose state. I stop. I think about the first time I met Scott, how we talked about the dragon on his hat, and the Welsh heritage of Malad Valley. I pick up the linen napkin again and wipe my eye.

"I just can't believe Scott is gone," I say again, almost in a whisper. "You would like him, Sam. He was so easy going. So laid-back. Acted like he didn't have a worry in the world. I remember wishing I could be like him. He was the salt-of-the-earth kind of guy."

"Well, so far you've echoed the complaint verbatim. I think we're in trouble and I can't say you didn't warn me." He holds up his empty glass to the waiter and shakes it, "want one?"

"I'll pass," He takes another bite of lamb shank, and pushes his plate away.

"By the way," Sam says, "where the hell did that cat come from?

"What cat?"

"The dead cat in the back of the U-haul truck."

I keep a straight face. "Beats me. Must have crawled in while we were loading up files in Idaho."

"Gawd, it stunk in there. Nobody'll touch those files. You said you gave Benny the key?"

"He was second in command," I tell him, "who else would I have given them to?"

"Why would he deny you gave them to him?"

I smile and don't say a word. He smiles too, waiting for his drink.

"So what happened on Olson's loan?" I ask.

"Well, Benny started out making some deal with Fuller, but Fuller backed out mid-October; so Benny started foreclosure proceedings. That's the only file he brought back with him, and since he won't work on any of the files in the truck, he didn't have anything else to do."

"Why would he do that? They had a Farmers Home Administration

304

loan approved to take us out. They were just waiting for an appraisal and a settlement number from our committee." I talk like I still work there.

"Well, I found that out after a member of our legal counsel and I met with Mr. Sorenson. That's when I found out you promised we'd write it off as reparations."

"I suppose I didn't have authority to say that, but honestly, Sam, after I drug him out of the cab of her truck and made him pull his pants up, I didn't know what else to do. I offered to go call the cops and have him arrested, but she begged Scott not to let me call. She said she just wanted to go home. She said her family had been through enough public humiliation. But Benny has a nose for figuring that kind of shit out, doesn't he? He knows how to attack the weak and vulnerable. I put all this in the affidavit I sent to you in August."

"Yea. I just re-read it for about the fifth time."

"So what happened?"

"Well, Mr. Sorenson told us while Benny was working with Fuller, who I guess is Molly's church leader, some President of something...,"

"Stake President," I correct him.

"Yea, yea, that's what he called him. Anyway, he called Benny to make an offer on the Olson's farm and two or three other farms that join them, and apparently Benny told Fuller she agreed to have sex with him in exchange for writing off their loan."

"That's bullshit!" Three people turn their heads to look at me.

Sam lowers his voice. "Well, then this President guy excommunicated Molly from their Mormon Church and took away her job playing the music. Sorenson told me it almost killed her."

I can't stand talking about her any longer. The lamb grease hardens in my gut and it hurts. I need to call Rebekah. I need to know how Molly's doing. It's funny it doesn't occur to me until several days later she is now single, and available. I can only think about the terrible things she's had to endure.

"You going to settle?" I ask him, trying to stay calm.

"I need to know what your testimony's going to be before we decide what we're going to do."

"You want to hear the rest of it, then?"

"Might as well, he says. "You gonna give me a ride home after we're done?"

"Sure." I don't smile when I say it. This job makes everyone drink too much.

"Good. Then I'll order another gin and tonic."

"Okay. Let me use the men's room, find a pay phone to call the bank and have Mom pick up Stacy," I say. "Then I'll start at the beginning."

It was nearly 5 o'clock when we leave John's Greek Restaurant. I tell Sam the story from beginning to end. I tell him about the funeral, about Scott coming to my motel room, and our drive to Pocatello. At about his fourth or fifth gin and tonic I confess to him it was me who bought the McDonald note and I'd buried their file in Grace Marie's grave.

When I look up, Sam is crying. Tears are streaming down his face. I think I should stop, but decide to I'll tell him about buying Dylan's lamb, and sending it home with him to raise instead of sending it to the slaughter house.

"It took an edge off," I said. "My problem at Malad is the job humanized me; which is why I had to quit. I could never be a good FDIC Asset Manager after what happened there."

"It must have been hell for you."

"Not for me," I said. "It's been hell for them. All of them. You cannot imagine the hell Molly Olson has been through. She lost her mother to breast cancer just over a year ago. Her father lost their three-generation family bank, four generations counting Molly. Her father's best friend killed himself after Benny Schnabel bullied the hell out of him. Molly's best friend's two-year old daughter got run over by a tractor and killed because the little girl's mother was distracted talking to our FDIC appraiser. Then, on the day of the

306

funeral, Molly is threatened and then beaten, and sexually attacked by our Assistant Asset Manager. He comes back to California with the Olson file and he lies his way out of the whole mess like he always has, but he's not satisfied until he convinces himself it wasn't his fault. He gets the woman he's defiled excommunicated from her church. The icing on the cake is her husband gets blown up on the job he has to take in order to keep their family fed because Benny's foreclosing on them. Tell me, Sam, just how much do you think would pay for that much pain and suffering? How god-damned much?"

The people coming in for early dinner are staring at me. Our waiter senses it's past-time for us to leave and begins hovering over our table where the bill has been sitting for three hours. He asks if he can get us anything else. I get out my wallet and hand him my credit card.

"I told you I'd pay," Sam said.

"Don't worry, Sam," I say as I lean across the table. "You're gonna' pay. I'm afraid you're going to end up paying for a lot more than you bargained for."

When the waiter returns with the credit slip for me to sign and my credit card, I put my card and receipt for two lunches neither of us ate, and five gin and tonics, in my wallet. "Now I need to get you home before I start drinking."

I pull up to the curb in front of Sam's house. "Are you going to be OK, Sam?" I ask.

"I will" he says. "I still have Sally, my kids and my home, at least for now. That's what's important."

That isn't what I meant, but it becomes clear to me what is weighing heavy on his mind.

"Those are nice people up there in Idaho, Jack. I can see why you care about them. I know you tried to hide it, but I could see it last summer, in the way you would advocate for them."

"Oh, by the way," he said, "I met Molly Olson's sister; the one who works for the attorney? The one who doesn't have a wedding ring on her left hand?" Sam talks like he is implying something. "She's is a knock-out. She told me if I ran into you to tell you 'hi.'" He winks.

He climbs out of the car and is half-way up the walk when he holds up his hand to me in a solitary farewell gesture. He is a decent guy, I think, who, I am reasonably sure, will be the fall guy for all of this. Despite learning about the tragedy of Scott's death, and I am truly sad for Molly and her children, the thought of Benny Schnabel in orange coveralls in the state pen in Boise, Idaho for the next twenty years makes me smile to the bottom of my toes.

settle. I don't think they want the bad publicity."

We talk a while longer. I ask him if he's dating anybody. He says he's not looking. He admits there isn't a day he doesn't think about Molly. I tell him it will take her time to heal, that he needs to be patient. "Molly's not going to stay single," I say. "And you have as good of a chance as anyone. But you'll have to join the Mormon Church," I say. Jack doesn't say anything.

"Well," he says, "it's been good to talk to you, Rebekah. I'm am truly sorry about Scott. I mean that. Please give my best to Molly."

"I know you're sorry, Jack. And I know how much Scott liked you. He kept trying to talk me into dating you."

"Well," Jack says, "I'm sure I'll be up for depositions and court unless Benny pleads guilty."

"Do you think he will?"

"No. Not in a million years. Mostly because he doesn't believe he is."

We say our goodbyes, I hang up the phone and finish my drink.

***

In March, FDIC settles with Molly and Betsy. Molly tells me they plan to open a new bank with the proceeds. Kenny says he'll take his share in stock when they get the bank open. Molly wants to focus on one thing at a time, and Benny Schnabel is her next target.

Molly is more passionate about bringing Benny to justice than she is about the money from FDIC. Benny hires a law firm from Idaho Falls; Mason and Smith. They work with his high-powered San Francisco attorney. Kenny says the District Attorney is going to have their hands full and he volunteers to help the Bannock County DA's office put their case together.

Jack flies to Salt Lake and takes a commuter flight to Pocatello the second week of May for depositions. We meet for dinner in Pocatello and talk past 10 o'clock. I get home late that night, and he flies back to California the next day. He doesn't see Molly that trip, but I tell her I talked to him. I tell her he asked about her.

Jack is subpoenaed by the Bannock County District Attorney as state's witness to appear in mid-July. He decides to drive to Malad from San Jose with his daughter, Stacy. He rents a room at the Village Inn and drives back and forth to Pocatello every day to attend the trial. Norma volunteers to watch Stacy while Jack is in court. On several different days Jack takes Stacy out to Melanie's to spend the day with Rosalyn and Lindsay. Jack says she is having the time of her life with her new friends.

Jack keeps his distance from me and Molly. He arrives at the court house at 9 o'clock every morning, disappears at noon, and leaves as soon as court is dismissed. He is called to testify the second week of the trial. It sounds convincing until Benny's attorney asks Jack if he is aware Benny is living with his ex-wife.

"Yes," Jack answers in a calm tone.

"Did you know Benny and your wife were lovers before you married her?"

"Irrelevant," the DA yells.

"I agree," the judge says.

"Okay, let me ask this another way," Tim Smith says, his condescending demeanor emulating Benny's, almost perfectly. He taps his chin with his index finger while he looks at the ceiling.

"When did you find out Benny and your ex-wife were living together?"

The questioning went on for another hour until Tim Smith was satisfied the jury understands Jack likely carries a vendetta against Benny and wants to make him pay. The attorney makes it sound as though Benny was having an affair with Jack's wife the entire time Jack and Camila were married.

Tim Smith finishes questioning Jack by asking him if he is jealous of Benny because of Benny's natural ability to attract women; women like his former wife, and Molly Olson. I hold my breath. I look over at Kenny and he is looking straight at Jack, slowly shaking his head as if to tell him not to answer the question. I can feel Jack's insides trembling and I pray he will let a calm head prevail. It takes him a few seconds to collect himself. He quietly says, "No, Mr. Smith, I am not jealous of Benny Schnabel in any regard, whatsoever."

The courtroom empties after what many had thought would be the final day of the trial. We stay in Pocatello, too tired to make the drive back to Malad. We just returned from dinner when Esther calls our room. I talk to all my kids. Rosalyn doesn't miss me. She loves her 'Auntie Esther'. Eric misses his Uncle Kenny, and asks me if he is close by so he can talk to him. Jason misses me the most.

"Mom, when are you coming home? When can we start being a family again?"

"Is this a guilt trip, son? I ask.

"No, I just really, really miss you."

I tear up. Molly watches me. The innocence and naivety of our sweet little Molly is gone. It's been an unbearable year for her, and here I am feeling sorry for myself. I take a deep breath and say "Jason, if you could go anywhere, do anything you want, where and what would It be?

"Hmm?" I hear him thinking, almost smiling to himself.

"Go to the ocean," he finally says. "I'd like to go to the ocean and ride in a sail boat."

He's never said anything about sailboats before.

"Well," I tell him, "as soon as this is over, and it's going to be very soon, we'll go to the ocean and I'll pay someone to give us a ride in a sailboat." I pause. "Just you and me," I add.

"Whoa! That would be awesome, Mom. Totally awesome. Thanks, Mom."

"Thanks, Jason. Thanks for being my strength and my support. I would have never have made it through this past year without you. And Aunt Molly feels the same way."

Molly holds out her hand and takes the phone from me. She says, "Jason, honey, it's Aunt Molly." She is quiet for a few moments, then says, "Hey Jason, I just want you to know something. When you were born, you were our very first baby in the Helland family and you made us so happy. Now you are the oldest grandchild, and I know it's hard at times, but it makes you special, and you are very, very special to all of us."

"I know, I know." She nods her head, like Jason can see her agreeing with him. I furrow my brow, wanting to know what he's saying. Molly smiles and waves her hand at me, like this is her conversation with Jason and it has nothing to do with me.

Then she laughs, "Yes, I know. That's great," she says.

"What?" I whisper, not wanting to be left out. "What are you guys talking about?"

"Hey, your Mom's a snoop, she wants to know what we're talking about." There is a long pause. "Yeh, I'm not going to tell her either."

She laughs again. "I love you honey. You take care and we'll all be home for good soon. K? Can you put Aunt Esther on the phone, honey? Your Mom says 'bye' and we'll see you tomorrow night."

Molly asks Esther if Kenny called her. I couldn't hear her reply, but guess he hadn't. "When he left the courtroom, he was headed to his old office to meet with the District Attorney to help him get ready for court. We all hope it's going to be the final day." She listens. "Gosh Esther, I don't know if I can go through everything that happened today, but it's not looking good for us," she says. "At least that's what I'm thinking."

Molly begins picking the lint off her soft pink cotton blouse and brushing off her skirt, like she was trying to get something off her that isn't there. I pull open the motel room curtains to let in some light. The view is toward back parking lot, mostly empty. Suddenly I see Molly look at me, "hang on a minute, Esther," and she puts the phone to her chest and points outside.

"Rebekah, there," she says, pointing. "What time is it right now?"

"Eight-fifteen, well, Eight-seventeen" I tell her.

"What's today?" she asks, then speaks back into the phone. "Esther, let me call you back." And she hangs up the phone.

"What is today?" she asks again.

314

I think for a minute. "It's August fourth."

"That night," she says, "it was August second. The day of Grace's funeral, or I should say the night of Grace's funeral. When I put the truck in park to let Benny out, the engine was still running. The clock on the dash board read eight zero five. I remember, 'cause when he had my head smashed against the door, I was facing the dashboard. It's all I could see."

I shake my head because I don't know what she's getting at, and I should have.

"Look outside, Rebekah. It's still light." She waits for me to tune in, but I'm not getting the drift. "On the stand, today, Benny said it was dark out. He said Scott and Jack wouldn't have been able to see what was happening inside the cab of that truck. The cook from the restaurant who saw us leave said we drove out of the parking lot from Remos at 7:45, and the guy from the Congressman's office said he left us sitting at the table at Remos at 7:30, maybe 7:35. Jack said he and Scott pulled into the parking lot at the motel at eight. It wasn't dark out. In fact, there were likely two or three more minutes of daylight two days ago than there are right now."

I look outside again. I can see every vehicle, every detail and I say to Molly, "let's go find Kenny."

Dad and Kenny are sharing a room next to us. I knock on the door. After dinner Kenny went straight to his meeting with the DA. His old law partners gave him a key to their office and told him to use whatever he needed.

"Dad, Dad, come here," I say when he opened the door to his room. I pull open the drapes. He has the same view of the parking lot.

"I don't know what you're talking about." He is standing in his stocking feet, his white starched shirt open at the collar, his face drawn. He is exhausted.

"Dad, Benny Schnabel said it was dark. It was one year and two days ago, right out there, in that exact parking lot."

Dad turns his face away, like I'd slapped him. I realize something I hadn't thought of before now. He had tuned it all out. All the horrible details, he completely shut them out of his head. He has no idea what parking lot they have been talking about in court for the last two weeks. He has no idea it is this one, the one he's been looking at from his motel room window. He only knows his baby girl is being ripped apart, degraded, and demeaned. He would give anything not to have her go through this. He asked her a dozen times if she was sure this is what she wanted to do this.

Molly told Dad that after she lost Scott, and the farm was being foreclosed on, the FDIC took everything from her except her children. She said if she had to go to hell trying, she wasn't going to let them run over her any longer. Dad promised he'd be there for her, but he hates it. He hates seeing her relive every horrid detail.

I feel her pain, more than I feel my own. I feel Dad's pain. I think about her file in the locked drawer at the Church House. I wonder who has read it, thinking those Helland girls are real floozies. But until this very moment, I hadn't thought about the one thing that can prove Benny Schnabel molested my sister. President Fuller told Molly that Benny, in his own words, said "he had his way with her." It would be in her file, in that locked drawer. Not in those exact words, but President Fuller is the one who convinced the High Council to excommunicate her for adultery, based on what Benny Schnabel told him. Now, under oath, he explicitly said he hadn't touched her.

I ask Dad for his car keys. "It's fine, Dad," I assure him. "You lay down and get some rest. Molly and I need to go find Kenny."

"Drive the speed limit," he says as we closes his door.

The door to the Hank and Ross Law Office is locked, but I can see a light on. I changed into my Wranglers and boots when we got back to the motel, so I told Molly to stay at the front door and I'd wade through the bushes and knock on the window. Kenny peers out. There is still a fading light, and he smiles as I point toward the front door, yelling, "Unlock it. Hurry!"

"What's up," he says in his normal drawl as he pushes open the door.

"Come here," I puff, and he follows me down the hallway to the lighted room.

"Kenny," I'm panting.

"Catch your breath Rebekah."

Molly starts to talk. "Kenny, remember when Benny said it was dark? That Scott and Jack couldn't have seen what was going on?"

"Yes."

"Look outside."

"Okay?"

Molly starts talking. "It was one year and two days ago, Kenny. And, it's eight-thirty now. It was 8:05 PM when we pulled into the parking lot. The sun hadn't gone down yet. Scott and Jack had full view of what he was doing to me," Molly says.

"Oh," I interrupted, "and here's something else we haven't thought of." I look at Molly. "Molly, what did President Fuller say to you when he called you into his office?"

Molly looks down. Talking about this hurts her more than anything.

"He said Benny told him he had his way with me."

I saw the muscles in Kenny face visibly relax to a point his jaw drops.

"Remember, Kenny. Remember when you told me you'd read my file?"

He saw where I was going with this.

"Do you know what an embarrassment this will be to the Church if I call President Fuller to the witness stand?"

"God, Kenny, who cares?" I yell at him. "Who the hell cares?"

"Sorry," I say, when they both glare at me. "I didn't mean that." But I do mean it.

"I'm not sure if I can subpoena the church records anyway," he says.

"Here's my point," I begin to say.

"I get your point, Rebekah." Kenny is angry. I know what he needs to do, and he doesn't like it. I am angry at him, for the first time in my life, truly angry.

"You can't sit here and tell me you'd let her dignity go out the door because you don't want to discredit The Church."

"It's more than that, Rebekah. It's really crossing a line I've never crossed. And it's going to take me some time to think about it."

"Well, you know what, Kenny? You can sit here all night and think about it all by yourself."

I stomp down the hall, push open the front door and let out a scream that comes from the bottom of my womb, the center of my plexus, and the innermost part of my soul. I can't understand, or comprehend what I just heard from the one man I love and revere more than anyone. I always expect him to understand where I am coming from, expect him to walk (proverbially speaking) in my pointed high-heeled shoes a mile, maybe two, to understand what it's like to be a woman in a souped-up male-dominated world. But I don't step into his world, or try to understand his angst. To turn on his religious leader would put him in a difficult position. I just expect Kenny to protect us, Molly and me, unconditionally.

Kenny is out the front door, Molly behind him. "Stop it, Rebekah," he sharply orders me. He turns to Molly, "don't let that door close or we're locked out." So, Molly stands holding the door open, not knowing what else to do. I don't know how to contain myself, how to not hate Kenny at this moment.

"Rebekah, come back inside. We'll figure something out. I've got another idea we haven't talked about."

I breathe deep until I feel my body hyperventilating. I feel the cool of the high mountain desert reach my lungs. I know I want Fuller in the witness chair because I hate him more than I have ever hated anyone, except Benny Schnabel. I want him to admit to the world what he did to my sweet, innocent little sister after she was raped. I want him to have to admit, publicly, he was making deals with the FDIC behind his parishioner's backs. I can't imagine anyone being hated more than I hate him. I can't see it from Kenny's perspective because my hate glasses are too thick and permanently attached to the retina of my eye linking the lens straight to my heart. I can't understand why Kenny doesn't hate anyone, especially Leon Fuller.

He believes his religion. He follows Christ's teachings, and he's learned to love his enemies. I just can't do that.

Kenny touches my shoulder. "Are you ready to come back in?"

I nod and take another deep breath.

When we are sitting around the conference table, Kenny says, "Rebekah, this isn't about you, or getting even with President Fuller for what he did to you and Molly. This is about winning this case. If the DA brings Fuller to the witness stand, it will be because it solidifies the case. But I can assure you, it will NOT be for vengeance or publicly humiliating him. Do you understand me?"

I nod my head.

"Our jurors are predominantly Mormons. If you attack their religion, we've lost this case. The fact you hate Fuller—and the Good Lord knows you have reason to—doesn't mean they will see this the same way you do. It's obvious to you, but it's sensitive to them, and trust me, they will resent having their Church disgraced. I think I might have possibly found a better way."

He pushes his glasses up with his finger, and says,"I was reading through a recent law journal tonight and there's a new DNA test. He stops to explain what it is.

"If there were any way we have anything with his…" he stops and looks at both of us. "Well, you know what I mean. If we had that, we could prove he's lying." I start liking Kenny again. He is so polite, so sensitive.

"Molly, are the seats in your pickup vinyl or cloth?"

"Vinyl," she replies, and Kenny frowns. "It wouldn't be there anyway, Kenny. It got on my clothes. Then she looks down into her lap and in a barely audible whisper says, "on my temple garments,"

"What did you do with them?

"I don't know," she says. Scott drove me to Lance and Melanie's house and Scott and Lance left while Melanie helped me get cleaned up. I don't know what Melanie did with them."

"Can you call her?" Kenny asked.

"Sure."

Kenny pushes the phone in the middle of the conference table toward Molly.

"Push nine for an outside line," he says, "and you'll have to dial a one, it's long distance to Malad."

Kenny looks at me and asks in a low voice, "Rebekah, did we know Melanie helped clean her up that night? Did you know?"

I shook my head. "No, I say. I thought Scott drove her straight home." I'm calm now with a clear head."I had no idea they'd gone to Lance and Melanie's."

"Lance, it's Molly. Is Mel there?

Kenny and I looked at her while she waits. She is staring up at the ceiling.

"Yes," she says, "it's going okay. How are the kids?" Melanie has been tending Molly's kids for the duration of the trial. We didn't want to overload Esther and besides, Melanie begged Molly to let them stay. It eases her pain of having Grace gone, she said. Especially this time of year.

"Mel, that night, after Grace's funeral? What did you do with my temple garments?" she whispered.

There is silence.

Molly covers the phone and says, "she thinks she put them in a bag and stuffed them in a drawer. She said she didn't know what to do with them. She's looking."

"You do?" Molly says.

Kenny holds out his hand and says, "here, let me talk to her."

"Mel? How you doing? You feeling okay? How's the baby?"

My gosh, I wonder, how he can be so calm.

"Melanie, listen to me. This is sensitive to all of us. But, it's important to Molly. We need those garments. We need them as soon as we can get them."

Then he asks to talk to Lance. It's more comfortable for him. They visit for a minute. Kenny explains the problem, and then hangs up the phone.

"Lance is bringing them up to Pocatello tonight," Kenny says. "He said the torn dress is in the bag with the garments. I'm going to ask for a stay tomorrow until we can get them tested. Then I need Lance and Melanie to testify," he says.

I frown. Molly frowns harder.

"You think this is less humiliating than bringing Fuller to the stand?" I ask.

"Likely not," he says. "None of this is easy, but let me be clear, Rebekah. I will not request President Fuller to testify just to satisfy your urge to see him crucified in public. I'll ask to bring him to the stand if I think it will win this case and put an evil man in prison."

"Fuller's an evil man," I say quietly, trying to get in one more jab. "He should have to go to prison with Benny."

"Well," Kenny says, "he'll get his when he meets his maker, and that's not for me or you to judge, Rebekah. I promise you, his hell in the next life will be far worse than prison."

I know I'm not going to get Kenny to buy into my fight.

"Now let's go back to the motel. It's getting late. We've had a good night of discovery and we all need to get some sleep."

"Oh. I about forgot. You're supposed to call Esther," Molly says to him.

"Yes. I will," he says. "You two go on ahead, I'll call Esther from here."

In the car, Molly grabs my arm. "I don't hate him, Rebekah." I know she is talking about Leon Fuller. "I feel sorry for him."

"You would," I say. "I hate him. I will always hate him. More for what he did to you than what he did to me."

"But hating him doesn't make it any different. It eats you up inside, consuming the best parts of you. The parts you need to keep to be a good mother, and maybe, someday again, a good wife."

"Whoa, don't even go there. That part of my life is over."

"What about Jack Whittaker?"

"He's my friend, Molly. Just like Kenny's my friend. Besides, he's in love with you."

Molly looks at me, drops her eyebrows and leans back. "What in the world makes you say something like that?"

"Because it's true. But I promised him I'd never tell you."

"It's too soon, Rebekah."

"I didn't say you had to, Mol. He knows you're not ready. It's the reason he's stayed away from you while he's been here."

"Oh. Good," Molly says. "I thought he was mad at me for having to come back to Idaho to testify."

"He'd go to China to testify for you, Molly. Heck, he'd go to the moon."

"Ohhhh." The inflection in her voice drops. "That's sweet." Then she's quiet. "Truth is, Rebekah, I was gonna ask him if he'd move to Malad and go to work in our new bank."

"Are you seriously going to open another bank?"

"As serious as I've ever been about anything in my life," she says. "With Dad, and you, and Kenny, I have all the talent in the world.

"Well, and if Jack would come on board, I think you'd put the Fullers out of business," I say with a big smile.

"That's not why I'm doin' it," she says. "I told you, I don't hate them."

"Hey," I say. "Maybe good things can come of all this. As Mom would say, stay positive."

"It's good to hear you say that, Rebekah."

"It's good to see you smile, Molly." I say back to her.

We pull into the Quality Inn and sit in the car behind the building for a long time. It's like Molly wants to sit there and let it release. "You know," she finally says, "I maneuvered the gun from under the seat and was ready to pull the trigger when Scott opened the pickup door."

322

"You're kidding me."

"Scott took the gun out of my hand and put it to Benny's head while Benny crawled off me. He beat me, he sexually humiliated me and made me feel filthy, but he didn't rape me, Rebekah. He was drunk, and he, well, just released himself all over me. He tried to, but he didn't because he couldn't tear my garments off. They wouldn't tear. They saved me."

I look at her, trying to see her face in the dark. She is staring at the corner of the parking lot where the truck was parked that night.

"Why'd you park back there?" I asked, already knowing the answer.

"Because he said he was sick and was going to throw up. He told me to drive back there by the empty lot." She points to the back corner of the large parking area.

"You know all this," she says to me.

"Yes," I say, "but I didn't know about the gun, or what you just said about your garments not tearing. Why didn't you pull the trigger?

"I didn't want his blood all over me, she says. I had enough of him on me already."

"So why didn't you tell us about going to Melanie's?"

"Because she's gone through enough. I hated going to her that night. She just buried her little girl. I didn't know where else to go, Rebekah. I couldn't come to you because I didn't want Daddy to know. And, I didn't want my kids to see my like that. When I decided to bring charges," she says, "I knew you and Kenny would ask her to testify, then that beastly attorney Benny hired would ask her if she was just being vindictive toward Benny because her baby girl was dead."

She looks beaten down. I take her hand.

"I've watched Kenny in court before," Molly says, "and the way the guys argue against him, I knew that's what they'd do to Mel. Honestly, Rebekah, I couldn't bear to see her have to answer that kind of questioning. She's been through enough."

"And you haven't?" I ask. "Been through enough?"

"But, this was my decision. I didn't ask her if I should do this before I made up my mind to go after him. Honestly, I'd forgotten all about the clothes. I had no idea what she'd done with them. She never said, and I never asked."

"Well, honey, I think she's going to have to testify for you. And I don't think she'll mind. I don't think she'll mind at all."

Kenny pulls up beside us and parks. We all get out of the car at the same time.

"You gals okay?"

"Fine," I tell him. "Just talking."

"I'm going to sit in the lobby and wait for Lance," he says.

"Stay out of the bar," I say.

Molly laughs.

"You too," Kenny says.

"Good night, Kenny."

"Good night, ladies."

"Thanks, Kenny."

Kenny chuckles. "If I had a nickel every time you girls told me 'thanks', I'd be richer than the Rockefellers."

"Likely," I say, "but having you as our brother-in-law already makes us richer than Rockefellers."

Our collective laugh is a welcome relief as we enter the back door to the motel.

"By the way," Kenny says grinning ear to ear. "Esther just informed me I'm going to be a new father."

Chapter Thirty-Three: Jack

On the last day of the trial, I arrive at the courthouse late. Norma agrees to keep Stacy for the day. Melanie telephoned her the night before to say she had been called to testify at the trial. Norma rapped lightly on my motel room door a little after 9 o'clock, after I'd put Stacy to bed, to give me the message. Since all the kids were going to Esther's, Norma and I agreed it would be best for Stacy to stay with her.

I see Rebekah and Molly sitting together, several rows in front of me. There has been such a turn of events, it's hard for me to keep up. The judge refuses to stay the trial for DNA testing on the clothing, saying it is new-fangled and hasn't be used in the U.S. The grocery bag with string tied around it sits on the prosecutor's table, unopened, until now. Inside are the same clothes several witnesses, including me, have described in detail over the course of the past two weeks. I have no idea where or how Kenny located them, but the ripped skirt and blouse, and soiled temple garments are sufficient evidence to prove Benny's story false. It is clear he told a bold-faced lie, under oath.

Kenny requests the new evidence be treated with sensitivity and expresses concern to the judge regarding the sacred nature of the temple garments. When Melanie is re-examined by the defense attorney, she is convincing and stern. Benny's attorney came at her from every side, leaving nothing sacred. But Melanie didn't wince, or break down, and she didn't back away. The harder he came at her, the more resolute she became. She told every detail of the night Molly and Scott came to them for help. When the attorney asked why she had kept the clothes for so long without turning them over as state's evidence, she said, plain and simple, "I honestly forgot I had them until Molly called me last night. I've never been involved in anything like this." She pauses. "And neither has Molly. We just don't understand what we're supposed to do or say when it comes to this kind of disgusting behavior."

I see the judge smile. I can tell by the expressions on the juror's faces, Benny's attorney is losing ground. The harder he goes after Melanie, the more their eyes narrow, and their frowns deepen.

The prosecuting attorney gives a concise closing argument. Benny's attorney tries one more time to paint Molly as a questionable character who was trying to get Benny to trade favors. The jury is out for less than an hour. The judge asks the defendant to rise. From behind, I see the back of Benny's head. I see him straighten his collar, readjust his tie, and arch his back. He puts his hands behind his back, and stands tall. When the verdict is read, I see him stiffen as he runs his hand through his hair. He is found guilty on all charges—aggravated assault, aggravated battery, willful imprisonment, and lewd and lascivious acts of a sexual nature.

There is a collective sigh and murmuring in the gallery. Rebekah and Molly stand. Rebekah winks at me. I wink back. The law enforcement officers handcuff Benny and lead him out of the courtroom. I watch until the door closes. As I walk past Lars Helland, he reaches out and shakes my hand. "Thanks for coming back to Idaho, Jack."

I don't know what to say to him. I wonder how much of what happened this past year could have been avoided if I had Molly's guts—but, here I am, slithering toward the door, trying to avoid her; not wanting to look at her, or shake her hand. What I really want to do is hug her and tell her how brave she's been. I start out the front door of the courthouse when I hear Kenny calling after me, "Jack, hold up."

"Where you going in such a hurry?" he asks, when he catches up.

"I'm headed to Malad to get packed up and head back to California tomorrow," I say.

"Did Norma keep Stacy today?"

"Yes. Since Melanie was here, I left her with Norma. From what I hear, Esther has the rest of the crew today," I say. "By the way, congratulations. I hear you're going to be a new dad soon."

Kenny beams. "Looks that way," he says. "Doctor says mother and baby are doing great so far."

"Well, congratulations."

"Thanks, Jack. And thanks for coming and giving us support. I know this wasn't easy for you."

"I'm just glad he's where he won't keep hurting people," I tell him. "But if I were you, I'd still have the DNA tests done and save the evidence. I know Benny, and he'll never stop fighting. I can guarantee you, he is convinced he's done nothing wrong."

Kenny and I walk out to the parking lot together. It's a hot August afternoon. The asphalt has absorbed the glaring sun; and so has my black sedan. I stand outside the car for a few minutes while I let it run, and cool off. We talk for a few more minutes. Kenny shakes my hand and I leave. That evening I take Stacy and Norma to the Deep Creek Inn for a steak dinner to celebrate. When I get back to the hotel, I use Norma's phone to call Rebekah.

"Hey," I say when she answers the phone.

"Hi Jack. You sure left in a hurry this afternoon."

"I suppose you went over to the cemetery and talked to your Mom when you got back."

"I did. And it's a little unsettling you know me so well."

"Well, I just want you to know Stacy and I are leaving first thing in the morning. I am not going to leave this time without saying 'goodbye.' Are you going to be in your office in the morning?"

"I'll be there at 8 o'clock," Rebekah says, "I've got about a month's worth of work to get caught up on."

"Good," I say. "We'll stop in before we leave."

"Sounds great," she says. "Talk to you in the morning." There is a click and the phone goes dead.

"I don't want to go, Daddy," Stacy wines, hugging Norma's leg. "I want to stay here."

Norma sits down, lifting Stacy into her lap, hugging her until I take her in my arms. I carry her to the room feeling like her world is a safer place to grow up in, thanks to Molly Olson.

I get up at 6 o'clock the next morning and pack the car while Stacy sleeps. I drive across the street to Ballard's Service Station to fill up with gas. I have Bob Ballard check the oil and air pressure in the tires. Norma opens her door and holds out a cup of coffee for me when I get back.

Stacy wakes at 7 o'clock. She dresses and we finish putting her important things in the back seat next to her car seat; like her blanket, her Elmo doll, and the books Norma gave her. We drive to Elsie's Café where she orders a pancake and orange juice. I get bacon and eggs and another cup of coffee. I see Rebekah walk past the front window. Vickie Thompson places the bill on the table saying, "hate to see you leave again, Jack."

I pull my money clip from my front pocket and set a twenty-dollar bill on the table. I extricate the rest of the money and put the roll of twenties and hundreds back in my pocket. I feel the sharp edges of the dragon head in my hand as I squeeze it.

The front door to the Sorensen Law Office is open. I ask Stacy to sit down in the large leather wing-back chair and hand her a Homes and Gardens magazine to look at. I walk down the hall, tap on the door. Rebekah looks up. I set the money clip on her desk. "For you," I say. She picks it up and looks at it closely.

"Does this mean you're staying?"

I frown at her.

"You told me last summer the only way this would stay in Malad is if you stay with it." She holds up the money clip and shakes it at me.

I laugh. "I want you to have it."

"Thank you." She smiles as she takes a ten-dollar bill from the back pocket of her wranglers, puts it into the money clip and pushes it into her front pocket. "So long as I have a few bucks in my pocket, I'll never forget you, Jack."

"Well, if you rub the dragon's head when you're feeling angry, or hateful toward people trying to destroy your life, it dispenses a little Welsh magic into your heart and softens it."

Rebekah laughs. She takes it back out of her pocket and rubs the clip, sticks it back in her front pocket and laughs again.

328

"Feel better?"

"Much, much better," she says.

I hear the front door open. Someone is talking to Stacy. Then I hear Stacy and another young girl talking. I give Rebekah a puzzled look.

"Someone else wants to tell you goodbye," Rebekah says. She walks out of her office. I turn around and Molly is standing in the doorway. She is wearing a soft yellow Swiss polka-dot dress, with a white short-sleeved cotton jacket and flat white shoes. Her dark golden hair is down on her shoulders. Her cheeks are pink, her dark blue eyes sparkle. "Were you going to leave without saying goodbye to me?"

My heart is pounding. I feel it pulsating in my neck and ears.

"Not intentionally," I say. "Well, maybe, intentionally."

"If you stay another day, we can saddle up the horses and I'll take you back up to Indian Head Ridge," she says.

"I would, but I've got to get back to San Jose before I get fired."

She steps inside the office and closes the door. I can smell her perfume and the soft scent of her shampoo. She touches my arm.

"Jack," she says. "You know I'm not ready to even begin to know what direction my life will take."

I am foolishly nodding my head. I look at the floor because I can't bring myself to look at her. I just stand there, shoving my hands deeper into my pockets, searching for the money clip, no longer there. I search for the words I've said to her a million times in my head.

"Scott was the love of my life and it's going to take time," she finally says in a whisper.

"I know, Molly," I say when the silence becomes painful. "And more than anything, I know why you love him. He was a great guy. I wish I could be more like him."

"I really like you the way you are," she says. "And, I'd like you to think about coming back to Malad and help me start a new bank with my settlement money from FDIC."

I look up, surprised. I stare into her face. She smiles at me.

"I'll have to process that," I say. "I suppose I'll have to process a lot of things."

"Well, nobody knows better than you about keeping the FDIC from closing a bank down," she says. She stands on her toes, puts her hands on my arms and gives me a gentle kiss on my cheek.

I wrap my arms around her and pull her to my chest. I feel her against me, and I hold her, not wanting to let go. When I release her, her hands are still holding onto my arms. I peer into her eyes. "I love you, Molly," I say to her, the tears welling up. "I realized last summer I have loved you since the first day I saw you."

"Yes, and you saved my life," she says, "Twice. I suppose the emotion of saving someone's life can be confused with love."

"No," I say. "Well, maybe, though I'd think it should be the other way around." I smile, and she laughs. I stand back and look at her in all her beauty, and I finally say with firm resolve, "My dear Molly. I suppose the rest of whatever happens here in Malad City will just have to work itself out." I take a deep breath and let it out slow with an audible sigh.

This time she hugs me. Not passionately. Not ravenously. But tenderly. The way someone touches you, or holds you, to make you believe with all your heart that, *all is well. All is well.*

The End.

Author's Note: Ruby

This story, like all stories, is an amalgamation of things I know, people I've met somewhere in my life, and things I have experienced.

ALL of the people in this novel are fictitious except two (not counting politicians, like Cecil Andrus, Congressman Stallings, and Governor Evans.) Some of the events align with what I remember of 1986, because I was there.

I WAS the appraiser hired by FDIC on the dairy that dreadful day, though it was a dairy north of Malad, in Bannock County. To the Baldwin family whose daughter would have been 30-years-old this year, my pain for your loss burns in my heart every single day.

www.ingramcontent.com/pod-product-compliance
Lightning Source LLC
Chambersburg PA
CBHW030401030726
47497CB00002B/435